TRADEWIND

Magda Sweetland

HEADLINE
REVIEW

First published in 1996 by
HEADLINE BOOK PUBLISHING

A HEADLINE REVIEW hardback

10 9 8 7 6 5 4 3 2 1

British Library Cataloguing in Publication Data

Sweetland, Magda, 1943-
Tradewind
1. English fiction - 20th century
I. Title
823.9'14 [F]

ISBN 0 7472 1572 3

Typeset by Avon Dataset Ltd, Bidford-on-Avon, Warks

Printed in England by
Clays Ltd, St Ives plc.

HEADLINE BOOK PUBLISHING
A division of Hodder Headline PLC
338 Euston Road
London NW1 3BH

TRADEWIND

1

It happened fast.

A call came through at 2 a.m. Hong Kong time – which was early on the evening of the previous day in Britain – and woke him up. Neal Langholm didn't object to that. He'd left instructions with the housekeeper that if there were any sudden or dramatic changes, she was to let him know at once.

And now the most dramatic. The old lady had died peacefully, without pain, in that state called merciful release. She'd been wandering in her mind for some months past, but he and Thomas had been spared any of the harrowing decisions about subjecting her to a degree of physical containment, such as moving her into the local nursing home, or about direct medical intervention. There were no tubes and no drips at the end. She was over eighty and went downhill fast. This was the best way out.

All the same, he was shocked by the suddenness of it. Edith was his grandmother, not his mother, although she'd raised him and his brother and been their surrogate parent, so that he'd admired her with complexity, rather than loving her outright. Strict – she indulged no one – but fair, she was a powerful arbiter, the court of last appeal in a household of men. To this day, he was in the habit of bringing key decisions for her to judge on, mentally, and had appropriated her critical method, which amounted to five minutes' consideration of the opposite point of view before it was swept aside in favour of the first instinct.

He opened the blinds. The city that lay spread out below the plate-glass windows of the flat was never dark and never still. From his vantage point at Mid-Levels, he could pick out the white wake of the Star Ferry crossing from Kowloon to Central Pier and, here and there, the outline of tall, illuminated buildings on both shorelines. The lovers were still hanging about the shadow of The Peak and the downtown squares, the public gardens and parks which came into their own as welcome, open-air rooms after nightfall, when the temperature and humidity levels in Hong Kong dropped back to the tolerable.

Eventually, the lovers grew tired of their secret kissing and went home with the daylight. At about the same time, the farmers out in the low-lying districts of the New Territories were loading up their bicycle panniers with chard and live chickens and wicker crates full of eggs, while the street traders rammed T-shirts cheaply printed with loose dyes, or delicate intarsia sweaters made from double-cashmere – whichever end of the consumer scale they were aiming at – into plastic sacks, and the great daily trek into the world's biggest marketplace began. Silently. The whole buying convulsion was so silent that sometimes it was hard to think of this Asian Manhattan as a convergence point for innumerable millions, the Sinian hordes arriving by every means of transport known to man for the business of exchange.

The bicycles began the movement, pedalling through a grey dawn that was already heavy with the crushing humidity of mid-June.

Concentrate. The now. He'd have to ring Thomas and looked at his watch. Two thirty in the morning. Instinctively, Neal glanced up at the wall on the right of the window – but, of course, it was in his downtown office that a dozen clocks kept time with the world's main trading centres. In Rajasthan, it would be around midnight. To hell, he'd had his sleep interrupted. Why shouldn't his brother?

He dialled. The phone rang for a time while he reviewed to himself the long corridors of the bungalow in Jaipur, the echo of sound from room to room like a dream he half remembered. Neal had thought it eccentric of his brother to rent the bungalow where they'd lived with their parents while they were working as Presbyterian missionaries in Jaipur, and took him for a sentimentalist. At the same time, he liked to have a mental fix on him, see him in actual, not imaginary, space, and when Thomas eventually did reply, bleary down the line, he could reconstruct accurately the slatted blinds and the deep surround of the verandah, dark at midnight, although by day it was a dusty, colour-washed pink.

'I'm sorry about this. I've only just heard myself. Edith died last night.'

'Ach. We thought it wouldn't be long.'

'Mrs Palmer will stay on for the time being, but we must go back pronto and put things in hand.'

'What things?'

'Details of the funeral. Reading the will. Selling the house. A few little things like that.'

Thomas, unalert, was still impressed by how smoothly his brother's mind had slipped into the forward gear. 'You don't need me for all that, surely. I'm in the middle of—'

'Don't tell me what you're in the middle of, please. As for myself, I can't afford a single day off-site. We're working to a contract with some hefty time penalties, not to mention the political ones. Who knows what's around the corner?'

Thomas groaned at the front-line-crisis tone his brother hit. He made out he worked to hourly deadlines and never overshot them. The new airport at Kowloon had to be finished before the handover to the Chinese – Beijing – government, and Neal would lay the Tarmac runways by himself, tooth and nail, if their completion targets were imperilled by one hour.

However, this urgency had worn routine with repetition. 'You know, we've got a few of our own dramas here, Neal. We've got enough potable water left in the city for eight days. Anywhere else in the world, it would be an emergency—'

Neal cut his brother short. 'That's a disaster, not a crisis. What can you do to help the helpless? It's insoluble, endemic in India. Now let's get on with this. I'm taking the London plane tomorrow at midday, no, it's Sunday today, isn't it? It will get me into Heathrow at six in the evening. And you can do the same. I had to check the schedules only last week for a colleague. There's a Delhi flight that leaves at one p.m. on Sundays. I'll put a reserve on it in your name.'

'Now, wait a minute . . .'

'I can't. I'm giving this a week. One week to do the business. Sunday to Sunday. I'm not taking the responsibility for this alone, Thom. I did it last time and it's not good enough to load it all on me.'

Thomas conceded that it had taken his brother all of thirty seconds to produce that moral blackmail. He hadn't gone back for his grandfather's funeral eighteen months ago, because he'd just arrived in India, and remained the unforgiven. 'Granted.'

'And I'll book the onward flights for us on the shuttle. Goddam that last bit. It's so fiddling.'

Separated by over two thousand miles of country and a greater distance in outlook, their minds still escaped at the same moment into the same thought: the downward cataract of the road towards

Langholm in Eskdale, which was as inevitable as the fall of land. It was their place as well as their name, and yoked them. In the eye of that image was also a shared regret, that the strong, calm man and his stronger wife would never wait in welcome at the door and that they were finally alone with each other in the world, brother to brother.

'So.'

'I'll see you at Heathrow's Terminal Three tomorrow, Sunday, tickets and any message in case of emergency with the British Airways desk.'

Lord, he was terrifying, that man. The sheer organisation of him, the mental attack! Putting down the receiver, Thomas stopped to ask himself if they really could be kin, wondered why his brother had so much of one quality and he another. But what this other quality was that he laid claim to he couldn't define, for it was exactly that, a lack of precision.

Today! How was he going to abstract himself from today? He was sure Neal had meetings and site visits and committees that he'd have to cancel, but he did have a secretary to help as well as the full infrastructure of teams and telephones that regularly worked. For himself, well, he could boast all he liked about being the water engineer for the largest site on earth, the Rajasthani desert, but that didn't count for much when not many people knew it and nobody cared. There was no glamour and no money attached to what he did. Disaster? Neal hadn't exaggerated; it was disaster on a daily basis, the ultimate crisis management. He must try snapping his fingers at Ajit in the morning to see what effect it produced.

He showered and dressed, jerking himself awake. The morning came slowly, creeping over the western plains of China, curving upwards with the camber of the land, and arrived uncooled by crossing the seas or the mountain ranges of the Himalayas. Thomas sat writing quick notes at his work table. A strong, marble-topped version, it had miraculously survived from his parents' day, through ten different tenants, simply because it was too big for the doorway and they were successively too lazy to dismantle it.

A week. All right. He excused himself on paper from forty diary engagements but noticed, in the phrasing of each of them, a hint of the valedictory. I may not be back for some time...

At six he shook himself, cold, chilled through by the night air and the marble work surface against his bare arm. A sweater. That would help. But he sat on, immobilised by the fact which had redirected him so suddenly and without warning. Edith was dead. He missed her immediately: the physical strength she'd given him even this far away and a personal style that was his own reference guide. She'd offered him a series of alternatives in life, in language, sex and her powerful opinions. Her native French pervaded his mental reference like a wine dispersed in sauce, strong and flavoursome. Neal had never been able to learn it, or his grandfather. It was their exclusive speech and a strong bond, the secret place they escaped to in a shared imagination.

It was hard to believe that she was dead. She'd lived so long he'd thought she was immortal. As she spanned the century like a majestic cantilever, arch on arch of decades past, he hadn't seen that her tapering off was into the finite. He'd paid too little attention and given too little time. His eyes filled repeatedly from regret and guilt, and then dried again with common sense. She was an old lady, and such a death wasn't untimely or shocking. He'd written to her every week of his life when they were apart, from school, at work, out of India. She was his double-mother. Tidy with her mind, tidy with her life, she did nothing to excess. He still tried to keep faith with her precepts, which stipulated that he give every man more than his due. She was a moral bank on which he could draw endlessly, without incurring deficit. He would love her for evermore.

But it was so inconvenient, mortality. He resented its intrusion into the practical flow of things. Penning each of his apologies in turn, he was able to predict its reception. Hand-delivered by Ajit or one of Ajit's plural cousins on a bicycle, it would raise an eyebrow in this department or that which he was trying to rouse into a sense of urgency about the water shortage, would give the addressee about five seconds' worth of annoyance that the schedule of the day was going to be disrupted, then be filed among the rest of the forgotten memoranda of Indian bureaucracy. Only his own presence activated things. Or was that the same egotism he deplored in Neal?

Only one apology was different and that one had to be made in person. No notes for Singh.

Its singularity dismayed him. After all this time, did he have just one real friend in Jaipur? The sudden crisis revealed the extent of an ongoing problem, which was his own relationship with

India. Neal was right, in one sense, that the long-term drought was so widespread that a single, isolated individual couldn't make any impact on it. Thomas was therefore dispensable, unlike his brother, whose daily output gathered influence to it with a measure of achievement, making him a very important person.

Neal worked systematically during the Hong Kong-to-Heathrow flight. He always flew Club Class and justified the difference on his expense sheet by totting up the work he'd been able to get through undisturbed.

He was a seasoned veteran of the route, going back to London once a month or so for debriefings and a management committee. He was working for a multinational construction company, in which he was the Far East representative with special responsibility for Hong Kong and Singapore. In-flight, he consumed none of the free alcohol and little food. He didn't try to sleep because, inevitably broken, it tended to upset the circadian rhythm. He'd perfected his own lifestyle and work methods, but two years in Hong Kong had added a few refinements picked up from the Chinese, who were good at self-management. Unlike the Japanese, they didn't suffer from burn-out or the Western stress-related illnesses. They were inclined to let technology take the strain instead of trying to outpace it. He simply slowed down, or became a marathon runner instead of a sprinter. Take a rest, Mr Langholm, you must take more rest, said his native engineers.

So he did. Out of every hour he concentrated for only fifty minutes. In the other ten he used a series of relaxation exercises, a kind of mental t'ai chi, if he couldn't physically get out of his chair or the building to unwind. He attended to his diet, which came close to the perfect Cantonese, ate no cholesterol, avoided dairy produce. Was sexually careful. Never angry. Never hurried. A Rolls-Royce life. He purred.

After he'd gone through his business files, he allocated one hour to the personal. He headed up a fresh piece of paper and divided it into four quadrants, each with a subheading, 'Funeral Arrangements', 'Bank', 'Solicitor', 'Sale of House', under which he made additional jottings. He had minute writing, not being a space waster, and could write a thousand words on the back of an envelope. He then folded the page, edge to edge, and on the reverse wrote 'Et cetera'.

The first side had consisted of a list of actions. He'd no trouble with those, moving along the path of fixed objectives, from the known to the known. But on the obverse he wrote two phrases, and they were both the names of people: 'R. Palmer', 'Caley'.

Ruth Palmer was his grandmother's housekeeper and, after a quarter of a century in their service, she'd entered the realm of being a family retainer. She was that person known in Church of Scotland circles as an indigent gentlewoman, well bred and well spoken, with a soft Highland fall in her voice, and wasn't in the regular servant mould. Mrs Palmer had been their factotum. Her appointment, when she was widowed in her thirties, coincided with the arrival of two young boys, orphaned out in India and sent back home to boarding school in Edinburgh, with their grandparents as guardians. It was one of the greater accidents of their five lives, to locate each other in a time of mutual need, Robert, Edith, Ruth, Neal and Thomas. They shared the tremor of these shocks of bereavement together, and made mutual compensations. The commodious house in Border country was the best shelter from outside perils that they would find.

First their maid, then cook, then housekeeper, Ruth had turned latterly into Edith's companion, nurse and friend. She'd kept the place ticking over. Without her Edith would have had to go into sheltered accommodation after Robert died, and the proceeds from the sale of her beloved Carterbrae be subsumed into nursing and attendance costs. But now Ruth would be leaving their employ without any pension beyond her state benefit. What was their legal requirement in regard to her? What was their moral?

That was an ethical conundrum he couldn't resolve alone. One for Thomas. He added three quick plus signs, meaning addenda, but as he looked at them, they turned into commendatory stars, or crosses, like a personal Calvary. He dismissed the fanciful idea.

The other name was more problematical still. When his brother first went out to work in India, Caley Brown had called herself Thomas's girlfriend. A marriage hadn't seemed impossible at that stage, but Thomas hadn't made a return trip to the UK in all that time, nor had she come out to visit him in Rajasthan. Neal wondered if anything intimate could have survived all these months of absence. Eighteen. Twenty-one. He totted them up. What was the state of play between them? Was the air clear? Were they still technically together? Neal didn't know.

But what he did know was that Caley had driven down to see

Edith from Edinburgh every fortnight without fail in these intervening months. His letters from the old lady were full of Caley, her doings, her odd work that was beginning to take off and show results, and chatter about the new circle of friends she'd developed since the brothers left to take up positions abroad. Irritating, really, for her to be so ubiquitous. Irritating young woman.

This thought absorbed him as he tried to analyse why, and what to do about her. Her name for a start. He was never sure he'd spelt it right, or what it stood for. Had someone been so inadvertent as to christen her Caledonia, or Calais, or was this a stab at *ceilidh*, and something Gaelic and fey, outside his ken? With that family, of course, anything was possible. He'd come across as many pronunciations of her name as spellings, and she answered to all of them, like a word in the *Concise Scots* with more local variants than meanings. It sounded like the trade mark of a beer licensed by a minor brewery, but the audible snort, which he couldn't control as that idea surfaced, was tinged with the knowledge of its accuracy. Caley was as well known, as popular, as cult endowed as any of the finer vintages or single malts. Those who knew valued her and kept a secret well.

Whatever, she was unavoidable in the days ahead. Intimate with the facts first-hand, she would almost certainly turn up for the funeral, and he foresaw a host of small social embarrassments to do with . . . her unstated expectations. The nebulous nature of these frustrated him as his pen hovered over the space behind her name. All he added was a question mark, and then he realised that appending the simple query had taken up fifteen minutes of his time and made him overrun into the following hour.

Thomas was lucky in planning his flight connections. A party of World Health observers from the UN, who'd been touring the northern provinces, was leaving Jaipur that morning for Delhi on a chartered plane, also onward-bound on the Heathrow flight, and he hitched a ride with them.

That left him just an hour to pack a bag and make his personal farewell. The bungalow where he lived was close enough to his office and he often walked to work. Sometimes he thought of these workrooms as his headquarters, sometimes a fully equipped laboratory, but, in fact, the building that was rented by World Health as the planning centre for their current Clean Water project in Rajasthan was an outhouse of the Jaipur clinic where, by eight o'clock in the morning, Dr Man Singh Nattawat was already busy at work.

Thomas wound his way across the dusty compound in front of the consulting rooms. The clinic was best known for an artificial foot it had developed, now called the Jaipur foot, light to wear and easy to fit, and so much in demand. People came from all over the northern provinces to have the operation. There were a few lepers in among the patients, but most of them were accidental amputees, men who'd been caught in the whirrs of old factory or farm machinery, women and children who'd fallen under the overladen carts and cars that choked the roads. A new foot would save them from a life of begging and make them useful in their villages again. While they were waiting for an appointment to see one of the specialists, maybe for days at a time, they camped out in the courtyard, usually with a female relative in attendance, whose job it was to wash and cook and care for the patient.

Many of these people in the courtyard salaamed to Thomas Langholm as he passed. Anyone wearing a jacket was a nominal doctor and, because they knew his work had something to do with public health and disease prevention, the mass of local people did call him Dr Langholm undiscriminatingly. He brushed up his Ph.D. and tried to look the part, although, with one half of his brain, he thought he was a glorified plumber.

He did look the part, though Thomas would have shrugged off any suggestions of an air of natural authority, thinking of himself as unkempt. But this meant he had a neutral social ease, had no cold or stand-offish looks and any of the patients could have approached him with a plea for help, for relief, for alms, and had done so before now. He was endlessly delayed by the petitions of the multitude. Today, however, he strode on and the people didn't detain him.

Down the cool shadows of the verandah a line of patients snaked, sitting with their backs to the wall, or lying down, or standing with the aid of a crutch or an accompanying friend. They quietly made way for the water engineer, while the old man who was being examined in the consulting room didn't protest at being left alone as the two doctors conferred in an outer room. He thought it was about his case, making him more noteworthy.

This early in the day, Singh was immaculately dressed, elegant and unhurried. Of course, out at Amber, he had three servants to see to his bachelor needs, but his primary asset was a physique on which the tailored clothes hung effortlessly. Singh came from a line of palace bodyguards who'd been chosen for their height. He also played sport for one of the All-Indian teams while he was still a schoolboy, basketball it was, and he was something of a hero figure in Jaipur. His blazers, of the institutionalised British cut, displayed one of these team badges, a small vanity which on him wasn't effete. He had energy and control of it, so that, coming into contact with him, Thomas was repeatedly impressed by the sense of something larger, known as power.

'You have an air of purpose this morning,' Singh divined.

'Yes. I've come to say goodbye. I'm flying back to Britain, now, at once. Edith died last night.'

Singh was quick and sincere in his condolences. He took Thomas Langholm's hand in his and covered the bond with his other. 'We have expected this, but it is always a calamity. I am so sorry.'

Thomas was suffused by the man's personal warmth, while the emotion at losing his ancestor, held in check by Neal's efficiency and the scrabbled arrangements he'd had to make for his own exit, rose and confounded him. In front of this friend he wasn't ashamed to feel and show it.

Seeing his emotion, Singh spoke more softly. 'She was very good to me. Wasn't she the most generous of women with her time? Always time to listen, time to talk. She stays in my impression as a great lady, and we have been fortunate to fall under her influence. I'm sorry. I'm saying the obvious. I should be thinking of something I can do to help you. What can I do?'

'Keep an eye on the bungalow for me while I'm away. I've cancelled my immediate appointments. The rest will have to wait.'

'And you will see Caley while you are in Scotland?' the doctor asked, quite tentatively, for they found each other's private life an impenetrable mystery. Singh's time in Edinburgh was overlaid with an impression of this girl, a flat at Bruntsfield with three young men and one exquisite creature drifting through its ugliness. She was what he liked in women, beautiful, quiet and subtle. He was riven with the memory of the forbidding tensions created between these two brothers, his unequal friends, and one girl. Without waiting for a reply, he added, 'Do give her my regards.'

'Of course. Now you'll have to excuse me. I'm expecting a lift to the airport any minute. I wish I had longer.'

'Today you go?' Singh glanced out of the window of his office next to the consultation room, looking to a horizon that was cut off to the north by a line of sandy hills edging the desert. By eight in the morning, the sky overhead was as hard and blue as enamelled metal, and gave off the same tinny resonance. Time pressed for both of them but they walked back through the chambers of the clinic together, prolonging moments. The doctor realised that the prospective journey was one-way. No date had been vouchsafed for his friend's return. 'You will come back, Thomas? You're not going away for good?'

'At this stage, I cannot say.'

The phrase was Singh's own, and India's own, often resorted to in a difficult situation, and Thomas had become expert at reading its multi-purpose nuances: I couldn't guess, or I have no wish to air my opinions, or I disagree with you entirely. It could mean any of those things and was the polite and anodyne response. Singh took it back without the least demur. 'And have you consulted the astrologer on the best time to travel? This may not be the most auspicious hour.'

'Even if it is inauspicious, I'm afraid I have no choice. Go I must.'

Singh bowed to the Western imperatives but shook his head with genuine misgivings. Throughout the rest of the morning's clinic, this notion of hasty improvidence came back to trouble him. It was their third such parting, he recalled, and each of them had been prompted by a death. First the Langholm parents killed in a Himalayan climbing accident, then his own father's death, which recalled him to India and his responsible place at the head of the family community of Nattawat, and now the old woman, Edith, had passed away in that little Scottish town which he remembered as a place so grey and dull and unremarkable that it hung on in his mind as a prototype. Deeply imbued with fatalism and the significance of numbers, Singh feared this third might be the last parting between them, and he wished he had added more to its sense of moment.

Thomas spiralled in the buzzing charter plane out of the Jaipur pink. The view below him wasn't reassuring. The city and its surrounding desert were one vast drab, against which individual points of colour were pathetically limited.

From the air he could pick out the farms where they'd sunk bore holes because they were ringed in green as artificially as with a fibre highlight pen. The agriculture was, at best, meagre. What they produced in the way of life-sustaining yield wasn't significant or useful. On his one visit to see Neal in Hong Kong – although he'd loathed the high-rise city like a cardboard pastiche stuck behind the indigenous junks and smacks and sampans bobbing in the South China Seas, a jarring culture-clash of modern and ancient – still he was impressed by what the Chinese could get out of their soil. Two crops a year, with no chemical fertilisers. Of course, they had the saving rainfall. His Rajasthani peasants were as expert in farming techniques, and conserved every last drop of water in their villages. The women dug irrigation channels to grow the millet and maize beside the roadway, utilising the shade of the natural embankment, and put in pats of dried cow dung for fertiliser, but the age-old agrarian system depended on the habitual monsoon. If it failed, disaster followed. With no rain, there was no growth. From above, the specks of vegetation soon petered out in the swamp of dust, and he was left to mull on the enormity of the encroaching desert.

Dr Nattawat paused on the clinic's verandah and listened, picking out the definitions of the high noonday. A train looped in a northwards curve towards New Delhi and the cities of the plain. In the distance, he could hear a dog howling. These melancholy noises tested the thin, pure air. A noise could travel for ten miles in good weather. The sounds of the plain metamorphosed themselves as shapes he recognised, a village, a corral with horses, a denser patch of vegetation composed of a brake of trees or maybe maize plantations coming towards harvest, according to how they interrupted the clear note given back by the dry and empty space of the desert, as the slow train chugged upwards in the ungiving country.

There was no industry and no pollution. The sky overhead was clear day after day, but what he usually boasted about made him catch his breath with fear. The climate was changing. The monsoons had failed for six years running. What if they failed again? Langholm had left. That was a bad sign because he was their water manager, a Joseph to ration grain in famine years. Another drought was imminent in Rajasthan. Eight days of water left. Tomorrow seven. The doctor knew exactly how the people would suffer if the rains failed again, and not just from dehydration. A small infection was enough to kill them, or dysentery from poor feeding because the crops were thin, and they'd no in-built resistance to disease: the children would fall victim first, then the old, then finally working adults.

The doctor wasn't tired of healing people. He was tired of combating the climate and the crushing terrain.

2

'Those two men can't really be brothers,' Caley said when Singh introduced her to the top-floor flat in Gillespie Crescent for one of their joint parties. *Surprise-partie*. Thomas liked the French term better because it often ended in the ultimate combination of surprises for him. The control factor was marginal: a happening. The three flatmates had a workable technique when it came to party-throwing. The Langholms supplied the men and the venue and the beer. Singh, who managed to have the reputation of a ferocious flirt without being indecorous, brought along the pretty girls.

'Why not brothers? Just because they look different?' His latest beauty amused him with her quick-fire judgments and the dark shadows that she threw into light. He'd never grasped the meaning of the phrase 'short shrift' until he met Caley.

'No. Because they *are* different.'

'But how can you know that just by looking at them?'

'They have a different specific density.' The idea was ridiculous, and so he laughed at her.

Neal was almost six foot but, stockily built, he seemed shorter. He'd well-made features, was neat, quick, organised in his movements, like the networker he was. He was going round the room efficiently, extracting something usable. What sort of contract was it? What were the entry conditions? Was it competitive tender? Honing his questions to the minimum. The point, the point, keep to the point. She thought he probably made notes, after a party, on the tradeable names and contacts. He was already a card-swapper.

But he wasn't unappealing. Caley could see that a lot of the girls in Bruntsfield would warm to this blunt manliness, a paradigm of the known. The room was full of pretty girls, nurses, undergraduates, the sports-club followers, but there was a culture-clash between them and their men. The men were old schoolfriends who'd looked after the Langholms and taken them on family holidays to farmhouses in the summer or on round-Scotland boating trips, always welcome, mucking in. They were the product of the practical departments at the university, had studied architecture, water engineering, medicine, thinkers and doers from Heriot Watt and the King's Buildings, hard-working and serious about their vocations. Neal was one of these archetypal clubmen; what Singh admired most about him, or what he repeated first, was that he'd played rugby in the good Border tradition, and turned out regularly for Fettes FP, reaching the standard of Hawick Seconds for one season – but never made Scotland. He looked strong and fit, a runner and a passer, a good scrum-half. A climber too, Singh told her. The brothers had scaled all of Munro's peaks by the time they were twenty. Yes, Neal Langholm was a man you'd trust to get you to the top of the mountain without too much hazard on the way. Map, compass, endurance: he had the full mental kit.

At the other end of the room, almost separated by antithesis, was his counterpart. Caley thought Thomas was the older of the two, because he looked so seriously drawn. Exceptionally tall and less tidily boned than Neal, he'd a face already haggard, with high, pronounced cheekbones like a Sioux warrior and intense, pale-blue eyes, not flat or calm but very fixed. A prophet, a preacher, he'd had the mission streak passed down to him.

It was darkling, a few weeks before Easter, with the lamps and candles lighting oblique corners, a sort of lambent intimacy in the air and people moving because it was a two-floor flat with a living room upstairs and down. They went between. But Thomas didn't move about. He didn't need to go grazing. Everybody was prepared to come to him. Stationary, seated cross-legged, one ankle resting on the other knee, he gave out a sense of laziness or timelessness like a slow personal vapour. But watching him, rather mesmerised by his capped energy, Caley could see he wasn't really inert. He was supremely concentrated into the act of talking. Each person who came across and spoke to him was the most interesting human being in the world for him. Thomas was consumed with his belief in that one person for that period of time. His eyes lit up, his body movement changed into the act of identification. I am listening. I am re-creating you in my mind. I am you. She didn't think this process was meant as flattery, and it certainly wasn't dishonest. He almost glowed with the wattage of his interest, and that was what endowed him with a spiritual air,

16

his self-effacement. His friends were precious individuals, and the strangers in the room were only potential friends.

'Caley?' He queried the name, when she sat down next to him in the current flow of the room. 'And what does that mean?'

She shrugged. 'It's probably a misprint. Ignore it. Accidental collocation of sounds with no known meaning. That's me. As well as my conversational style.'

He roared out loud at an idea so outrageously self-rejecting, a full-capacity sound that stopped the room's talk for a second while other people looked around at the two of them leaning together and smiled. 'That's too dismissive. There's a word like it in French that means "very bright", to be a wizard at something. *Calée*.'

'Well, there you go. It's possible to be wrong in two languages.'

'I saw you coming in with Singh.' He was trying to graph the layout of relationships.

'That doesn't mean to say I'll leave with him.'

'Who will you leave with, then?'

'Who knows? I may not leave at all.'

This was faster than Thomas's natural running pace and winded him. Stop on the way uphill and take a deep breath. He looked sideways at her, wondering how much of her blasé phrase was meant, how much was a pose. 'So you're one of the itinerant homeless and will bide anywhere?'

'Homeless? Emotionally, oh, yes. I'm looking to abide.'

The woman had enough personal charm to get away with this. She was strong, not slight, in her mental demonstration. Thomas was caught off balance. My God, he thought, she is terrifying me. I'm not going to get away with being casual about this. 'I meant the physically homeless.'

'Are they different, body and mind? Dislocated people can't usually connect either way. Or they don't want to. They want the freedom to rove. Strange, that's an amorous term too, the roving eye.'

When she said this, she detached herself from the rest of the party-goers and focused in his gaze as forefront, close-up material. Thomas was used to being interested in other people, not in being searched himself, not in being upset or even challenged. He knew he was regarded as a guru in his circle and rather worked on this because it was an easy mask of anonymity, to be aloof and remote. Caley slid up and round this mask and fixed on his very self.

She was also implying in her off-hand, jocular way a random

17

promiscuity which was part of the aura that terrified him, for he kept his sexual history well hidden but, as he looked into her face, he couldn't believe this woman was other than pure at heart. Large-eyed, frank, open, all the metaphors of honesty applied. She had a power of attachment to other people no less than his own. She also carried a sexual charge that shook him or took him in its path, although it wasn't overt or vulgar, rather the reverse. Compared with most of the girls in the room, she was covered up, liked wearing long, dark clothes, was personally modest – but even as he thought this, his eyes undid. He realised that her easy-going sexuality was as much a mask of convenience as his philosopher-king status, and something she played up to because it was a ready-made role, acceptable and attractive for the same reasons. It was a crowd-puller and they both loved a crowd.

Which didn't simplify matters between them at all, that their motives were crossed or that they projected a public image simplistically different from the private one.

'I went to Cowdenbeath today,' she said into this silence, like scaffolding into empty space, defining it. 'There's a man there called Jamie Drew. Have you heard of him? He collects fossils. He's a miner's son, left school at fifteen. Completely self-taught. He's got this one fixation, fossil-hunting, and he's stumbled on a site in Fife. It's a rich seam he's found, his personal oilfield. He keeps it to himself, and why shouldn't he? I went over there today to buy some of his samples, although he wasn't very happy about selling them to me because I'm going to dissect them and frame them with silver as brooches and buckle pins. Funny, he thinks that's barbaric of me, and maybe it is. But if he were an absolute purist, the fossils would still be lying in the ground and nobody would ever see them. Once you interfere with the natural cycles, it's hard to say where the process stops, isn't it? To make the dead thing beautiful and make it live again, well, what else could I do with his fossils that would be better? We argued about it politely, but he still doesn't approve.'

'I'd like to meet Jamie Drew. I'll come with you the next time you go to Fife.'

It was the promise, made and then accepted without conditions. It stretched into the future. It took her word for things. It was a contract.

No, she didn't leave Gillespie Crescent after the party. She told him she was tired and wanted to lie down. It was that straightforward. His room downstairs was large, his bed big enough to accommodate them both. Behind the wooden shutters, she undressed for his eyes, peeling off the loose knitted layers effortlessly. The body whorls ran like the curving ammonites she'd talked about, while the nodes of vertebrae that ran down the length of her tapering back were visualised for him all over again in the three-dimensional. She curled round his clothed body, immensely pliable, not hard at all. He resisted her, somewhere. I don't go in for this, he thought, I just don't do this sort of thing. I do not sleep around. But when she kissed him, he capitulated, because she wasn't outside him any more, she was inside him, and it was impossible not to act out what he was thinking.

The effortless slippage of it! She was only embodying the erotic images that had played around his head, unfulfilled, for years and was able to guess them quite accurately, to judge by what she knew to put where. He thought it: she did it. Her flattering hands, in dropping down his torso, made him what he most wanted to be, magnificent, slow and intensely cerebral. She actually thought about what she was doing and keyed into the connective rhythms of body passion as if it were a conversation. She listened, then responded, and gave back something extra to the dialogue. He was devastated by her and by the experience wholly new. Saturday. Bruntsfield. Midnight. A new woman as sudden as a landfall in his life, as composure-shattering.

She did strange things. She stopped mid-track, got up from the bed and put on a shirt again. Was that because she was cold or shy, or was it just a provocative gesture, tormenting him to find her under it again? A sexual hide-and-seek. It was his shirt she found. It was as if she was putting on him. The gesture doubled up, confirming her identify with him, as well as the differences: see how differently I fill it, feel how. And when she did settle on him and he arced at last into the lonely interior of another person, he discovered the last surprise. That he hit a sac of pleasure so strong it was almost its own justification.

Caley had no hesitations. She loved his body, loved his mind, the rangy straggle of his persona into which she cleaved herself for good. As she got to know him better, she realised that he was often moody, enclosed and depressive, and deeply solitary at times, however gregarious at others. They spent long hours talking politics and social ethics and what was owed to others, good diversionary tactics from the kissing and the undressing and what was owed to self. Highly motivated and correct, he was the best sort of man to seduce. She enjoyed planting lecherous ideas in his mind and watching them grow, teased him by throwing out spare lewdness, dirty talk he hadn't imagined on those classically modulated lips, and then she diverted him with a thought or idea so novel and intriguing that he was beside himself wondering which path to follow. Take or talk: the variants on the themes of interplay were endless.

But it wasn't pleasure without pain. Not a prude and not a Christian, Thomas had still made very simple vows which happened to include chastity and monogamy. For the practical reasons he called moral, to do with habits of conduct, mores, he'd resisted the casual love affairs that were on offer round the Old Quad and the Meadows. He thought once would be enough. It ought to be the best. But for once to happen in this way, when he was least expecting it, for the woman who fascinated him to walk in with his friend and sit in his brother's chair and latch on to his mind, was so bemusing it weakened his resistance. A cold cell in his brain was not impressed with himself. Just what has happened to my principles, he thought, and my sense of dedication?

Caley located the fastidious aesthete that lurked in Singh: she listened to his description of the songs of Indian *raga*, whose structural limitation he admired, and said they sounded like the traditional Scottish ballads, short, narrative, powerfully metred; she went with him to see his tailor at Gieves in George Street, where he had his suits made to measure from bolts of Reid and Taylor cloth, out of the Langholm mills; she discussed architecture and form with him. When was a dome Eastern and when was it European? What really was the difference between the Muslim and the Norman arch, and was that difference religious, or due to mathematical sophistication, or something much more basic like the grain in the local stone, water-retentive like limestone, or repellent like marble? The materials conditioned what you could construct. She showed him her jewellery designs, which he found Celtic-crude, and he explained to her in turn the higher refinements of gem cutting and setting as practised in his native city, Jaipur, pink of pinks.

But it was with Neal that she engaged in the most excoriating review of self called passion. Through passionate dislikes, and impassioned differences, they flirted with hatred.

One day, she was so angry with his snubs that she found herself writing out a list of his good points, and his bad. The latter was long, the former restricted to one – that he happened to be Thomas's brother. He was a man she wouldn't have spent one minute with otherwise. She didn't argue with him, or even openly disagree, that wasn't her method, but she set about correcting his pompous tendencies with the apt, deflating term. Know-all. That's the official view you've just given us, is it? Been boning up from the weekend supplements again? All those cut-out opinions, prescriptive thinking. Once she called him smarty-pants, for he was smart. Someone told her that the best insult was laughter, because it was unanswerable, and so she continually laughed at him.

He writhed ineffectually against her barbs.

For his own part, Neal would have liked to overwhelm her more. When he carried out his own tally of plus or minus points on her, there wasn't such a vast imbalance. Sometimes, when he looked back on these flurried skirmishes of theirs, the sceptical look she threw him, the hasty or inconsistent word – because whatever he said, he knew she would support the converse – the actual reason for their disagreement was minimal. They were both tidy-minded and despaired, between them, of Thomas who sprawled his debris into every corner of the flat, and of Singh who waited for a serf or sepoy to clear the floor. But they didn't approve of each other's form of tidiness either. Her systems were human: she threw brilliant, quirky dinner parties in the flat, tossing people into the spectacular *mélange* of something never to be repeated. Don't ask for the recipe. She didn't know it. It was the moment, today, the mood as it took her.

But after the guests had gone, she slumped, her energy played out by being life and soul and cook and hostess to so many talents. Then, for reasons Neal couldn't locate or condone in himself, he nagged at her. He wanted the dishes piled up ready for washing at two in the morning, the windows opened to expel the smoke and the twice-breathed air, to sanitise the place of people. Caley, on the other hand, wanted to protect the aura of well-being which she'd worked so hard to create, keep the mood on high with Thomas and with Singh, who needed no encouragement to languish and pass the time of night. His system was things, cupboard doors closed, surfaces wiped clean, and when she cut across that with her liberality, he felt the result was squalid. Too much. Too long. She cleared rooms for people to flow.

He cleared rooms to stop them. He thought that she didn't know where to draw the line between what was owed to others and to themselves.

Or was he greedy for her, to close her up and keep her to himself? When she came back in a taxi full of flowers before one of these parties, meaning to decorate the place from top to bottom with a magnificent, throwaway largesse that brought the hothouse spring indoors, he said miserly – How much did those cost us?

Oh, cost. Nothing. They were clearing out the stands after the Ideal Home Exhibition at the Waverley. These were headed for the dustbin, and I charmed the doorman into letting me have them all for free.

He found he was charmed in turn. When she'd arranged them in jugs, mixing bowls, buckets wrapped in silver foil, until the dull, grey, solid flat beamed behind arum lilies and gypsophila and white hydrangea heads, he wanted to cancel the party. He wanted to smell the blooms alone, not share them, or have the impression blocked by other bodies in the way. Day after day, she could create an image of perfection that defeated his analysis, extravagant with her energy, consideration and an ingredient it took him several months of knowing her to place, a native instinct for happiness, an ability to be satisfied with little. Why did she behave like this? Why give so much away? Why didn't she put her time into her own futures box, and hoard it, gathering its solitary yield? He admired her and despised her, knowing she wouldn't be one of life's long-term gainers.

She cooked to soup-kitchen requirements. I'm not really a cook, she confessed, I'm more of a caterer.

And what's the distinction, pray?

I've no sense of quality, only quantity.

That was to underestimate her skill with batches, or ignore the other magic essence which was so strong it hid any jarring blend of tastes. She loved communality. She was a sharer, and that was the lasting impression after her parties, of harmony and of people who were engagingly good-natured, as long as she was with them.

But as head of this household, Neal felt he was responsible for upholding their standards: she persistently flouted them. He imposed economy: she bust the bank. He locked up the brandy: she unlocked it again as soon as he went out. He was appalled at the squanders of her life which must lead in the end to an emotional bankruptcy. But what are we saving ourselves for? she cried. For posterity? She laughed and chided him and was, at times like these, in the impress of her personality, his mentor and his mother, but it also struck him that she was the corporate mistress of them all, all three, holding each in one form of suspension or thrall.

'Who are you going to marry, Singh?'

'My grandmother is looking around for me. It is her chief activity. I am very hard to please.'

'An arranged marriage?'

'Quite so. Better than your disarranged ones.'

'There's no divorce in India?'

'Oh, tactful absences among the well-to-do. Spouses in different houses at different times of year. Very discreet, a slow, rotational system like crops, to benefit the social soil.'

She looked into the middle distance. 'I'd like to see the man my parents chose for me.'

She dropped a stone into a very deep well. He waited for it to strike bottom to test its resonance. They didn't doubt Caley had a family somewhere, but she was coy about them and other details such as their address in town. Singh had not been introduced to her family and therefore he could not know her. For all his Western licence, he was shocked by the young women who drifted through the flat. Their clothes were too provocative, short skirts, tight jeans and the thing they called skinny rib, and their manners bold as they talked about rolling on their penny-plain and tuppence-coloured. He adored Caley, except that she was the lover of his friend, and his social modesty had not prepared him to respect women like these. The clingers he could ignore, but Caley was free-standing and, among his cousins and his cousins' wives in the higher echelons of Rajasthan society, there was none such. He realised when she asked, Who will you marry, Singh? – and nobody else would dare to venture on to such sacred ground with him – that this was the question asked by a woman friend. Indians didn't have women friends. Colleagues, cousinage, but no access to such a formal intimacy.

She was very clever at befriending him. She didn't touch him or presume. She treated him with dignified reserve as if he were a princeling which, in less democratic days, he might have been. This aloofness brought some degree of privilege. He took her to his tailor because he trusted her judgment, her infallible instinct for the best, tempered by a strict sense of budgeting, whatever Langholm senior thought. She was beautiful and it was flattering to be accompanied to your tailor by the beautiful, while he wasn't above relishing the small scandal of their appearances together, the assumptions made as they sauntered side by side along George Street, her skirt floating across his legs. Tall and dark, she had a sculptured look that went well with his. They wouldn't have been a bad couple, he often thought, and sometimes the sight of her shapely legs crossed below a chair distracted him from architectural form. But mainly he took her with him because she wouldn't reveal the secrets of the fitting room to anyone, that one of his shoulders happened to be higher than the other, or disclose the effects of a sports injury which made his back unsupple. His fullnesses were private. She was, in spite of the odd incestuousness of their arrangement, a very private friend.

Neal had a cruel genius for exposure. He came across a letter in the *Scotsman* and read it out. 'This little twerp from a public school complains about the punishment doled out by his sixth-form prefects, and mama rushes into print to defend him. Why did she pay so much a term to have him thrashed? I say. Probably because she couldn't exert the needful pressure on his backside herself.'
  'Which public school?'
  'Oh, guarded on that one. Not Fettes, I trust.'
  'Will she pursue it to the Court of Human Rights?'
  'She does sound the type! A warmonger.'
  Caley was silent. Picking up the paper later on, when they were alone, Thomas saw it was indeed signed by a Mrs N. Brown, Buckstone, Fairmilehead. It was a well-construed letter, in a fine heckling style, but not destined to calm a situation already on the verge of the hysterical. It offended the libertarian in him to admit it, but Thomas knew first-hand that school punishment was endemic, like the sexism and racism which went on in most of the city's private clubs. Beyond easy law enforcement, beating by belt or slipper or clackan was enshrined in the moral constitution of Great Britain. Submitting to being walloped was only a test of one's willingness to join the great success club, and be a walloper in turn. It was the ultimate initiation ceremony.
  'Your Browns?' he asked her.
  'Unfortunately.'
  'It's not your misfortune anyway.'
  'Why not? I don't dissociate myself.'

'Perhaps you should.'

Caley thought that was easy for him to say. They'd a cold-blooded streak, the Langholms, or were related only to people they were proud of.

'What's behind this letter to the paper?'

'He'll be expelled before long, I think. This is good cover. It will make it look as if he chose to go.'

'Why expelled?'

She gestured. 'Because he doesn't take the punishment.'

He thought for a while, guessing at the details she didn't impart. 'Don't tell Neal,' he warned.

'Oh, don't worry. I wouldn't deplete his store of compassion.'

Afterwards, Thomas wondered about that injunction to be silent. Because he didn't want to be connected for his own part with expulsion-material sons and a shrill mother? Because he was a latent beater himself? Or was it a kindlier impulse, to just be quiet and let it roll? Or a solemn premonition of the way things did fall out? Whatever the reason, he knew he shouldn't have said it, because they weren't naturally secretive and his warning served to extend the error, implicating them in another's mischief whereby, in trying to cover it up or not speaking outright, they were sure to be exposed.

Singh put another newspaper cutting in her hands. It was twenty years old and fell out of one of his books in the reading room, surprising him as much as her before he passed it over.

Hundreds of friends and professional colleagues heard with real sadness of the death ten days ago of John and Mary Langholm, while on a walking trip in Nepal. John came from a family of Church of Scotland missionaries who also numbered several Hebrew and Hindi scholars. His great-grandfather (Thomas Langholm, 1823-76) is best remembered for his extensive work on a Hindi dialect which he learned fluently and recorded by hand transcription in a famous work of Indian lexicography, thereby saving it from extinction. His father, Robert Langholm, also spent several years in the Far East, and was a lecturer in Comparative Religion and a former Moderator of the Church of Scotland.

John and Mary met at the College of Theology in Edinburgh and married shortly after graduation, determined to spend their working life abroad in the service of the

Church. Their first posting was to Sri Lanka, where they revitalised a rural Christian community, but John's expertise in Hindi meant a long spell of duty on the sub-continent was the best utilisation of his talents by his parent church. The couple spent five years subsequently in Mangalore before being posted to the Rajasthani community based in Jaipur.

Here they made very many friends, respected for their hard work and commitment, and a determination to expand their normal duties with social work among the poorest of their parishioners. V.J. Nattawat, the New Delhi diplomat and longstanding friend of the family, writes: 'Their exceptional quality was at once apparent in the ease with which they mixed at all levels of the community in Rajasthan. The role of the missionary in post-Independence India is not a simple one. Too much preaching meets with quick resistance, and the gift John and Mary possessed was to embody spiritual beliefs in the widest context of humanity and charity. They were wholly admired and supported in their work in this state and will be greatly missed.'

The couple were also gifted amateur botanists and had spent most of their summers in India collecting specimens of flora among the Himalayan ridges and foothills. They discovered a gentian which was named *Gentiana clusii* 'Langholmii'. This was transplanted successfully to several European slopes, where it has proved resistant to disease and frost, and continues to thrive.

The exact cause of their death is not yet established. They had fallen down a small ravine and are thought to have died of dehydration, not being discovered for some three days after they went missing. Rumours of foul play are not credited. The couple leave behind two young sons who will now return to Scotland to complete their education.

'They never talk about it. This is all I know. An official obituary.'
'Was there foul play?'
'Oh, that was a politically motivated rumour. I doubt it. But there was no evidence, as I remember. Three days in the mountains. They'd had a Parsi funeral anyway. Nothing left for an autopsy.'

'What are you thinking?' Thomas asked Caley one evening when he came across her laying out a game of draughts by herself, preparing to play both sides. The board was leather, part of an Edwardian games box he was fond of.

'Oh, I used to play like this a lot when I was a child. Boring game, really.'

'But you're looking – sad.' He stroked a desolate cheek.

'Something I'd forgotten.'

'So, tell me.'

'I don't know how I learned to play draughts. Somebody must have taught me the rules. I expect it was my grandfather. It's their function, isn't it? To pass things on. We didn't have a draughts set at home, so I made myself a board out of some corrugated paper and I coloured in the squares with felt-tips. Draughtsmen? Oh, I just used different buttons, white and black, plenty of those knocking about in drawers, and I used to play by myself most of the time. There was nobody to play with. I didn't mind. I liked the game, not the winning. Then, one Christmas, I think my mother must have noticed this was a bit peculiar, pushing buttons over a bit of stiff paper, and I was given a compendium of games as a present. It wasn't as lavish as yours, of course, just a cheap cardboard thing with plastic pieces. These dominoes,' she rubbed the ebony and ivory oblongs riveted with brass, 'they're almost too good to play with. I was thrilled to bits with mine just the way it was.

'Anyway, after Christmas dinner that first day, I sat down to play with my grandfather. The fire was burning, the tree was lit, the standard idyll about how things ought to be in families. We were coming to the end of the game when, without any warning, my brother came up – he was only two or three – and snatched one of the draughtsmen off the board and threw it straight into the fire. It was made of chalk and it fizzled into nothing in the flames, although my grandfather leaped up and even tried to put his hand into the fire to snatch it out. But it was powder in seconds. I cried then. He took the tongs but he couldn't get it out in time. They were shocked because I was the child who never cried, but I was so dismayed that my lovely box of games was spoiled when I hadn't even had it for a day.'

'And what did they do about it?'

'Oh, my grandfather made me a replacement piece, as best he could. It didn't match, of course, just a plain lump of wood, but it served. I went on playing by myself, until I realised what a boring game it was. Nobody knew the rules of chess. I had to teach myself those later on, from a Teach Yourself handbook, but I never got very good at it.'

That wasn't what he meant. He'd meant, did they thrash the living daylights out of that malevolent brat? Two years old and the bearer of a large share of original sin. Why would an infant be so instinctively spiteful? Probably he couldn't bear to see the clever acted out in front of his eyes when he couldn't understand it, couldn't bear to see his sister enjoy something with their grandfather which he couldn't share. Couldn't grasp why eight squares by eight should be absorbing, or the conceptual arrangements that were possible in empty space.

'What do you think about it now?'

'That my life was perfectly normal and yours was abnormal because you were so privileged. But you don't know it yet, and that's maybe why we can't learn from each other.'

'You mean I'm a posh kid.'

'I mean it hasn't dawned on you yet how unposh I am.'

3

Edith took her letter out to the garden to share it with the man who was busy weeding the asparagus beds which were his latest craze. Robert Langholm focused exclusively on one thing at a time, reading it up and experimenting with new strains, then, when he discovered all he could, lost interest and moved on to something else.

'Thomas is coming down at the weekend.'

The man stood up from his hoe, his face quickened with interest. 'With Neal?' The brothers didn't often come together nowadays.

'No, with a girl.'

Robert drove the hoe into the border and rested one foot on its shoulder as a mark of his surprise. 'Well. And what is her name?'

'He doesn't say.'

He took the sheet from her to check this omission for himself. It proved to be the same as all of Thomas's letters, a photocopy of one of his diary entries. He had a fine hand, the old man conceded to his grandson. It was hard to think how anyone so disorganised in his person could be this elegant on paper. The script was dictated by the broad nib of his pen, the thick and thin strokes, the jet-black ink. His handwriting came out like print, edged and firm, and was the best of him. The twenty lines were scrolled immaculately down the page like the manuscript of a poem, and often read with as little logic, being shorthand notes to thoughts whose expression hadn't reached fullness.

It didn't convey anything useful to prepare them for the joint visit. 'What does her father do?'

Now Edith had come by the answer to this, if not through honest means. Neal had made inquiries and, anxious, passed his findings on. 'She doesn't have a father. She has a stepfather who is a draper and a Jew.'

They were Christian liberals. They didn't judge men by their station or their creed, but the combination prompted their misgivings all the same. A match, if one was being made between their much loved Thomas and this girl – and presumably something was afoot, as she was the first girl he'd wheeled out in front of them – a match assumed some degree of parity. Had he fallen for a lass who was desperately unsuitable?

'Ah. In trade. And it was Neal who told you so,' he deduced sharply enough. 'What does he think of the young woman?'

'That she is very personable indeed.'

'A great misfortune, that. It does blur the edge of common sense.' A scene he'd witnessed at an adjacent dinner table leaped to mind. It was north of Boston, in conservative New England, where he'd gone as a delegate to a Presbyterian conference. Six people in the dining room of his hotel were celebrating an engagement, in a way. The young man was clean-cut American, his parents the successful stockbroking, homestead-owning paragons, so upwardly mobile that nobody in their circle knew where they had come from to begin with, or cared. His mother had been coiffed for the evening, was tactfully dressed down to match the present company but still her jewels were weighty.

Across the table were their prospective in-laws. The young woman, oh, she was very personable. White-suited, she was chic, with a ravishing figure and long, black, glossy hair. She was a newly qualified lawyer to judge by her clipped, super-slick dialogue about the local real estate and how big a yard she wanted with her first house. Mexican to boot. The father at her side had been maybe a steeplejack, maybe a farm hand. His face was weathered, his hair white, his jacket sat on him unfamiliarly. His wife had some problem moving her left leg. She was wearing a buttoned, hand-made cardigan to dinner in the best restaurant in town, probably her first time through these doors. She was saying very little, which was wise of her. She was away from the table for a long time towards the end of the meal, limping while her man helped her through the glass doors to the ladies' room with an obsolete courtesy, because he loved her and was going to stand by her whatever. The dignity of those two, he would never forget it, the dignity of their shame that they weren't good enough to be seen in public with their child.

Well, well, what a thing to be so educated that your folks spoke in a strange tongue. How would it go? The bright miss would be streamed into her new family's onward success, leaving the trash behind, although Robert Langholm couldn't help observing that the young man, who was besotted with her, had no idea that every word his darling spoke made his mother cringe and curl with her own disdain. The marital quarrels ahead! The snubs. The whisperings at the country club about his mulatto bride. He had yet to learn, the innocent, how cruelly the world would treat his predilection for the swarthy.

'We will welcome her just as she is,' the man decreed, 'and be pleased, whatever he decides, because there's no changing it.'

Edith planned lunch on Saturday as an informal little meal – no silver and no fuss. They only had one room they ate in, a chamber forbidding in its vaulted size, but not in mood. On warm days like this, they pulled the table forward and with the French windows fully opened, they were *en plein air* as much as it was possible to be, sitting under cover.

She meant it to be a relaxed first meeting but was anxious, anticipating that the girl would be even more so. However they defined it in politeness, it was a viewing on both sides, and Neal's facts stuck glumly in her mind.

But Caley smiled at her, radiating easy happiness, and she was won over although Caley had smiled not to charm anyone but because she was genuinely delighted with the woman who came out to meet her in the driveway. Almost eighty, she was impressively put together. With a rather boned and hawkish face, Edith Savoyard traced her family and features back to the Revolution when, as lawyers and financiers, they'd sacrificed their lands to the democratic surge, but not their principles. She'd been keeping something of this two hundred-year-old history alive, some potency of anger and forgiveness. She was very straight about her person, with strong white hair knotted at the back, and a dress so sombre and restrained it took some time to realise it was a sprigged print. *Foncé, à la mode anglaise, ah, je m'excuse, écossaise*, she said in answer to the compliment.

After an interval, Robert came inside and joined them, walking up some steps from the slope of the garden as he rubbed his hand dry of soil to shake their guest's. He was a man unaccustomed to shed his tweeds and wore some working thornproofs that were his father's breeches. The air changed and went dark. Hard-handed and headed, Robert Langholm had nothing at all of the charmer in him. Caley would have to convince him by other means than smiles. He was shorter than his grandsons, but dark and strong, his face lined from punishing summers in the East, where dealings with his fellow kind had left him severe rather than indulgent. He was an Old Testament man before he was a New. They seemed not the most natural of couples, a French *grande dame*, a dour Scots Presbyterian, but made the auldest alliance all the same.

Edith worried needlessly. Caley had no social nerves, no anxiety about her skill in handling people, at any rate until she arrived. It was the house that unsettled her. Thomas, in suggesting the ramshackle, had left her unprepared. Carterbrae stood on the edge of a breathtaking escarpment, surrounded by the arena of low hills round Langholm town, Tinnis, Hog, Crumpton, Whitecleugh and Carlesgill in a circle. Below it, there was a long, dropping view across the River Esk that gave the grounds drama. Fertile, warm, secret, the house was built of stone, as if the hills were cut down into blocks, with the local oak hewn into doors and lintels, the forest pine making a stretch of pitch floorboards which, through open doors, gleamed down the length of a well-polished interior. The restraint of choice in a native setting added up to the undefinable quantum known as class. This was their ancestral home.

It was the strangest place, all the same, almost museumised except that it was scrupulously clean and bare along the resonant floorboards, the sound of feet muted with oriental rugs, though even these could have been samples of different knotting techniques, different designs, put out for show. There were a lot of objects in glass cases, Caley noticed as she went to find the cloakroom, Indian silver scrolls for holding parchment and documents, inscribed 'in acknowledgment of our blessed esteem . . .' In the right mood, Singh could hit the same afflatus with the English language. Every room teemed with books, old, leather-bound, gold-stamped bindings, those outsize tomes she'd seen only in stately homes before, also locked behind grid doors for security. What could they be worth? Scots history. Maps, annals of the Church of Scotland. Dictionaries abounded, French, Hindi, Greek and Hebrew, Scots. A first edition of the Waverley novels. Great testaments that would need a library table to support them. A *Young's Concordance* left out for regular reference while the Bible itself was a daily presence in this household. And strangest of all, in a roomy hallway that she crossed, a small church organ had been installed under the stairwell.

It was pleasant but bizarre: part family repository, part library, part church.

When she got back to table, they were standing behind their chairs, waiting for her in some solemnity. Robert said grace. He varied these each day according to his present sense of ease with the Almighty, sometimes formal in his terms of address, sometimes couthy.

> Some hae meat and canna eat,
> Some nae meat that want it.
> But we hae meat and we can eat
> And so the Lord be thankit.

Occasionally, in familiar mood, he slipped in his favourite offering, James Stewart's thanksgiving as paterfamilias in the western film *Shenandoah*: 'Thank you Lord for what we are about to eat, but we worked bloody hard for it.'

Their talk was fragmented. Caley, who could converse with anyone, found it hard to concentrate on her own speech because of the effort of peripheral listening. Thomas chatted to his grandmother in rapid French, good for him, agreeable for her, but Caley's school-textbook stuff wasn't up to it. The sounds rushed by her ear like a millrace.

Edith brought out a plate of asparagus freshly cut that morning, and steamed in her bain-marie to seal the flavour. There was a pile of green plates made like leaves, very old and costly as well as hideous, and the spears went down on these with a butter sauce. Caley paused, remembering there was some ritual about eating asparagus she maybe ought to know. She'd been here before, hesitating on the correct form. Six children of a professor sat down to eat drop scones which their mother cooked as fast as they could demolish them, off through a hatchway. Innocently, Caley had spread butter and taken jam, while a ripple of disapproval went round the table at her self-indulgence. One addition or the other was their norm. The act, which she didn't repeat, made her look spoiled, or not like one of them. Now, she watched attentively to see how they did it. No knife and fork were supposed to touch the asparagus. They slopped the spears about in dribbles of clarified butter and ate out of their hands. She followed suit, askance at the habit, for she didn't favour finger-food at the best of times.

'Are these the Lucullus you wanted to try out?' Thomas asked.

'No, no, they're the later crop. I sent away to an English nursery for these crowns. Martha Washington. What do you think of them?'

'A bit watery, aren't they? Need a heavier soil.' Thomas had marginal interest in the eating, more in the growing.

'Maybe so. I'll make a note of that.'

And so he did. Robert got up from the table and went to the side of the room. He picked out a notebook from a bracketed shelf that ran across radiator tops and wall panelling. It was one of thirty or forty such cahiers, all black, distinguished by titles written down the spine. He kept a note of what he grew and when he harvested it, studiously added these details as his manual for next year. The same for the freezer contents. Car costs. Household expenses. Tax statements. These were the current manuals, but there were also jotters going back the whole length of their marriage and, for all Caley knew, similar archival documents were stored elsewhere, detailing the purchase of the house and all its fittings. Mahogany toilet seat. Five shillings. These were people who annotated their lives minutely. She knew that Thomas kept a daybook for his thoughts, diary was too skimpy a term, but to pass your entire existence through this mesh of recording was the oddest thing Caley had ever seen.

Moreover, potato was a generic term to her, with white or red, new or old her only refinements. She hardly knew that different varieties existed, and certainly didn't care. She realised she'd no finesse in cooking compared with Edith's *batterie de cuisine*. Every dish perfectly prepared and served correctly. It was ordeal by eating. Her batches looked more hashy by the minute.

'You've made a long journey,' Robert commented against the background flow of French. 'And we are pleased that you could make it. Did you drive?'

'No. Thomas did the driving while I kept watch.'

'And what did you see while you kept watch?'

'I saw the ballad country. And I sat and listened to it. I think the ballads are still being spoken in these hills, and probably lived.'

She silenced him, but not in complete approval, for he was a literalist. 'And which ones did you hear?'

'"Thomas the Rhymer". Seven years' slavery in exchange for the gift of truth. That always seemed a hard bargain to strike. Or do you think their years were shorter then, like the biblical ones? Surely Jacob didn't have to work seven years for Leah? Who's worth that? Who's worth waiting seven years for?'

Robert shot her a summary look, thinking she was teasing him about the verities of Holy Scripture. 'Do you know Abbotsford?'

'No. I know the books, but none of the places.'

'And Thomas says you haven't been to Langholm before,' Edith cut across them. 'You must come back for the Common Riding. It's the big event in the town. They reassert the boundaries. Quite fun to see it, just once, like the Tattoo. Come back then. The last Friday in July.' Her speech was gracious in its invitation, but overlooked the hugeness of the imminent. In those five weeks, it would all have been decided, and Robert confirmed this fact as he looked up from his plate.

'Why, Thomas will be in India by then. Sonal Nattawat is expecting him. I've had a letter from her. You must reply to it at once because you'll need her to secure a house for you. But you're welcome to come back all the same.' He spoke undiscriminatingly, addressing each in turn without moving his head one way or the other. There was something very judged about this, and unshakeable.

If Caley had been tense, it wasn't in awe at meeting Thomas's grandparents, but because she was on the verge of her own crisis with him. Even by the time she met him, she sensed it was too late. They were shutting down their systems at Gillespie Crescent, Singh going back home, Neal signed up for Hong Kong. Only Thomas wavered, and sometimes she felt she wasn't capable of counteracting the magnetic pull of the Far East, because that was the direction of their general exodus. Planned long before she arrived, Thomas's career would evolve inexorably without reference to her. Events foreclosed.

How was she going to hold on to him? She located allies in the struggle, but Neal wasn't disposed to be one of them. He put the Appointments page in front of Thomas every morning and said, 'Apply for that one.' And Thomas did as he was told. The interview appointments flowed in. He was offered posts but didn't finalise, while Neal hung in the background, calling out, 'Decide. And do it now, or you will lose your chance in life.'

There's no work for engineers in Britain, Singh told her honestly. And they're shamefully underpaid. He'd have to get his experience on major projects abroad. The options narrowed before her eyes and Caley saw herself losing this man by default. What have I got to offer him in return for all these lost opportunities except myself? His family's expectations of him were immense. There were no free choices for Thomas Langholm. His life was already written into the continuum of those spine-designated notebooks, a CV rolled inside the parchment scrolls to add to the other scrolls. She realised that he was essentially a linguist who had taken to engineering and the sciences because they were more useful, or had a higher charitable status, and that he was being forced to masquerade as someone he was not, to fit his lineage.

'What do you do, my dear?' Edith asked directly. She liked the way this girl gave herself no airs. She walked straight into the scullery with the dirty plates and asked for a job to do, was no stranger to work, and looked agreeable about the place, pleased with what was offered her. Neal had once brought a girlfriend back who washed her hair every evening just before supper time, and asked for the iron and board to press her clothes when it was most inconvenient. A fashion plate and useless.

'A bit of everything. I read geology at Edinburgh,' Caley said. 'I was in one of Neal's classes, although he doesn't remember that coincidence, or he chooses not to.'

'Why would he choose to forget?'

'Because my marks were better than his.'

'Yes, that might well irritate him.'

'So, you're a geologist?' Robert broke in for the facts.

'No, not now. I'm training to be a lapidarist.'

'And why would you change to that?'

'I'm studying silversmithing and design, and I'll be a stone-setter. Because I like to unlock the stones, and let their beauty out.'

Edith turned about, lifting her salmon on to the curved blade of the fish knife. She knew that she had heard something strange, an original point of view spoken out loud by someone who also listened to the border ballads reverberating in the enclosure of the hills. 'I saw you had unusual ornaments.' She hesitated to call the polished discs which Caley wore pieces of jewellery. 'Is there work to be had at this?'

'Maybe not here. British women don't buy serious pieces, unless it's an investment, and they prefer to go in for safe designs. Garrard's. Asprey's. Hamilton and Inch's. Then they can trade them in when their husbands lose money at Lloyd's. But there's an export trade. Europe, North America, it's a different outlook there.'

'What is your – style?' Edith floundered with a new vocabulary.

'I stick to the Celtic. I like the geometry of it, the sense of structure. The Christians came along and adapted all the ancient forms to suit their needs, but the devouring beast came out of Norse mythology first and hasn't got anything to do with Adam and Eve and the serpent. People adapt their symbols just as easily as buildings. They tell me, too, the swastika was a Hindu symbol

36

for peace to start with. First it was a synagogue, and now it's a church. I must see Cordoba.'

Edith looked at the brooch she was wearing. Now that she examined it, she could pick out the head and tail of the serpent, but they were centred and the body was inscribed at a different angle in each of the four quadrants of the Celtic cross, like a maze that amused the eye as well as blocking it, a mathematical puzzle. Rather clever, she thought, rather pleasing. 'And did you design that?'

'Yes. Singh thinks it's an awful lump of stuff. He's into diamonds. But I can improve on it, can't I? I can always try to get better at the thing I do.'

On Sunday evening at six, they came together before dinner in the hallway. Ruth Palmer, who had the weekend off, came back and rejoined the family without comment. This was a house of silent accord. Things ran by clockwork, which Caley conceded was deeply boring as well as deeply supportive.

Out of all the perfectly collected rooms at Carterbrae, she liked the hallway best. The double stairwell curled back like ram's horns and, behind the alcoves that were formed by it, the reed pipes of the organ ran up the full height of an internal wall. Overhead was a cupola, making the space as light and airy as a presbytery, shedding sun on decorations that were restricted to blue and white and pine. With a good drawing fireplace and steady daylight, the family used it as their second living room, which meant it was their favourite space and attracted the objects they used most; it was the warmest of the rooms downstairs, in temperature and its enclosing mood.

Robert took up his position at the keyboard of the organ while Caley eyed him warily. Were some family hymns pending? Please don't ask me to sing along. I'm tone-deaf and will shame us all.

But, although they came to a silent attention, Edith weaving a matching darn into the elbows of a work pullover, Thomas constructing the reply to Sonal Nattawat, alternating paragraphs of Hindi with English, she looking through an old book of coloured lithographs with names like 'Amber Palace' that cast a remote, dream-laden spell, it was to a recital they had come. Active participation wasn't called for.

This organ was Robert Langholm's joy and only self-indulgence. When he retired from active ministry, he bought it from a derelict chapel in Carlisle and installed it with his own hands. It took five years to complete the work, in an operation as complex as plumbing and central heating and rewiring in one go. Three thousand feet of reed piping underneath the floorboards. Two bedrooms out of the original eight had been turned into organ stops. A pump, control room, amplifiers, speakers, transformer took over. It was the world's first and biggest personal music system.

The man sat ramrod-backed on the organ stool, and played something stern and unsmiling like Crimond, or one of the metric psalms, to warm up his hands and the machine. He disdained the more tinkering hymns, some of which were downright ungodly – Blake's 'Jerusalem', manic if visionary, shouldn't have been adopted into the hymnary in his view; or unseemly, like 'O love that will not let me go'; and sometimes badly written, his most condign charge, like 'Onward, Christian soldiers'. But his congregation were allowed to ripple over 'O God of Bethel, by whose hand thy people still are led' and Milton's crystal spheres, ''Tis only the splendour of light hideth thee'.

The house puffed and wheezed on the border hillside as Robert slid backwards and forward over the long polished bench, pulling stops, his feet pumping, his hands flying over the double keyboard, mind and limb envigorated by the five-way movement. He gave a commentary while he was playing. This note is coming from the dining room. This stop's under the bathroom floor. And there, you can hear Vox Celeste, that's in my study.

After his introductory preamble, the organist grew serious. The pipes were warmed, his audience was primed, his spirits flew to match. There was a pause of receptive silence – Caley had no idea what to expect – and then his fingers came down on a sequence of notes that was happily familiar. It was still church music. Bach. At school, the orchestra had played this allegro quite often as an exit theme from its extensive repertoire. These exits were her only musical training but she was a careful listener, a careful everything, and soon the musical tensions of the piece forced her to notice, so that the pages of the picture book on her lap went unturned.

What was this music? It was the fifth of the Brandenburg Concertos. She knew it as hazily as she knew the pattern of church bells, more mathematical than melodic, and so more likely to appeal to that sense of geometry she had. Locked on to it, however, she was so totally involved, breathing with the airflow in the pipes, concentrating on the re-emergence of that haunting motif that the striking of the hallway clock, the clanking of the metal radiator as it cooled were cursed distractions.

Caley sincerely marvelled at the piece and, if she'd been hearing it for the first time, would have recognised its genius in tonal structure, build, variety, pace, the sheer emotional impact achieved by the level left hand and the excitable right, the balance between what is known or safe and what is guessed at in life. Her heart almost burst in anticipation of the final chords. What a jubilant noise it was! If this was religion, it was the best conversion tool the ministry possessed. Heathens subdued, doubters won over, herself included.

The others were less swept by the phrasing than she was. It was their daily fare. That was the distance between her and them, not their ability, not even the quality of their response or their power to analyse it, but their ingrown familiarity with the raw material. They were bred to it. Caley knew she could never learn to read music any more than she could learn to write Hindi. These two occupations pursued in her presence by grandfather and grandson, sophisticated, rare, sweetly compatible, represented the breach between their separate sets of endowment and what was unreachable along the arc of her own attainment. That set up an ache of envy in her, that they were so accomplished and she so dull. She might be a fast learner, but they already knew it. She didn't want what they had, but she wanted whatever it was they were.

The twenty minutes or so of the concert were soon ended. The player rubbed his fingers. I'm getting stiff, he complained, and coarse as a tinker on the notes. They all yawned and stretched. It was an interlude before something else. The older women rose to prepare their communal supper. On Sundays, Ruth always ate a cold meal with them. They weren't fundamentalists when it came to cooking on Sunday but respected their neighbours who were and, having no need of motorised transport to the kirk, forbore like Wee Frees to labour on the Sabbath day and kept it holy.

How could she hold on to him? With the paraphrases of her body.

They kissed in the small bedroom at the end of the corridor, so steeply sloped under the coomceiled eaves it left them only a strip three feet wide to stand upright in. Their kisses dragged and seemed unendable. If they went on kissing standing up, she felt she was going to faint because he had a way of drawing something out of her, like good sense. Or maybe he was so tall, she toppled to reach up to him, and that made her dizzy.

The sitting was easier. The lying better still. They lay for a long time in the strange, crepuscular light of the Scots midsummer, warming each other, cooling, taking off and putting on. Undone, Caley was voluptuous or the bones carried the flesh well. Time and time again she detained him.

'I'm going to send that letter to Sonal Nattawat.'

'There wasn't any point in writing it otherwise.'

'There's a job waiting for me in India, a good job, I mean to do good work. And she'll find a house for me not too far away.'

'She's a house-finder, is she, Singh's mother?'

'She's an everything-finder.' They were quiet, absorbing the burble of the river. 'You should come out.'

'To India? What's there for me to do in India?' Was this a visit he was suggesting or a permanence?

'In the way of work, I don't know what there is. Something. Maybe I need to see the situation first-hand and tell you.' This was Thomas's idea of a proposal.

'But I've none of those useful skills. Paramedic, social worker. That's not me. I couldn't help you out there. I couldn't help anyone.'

'You could teach. Everyone can teach English. Or you could work with crafts. The women make things but they have a hard time selling them on the domestic market. Textiles and handiwork. You could shape up their designs to Western standards.'

She juggled with the idea, but it contained a hugh conceptual leap. Like the music and the script, she could only guess at its outlines. The actual meaning, the reality of it, was hidden from her. And he didn't make any sort of plea. He didn't even ask her. He put forward the momentous casually, take it or leave it, and while she was drawn to his liberal approach, she would have liked the strong persuaders, love, need, the passion for a shared life, or for him to convey he had the situation under control and would smooth her way. He knew the shape of that future. She didn't and he couldn't describe it convincingly enough.

'It would be expensive for me to fly out, wouldn't it?' She stalled on the most basic detail. How would she pay for it? What did she own that she could sell? A beaten-up car, some jersey pull-on clothes and a skill. Not even that – the pathway to a skill as yet undiscovered.

He heard her negative excuse with some dismay. Money. Wasn't that the middle-class pretext for not doing anything, that it would cost hard cash? He was disappointed at locating the ordinary streak in her and, not understanding its source, thought she was reluctant for the joint adventure.

Edith stood at the open window of her bedroom, lightly shawled. She heard him pass along to the room at the end of the corridor, creaking on a loose floorboard as he went, and waited for him to return. But he did not. He slept the night in Caley's bed. What do I think about this? The woman jumped fifty years of attitude and wasn't shocked. What was carnal knowledge, after all, but a description of degrees? She'd lain on the upland hills and clasped her own man ahead of banns, so was unshockable. This was the house of the Langholms, and if she didn't forbid their union by going along and standing at the door and physically parting them with her own hands or words, then she condoned it. Besides, she'd no objections to his choice of woman. If they didn't love each other under this roof, then they would go somewhere else to love. So she stood on, chilled and anxious and remembering what passion was.

'What did you think of Caley?' Edith asked her husband first thing on Monday morning, when the house was empty again and their visitors had gone back to Edinburgh.

Robert thought for a long time because, although he'd known the question would be asked, he had no ready answer. Beautiful, charming, welcome in their family group with or without the hangers-on, these were the easy comments he rejected. 'I think that she will under-serve herself. She has such a great gift for communicating that she has no need to impress other people by any other means than talking to them. And that is not enough.'

Ruth was more discerning, at the kitchen sink. 'There will be no other woman for our Thomas. He is a once-only man. But that doesn't mean to say they will end up together. She is multiple.'

4

Dear Edith,

A quiet week in all. Thomas has seen home his thesis into his Director of Studies' office and on time, wonder of wonders. Singh holds his head in his hands about the finals paper on surgery techniques for osteoarthritic joint replacement – or something such. This is the last, desperate ditch for him. Being farmed out on the wards of the Infirmary hasn't been so gruelling. I think he will be a brilliant surgeon, but he finds the bookwork a chore.

I'm thinking ahead myself, and won't do a day more than my contractual three years' pay-back to Costain for my sponsorship. I sometimes wish I'd snapped up one of the fat Middle East contracts earlier, and taken a chance on paying the penalties for crashing on my agreement with them. But I suppose they could have blacklisted me for breach of contract, and it's not been too dull, seeing my time out like this, or hasn't over-exerted my imagination. Thomas has found the new hydroelectricity plant interesting and we've had several days on site recently. We arrive at a pedantic distinction that for him water is a source, for me it is a resource. We have hours of fun on that, punching each other senseless with words.

It strikes us all that we're winding down on this period of apprenticeship. At the end of the summer, the three of us will have been in this flat for eight years altogether. By a coincidence of timing, that's the span of Singh's medical degree and my rather desultory changes of heart about architecture as a useful means of earning a living, which has put us in the same chronological boat. By September, we will all be out. That's strange to contemplate, being three totally separate entities again, instead of a hydra.

The main event of last week was the visit Thomas and I

43

made to Caley's family in the suburbs. I started out feeling equally disposed towards the invitation, and I intend to be as dispassionate as I can in telling you about it now – for no one else would I ever tell, or could. It was billed as Sunday lunch with her family. We roll up in the Esprit. Thomas has gone into his silent mode, the space-staring we know so well. I see I will have to make the small talk. Arriving early from wherever it is she hangs out, Caley is producing a meal very quietly when we arrive, very organised as usual. It smells good. But she's alone. Where's the reception party to greet us? I don't ask in case there's a strategic problem, like not being wanted or a family row which is raging in one of the back rooms. It has that feel, you know, a place of veneers that quickly peel.

Being alone gives me a chance to sit still and take in the house, however. Fairmilehead – did I tell you? – a Twenties house in decent grounds, not bad stuff really, with a lot of heavy pine panelling that's got a hint of Lorimer about it, a sort of watered-down Lutyens. But the décor they've flung on to its sobriety! It was all quite shamingly bright. Someone's gone round with the colour chart and chosen the most garish things. The room we sit in is, I suppose, Chinese-yellow. Great in China, but we don't have the sunshine levels to balance out those chromes. It's hideous on the pallor, and I feel I've come down with a bad attack of jaundice. Everything the eye lights on is showroom-new and still price-tagged. I begin to scent the nouveau, and this is confirmed when madam makes her entry.

How is Caley the way she is and her mother is so tacky? Mystery of genetics. Not stupid. Not ugly. Just tacky. She's a woman who doesn't wear clothes but outfits, colour-matched and on the bright side of her walls: heliotrope, aquamarine, an arctic blue, all the rainbow shades but the storm factor is prevalent in the display, not the after-calm. All the time she's talking to you, Nina Brown is quietly running her eye up and down your own clothes to work out what they'd cost. Where are you on her graph of worthwhile people, wealth one way, influence the other? Thomas she's already discarded as untradeable, but I puzzle her because she's astute enough to know I have the mark-up value of a gentleman. I pump this weakness up unashamedly, telling her about the famous scions of my family until she squirms with unrequited jealousy and starts to tell me about the man who married one of her aunts and is somebody I must surely have heard of. I have. Even more bizarre. She *should* know better.

This is a wicked game to play with strangers, family one-upmanship, but she forces the basest attitudes on you because there's no range, no reach, in the woman's mind. She is stuck at the doorway of acceptability and may shout for entry to the skies, but no one inside will let her through it.

They tell me that she runs her own business, a rum sort of place called 'NB' in a prime site in the High Street. It's acquired some status, so they say, among nightclubbers and the disco-dancing fraternity. She sells second-hand clothes, quite upmarket, words I don't know but borrow where I can, with sequins and bustiers and American authentics, for which she scouts round the charity shops in the Grassmarket and beyond, snapping up little bargains they haven't spotted. Has a furrier at Marchmont who repairs the hundreds of coats she cold-stored during the anti-*fourrures* campaigning years and brings them out to meet a starved demand. All the blue fox and Persian lamb you could wish for, hanging on the rails like so much dead flesh. And she can lay her hands on second-hand cashmere, finding poor girls newly out of design school who're so desperate for work they'll recut it and make new from old. That's quite clever in its way, to have the designing eye. Almost an original. 'NB' stands for North British, which is technically correct, or *nota bene* for the benefit of the college girls who drop in, or, more egotistically, for Nina Brown.

This is the way she trawls people, to use and reshape them for some future purpose of her own.

Time goes by and we wait on. The lunch is switched down to simmer point. Nina has a pre-dinner drink too many. Eventually, about three o'clock – we have walked the entirety of the grounds by this time, and been ushered into the most private recesses of their bedrooms to admire the new wallpaper – a car pulls into the drive.

Father and son emerge. Maurice and Oliver Brown we are introduced to. (Braun, in fact, German Jew. Why have they changed it?) These are the draper plus the public-school boy, Caley's stepfather and stepbrother. The brother is much younger, a good six or seven years, a tall, handsome, green-eyed boy who has obviously seen her off in terms of cornering the family's massed regard. She is clever, so what? Works hard to keep them centred, at least during their erratic mealtimes, so what? Is deeply loyal to this impossible, embarrassing trio, so what? He is the Star of David son, the be-all boy. At one point, later in the afternoon, this Oliver comes up with a half-baked, unworkable scheme for how the Faskally Dam could have been better built, if I recall, having read about it in his anachronistic geography book. His father, smirking at his borrowed cleverness, is moved to say, 'You're just like me, son, you can do no wrong.' And no one laughs. They are serious in their misplaced regard for this stripling's recycled thoughts.

It transpires they've been at their draper's shop all morning, and much of the afternoon too. Jewish, they are, of course, exempt from observing Sunday trading laws and keep open shop every day of the week, *nem. con.* Oliver is taken along to tidy up the stock that's been dishevelled by Saturday's frenzy, and he has that bored, sullen look which neither his parents nor his schoolmasters can thrash out of him. The father, master draper, is dressed in rags, literally – his cardigan is in shreds, his shirt collar worn – and he is completely unshaven with a grey hoar line I can't drag my eyes away from. On a Sunday, at three thirty in the afternoon. We are talking about a different culture base. I have no point of comparison and mark this behaviour down as aberrant.

'If you would excuse me for a moment, I must go and brush up,' he says, opening out a pair of grimy hands that wouldn't be remarkable on the dossers down the Salvation Army hall in the Grassmarket. 'Would you care to wash your hands?'

He has a curiously pedantic mode of address that isn't unpleasing, but we still decline, in case the offer is intended to be communal and we'll be all bums together.

Caley serves a lunch that is as delicately cooked and presented as two hours' overtime permits. The conversation is, well, non-existent. Actually, the draper isn't bad in spite of coming to table as raggy as he entered. He's rather hospitable, *Do have some Goldvasser. These are pieces of real gold in it.* You'd be dead if they were, but never mind the inaccuracy, there's a touch of Cleopatran splendour about the notion. The man's been around a bit and kept his eyes open, has seen the Middle East and you could probably extrapolate something from him like a pithy observation, if not an idea, if his wife would only let him be. She interrupts constantly, hacking off the end of other people's sentences – is she deaf, or just drunk to the point of being numbingly insensitive? – and postures with her own opinions, as grandiose as they are ill founded. She is somehow unsilenceable and, as she talks, I fixate curiously on her Adam's apple which, enlarged like a man's, bobs up and down, and I am overcome with a desire to throttle her at that exact point and stop the flow of verbiage.

Man and wife bicker unremittingly. I have never been party to this sort of social indecency before. Marital banter, yes, the private in-joke, but this is just too grim for words. Maurice picks up the cream bowl, a hand-engraved crystal job, while she goes into raptures telling us whose aunt it belonged to, as if we care whether this is the one who married the famous man or the one who didn't. As Maurice is serving himself, her face writhes in an agony in case he drops it or marks it or damages her precious object in some way that's implicit in using it. I see what shapes Caley in this scene and promise that I will be more careless with the immaterial from now on. And then, when he is done, she takes the bowl back into her own safe hands and scrapes it perfectly clean with the ladle, licking same!

The son, meanwhile, bored with a family pageant he has probably seen enacted every day in life, wanders away from the table to play with the television set in the adjoining room while we are still finishing our meal. Remonstrance makes no difference. Command falls short. He carries on and, eventually, opens the connecting doors and wheels the set into the room as far as its flex will go, so that he can watch it while he eats, pawing disdainfully at Caley's meal. What's this supposed to be? And, in part, I sympathise with his desire for an alternative entertainment, dull as the table talk is. But this is what they are spending six thousand pounds a year to educate, to send out to tidy up the shop on Sunday and to launch finally into the family drapery by way of his career. Anyone more unsuited to serving others I cannot imagine. Nina has married Mr Money Pots, and she don't like the end result.

After we finish lunch, Oliver starts to pester me about the

Esprit, first compelling me outside on to the driveway to show him how things work and then demanding to be driven around in it. So I take him for a spin. It's light relief, actually, to be out of the emotional consternation of that house and we go along the back roads to the Braid Hills and circle round by Comiston. He starts to want to take the wheel. I've got a provisional licence, he assures me, but I realise that I don't know his actual age, whether he's sixteen or seventeen, I'm not sure – and wouldn't trust him to tell me the truth anyway. He goes on and on and on, the quality he's inherited from Nina and Maurice, a blunt insistence, which is why they give in to him rather than putting up a fight.

I've driven across Europe in my father's car. Well, not in mine, boyo. The argument I produce, that it's insured only for me to drive, cuts no ice with him either. We have comprehensive for every vehicle, business regulations. I'm already covered. Just five minutes. I'm a very good driver. We'll go out on the Penicuik road, I know it well. I'm almost taken in by him, am shaking with a spasm of rage that my logical argument makes no impression on his suave and painless features, that he's simply untrainable as a human specimen and doesn't know his place in the scheme of things. Even if I'm rude, I won't dent that insensibility. He's a creature possessed by the power of what it is he wants at that moment.

I turn quickly through Buckstone and back to Fair-milehead, pocketing the keys without a word. I wouldn't put them down in that house, not with Oliver filching and making soap impressions or taking maker's codes. Not one inch would I trust that boy. They lock things up like warders, door on door on door, and I'm not surprised. I tell you, he gave me a fright because I've never met anyone so dedicated to being a nuisance before. That boy needs a one-way ticket to somewhere distant.

Caley, meanwhile, how is she taking all of this débâcle? She is very calm, unflappable, keeps smiling and trying to make a go of things somehow. I have a sense that she's often been pressed to say please and thank you, to be humiliatingly grateful to the man who had saved her from a fate worse than death – that is, being excused his daily presence – and that they have Cinderella'd her quite extensively. There is a touch about the corners of her smile that's set, and suggests endurance rather than happiness. When we get back to the house, she's serving tea by the television set, with Nina sitting glued to it this time, while the dining table in the next room has been cleared of dinner plates and covered again with piles of banknotes, Saturday's takings and today's, which Maurice is sorting into the different bank issues and denominations before putting the locked bag into the night safe.

Thomas and I take our leave and drive back to Bruntsfield without saying another word. What is there to say that wouldn't humiliate either of us? Am I a snob to notice how far adrift they are from anything we would recognise? Am I wrong to fear that Caley will, at some point in the future, have to make the insupportable choice of seeing those people alone, or not seeing them at all, because they are not presentable? That's not for me to judge. I'll stay staunchly silent until I'm asked.

Forgive me if I've burdened your patience with this long outpouring, using you as my sounding board. I'm distressed, and angry, at a loss for how to think and turn to you, as always, as my best adviser.

With my love,
Neal

Edith had walked outside the confines of the garden wall, on to the hills behind the house. The fatness of Neal's letter had warned her there was some reading in it, and she was glad to be alone during its perusal, for she cried out loud several times, in pain, in grief and sometimes in laughter, at the accurate slights he made. He had a wicked turn of phrase, that young man, and a wicked seeing eye.

But he had indeed burdened her patience. She wasn't pleased with him for having committed these thoughts to the indelible. So what? the emphasis of her experience tended to ask. Was this the end of the world, what he described? She knew exactly the set-up outlined, had known a girl at school who'd had the same shopkeeper's background and on Sunday morning had sorted the socks into pairs by scraping off the half sizes printed on the toe piece and stretching the smaller one to make a saleable duo out of a mismatch. There was no reason to suppose that Caley had been exempt from that small act, or harmed by it. Where had her common sense, her graft, come from other than by example? Dirty hands? Pshaw, boy, time your own were soiled. Down to the Salvation Army halls and expose thyself to feel what wretches feel.

Neal was trouble-making intentionally, and had succeeded. He troubled her. She knew she'd never clear her mind of this ready-framed record of events, distorting her response like a bad rumour he'd repeated maliciously. Not the effect but the intention harmed her. That was the first cause of her distress, that he was so belittled as to notice whether they had yellow-painted walls and crystal cream bowls. What an old woman in the making! What a spyhole he made on the larger truth.

The phrases wounded her all the same. They hadn't hesitated to educate their son's sons after that cruel accident in Nepal, although there were younger kin willing to take it on. Those re-created, boyhood years were golden in her memory, the more so for being unexpected, years of happiness they'd had with their grandsons, like a second crop out of the same ground. But raising a grandchild had a special sort of strain attached to it. She often felt that they were out of step, too forgiving of the inherited family traits because that was the tie that bound them, and too intolerant of youth's. As with any fostering, Edith suspected she'd misshapen those boys or could have done much better. Once at child-rearing was enough. She should have raised Neal differently, although, in her heart of hearts, she thought, 'He's more like his mother's side than any Langholm man I ever knew.'

At each mention of Caley, her mind contracted in a spasm, not from the antipathy Neal had hoped to arouse, rather the reverse. But I love her, she cried out, and I love her more for this. I want to go on seeing her. Don't deny her to me. She's Thomas's future, and she's mine. Why, if they went about it in a hurry, she could live to see a new race of Langholms, a new regeneration. She quickened at the thought of the parents the two of them would make: strong, strict, loving, fair, compassionate, creative, all of the best. Please hurry to do it before my time runs out, and put a new child in my arms.

The seizure of fear that this natural outcome might be thwarted highlighted something else for her, that it was Neal's intention to secure her as his ally in a concerted family rejection of Caley. What a piece of vanity on his part! They weren't so wholly wonderful, the Langholms, or she must have been too reticent about their own black sheep. What did Neal know about how Caley felt in all of this, and what did he care? No more than those he castigated for insensitivity. Had he jumped and offered to relieve her of the burden of serving such an ungrateful crew? No, he would sit there and gloat behind his hand. But his parodies gave rise to many questions all the same. If Caley wasn't Brown by birth, or Braun, what was she to begin with? Had she sacrificed her own name voluntarily or been pressurised into it? Wouldn't it all be easier if we had the same name? To a hapless, under-age child that might be a tough argument to resist.

But the fact that there was ill feeling at large among these three people close to her had to be addressed. It fell to her to alter in maturity the attitudes of a man who had forgotten that he'd previously met a woman who overtook him in one sphere of excellence. He sidelined well. It was probably too late to rectify the imbalance between Thomas's precepts of charity and his brother's. One under-driven by ambition, the other over-driven: who could sort it now?

The letter fluttered on her lap in a summer wind. Neal hoped to enlist her sympathy but achieved the opposite. She wouldn't even have the malign document in her house. She tore the four, close-written pages of the letter into tiny shreds, until no more than the odd word was left legible, and she flung it disdainfully down the hillside and out of her sight.

But a fickle wind caught it and whirled it round again, as lightly airborne as confetti petals, and drove it over her head in a cloud before dispersing it downwards, some of the minute scraps reaching to the edge of the town on stronger thermals. Seeing it broadcast like this, she felt its message had spawned and grown and was unstoppable in evil influence. She wished she'd burned it in the kitchen stove or contained it in some way that was more finally destructive.

Neal waited for his grandmother's reply, but none came. He knew that he was censured by her silent reproof, but exactly why, he never understood. She made no reference to it, and often, in their subsequent dealings, it formed a raw space chafing at the pair of them with both too proud to clear it.

Caley didn't fare any better in terms of her family's response to the dismal lunch. Nina was very unimpressed. She sat at her dressing table, in a Wedgwood-blue bedroom, while Caley combed her hair. The woman often asked for this service, asked Caley to even up the cut the hairdresser had given her, to check why the crown wasn't lying flat, or to perm it, and Caley did so when she was at home, just because it was asked. But it made her squeamish to touch her mother at all, when even the pimples on her scalp gave rise to feelings of antipathy.

'That Thomas of yours hasn't much to say for himself. Now his brother's got more gumption. You can get some sort of response out of him.'

'Thomas is thoughtful to himself. He doesn't have to think aloud.'

'Well, maybe he should try it. He'll get nowhere in the world like that. He's a man who's made to be put upon. Whereas Neal will go far, if I know anything about it.'

'So you think I ought to switch the brothers round and go for Neal instead?'

This was further than Nina had moved along the path of her own reasoning, a trajectory she seldom followed to the end. She only meant to disparage Thomas, principally because she thought Caley ought not to be tying herself down to any one man in particular. She'd strange notions of betrothal, thinking Caley might look very high if she'd a mind to. Keep your powder dry, she often said. 'I might prefer to chuck them both. Take your time about it.'

Caley had no such concept of lineage. Brown, Braun, a nameless somebody before that. She didn't think much of names. In the last hundred years, the two sides of her family had produced between them a street scavenger, a cobbler, a bankrupt builder and an illiterate, immigrant pedlar, two of whom were alcoholics. That they'd escalated socially – producing bright and bonny children – was a matter of some interest to her, while she wondered where the power to rise came from. Perhaps people were like water, and rose under pressure to their own levels? Was she ashamed of the ragtag? Not on your life! She was suffused with pride that in her bones was a goodly quantity of dross, the energising compost in which rootstock took hold and flourished.

Listening to the sharp advice, Caley was diverted from her own purpose for no more than a second, and merely gathered the useless, idly given opinion like a stray thread, gratuitous on the carpet. She put it in a lapbag with many others and in time would sort the thrums to something usable.

If she'd been privy to Neal's letter, she wouldn't have disagreed with it in one iota. It was the real, unvarnished truth. She would even have chided Edith for censuring the account. After all, he'd been to see the pantomime, and wrote about it in caricature. But the distance with which she saved herself, the buffer zone she'd made to stop her family crashing into her too often, didn't ease the pain of having to apologise for them to outsiders. The Browns were unreachable and she knew it. Maurice had in truth saved her from a fate worse than death. He'd rescued her from ignorance and self-deception. He sent her to one of the city schools where they played Bach at morning assembly, and showed her fossils lying curled inside cold stones, and she rubbed shoulders with the mainstream of the capital's clever young. She met the sisters of the same families who'd befriended the young Langholms when they were stranded in the long summer holidays at Fettes. She'd been taken on the same boats and to the same farmsteads, at varying times. She'd caught rumours of the brothers long ago and wondered about them. Sometimes, hearing Thomas's tales of dislocation, about living abroad, the difficult of relocating into the different thought climate back in Britain, she felt sorry for him. She'd been down that same path, but from inside the island shores, not outside. Her story, although it ran parallel, had a different ending. She'd rather have been brought up by those two strictly loving grandparents down in Langholm than be adopted into Buckstone, any day.

She'd learned to self-protect as a child by developing two separate characters: the extrovert, sociable one outside the Buckstone walls; the quieter, withdrawn home bird. Neither of her personalities knew the other. As an adult, she was still surprised by the extremes of her own response, which could be either outspoken and bold or dutifully submissive. The two halves of her often looked over a dividing line and said, How could you be so outrageous in public? or why didn't you put up more of a defence? Why be so cowering?

At times she'd tried, but three to one weren't fair odds. She'd been on the point of walking out of the Brown entourage half a dozen times, for good enough reason. But something held her back from dismissing them altogether. She was the only one with mental mobility and she earnestly believed that, as long as she was with them, they might improve and learn by her example. Nina could turn sweet-natured, Oliver take to work, Maurice become wiser in his judgments, viewing the shop as a means and not an end.

They were a violent family. They expressed themselves in aggressive words and acts. She'd had several uncalled-for beatings as a child and witnessed many more. The letter to the *Scotsman* brought that nastiness back to the surface again. They were people in whom the grain of beating was deep and pervasive.

More than once she'd stood between the man and wife, or stood between the parents and their mutual child, and pleaded for clemency, bound their sores after they'd hurt each other, offered them balm and compromise through her. She was their access point, and she mediated to the best of her ability with a soothing presence. And what was her reward? To get in the way and be beaten in turn. Quite recently, in a fit of rage, Nina had smashed a hand mirror down on to her wrist. Even Maurice, seeing the hardened swelling, the red pain, was moved to sympathy. 'You know what she's like when she gets into these moods. You're best to keep out of her way.'

But where? Where was safe from all of them? She stayed away five days out of seven, working, driving over to Cowdenbeath, seeing suppliers and shopkeepers, but wherever she went, the noise of an angry family dinned in her head and she couldn't shake it off.

5

A couple of weeks later, Oliver came across a duplicate Esprit parked on Castle Terrace. It was a white car, which rated a lot higher than Neal Langholm's red, and it was a more recent model too, with bigger headlights, an open top and not just a wind-back sun roof. It was eight o'clock in the evening. Friday. The street was quiet. No one about. Oliver reckoned that the owner had gone into the Usher Hall for a concert, or maybe the Lyceum Theatre round the corner. Plenty of time for him to take the car for a spin and have it back again without anybody noticing. No harm done.

He'd done it several times before. He'd got a friend who worked in the Lotus garage at Church Hill and he'd managed to get hold of a set of skeleton keys when his back was turned. A sports car was quite easy to get into anyway, and easy to drive away. Part of the fun was getting it back undetected, just sauntering along the back roads under the noses of the police sitting in their patrol cars. He looked older than his age. Nobody had stopped him yet. He smoked as he drove, wore his Ray-Bans, and he knew that people who borrowed cars for fun like this usually went out in a group. He always went alone.

He opened the door without feeling at all nervous. His hand didn't shake, although his heart was pounding with excitement. He eased into the driver's seat and, finding he was longer in the leg than the owner, pushed it back six inches. That was a better fit for him. He adjusted the mirror and checked the back angles in the wing mirror. Nobody behind. Nobody watching. He put the garage key masterfully in the ignition and turned it. The engine roared and, as he gripped the steering wheel, shifting the gears, releasing the handbrake, touching the accelerator pedal, Oliver was energised by its 2,000cc power, and transformed.

He was in control at last. He manoeuvred skilfully out of the parking space and turned back up Lothian Road to head along the broad southern avenues of the city. He idled at the traffic lights, swung into the lanes of fast-moving cars, signalled lazily as if he had all the time and resources in the world. He watched the long-legged, hair-tossing girls on the pavement and they watched him.

Past Church Hill, thank you, Lotus, past the clock at Morningside, the Braid Hills Hotel high up on the left, and through Fairmilehead. The street widened all the way as the houses thinned, and he laughed out loud as he passed the entrance to their own driveway, thinking the rest of them had no idea what a good time he was having. Some boring meal and some boring programme on the box. Homework – goodnight. He'd left all that behind.

He sped. The evening light lowered in intensity but was still strong. He ticked off the inns on the route out to Penicuik, humming at an even speed between eighty and ninety miles an hour, gliding effortlessly through air like a rally driver, taking bends without having to change down because he knew the road so well and calculated his gear ratio to milliseconds. Eventually, he found he'd run the course of his allotted hour, and then he executed his favourite detour down to Roslin chapel. The car park there was wide enough for him to turn in, single-handed, pulling on the wheel like a ship's captain at the helm, wheelie on his bike. Brilliant. He was just brilliant at this.

He ought to have been a Formula One driver really. He always knew how to get the best out of his machine.

The verger spotted him from his kitchen window. He'd seen this little tyke before, skidding over the wayside stones and churning up some of the carefully planted flower-beds with his racing wheels. He'd tried to report him in the past but the Midlothian constabulary had been slow on the uptake and asked him for fiddling details of the car model and the number plate which he hadn't noted down. This time he was at the ready. He picked up the receiver to dial and in seconds the message was relayed to a patrol car circulating near Loanhead.

The boy was easy to pick out on the highway. Alone. A white sports car. Driving not recklessly, but too fast for the dimming conditions. He was the classic joy rider. They put on their sirens and gave chase.

Oliver didn't panic. He was sure he could drive faster than their potty Vauxhall. He knew these roads better. Could dodge and weave. Dump the car and run up somebody's garden. They'd never find him after that. He knew he was afraid of something, but it was only of losing the game or being outwitted. He knew he'd not be caught.

He clocked a hundred. What a little fool, thought the following policemen, as they watched him courting death. There was a stretch of dual carriageway at Burdiehouse, and Oliver put his foot right down to the floor to shake the police car off. He saw the film rolling faster on the screen, himself piloting across it, stick in hand. The road narrowed suddenly into a single lane and he found himself blocked by a little Mini crawling along at twenty miles an hour. He jumped on the brakes. The sports car swerved violently, his power gone into useless spinning Gs as he hit the high kerbstones. Behind him, the two officers in the patrol car watched helplessly while the Esprit rolled over three times down a bank and came to rest upside down in a field of ripe grain. There goes another one, they said, as they waited for a burst of flames to engulf the chassis from an exploding petrol tank.

The young man didn't die. He wasn't even hurt. A little whiplash and some bruising on the ribs, although the white Lotus Esprit was a write-off. The only people who were shaken up were Maurice and Nina.

It was all Maurice's fault and so she screamed at him. 'You should never have let him drive on holiday. That's what started off this craze.'

'Two thousand pounds a term in school fees I'm paying to keep this boy out of trouble. What more am I supposed to do? It's you who ought to be staying at home and seeing he does his school work.'

Caley listened at a distance, escaping to her old bedroom which had a window and a bed and a door with a key in it. She could always imprison herself in there and let time pass on the inside. She turned the quiet pages of a book, looked at silent stones and their engraved life, burying herself in the inert and passive reaches of herself, like an island castaway.

'I've told you time and time again that something like this was bound to happen. You need to supervise him.'

'It's you who should be here in the evening, paying attention to your son. Why do you have to keep the shop open till eight o'clock at night? I can't be with him every minute of the day.'

'And how are the bills going to be paid if I don't keep it open? And Caley ought to be here all the time. She's always off. What's she doing with her time? Besides, the boy's past baby-sitting age.'

They went round in circles like this, pivoting on the central point which was that they were too different to resolve any domestic issue.

To Oliver, this new problem was a physical maze he had to get out of speedily. It was uncomfortable. It was confining. It limited his free choice. He'd puzzle and worry, but about the result of his action rather than the cause of it, not thinking he'd done anything very wrong. He hadn't hurt anybody after all, and he was quite sorry when he saw people were upset like this.

The police came up to Fairmilehead to take details of the incident and made out a charge sheet. Driving without a licence. Driving without insurance. Driving in excess of the speed limit. Failing to stop when challenged. This was posted in the police station in the High Street, from which daily notices were automatically printed in the *Scotsman*. The Procurator Fiscal, however, had views on such cases cluttering up the panels – that rich boys did play about with cars, that imposing a fine hurt only the parents, that not making too much of a fuss might get the youngster back on track. This man was called Lionel Cohen, although he'd gone through the same vowel shift as the Brauns and preferred to be known indigenously as Cowan. A first-generation émigré, his father had also been the Chief Rabbi in the city and, although the Procurator Fiscal hadn't been inside the Salisbury Road synagogue for a long time, he didn't like to see the community fall into disrepute. He interviewed Oliver Brown and his parents privately, delivering a stern but informal warning. No records were retained and the charges were withdrawn.

But the headmaster, who'd already had his punishments flouted and then mocked in the columns of the press, wasn't so easy to placate. He wrote a letter to Maurice Brown advising of his displeasure at having one of his scholars highlighted in this way, and suggested a suspension to the end of term wasn't inappropriate. Maurice, who was afraid of another bout of arguments and recriminations with Nina, quickly scrawled 'Agreed' across the bottom of the sheet of paper, and sent it back in a brown bill envelope. Oliver had the job of delivering this to the school office by hand. Not even a stamp. He was enjoying flaunting his escapades to his fellow pupils. The car, the law, the school: he'd beaten all the big systems. The headmaster, foreseeing the danger of hero-worship rippling out on a bigger scale – for, oddly enough, the boy was a competent musician and had started up a school band that played for local charity events –

took remedial action and expelled him. Brown was over the school-leaving age. He was a poor student and a first-rate nuisance. Better to part.

The third calamity was financial. Somebody had to pay for the written-off Esprit, otherwise the owner's insurers would start their own proceedings for civil damages.

Maurice threw up his hands in despair. For days on end, doors slammed at Buckstone, voices were raised, tempers frayed. More money, he exploded, endless expenses. When would it stop? The business was going through a bad patch. The takings were down. People didn't buy clothes or household goods in the summer. The shop was in an area behind the university, marked for redevelopment. He couldn't afford to improve the building independently. He couldn't sell it. He had two sitting tenants in the ramshackle flats above, whom the law protected from eviction and from paying realistic rents. Strapped he was, and cashless.

And then, by a stroke of that good luck he called divine intervention, Caley's annuity fell due. A week after the crash, the insurance company sent him a reminder about its nearing maturity. He'd been paying an annual premium for twenty years in Caley's name. It was one of the conditions her grandfather suggested before Maurice married Nina, hoping to secure some future provision for the child, for he doubted the man's instinctive kindness towards her. She was a mere girl, a child by another man, a child born outside the faith and therefore inconsequential, which was a heavy penalty for being adopted by a man inside it. But now, on her birthday, the policy came to fruition and all his bonds were made good.

That fact of the policy reaching term didn't make it Caley's money, however, all ten thousand pounds of it. What could she possibly need ten thousand pounds for? She still had a room at home, when she chose to stay in it. She didn't even pay towards her keep and seemed to have been studying or training for ever. It was time she got on and did more for herself. She'd no real outgoings. Maurice decided that he'd borrow the money from her. Some time, when she was doing something big, setting up her own business, getting married, he'd pay her back. Her stepfather quickly sent off a note to the insurers saying the sum should be paid directly into his business account, over which he had sole charge, and Nina, seeing peace loom at last at the small price of Caley's disadvantage, didn't offer one word of disagreement.

* * *

Robert put down the copy of the *Scotsman* which contained the notice of police charges. Neal had saved it carefully for a week and, remembering that he'd produced a blank response from Edith last time he complained about the Brown family, he applied directly to his grandfather as head spokesman of the Langholms to drive up to Gillespie Crescent and discuss the crisis in person.

His grandfather greyed visibly as he read the report, felt his strength ebbing away to the point where he couldn't resist the force of Neal's personality. They had blackguards in the family, but no convicted criminals. 'What does Thomas say to all this?'

'Thomas says nothing. Who does he confide in? Not me. Does he confide in you?'

'No,' replied the older man, who felt he'd been herded into making an accusation against his will. 'Does this really matter? I mean, the boy's obviously a scallywag, but is it any worse than growing pains? Judge not—'

Neal cut short the moralities. 'Well, I've asked around. I've never understood why this Maurice Braun went to the trouble of changing his name to Brown. It transpires that twenty years ago he was charged with reselling stolen goods and found guilty.'

'Resetting,' Robert amended gently.

'Two years in Saughton. Served thirteen months with remission for good behaviour. About the time he met and married Nina. It's in their blood, thieving. And eight pints of transfusion won't flush it out.'

Robert went to the window and raised one of the beige linen blinds that shaded the front rooms of the flat. He was feeling hot, had forgotten how hot the city was in June and had come up in the car in country tweeds that served him ill along the baking roads and pavements. He prickled all over as if he had a skin rash. How had Neal managed to exhume these long-forgotten facts? Twenty years. That was some pile of documents he'd had to sift. But he didn't for a second doubt the results of his research, for he would be methodical. 'What do you want me to do about it?'

'Make Thomas see sense.'

'And what is sense?'

'Is that a question we need to pose? Sense is moving into the centre ground of his potential and realising it. He's more able than I am. I wouldn't deny that. But I've had to chivvy him every day for the last two years to put pen to paper to get his thesis down. He's succeeded. He's got his doctorate. Great. Now what's he going to do? Sit back and fritter his time away. He has the greatest obligation to use his talents to the full.'

Robert watched his grandson as he declaimed in this way. Neal had the expression found on many athletes, with something strained in the look around the eyes, as if he had a goal or a winning post permanently in sight. He wanted to win very badly. It was an eager and combative face but, to the man's mind, its determination militated against a fuller development. How would Neal cope with age, or failure, or the other maturational tests? He could only guess, as he replied with some annoyance, 'I thought he'd already accepted that job in Rajasthan, with World Health.'

'Talked of accepting. It's not done yet.'

'Well, I will ask him what he is about.' But it was clear to Robert that they were talking at cross-purposes. Neal, starting on one line of proceeding – that the Browns were to be shed as contacts – moved quickly to another, and the gulf between the two prongs of his attack was Caley. Neal wanted to oust her, although, logical on every other subject, he was obscure on the reasons for his enmity towards her.

This is your bounden duty. That's not a thing you can negotiate on. It's stated, laid down. The fact that you've lost your personal inclination for it makes it more incumbent on you to fulfil it. It is what the Langholms do, serve abroad. A year, five years. That's not for ever. There's no fixed time-scale. But you cannot skulk at home, or shirk the obligation. We have expected it of you, Edith and I. Your mother and father would have wanted it, if they had lived, and if you're honest it was your own wish until very recently. You've been taken up the mountain and shown the lands of the earth. Do not cast yourself down or barter with temptation in any assumption of your own greatness. For God's sake, go.

'How can you let this happen to you and make so little fuss?'

'Because making a fuss about it will do even more harm.'

Thomas didn't follow Caley's deduction. They were walking along the paths that crossed Bruntsfield, where groups of people were playing a round of putting on the Links in the low early evening sun. Increasingly, their love affair happened outdoors, which made them feel overly young and vulnerable. They snatched moments either in a car or in a public park: they'd no other private place because the flat had begun to be invaded by half-filled packing cases, reminding them that things were on the move while they stood still, inert in the limbotic trance of indecision.

They even moved very slowly. Each had been thought lazy at one time or another because they conserved their body energy when they could. It was anyway a warm and languid day. Caley wore a knitted cotton skirt and a striped top in which he, and several others passing by, admired her very much. Admiration had its own special slowness, although she began to look fragile and nervous too, on the verge of losing her serenity, or her place of safety, which was him.

'You could try making a fuss.'

'But I've no rights to try for. You don't seem to have grasped that. All your life, you've dealt with people who are fair-minded. They operate on levels of natural justice. But I'm working with people who don't know your rules. Your power base is being kin, my kinsman right or wrong, and I just don't have that leverage. What position do you think I hold in my family? Firstborn. Beloved daughter. Don't you believe it. I'm an interloper. I'm another man's child and I've been made to feel that most days. I've no clout, and no function apart from being an unpaid housekeeper. As for myself, for what I am as a person, they don't know the first thing about me and maybe I want to keep it that way.'

This moved them on to an emotive issue, and he pulled her back to the simple, practical one. 'You've got two choices, Caley. You can put up a good case for your dues. I mean, your grandfather tried to guarantee your portion in life. Why should you be cheated of your opportunity so they can pay for the car Oliver's written off? Or you can leave for good. Walk out. Come with me. There's nothing exactly life-threatening in these alternatives, but you duck them both. You won't decide. You won't take charge of your own events.'

She heard a stray note in his invective and recognised it as Neal's. Neal must have been getting at him again. 'Yes, I always take the line of least resistance. So that's weak of me, to try and please others and put my own pleasing at the bottom of my list. Is it any less weak to walk out and leave them to it? I owe something, you know. I don't know what it is, a debt to the ideal that people in families ought to matter to each other, but I can't walk away from it, or not yet.'

'Last month at Carterbrae,' he reminded her, 'you complained you couldn't think of going out to India, or said you'd no actual freedom to operate, because of lack of cash. But when you have the chance to secure that money, which I understand is due to you, you won't fight for it. What am I to make of that? I think you're using other people as an excuse to mask your own desires, or your lack of them. You don't actually want to come with me, and I'm disappointed about that, as well as annoyed.'

Restive at being told a truth about herself, Caley became more heated. 'Well, you're the same as they are, ordering my reactions. Why do you think you can tell me what to do? I want to be what I want to be, even if that's obtuse.'

'Then that's something I don't understand.' He thought privately that the relations she was trying to harmonise might not either. She was too prone to wanting to be liked. Even when she was arguing with Neal, she didn't let things become acrimonious but smiled in the middle of bawling him out. She'd no confrontational skills, and often expressed her anger indirectly, by letter, by proxy or simply by absenting herself. To keep on good terms with everyone was her first principle, as if being often constrained in her youth had made her too pliable. Anything rather than a shouting match.

'We're ignoring the common points,' she said, ever conciliatory. 'We want to be together, but timing and place aren't on our side. Can't we rethink it? Do you have to go to India? You talk about doing good work as if that exists only in the singular. Can't you stay and locate goodness here? There must be . . .' She trailed off, waiting for his supplement of alternatives.

That invocation to duty, intoned by a grandparent as solemnly as a death knell, was still ringing in his head. He owed something too, the tithe of his working life to India, and that concept was so deeply implanted that he couldn't argue against it any more than he could change his name. 'Stay here? But that's like settling for cushy retirement at thirty. I need some bigger skies.'

Caley recognised an impasse. The arguments were familiar. She'd grown up on them. You versus me. No middle ground. She gave up.

'If you're absolutely sure that's what you want.'

'I'm sure. Will you wait, or come later even if you won't come out with me now?'

'Yes, I'll wait. So be it,' she concluded. 'My sense of duty is at odds with yours. Mine is family. Yours is – service, people at large. I can't manage the focus you've got on the whole of the human race or your world issues. You're macro. I'm micro, but the essence is the same. These three are my own people. They're not great, they're certainly not good, but they're mine, and until I feel

I can't do any more for them, I stay put. This is their crisis and I'm the lightning conductor. I may still be wrong, but it's a better wrong than most people's.'

Thomas was silenced, seeing they made no progress except to deepen a theoretical difference. He hadn't stooped to criticise the Browns, being largely non-judgmental, but thought hers was a wasted effort because they were individuals who, not acknowledging her sacrifice at the time, would not remember it either. Besides, it wasn't enough in his view to love out of duty. You had to love outright.

'The cat has run away,' she added, getting up from the park bench where the long shadows under the plane trees started to grow cold. 'I liked that cat. It was a good cat, clean and clever. But even it has deserted us. I swear I'll never let myself get fond of another cat again.'

The evening lengthened out at Carterbrae. Edith waited for her man to come home, puzzled that he should have elected to spend a day away in Edinburgh when the gardening weather was so mild. The hours dropped slowly. Nine, ten o'clock. The light waned and she started to grow fearful, for she didn't know what business he'd gone on to town, or who to contact in an emergency.

That word chilled her to the bone. It was hard to credit, but Robert would be eighty in September and she wasn't far behind. The future and its potential change seemed illusory in these moods, as she walked inside the protective garden wall the way she'd done for more than half a century, pulling out stray weeds. The town saw fluxes, but they were only of fortune. The wealth of Langholm and its enterprise was still in the farming and the weaving mills which drew on an unvarying formula, wool and water, sheep and the persistent rain on the gentle, leeward hillsides: the combination was written in the climate and therefore survival was secure, whatever fashion swayed.

Nor, while she lived in it, had anything altered inside Carterbrae. The house with its cluster of family objects, the throughput of people were a continuum that had held good for two hundred years. In that fixity, however, she sensed an end. She was ignoring signs of change, but they were manifest. Her grandsons had none of the Langholm missionary tendencies. They rather scoffed at churchiness and were lost to faith. She fretted, rubbing her hands against an apprehensive wind. She wouldn't have felt this way if she still had her own son alongside her, her own heir, John. Ah, she never stopped grieving for him because he was the best of the line, the actual last. She had a sudden sight of her dead son's face, features made like a composite of his two boys, as if a whole had been split into disjunctive halves after him. She walked often in the comfort of his shadow, a larger man than they, listening to old talk.

The car came into sight at last, and put an end to such dismal thoughts. The man who stepped out of it on to the gravel drive carried his own share of depression, however, and they had only a brief respite from the querulous mood, in being so happy to see each other that they held hands until they reached the open door. Days apart were harrowing now because they foreshadowed the longer separation.

'No, I'm not hungry,' he answered, head down to her solicitude. 'Some tea, perhaps.'

She fastened up the bolts after him and found his indoor shoes while Ruth, who'd waited up to make sure that he arrived back safely, added a busy layer behind with kettle and tray.

'You're tired.'

'I'm out of touch with the city, that's all. The crowds are very tiresome.' He took off his woollen jacket and, on an impulse, went over to touch the keys of the organ. Without current, they responded only with a tuneless clatter but the sound revived him all the same. On the music stand was the score of the Sixth Brandenburg, which he had been practising, and he hummed a complex trill from the second movement. Tomorrow was for pleasures only.

'You saw the boys?'

'Yes, separately. They're all at odds now in the flat.' He hadn't meant to give the impression of dissent, only disarray, and saw her anxious eye. 'They are for the off. I saw to it that Thomas put his contract in the post. Why, he has been carrying around that letter to Sonal Nattawat, asking her to find a house somewhere near the clinic, since he was last here. To do the hard work and then omit the easy – strange of him.'

'And did he want to put his contract in the post?'

'I think so, on the whole. Nothing is absolute with Thomas. He often doubts.' The doctrinal quip was a standard family joke, but Edith wasn't inclined to see the funny side of things this evening.

'Did you put pressure on him?'

'Well, he's got himself into rather a cleft stick with this girl. It does no harm to simplify.'

'And how did you elucidate his problem?'

He thought she was being confidential with him or didn't observe, as she bent herself to pour his tea, that her face was puckered with distress. He said the incautious. 'This girl's family are a rum set. Distance may cool things and give them both time to reconsider.'

'Is that for you to judge, or even Neal?'

He caught the drift of that all right, that he had jumped at his grandson's bidding. 'No, it is for Thomas.'

'As well as Caley. She has a vote on this, or should we each trample on her in turn?' Edith had a momentary impression of the girl's reticent face, the eyes downcast to shield their disappointment, that close, corner-clipped smile of hers. Endurance not happiness.

'Hardly that. They're both quite free to choose.'

'But you've blackmailed him in some way.'

'No. I only outlined his obligations.' Saying this, Robert realised he had made the same leap as Neal between the two different sets of constraint as if they were direct alternatives. Stay or go. He saw they'd panicked and maybe needlessly added to their long-term problems.

Tired, distraught with waiting over long hours, the woman suddenly brought this issue into the focus of her own life. Today was like all the days of her marriage: her man disappeared on his business without giving an explanation and she was left hanging on his return. It was the fate of Langholm women, to pack up and go, or to pack for others and stay behind. The Church of Scotland was a career very like the military, whose conscripts were posted to remote stations, without choice in the service of God. She didn't blame Caley for balking at the presumption that she'd up sticks and follow a calling she'd no sympathy with. Family was as good a priority as any other to stake that refusal on, or the conviction that she should serve her own talents first, or her own country. All that personal wishfulness Edith had subsumed for her own part in Robert's itinerant life. Ten years in Africa, four in India, five in China: different ministries but stable in one calling. The mission women faced the same, impossible dilemma as colonial wives, to be with their children at home or the husband abroad, but never to have all of them together, and so they suffered disproportionately from the fissure.

Edith had already lost one son to India. Must she lose a grandson too? The apprehension seized her that if Thomas went away, she might never hold him in her sight again, or in her arms. The three young men would disappear over the horizon of the earth and leave her old. That was the unspoken change she'd dreaded this evening as she waited, that she was too old ever to be needed again. No wonder she'd thrown her weight behind Caley, to help to keep her youngest offspring at home, and the living future in her grasp. Live on! Live now in simple human happiness.

'I would have liked to be consulted before you outlined his obligations for him. But you haven't seen fit to ask my views ahead. Don't ask me for my advice again on any subject, for I suspect you would only spurn its application.' She rose, furious beyond being properly coherent.

Robert didn't feel that anything he'd said or done had justified this display of wrath, and anger was injurious to health. To calm her down, he diverted to another topic, outside themselves. 'I should have told you at once. Bad news came while I was at Gillespie Crescent. A telegram for Singh saying his father has died. He'll go back at once and take over the duties of his mother's household. Funerals are big things there. He was almost ready to go but this precipitates his leaving. He sends you his farewells and says he's no time to come in person. He's very sorry.'

She looked at her husband askance; this was neither the time nor the right mood in which to impart such desperately sad news. She recalled Mr Nattawat as a very formal gentleman, suited and waistcoated and fastened to the chin with high, old-fashioned collars, who had visited them once with Singh. He'd exquisite manners and a perfect English accent, Oxford-honed, and the moment was an agony of regret for her, because of passing days and the great people of her own era who slowly melted away. The thing she feared, to be left alone in her advancing years, was happening before her eyes. Robert, too, felt a tremor round the heart even as he spoke of it, which he thought was heat exhaustion, but was the first knock of his own mortality.

6

The same evening that Thomas Langholm left for London Heathrow and Delhi, Man Singh Nattawat stood looking down on the heat-embalmed city of Jaipur, waiting for a change in the wind direction that might signal the onset of the monsoon rains. The heat went booming over the city like a gong which had been struck with a metal hammer. It came out from one of the courtyards of the City Palace, flew over the high walls and, finding no resistance in the flatness of the city, surged ahead as far as the hills at the edge of the desert plain, where it reverberated like a triple echo, pulse after pulse, wave after wave, and sent back a shock of head-splitting and ear-ringing heat from which there was no escape.

When he was a small boy, Singh had been prone to imagine that the summer was the personification of a dragon which had stirred from its slumberous lair in the mountains, and came down to destroy the villages of the plain with some sort of climatic fire-breathing. In his teens, that image hadn't entirely succumbed to common sense: rather, the impetus of current events reinforced it. The dragon was replaced by the threat of China behind the curtain of the Himalayas, coiled like a serpent's back before it swept round for the kill. The Tibetan refugees who congregated in the Jaipur streets and marketplaces proved the power of a dis-placement theory even this far away. Then Afghanistan, Pakistan, the sword-rattling states of the Punjab and Kashmir spilled over with the conflicts of Independence. Every year the summer months brought a new outbreak of tension along the northern boundaries, and he couldn't separate the crushes of heat from armies. He hadn't laid this personal mythology to rest and feared the pre-monsoon temperatures of June with more hate than reason. The gong signalled a war.

Starting out in the early evening, he drove across the plain towards his mother's house. Built at the edge of the desert, it was one of several hunting lodges that had belonged to the late maharajah and had been given to his family as a pre-Independence favour. The ruler knew that his personal hour was drawing to a close and, anticipating that Delhi was going to suspend the long-guaranteed privileges for the princely states, he quickly distributed the smaller properties to his loyal servants of some standing. Better a friend should punt the lake for duck than some New Delhi state official make it his provincial residence. Better a friend than tourists.

It hadn't changed since then. Nothing had changed from the beginning. The lodge was enclosed in the Rajput tradition of building, a square beside another square beside another. The Hall of Public Audience led to a Hall of Private Audience, which led, in turn, to a Hall of Pleasure. It was the unvarying formula for a palace, however reduced it was in scale. It resembled the motif of their hand-made carpets, multiplied edge to middle. No matter how subtle the interplay of the design looked, when you broke it down it consisted of a handful of colours and shapes, the fir cone, the flower, the leaf, the arch. Infinity from a speck; that was India. The lodge beside the lake held all the emblems of antiquity in poise, as beautiful as its hand-carved chairs and every bit as uncomfortable.

Ajit's father was the last of the houseboys whom the Nattawat family had taken over with the property. As the servant led him ceremoniously down the colonnades to the inner library where his mother was holding her party, the servant opened the double doors so that the doctor should not have to trouble himself with turning handles. 'You have heard from Doctor Thomas, when he is coming back?'

'No, he's only just left,' snapped Singh. He was brusque in order to curb Ajit's interest in the water engineer, and to remind the father of his place. Thomas had encouraged too much familiarity with his assistants, too much equality. 'They may be appointing a new man before long. Or no one at all. Who can tell?'

The man bowed his head gravely on receiving the rebuff. Who would Ajit work with then? How would he use the skill and training Dr Thomas had lavished on him? The servant retreated silently, padding back in low-heeled slippers along the length of the corridor to wait for the next caller at the main entrance.

The room Singh entered was long and low and very cool. The reservoir bed of the lake supported a small enclosure of trees which made it a shady spot in which to build a retreat. Wooden panelling acted as insulation. These private rooms had no outer windows. They were lit from the courtyard side where the air was kept cool under the verandah. In the great days, fountains used to play among the waterlily beds, but they had dried out and Singh felt the heat was threatening to invade even this sanctum, as he thrashed up the yards of carpet to where his mother sat. She would not install air-conditioning. Too modern and expensive. She would not have it.

Sonal Nattawat watched her elder son as he came in frowning, most handsome of her children, most able and the least known, as if possessing these assets diminished his needing to be liked. Along the panelled walls were portraits of his illustrious ancestors, who were good rulers or good advisers and, passing them, his frown occasionally lifted with his eyebrows in dutiful acknowledgment to soldiers and statesmen, but that furrow was becoming engrained, she thought, as she raised her hands to hold his beloved head while she greeted him.

'See, your uncle is here and your cousin. Greet them.' She held on to his hand for a moment, none the less. 'Remind me to have a quiet word with you before you leave.'

She smiled. He passed on to the retinue of relatives and friends waiting to welcome him, but she had set up a chill in him, or a fever, and she knew it. He fell into an instant sulk. Yes, he was aware the family would mass against him, but their collective complaint that he was not doing his duty he felt was minimal compared with his mother's lack of graciousness in inhibiting his enjoyment of the evening she'd arranged, and at which his attendance had been mandatory.

Four *raga* musicians had come to play for them from Jaisalmer, where they had been filming during a festival; they said the man on the zitar was a famous musician and composer, while the vocalist had made recordings and performed on All India Radio. It was a very significant honour, and Sonal Nattawat had obtained their agreement with the greatest difficulty. The intellectual life of Jaipur had travelled out this far to the lake in order to salute her skill as hostess as much as the players'. But they all sat and waited for something to begin, immobilised in inertia.

'They say they will be a little late starting,' said his uncle V.J., 'but this will not impair our entertainment.'

Singh grimaced and looked at his watch. 'I mustn't be late back. I have a clinic tomorrow and a class of student doctors.' Western punctuality gripped him. Eight fifteen. Two hours' playing time. How many encores and bravos would be added? Then the interminable refreshments and chattering. The saved-up scolding from his mother. He would be lucky to reach home by one in the morning.

Sonal, watching him always warily, thought the consultation of his watch a rudeness. Hardly arrived and he thought of going.

His uncle ignored the time strictures and went on with his interrupted conversation. 'But I am telling you, C.P., that we were better off under the maharajahs in the princely states, or British India as part of the British Empire. Take my word for it. This is not idle opinion. I am old enough to remember these things as facts. What has democracy done for India?'

'Better health,' interjected Singh.

'And so everyone lives longer and has more children. The population doubles in forty years. This is progress? No, this is self-destruction when we cannot feed ourselves,' the older man declaimed. His uncle V.J. depended for the style of his discourse on the rhetorical question, and so did the nation. Question without answer without end.

'Saying democracy doesn't work is what makes it unworkable,' answered C.P., starting to raise his voice and agitate long, thin hands over the cream cloth of his suit. 'We have got to get out of this servile frame of mind and take responsibility.'

'My dear C.P., until we break the hold of the caste system completely, we will get nowhere with this voting business. The professional politician is the new mogul, the new invader. It is in his interest to keep the other eight hundred million in a feudal network. And, sadly, it is the intellectual élite who are disillusioned. We have lost our fight, and the means to fight, because our New Delhi politicians are more corrupt than the moguls, more corrupt than the maharajahs or the British. There are far more of them to be bribed and to impede progress. That is the point. And the educated man says to himself, in his heart, how can my vote possibly be worth the same as the vote of an untouchable? I will not use my vote because to use it enhances his. I abstain from this egalitarian business of democracy when it goes against Hindu teaching.'

The assembly dissociated itself from the unpalatable and seldom-voiced truth. Sonal clapped her hands in their direction. 'No religion. No blasphemy. Those are my house rules, gentlemen. Obey them.' She had ridden on howdahs through the jungle, when she was young, to shoot the tiger. Why should she fear their drawing-room snarls?

Singh rose and moved over to an empty chair beside Lata, his cousin's wife. She was considered a beauty when she married five years ago. Two small sons and the running of a household, which included her husband's unmarried sister as well as the argumentative V.J. and his wife, had aged her prematurely. She had developed the deep panda rings round the eyes which marked most Indian women over thirty and, he noted depressingly, she had let her figure go. The sari was unforgiving on the less than lithe.

'My grandmother tells me that your cousin will come out to visit you at the end of the hot season,' the doctor said lightly.

Lata widened her eyes. In the tense matrimonial climate which surrounded Singh, the comment showed so particular an interest that it amounted almost to a proposal. Yes, her own cousin's name had been paraded to the matchmaking grandmother in Jaipur, but the grandson hadn't shown more than his normal uninterest. How should she interpret this move? Impropriety? A wish to get something more out of her than the usual brokerage allowed, which was limited to the bland, careful and unspecific? She stiffened, all the matron, but at the same time didn't want to inhibit a liaison if it might come to fruit.

'This is so. It is not the best time to come to us but, of course, she is restricted by her new employment. She has qualified now from Bombay University.'

'I know,' Singh said, as if he had been making independent inquiries. 'Does she ride? I have some good horses. They are stabled out near the polo ground. Do borrow them if you want to go into the desert.'

This was so friendly, it was fast. Convention allowed that sometimes, after preliminary details were exchanged and a loose negotiation had been entered into, the couple might meet very briefly but not, of course, unsupervised. Lata panicked, thinking the post of chaperone might fall to her, keeping the customs of East and West strictly segregated. What might the doctor expect in return? Was the loan of his thoroughbreds a bribe to leave the couple alone together?

'How very kind of you. I will remember your offer,' she said as frostily as she dared.

Absurd, thought Singh, acting as if purdah were in force. The girl had been to university. I might have met her on the campus, been to the same non-segregated classes. Why does my family persist with the outdated forms? Why are they so absurdly old fashioned?

As Lata looked into his face, she didn't think that on the whole the offer was presumptuous. Of course, they say he will not marry, she had repeated months ago to her cousin, forestalling any disappointment on her part. He has a problem, I understand. He loves the water-man and has loved him since they were small boys. He has a mistress who has entangled him. Now she was ashamed of her repetitious gossip, finding him not arrogant at all but a little sad. And he does have such comely eyes. She and her cousin had laughed together like children.

The musicians arrived at last and settled themselves, cross-legged, on a platform covered with a rug which had been set up in one of the double doorways. Quietly, the servants positioned themselves along the backs of corridors, where they were out of sight. The lamps came on, forty glass domes suspended from chains, signalling the moment for concentration and for talk to be abandoned, but it hung on querulously in the heavy air between the portraits and the pillars.

I am a stranger here, Singh thought. I am at odds. These are no longer my people. These are not my ways.

Raga was one of the ancient forms of music, and arose from an oral tradition so remote that nobody could define its beginnings, although everyone had a go. It was absolutely fixed – composed of at least five notes – and absolutely fluid, allowing for improvisation during play. The music was meant to represent the perfect balance of man and woman in Creation, and the songs that evening stung him into emotion, lyrical and poignant, enigmatic because they were so brief. *I love you. I have gone into the hills. I know you will not follow me but as the days break I hope.* What did they mean? The words set up the barest monologue around which his mind hurried to fit a setting and characters, while the emptiness in his heart was because he hadn't finished his own narrative before the notes of the song ended.

He felt exhausted by the sustained eroticism of the melody, male instrumental leading, female vocalist elusive down the scansion, the two not quite in perfect synchronisation. The stimulus to his thoughts wasn't either Lata's heavy-browed cousin or his absent friend but the third character whom rumour had attached to his private life. She would not come with him to his mother's soirée this evening, could not come with him in any declared sense, but she throbbed in the shape of spaces. He had gone up into the hills of his mind where she could not follow.

This was not a calm mood; the performance excited him but didn't fulfil, flirting only with the passions. He told himself it did not, unlike Western orchestral music, build and crash and build again with those torrential notes that had filled the Usher Hall when he was a student. It was local, not universal. It was not the great experience. The comparison cooled him. Cool, cool as the evening that passed the transitional to night.

Round the library, Sonal's fifty guests nodded as they listened to the performance. There would be experts on *raga* in the room, men who could pick up the themes like weavers' threads and say, out of alignment, broken pattern, not the fullest range of inventiveness here. Yet others who would judge that the choice of music wasn't perfectly attuned to the season or the hour. *Raga* ought to be inspired by astronomy, palmistry or mood like the medieval humours that controlled the harmony of the body. This talk of music irritated the doctor every bit as much as their clichéd conversations about politics and the unidiomatic English which his relatives used, as cloudy as rancid butter and thick on the tongue.

Even their names were written in this cryptic jargon, V.J., C.P., his younger cousin M.I. He was M.S. in the family group. It was considered a mark of respect not to refer to the full name, but was this really the desired effect? He personally knew at least a dozen V.J.s. It made them anonymous, rather than individual, and therefore insignificant, one motif among many, one note lost in a chain.

Sonal was a gracious hostess to the end, as well as a friend to the members of her family. Before they took their leave of her, she smoothed her brother's temper, told Lata she was a wonderfully clever mother to her little boys, and patient beyond endurance, thought M.I. would surely win his promotion before long, smiled at the critics of her soirée, deprecated too much praise.

'You are the all-in-all,' said Singh, watching from a doorway how the gold hem of her sari fluted against its turquoise ground. Not Rajasthani born, she didn't wear the full skirts of the state costume and was more glamorous than the other women that evening, slight, strong. Every hair in place. 'You are magnificent at it.'

'Bombay sneers at us for being provincials, but we have heard something this evening we will not forget.'

They touched hands: he kissed hers with reverence.

She turned back from the verandah where she had said goodnight to her guests, noticing with her skyward glance how humid the hour was. 'So late you have stayed. What was it I was going to mention to you? Oh, yes,' she added after the slightest hesitation. 'We must find you a new servant when Shalini goes back to her village to have her child.'

The gong beat. The conflict was joined. The elements formed somewhere higher and came down into the plain to be resolved. Storm. Stress. The war was his.

'Which village is this? Her husband's village, where they stoned her for being a witch, or her own village, where they cast her out to starve? She has a choice of villages. Which one do you suggest?'

The woman eschewed these obvious statements as vulgar. They had circled the problem of Shalini for months, a year now, because their excessive politeness, and regard for each other, ruled out the direct approach. 'It is unsuitable for her to stay,' she objected. 'If you prefer, I can place her with a family of good character.'

'Why would such a family take her?'

'Because they are good.'

The talk ran like this in circuits. For all her sophistication, Sonal went in awe of her elder son. Technically, he was the head of her household and soon to be head of the vast unwieldy caravanserai of their extended family, once he was married. It was his implicit duty to take a wife and, at least in theory, provide her with a home in old age. Social reforms, state pensions, the equality of the ballot box could not loosen the obligation which, in caste terms, was akin to the sacred thread of the Maratha, the sword of the Sikh: honour without which there was death. His servant's status in his house proved that Man Singh Nattawat was an infidel and that his mother had failed to educate him in right-thinking. She could not discuss it with him because she discussed it with no one. It covered her too with shame.

'She cannot go.'

'She cannot stay either. She is an impediment to your progress in life. I can imagine that you contemplate several ways out of this. You think you will escape back to Britain with her and your child and live as you choose there, forgetting who you are. Or you will hide yourself in your work and see no one but her, not even me or your brother and sister. But these are not real solutions because they ignore too many contingent elements, not least your own character, which is sociable and open and principally dutiful. Think about it. You have infinite choice but only one option.'

How odd, he thought, the blame is not moral. She doesn't say I have done anything wrong but urges me to do a greater wrong and put this woman away. At the same time, he appreciated her delicate diplomacy. She brought the best of himself to the surface and blackmailed him very gently with that. He felt whipped with kindness.

'It's June,' he said conclusively. 'The monsoon will arrive any time now. On the first day of the rains I promise that I will give you an undertaking.'

She picked up a book. 'I will read a little before I go to sleep.'

7

A man, who happened to be passing through Turnhouse that Sunday evening after a routine flight from Manchester, caught sight of an interesting face in the airport lounge and did an about-turn. Hello, who's that? There was nothing urgent pending at home, nobody was expecting him. He'd follow this one up. The woman who'd taken his eye was sitting by herself at a table, reading a book while she waited.

He watched her for a few minutes, and bought a coffee and a Sunday newspaper as cover for hovering at the table next to hers, but he kept her in his sights over the top of the cup and the newsprint. She'd an unusual face, all bones, and deeply shadowed under a high forehead and wide eyebrows. Abrupt hair too, cut in a cap with edges to it like her face. She had a cast head that was full of angled geometry. The effect ought to have been hard but it wasn't. The look out of her eyes was mild. She was also wearing unusual clothes. Fit for summer, they were loose but dark, which suggested something sensible or not flimsy in her. A long jersey skirt, a long T-shirt, shaped in with a belt, and some interesting jewellery as if the whole plain set of the rest was a framework for the strong ornaments and the strong face. He wasn't a man who saw these things as a rule. He surprised himself by what he noticed.

I want to get to know this woman, he thought, but how do I go about it? He wasn't a lecher, and didn't know lecher's ploys. What was the natural way to get into conversation with her? He spurned the obvious tactics. Have you got a match? Do you mind if I borrow your spoon? She looked as if she'd dismiss those openers as uninspired. One part of his mind was rolling ahead to what he ought to do next, but the other moved backwards. What had brought her here? Was she travelling by herself, or had she come to meet somebody off a flight? She didn't have a suitcase with her but she was carrying a bag large enough to be an overnight bag. Had she spent a weekend away? His mind raced furiously. Respectable, forty, a man who had a reputation for insight and judgment in his own field, the cornerstone of city respectability, he wasn't used to being thrown off course like this, but he'd lived long enough to know that the unique called for some exceptional risk-taking.

Before he could advance any definite strategy, however, he was overtaken by events. The Heathrow flight arrived and, being internal, it quickly disembarked. The woman waited calmly, checking her watch, closing her book, until the person she'd come to meet appeared at the exit gate. Then she got to her feet. He went on watching her compulsively, as the best thing to appear on his horizon this twelvemonth, and wondering why she didn't smile in anticipation of the meeting. Something more guarded came across her features, with a look of sadness, although the face wasn't inimical to sadness or greyed by it.

She stood up, and went forward to greet not one man but two. And, turning his attention to them with an obscure jealousy, the stranger thought, yes, they're about right for her. Distinctive people too. One of the men was exceptionally tall, swarthy and bearded like someone who'd often been exposed, the other tidy with himself. She kissed the tall one, shook hands with the other who addressed her with a curtness that was almost hostile.

'How did you know to come and meet us? Did Thomas ring you? We were meant to go to Glasgow but that plane was fully booked.'

'I just asked what flight the Langholms were on. I thought you might need a driver.'

The other man headed off a quarrel. 'That's very kind of you, Caley. It saves us so much time.'

They passed him by, unregarding. A vapour went with them. Animus, that odd word, came into his head, and the stranger spent a second splitting it into its atomic meanings. Spirit, yes, and animosity and something basic of the animal in these three adults who were so entirely composed, so physically real and shaped and hard that it shocked him as if they'd delivered a sideways blow to his head, stunning him.

The woman had forgotten her bag. It sat tucked under the chair. In spite of her apparent cool, she was flustered. Leave it there, he said to himself. You can rifle it later for her address. Then return it, under more conducive circumstances, wherever. He'd drive to John O'Groats to see her again. The worst of his instincts prompted him, but the honest man finally prevailed and, before the trio reached the swing glass doors, he'd caught up with them.

'I think you've left something behind.' He held out the portmanteau, more impressive than a handbag, and she took it by the long shoulder strap, avoiding contact with the handle by which he held it.

'Oh, I'm sorry that I troubled you.'

No one said thanks, and still she didn't smile. He hung on the timbre of her voice, which was unnaturally deep and resonant.

Neal had been right about the embarrassments. They began at once. Caley had a car parked outside and she came prepared to drive them all the way to Langholm that evening. Most of him collapsed in a heap of gratitude at not having to hire transport for himself, get out his driving licence, find his credit card, take the wheel and all the rest of it. But something obdurate resented having gratitude enforced this way. Caley always made herself indispensable.

For a start, he didn't believe that she'd rung British Airways for the passenger list. Ruth Palmer must have tipped her off that they were coming, and he thought it was officious of Caley to interpose herself in the first place, as if she were claiming equal status in arriving at Carterbrae at the same time as they did.

She drove the car. Thomas opted for the front seat while he was relegated to the back. Neal could have relaxed and enjoyed being chauffeured, but the triangle composed itself into two adults in the responsible front and one insignificant passenger behind. They talked in murmurs just out of earshot, so he had to crane forward to join in, head up like doggy in the back. And it was such a boneshaker of a car! Any older and it could apply for veteran status, the Morris Oxford she'd been nursing along for years, an estate model with wooden bracing which made it prone to rust. He could actually see daylight through these spars. Would the old banger actually make it down to Langholm without a pit stop?

Neal fretted at being endlessly beholden to her. It transpired she'd first-hand news of Edith and Ruth Palmer, was with their grandmother as recently as last weekend, and passed these quiet, personal details on to them. She assured them all the arrangements were well in hand. The funeral was scheduled for Wednesday.

'And who decided on Wednesday?' he interrupted from the rear.

'The minister, actually. He came to see Edith almost every day when she fell ill. Perhaps you'd like to take it up with him. Ruth made the practical decisions, as she's had to for the last couple of years, but you may wish to put a stop to that.'

She silenced him. Caley had a way of insinuating something in the fall of her words that threw him off balance. A lift in her voice. An inflection in her choice of words. She got under his skin with innuendo. She implied that Ruth made the decisions because neither of them was there to see to it. He'd done his bit, hadn't he, by coming back, not on every roundtrip from Hong Kong, admittedly, but it was Thomas she ought to be upbraiding for neglect. He'd never made it home once. Then Neal caught the self-righteous whiff of these excuses and prickled all over with the discomfiture created by her nearness.

Thomas would second that discomfort. Everything in him clenched at the sight of her. He'd been in love with this superb woman and then abandoned her for almost two years of spent ideals: that was a lopsided equation. You fool, he muttered to himself. You utter fool to let that chance of happiness slip. He was shy of noticing her entirely, and saw her clothes instead. She'd always worn knitwear, cashmere winter, cotton summer, blocks of things for easy movement. Now, he observed the details of construction, a gathered edge, a placket at the neck, some contrast trimming, and put the garments into the context of a new knowledge: what cashmere was, where cotton grew, their natural properties, shared and disparate. In other words, he saw her more clearly in the new light of his own experience, by which she didn't fail.

The effect on him was devastating. His first meeting with Caley had shaken him: at this reunion he crumbled, dismayed by the power of an attraction that was stronger than their sexual appeal. It was need. It was as if a shutter had flipped open, revealing the emotional dependence he'd been masking all this time. Away from her, he could sideline or effectively forget her. He was a man who could easily hold his feelings in suspension, or sublimate them to work and duty, in order to live off canned memories.

He recognised the outside of her, but not the in. He felt she'd changed vastly in his interval away. He'd written to her as often as he'd done to Edith, and by the same method. He photocopied pages of his journal, keeping the originals. He knew these made for very impersonal letters, however, done for speed, and he imagined how Caley would have turned his pages over with less curiosity than her mined ammonites, dead long ago and far away. To make them a living entity again would require a superhuman effort. Besides, Caley was a presence. She didn't have the mental projection for love in theory, was warm, urgent and essentially practical. It had taken him all this time to recognise that the relationship was doomed the moment he put his contract into the letterbox at the end of Gillespie Crescent.

'Singh sends you his regards, as of this morning.' The voices went on murmuring.

'Ah! How is he?'

'Very well. Very successful. He's turned out a gifted surgeon. He's building up a huge reputation.'

'And how's the matchmaking grandmother? Is he still thwarting her designs on lineage?'

'Quite deftly.'

Thomas now fell into his own thoughtful reticence. She prodded him just as much as Singh had done when he said goodbye, he prescient, she truthful. Her questions still had the tactlessness that his brother had often complained about. Direct and frontal, she asked the penetrating question out of innocence, in the same way that she answered Neal's query about the funeral, not intending any of the guile he ascribed to her. How could she possibly know that Singh was on the verge of his own domestic crisis, that this very evening, at his mother's house by the lake outside Jaipur, the massed ranks of Nattawat would close and compel him to meet his filial obligations at last? Thomas cast his mind back halfway over the world and wondered what was happening on the other side, as always.

'How *is* business?' he asked, shifting on to less personal ground.

'Mine? That's an elevation in terms. I make enough to live off, but that's about all. I've been working mostly to commission. It ticks over. There's so much mass-produced stuff around that hardly anybody's prepared to pay for hand-made pieces. Or it's cheaper to stump up the air fare to Eastern Europe and find a one-off there. Cheap materials, nil trade tariffs, low wages. How can we compete?'

'Or Hong Kong?'

She smiled wryly. 'Precisely. But I'm not going pearl-diving for anyone.'

'Did you make your bracelet?' It flashed under his eyes as she changed gears. 'What stone is it?'

'Well, it's only a bit of granite, but it's a nicely veined piece, isn't it? The grain came up well with polishing.'

It was a large oval stone, the size of a Victorian cameo, but was striking and modern, a dull grey granite shot through with parian white, and summed up his taste in things. She had improved a great deal. In her letters, she'd described small surges of success, one good gift fair or an article in an English daily paper that brought her in a small spate of orders, which hadn't, as yet, built to the self-generating, word-of-mouth level.

'And what else has been happening?' He tested the huge unspoken.

'Oh, quite a lot else.'

She was painfully honest. When she stalled, as he did in talking openly about the predicament of Singh's private life, it was because of the third party in the back seat, all ears, critical, jumping to the wrong conclusions. The truth she put on hold.

Neal found the cooped enclosure insufferable, and wound down his back window to the sill, blowing them about.

Ten miles out of Edinburgh, he was able to calm down, admitting that his fears about the roadworthiness of the car and its driver were unfounded. It was a long road and she drove it well, knowing it and the car engine to capacity through many journeys. They were travelling down the A7, traversing the small Border towns of Dalkeith, Galashiels, Selkirk and Hawick. Great names for awful places. The repetitive stone-grey dunned at him, with the traditional, unchanging style of decorated gables and dormer windows, which had an overall littleness implicit in their design, something shut against the hostile inroads of the weather, like the people who chose to live in them. Neal thought of existence in these towns as a living death, with the low, rolling horizon bounded by inmates who knew each other too well. He favoured the big-city life, just because it was anonymous but highly coloured and highly charged, rotating like the motes in a kaleidoscope. Still, with luck, this might be his last time around the parish boundaries. Sell up and move on for good.

In the driving mirror, Caley caught his bored eye and asked, out of politeness more than interest, 'Are you on schedule?' and then reflected she could have asked the same question at any time since they'd met, varied only by the particular circumstance.

'We've managed to get four days ahead on our contract.'

'Four days? That's good.' She judged its merit by his tone of voice and not by the fact, which seemed an infinitesimal gain to her. Days in stone-setting weren't quantifiable.

'It's on the right side of the deadline, but only just. We're working all out. It must be finished by the handover.'

'Why "must"?'

'It's imperative. And I've booked myself on the last flight out of Hong Kong.' Neal had often said this elliptically, but knew he'd take a long tour through Malaysia and Borneo and Australia after his contract ran out. The entry stamps on his passport were a sort of credit rating. He'd been everywhere and done everything.

'Why don't you stay on after the handover? You must have worked with Chinese engineers before.'

'Only as my employees. When they're the managers, the Chinese always hire their own people. We'll be *personae non gratae* afterwards. That's the way of it. We won't get a look in at a contract. For centuries, the struggle in China has been against invasion and foreign imperialism. In their view, the *gweilos* always exploit. I won't complain when my time comes. I'll have had a good three years out of Hong Kong by the end.'

While he was speaking, Neal's eyes came to rest on the shoulders of his brother in the front seat, which forced an ostensible comparison between them. He reckoned he was doing rather well: Thomas did less well. He was starting to look an oddball. Neal had been shocked to see him bearded at Heathrow, and hadn't actually recognised him until he spoke. For himself, he didn't like facial hair. Working with the Chinese, who hardly ever grew beards, apart from old men on whom it conferred an aura of Confucian wisdom, had made him think of the hirsute as untidy and probably unhygienic. These silences, these intense spells of musing Thomas fell into, were very off-putting and increasingly eccentric. The old clothes too, mismatched suits and jackets trotted out year after year because he'd moved into a downbeat society that had no formal structure. Thomas never had to attend a board meeting, never made a presentation or a submission for competitive tender, where his image and personal smartness counted for something, as tokens of reliability. OK, appearance wasn't everything, but it was a measure of efficient dealing.

Thomas had indeed fallen silent again because the phrase Neal used appalled him. His own statement might have been, I've given two good years to India, though even that sounded egotistical and pat. Defining your self-regard was overly smug. He wasn't in the habit of chalking up his own career points.

'Just how good have they been?' he forced himself to ask.

'Well,' drawled Neal, only half-reluctantly, 'I could afford to retire at forty. The tax advantages are the incentive to stay out there to the bitter end. I'm using all the tax havens I can find.'

'And what would you do then? At forty?' Caley wondered.

'A bit of consultancy work. Three days a week would suit me. And I wouldn't say no to a directorship.'

'Whereabouts?'

'Oh, where's next for development? Somewhere in the Far East. Singapore would be acceptable, if they manage to oust Hong Kong as the South-East Asia stockmarket. I've made some good contacts there.'

Thomas listened on the surface, easily distanced from terms he found too smooth and complacent to allow of entry, too finished. He also found it hard to concentrate because he was cold to the point of shivering. It was the week before midsummer, but he'd forgotten how the evening temperatures plunged this far north, 80°F midday down to 40°F overnight wasn't uncommon. Neal, he noticed, had sensibly changed at Heathrow into worsted, whereas he was still wearing the tropical jacket he'd set out in that morning, walking from the bungalow to the clinic at Jaipur to say goodbye to Singh.

It was hard, anyway, to focus on something futuristic and practical. The sky overhead was turquoise, with a crescent moon which lit a corner of the windscreen while the trees bordering the roadway were a navy blue, stark and surprising so that he found himself thinking, this could be the African veldt. Huge, open unspoiled spaces. The scenery was both exotic and mundane. It continually distracted him. Its outlines were his own anatomy and his own character, so intimately known that changes to the contour were shocking because they defined his personal ageing process. An overgrown beech hedge, a church reroofed since he'd left denoted passages of time in which he was inconsequent. All the same, he was nervous about seeing Carterbrae and Langholm town, transporting home his sense of failure, or of non-accomplishment, which arose from temporary fatigue as much as anything. Evening set in but it was still daylight in this interminable thirty-two-hour-long day. His body clock was wrong, his mind clock too. Please let me arrive in the daylight. I don't want to see it for the first time in the dark.

The last corner unwound and they drew inside the limits of the burgh. It shrank on each adult return. Blink and you were through it. The municipal park on the right-hand side, the humpback bridge at the meeting of the waters of the Esk and Ewes, the stone-built square ahead of them, slightly skewed with the clock tower at one end, a run of shops and the Thistle Hotel, all overhung with the greenery from trees that drooped with the weight of their own lushness. Then they turned right over the iron bridge, drove past the mills of Reid and Taylor and sped on, rising all the while into the fastness of the hills.

Thomas had shrunk from confronting any dramatic changes which would have ousted him, but there was none. At Carterbrae, the door of the porch was standing ajar, leading to ancient lights. The hallstand sprouted the same wet-weather gear as always, a sheaf of Fox frame umbrellas, malacca walking canes, boots he'd worn, jackets he'd snagged walking on the hills. And Ruth Palmer came out of the kitchen, down the long access of the hallway, as if all was well and welcoming, smiling in cautious joy at seeing the three of them assembled at her door. She was a tidy body still and neatly buttoned up. The clock ticked, the radiators were warm, the organ, which was empty of music, nevertheless waited for somebody's input and hadn't been dismantled. Nothing had changed in essence.

I'm worn out, he thought, reading his own emotional state as precarious. There's nothing the matter, and I am just back where I belong.

'Will you stay over?' the housekeeper asked Caley as they went to put supper on to trays.

'I don't think I will. It's awkward, isn't it? I'd better go.'

'But surely you can't go all the way back to Edinburgh tonight, so late? And I've made up your room for you.'

Caley reflected that this being their customary practice when she came to see Edith would hardly endear her to Neal, while Ruth sensed that her awkwardness had other causes. 'You haven't told him, have you?' she challenged.

'Hardly. Not with Neal listening in.'

'Then you must stay until that's said. Besides, you may be called upon to keep those two apart.'

'They're only niggling at each other. Only jibes.'

'As yet.' Ruth paused in assembling the worn pieces of the dinner service on a tray. She didn't readily add her own emotional weight to the plea. 'I would deem it a favour if you stayed and helped us through the next day or two. If you're not comfortable staying with us in the house, the gardener's wife has room to spare, and will be pleased to take you in.'

That this was an offer plotted beforehand measured the woman's emphasis in making it and sealed Caley's consent. Both women, threading their way back through the lofty rooms to where the brothers waited, adjusting their own mindsets to present demands, felt apprehensive at the stress of the week's impending business.

'Can I be with you?' Thomas stood at Caley's door at the end of the long top corridor, looking forlorn. Under the beard and the dark colouring, he was actually more emaciated, and her heart went out to him.

'Oh, Thom, this isn't sensible. You've been travelling all day and there's still a way to go.'

'I appreciate that. We've got so much talking and sorting out to do. Don't throw me out yet. Just let me be with you. We won't make love but let me sleep beside you.'

Wasn't that her fallibility? Someone asked her for a favour or for a touch of human comforting, and she gave it, not sparing anything to meet the need. Her resolve weakened. He looked cold, hungry, whipped. A little kindness could remedy those miseries. You shouldn't be doing this, she warned herself, but went on undressing as if the last time they'd lain in this narrow room was yesterday and there hadn't been half a dozen revolutions in their lives since then. He turned away, needing no immediate recall of her shape when the picture in his head was highly defined.

As he eased into the iron bedstead alongside her, he could feel the real differences which his eye had guessed at. She was thinner, like himself. They'd shed their plump ideals and were left lean and close together, skin-fitted. In the language of his thinking, he said, *'Maigrichon, chétive, pénible amour.'* He murmured the words in her ear, which received the sound from a conducted pulse rather than on air waves. For a while, he only moved his lips slowly across the lobes as if he were speaking directly down into her bones.

In spite of her good intentions, Caley was swept by a sexual memory at least as powerful as his. At one moment she resisted, saying sternly, don't feel this way! Don't react to him! How can I have got myself into such a mess? It's over. Over long ago. And I've moved on. At the same time she could feel the corded sinews of his bare legs along the length of hers. She used to enjoy lying beside him in this position, where he bent his knees and she sat against them as if they were her chair, as warm and encompassing as thick upholstery. The sapped energy in him revived, and she remembered how good it was to be tight with him.

The lips stopped moving on her lobes. They compressed together, trapping her skin and the fine hairs against the warm inner tissue of his mouth. The pressure grew and spread and changed imperceptibly to kissing. As if there was something very important to say, which had been interrupted mid-sentence, Caley turned to him in order to relieve his mouth of whatever urgent message it was trying to communicate.

Interaction was very different between them now. Thomas had kept his values intact. One woman. The best was attainable if you kept faith with it. So the act of love carried many idealistic burdens for him, relief at the end of his journey, a welcome home, the powerful triggers of her immediate emotional acceptance. In this state of mind, Thomas was particularly vulnerable. At the moment of release, fraught with the impact of several tensions, he made a noise she would never forget, harsh, rasping, an outpouring that was closer to tears or pain than joy. It was beyond his control, at any rate, and frightening in its new demands on her.

Caley was dismayed as he shuddered convulsively into her shoulder. He wasn't unhappy, surely, only relieved. She stroked the nape of his neck quietly in the dark, soothing, soothing, as if stress or angst were a spot that could be worn away. What folly have I committed, she wondered, to let us get so hopelessly ensnared like this?

Neal listened for the footsteps that didn't return again along the corridor and lay awake afterwards for hours, more jet-lagged and jittery than he would readily admit. Well, well, back at that again so soon. They weren't noisy, gaspy lovers but often in Gillespie Crescent he'd been on edge deciphering their murmurs through the thick walls. In their sleep or lovemaking or talking, they spoke the composite, together-language which excluded him. French with Edith. Hindi with Singh. Love with Caley. The lucky polyglot, to have the advantage over him with so many people.

At last, he fell asleep, but it was a turbulent, restless night. He dreamed of Lin, who walked on through his head, easily naked in the way that Chinese girls had. Her agility stayed with him, with a sense of movement remembered from a Shanghai circus act

where the girls vaulted before his eyes into impossible
contortions; there was something brave as well as something
foolhardy in her single-mindedness, so that even when he was
tired, she could arouse him and impress him to encore. But, on the
whole, his waking mind knew it was an entanglement to be
avoided. A lot of his European friends had succumbed to the
charm of Chinese girls and actually married them. Those pliable,
unbreakable blossoms turned into fire-breathing dragons
overnight, apparently, not sweet or coaxing lovers any more but
instant matriarchs.

His mind, however, still did the cartwheels to her bidding.

8

Thomas was standing in the back scullery, looking at the three taps set into the wooden fascia board behind the stone sink where Edith used to steep her whites. Three taps? Yes, there was a hot, a cold and a mains outlet. The hot and cold were moulded in pre-war stainless steel and had china disc insets to distinguish them, the letters rather worn and chipped. The mains tap was much older, maybe Victoria and made of brass, and Ruth kept it polished to an impressive brilliance.

This sink had been his favourite play area at Carterbrae. He'd poured and measured and tested the viscosity of the spring water until his fingertips were wrinkled and pale as a washerwoman's from the constant immersion. Which objects sank and which floated? And why was buoyancy something different from specific density? He'd filled a series of glass milk bottles up to various levels to make a scale of chimes. He'd proved for himself the contradictory qualities of water, how it vaporised in steam, solidified in ice, blobbed like glue under certain compressions and was as frustratingly elusive as drops of mercury in others. Great stuff.

Now he turned the brass knob and put his hand under the spring water that poured obediently out of the faucet. He remembered this mountain water. It had a special feel against the fingers, as if H_2O wasn't an exact enough formula for its distillation. Collected from the soft Lowland rain, filtered through heather, bracken and peat down the Ettrick hillsides, it had a particular taste as well as feel, with a higher proof than the Water Board's purified solution, and was a bright and beautiful colour, almost blue, sparkling with bubbles, transparent and absolutely natural. No chemicals had come near it. He was surprised to see the outlet was still in place, vaguely sensing that it might contravene some European Union standard on potable water, not having passed through the processes of a filtration plant. He lifted

91

his palm in which the drops gleamed like blue diamonds, bouncing prisms of light on to the ceiling, and drank from his own hand. Superb. It was as cold as the hillside and the burn outside, clear as the sky.

'Take some,' he offered Caley, and scooped another handful up for her. She drank it but tasted him rather than it, his salts, his own condensation.

It was five o'clock in the morning. Wide awake, they'd crept downstairs and made free with the early hours. The kitchen, which was ranged with old-fashioned cupboards, glazed above, painted below, was empty and cool underfoot on the quarry tiles. 'Are you hungry?' she asked him.

'No, not yet. Just thirsty.'

He let the water splash across his outspread hands with a sense of profligate waste. 'I wasn't able to do that in India, you know, or not with a clear conscience. I used to restrict my fluid intake so that I didn't waste water. One litre a day. A litre and a half in extreme conditions. How can something so basic start to rule your life? I swore I'd never take tap water for granted again, or said I wouldn't turn it on without saying a prayer of thanks, but I suppose I will.' The spillage syphoning down the drain proved his point.

Although he hadn't slept for more than an hour or two, disturbed by travel and memory and the continuous erotic prompt of her haunches resting in his lap, he was refreshed by the cooler northern air and felt brighter than yesterday. He'd pulled on a pair of shorts and a sweatshirt and was tousled in a way that Caley found American, or international. He could have been an Israeli except that he was too tall, or Swedish apart from the burnt colouring, or South African if he weren't so lean and meatless. He'd become one of the indeterminates, the much travelled men who picked up their clothes and habits where they could. She didn't dislike the lines of the edging beard or the blue-brown sheen on his skin. He was all trim, honed to basics like a mental backpacker. He had a different smell too from the one she could remember, slightly astringent or with a chemical base of alkali or one of the chlorides, which she bent into him to test along the frontal taste buds of her tongue.

'What are you doing?' He softened as she touched him.

'Being a fool about you. Wondering where you came from, which makes me feel I know a stranger this well. You're like a book I know inside out, every word, except that it's got a new cover which has thrown me temporarily. I'm starting at the first page again. I seem to know the style but I've forgotten the plot.' She sighed, rewriting several possible outcomes.

'I'm sorry about last night.'

'Inconsolably sorry?' she teased him, her face tilted back without resistance.

'I'm sorry I played on your sympathies.'

'Or my susceptibilities. We've made a mess of this one, haven't we?'

'You've got regrets?'

'Oh, yes, immense regrets.'

They didn't risk that path just yet, until they grew comfortable with their new personae, and for long moments at a time the draw of their own mutuality stunned them into being still and quiet. They each thought of the other – 'You're such a remarkable person. How did I mislay you?' – which kept up a distraction in their heads: to be together was enough to re-create the hallucinogens of glory that blotted out the dull and practical matters waiting for their decision.

The scullery where they were standing also housed the boiler, which came on automatically at six. Thomas opened the cupboard door and leaned against the insulation padding to relieve the early-morning chill on his unaccustomed limbs. She pulled up a chair and placed her bare legs on the same spot. His shirt of yesterday served as her dressing gown.

'You used to write to me about almost everything in India except the work you were doing. That made me think it must be very hard for you, or was it just very engrossing?'

'Hard, well, it certainly took up all of me with nothing to spare, if that counts as engrossing. It turned out to be the undoable work. Or that's maybe my excuse for not being able to do it. You couldn't make out a job description for what I was supposed to be. I was a paramedic and a social worker and a well-digger and a dambuilder and everything else you can think of thrown in. The villagers called me the water-man, the way country people talk about the rain-man. And I attracted the same sort of mystique, out of superstition. They thought that if they begged me or made offerings to me, revered me in the end, I'd produce the goods or sink the bore wells into some magical oasis waiting underneath the desert rocks and hit the spring. Then it would gush forth the white gold they were all waiting for. It was far more precious to them than the black stuff.'

'And why didn't you find the water? What went wrong? Was it the geology or the climate?'

'Both. Everything was wrong. It was sandstone and porous, without natural aquifers. Low rainfall, one of the lowest in the world, and it's still falling. The monsoon's been sporadic for a generation. Heat like an inferno, just scalding, month after month without relief. Rajasthan's one of the hottest places on earth where man can live continuously. And as for motivating people to counteract all that, I ran into poor local management of resources and no national infrastructure. In India, you've got to understand that there's endemic bribery at every level of the civil service, coupled with political inertia. You name it. I was combating all the Third World problems in one place.'

She watched his features carefully, reassessing them. When he was speaking, the rapid flow between the eye and its emotional register in the brain and his strong command of language was so intense and emphatic that he was compelling and quite unstoppable. This was the Thomas of old who could draw a crowd round him at Gillespie Crescent, the committed firebrand socialist who burned with the passion for doing good. It is a good job, he had said. I mean to do good work. But since he made that mission statement, his idea of good had undergone a subtle refinement into what was realistically good. She'd called him pan-national, indeterminate in his looks, a broad adjective and broadly right. It applied also to his age. He was no longer young, had suffered through the blockages of failure and inadequacy, underachieving against his own superhuman set of goals, and had aged by more than simple chronology in the process. He wasn't old, but he was much older than when he went away, mentally played out with the burden of his responsibilities.

'What sort of problems do you mean? Give me an example.'

'Just one?' He ransacked the catalogue of thousands and chose the nearest. 'The day before I came away, I had to analyse a water sample in the lab. It was from a lake outside the city, near Sonal Nattawat's house, as it happens. One of the landowners had diverted the stream from a natural spring without consulting the authorities, and that was all it took to change the level of the water table. It had been falling for a month without anybody noticing, so the effluents stayed below the drainage outlets in what was one vast septic lake by the time I got to it. The intense sun, at 120 cloudless degrees, had brewed a soup. Algae were multiplying out of control and bacteria alongside. Not just unfit for human consumption, actually dangerous just because of one thoughtless act. But it was still the water supply for twenty villages downstream. What else was lurking in that sample? Cholera? Dysentery? Whom should I have notified? What was I supposed to report, and who would take action even if it was liquid poison draining into their wells? This may sound an extreme case to you, but it happened almost every day I was there, in some form or another.'

The scale of the sub-continent was still outside her range. She couldn't believe his hopelessness. 'But you must have had some successes. Things must have improved because you were there and supervising events. Or were better than if you hadn't been around.'

'Oh, yes. I did build a few drains, and I got the money from a UN development fund for a reservoir that hasn't been built yet, but you're up against inbred ignorance at every level. I had to explain the most basic principles of hygiene to the villagers. That they ought to wash and cook from separate vessels. Not draw their water when it's muddy. Boil it. There's a foolproof method for clearing water of the common coliforms, by standing a glass full of water in sunlight for twenty-four hours. Simple. But I couldn't get that message across. I couldn't put the practical chemistry into small enough words for them to understand it.

'The women still go down to the village well every morning to pump the day's water. But resistance to piped water is widespread and quite subtle. The castes still want separate wells, otherwise the untouchable pollutes the others. And the purist brahmin only uses water that's been hand-drawn from the well that same day, straight out of the earth, with no machinery involved. And attitudes like that are impossible to overcome because they're not reasonable, they're not accessible to logic. You can't argue against them. I started an education programme in the villages that ground to a halt from lack of money. I tried to liaise with the local doctors to get them to spread the word about water purification, but all they said was, This is their way, Mr Langholm, we cannot change the habits of past centuries overnight.'

'Even Singh? Surely he pitched in?'

'Well, it's funny, but when you're so similar, the little differences are exaggerated. Singh was quite fatalistic, or self-deceiving. He's sophisticated in a lot of ways, but quite naïve in others. He still believes in augury. As I was leaving, he wanted me to consult the astrologer. I ask you! It's escapism, like believers saying a prayer to St Christopher before they set out on their travels. If I ever quizzed him about it, he'd answer, Many things have been foretold that have come to pass. But he ignored the ones that haven't. You can't argue with an Indian about the law of averages or probability. I just made no impact. What I grew tired of,' he said, sighing at length, 'was trying to educate eight hundred million people.'

'But that's too messianic of you. To educate one man is enough.'

Ruth came down to the kitchen to make breakfast and found they were sitting huddled by the cylinder for warmth. 'What early birds you are today. Are you famished or can you wait for me to light the cooker and fry you something?'

'Some crumbs will do.' Thomas rummaged for bread in the bin and ate it dry. 'We'll wait till Neal's up and about. There's no call for you to serve two sittings.'

He went outside through the glazed door that led into the kitchen garden, where they saw him poking around, disturbing dormant roots and overgrowth. Caley couldn't leave the woman to make their breakfast single-handed, and so she worked alongside her for a while, companionably.

It was always easy-going between the two of them. Ruth warmed to her handy touch as much as Edith had done. Nearly twenty-five years she'd passed under this roof, and who was to say that the last two hadn't been the best of them? Three women were couthie together. The two of them alone, day upon day, might have turned heavisome and dull, wearing out their store of talk until they were threadbare of ideas and peevish with each other. But with Caley coming every other weekend – every second Sunday she had come without fail since Robert died of his sudden heart attack, in the September that the men all went abroad, and sometimes she stayed over to the Monday morning – they'd had news aplenty. Her letters from Thomas eked out their own, and they shared their common interests: a love of the old ballad poetry books, which were dusted off the shelves, and cooking recipes cut out from the newspapers, and flowers to pick and arrange indoors in gorgeous displays to match the season, so that the unlikely friendship between the three women, more than half a century adrift in age, went on a firm footing.

And they drew her inside it generously. If she had become companion, nurse and friend, then that was Caley's doing, quick to locate the higher motive in the people round her. Expecting the best, she always found it. When the boys grew into men and left,

Ruth had half thought of taking an easier position, a smaller house to care for, a bigger town to spread herself in. Her home was Tain in Sutherland, and sometimes these little hills oppressed her as too low, and the folk too busybodying within them and too ready with the clack. In the north, the peaked mountains rose and cut the people into standing stones, more monumental and aloof.

'But why do you want to start again where no one knows you?' Caley asked.

It was the argument of attachment and Ruth heeded it. It was too late to fashion new friends, which was a lifetime's work. Edith and Caley were her friends, and who needed more than two? She didn't think that was putting it too high, or presuming. Ruth knew it was her own lot and skill to see nothing and say nothing out of place, to be subservient, but Caley wouldn't entertain a relationship of inequality. She levelled the talents of others upwards, but had a saying that was moving on the lips of such a young quine, wise and strange: all words are noble, nobly used, and all men.

See how she worked beside her now, her cloth in hand, her smile at the ready, the two of them like woodsmen cutting with a double-handed saw until the log was cleft. Caley had broken down those mountain walls of reserve and distance until Ruth would sometimes be persuaded to take the ballad book into her own hands and read out loud from it, for she phrased the lines well – her father had been a preacher too – while her Highland lilt pervaded the stanzas with a new softness or a new heartache, that men should go to war and women wait for them.

She felt drawn out of herself, and admitted for the first time that she hadn't been heartbroken when her husband died. She didn't like the sex of him, the weight of his opinion contradicting hers, his push about the place. She spoke her mind more often in Carterbrae and was taken as a seer. That was very seductive. She began to wait for Caley's Sunday visits with a keenness that became dependency, knowing that she would notice her new blouse or that she dressed her hair in a different style, and commend the change. Together they shared the care of Edith, who sank under a hollow loneliness in her remaining days without her partner, and the sense of guilt that he and she had fallen out more than once after Robert had redirected his grandson by his meddling, as she called it. Edith hounded him because of the shortfall between word and deed. He'd said ahead of meeting Caley, We will accept his choice, come what may, because there's no changing it: but he had changed the circumstance and his own promises thereby.

So, for long hours, Ruth had listened to the couple argue, the only quarrels of any length or substance she remembered in Carterbrae. Robert, uneasy himself, would fire back double volleys wherein she caught him crying, Why, woman, you care more about that second-generation son of yours than you do me. You give me no peace with your haranguing when all I want is quiet days. He turned for solace to the organ, whose chords drowned hers out. Very sad, Edith was, when his time came before they learned how to agree again.

Maybe Caley came month after month because of her own desire to reduce that guilt. Who knew what her motives were to make the long journey less tedious? To fill a space? To keep her own contact with Thomas and his family? To prolong her genuine fondness for Carterbrae and its mellowing antiquities?

All of this backlog ran in Ruth's mind, like an overloaded dam that put pressure on her when she saw the young people take up with each other all over again without restraint. It wasn't her nature to speak out of turn, and so when she said, 'You will take every care, won't you, as far as Thomas goes? It isn't given to many to have their second chance,' the statement was out-rageously impertinent in her taciturn context.

Caley came to a halt in her wiping, and leaned on wide arms against the wooden drainers. 'I knew the dangers, Ruth, and didn't want to stay here. You asked me to stay, and Thomas asked me, so I stayed. That's the way it is.'

'You made a guddle of it, last time, between you.'

'And may well this.'

'Well I—' The sentence was unfinishable, even in the woman's unspoken reach. I care for you, as I would care for my own child, and don't want you to be needlessly unhappy. That would do. The ironies of their common situation weren't lost on Ruth: the wrong people were parents, and some children spent all their lives looking for their natural family, borrowing, adopting, seeking to be fostered. Why else did Caley burrow into the sheiling of Carterbrae, the lamb out of the blow? Because they mothered her and were her sort of people. 'Well, you know I wish only the best for you, and whatever you resolve between you, I agree with that.'

Thomas came towards her when she stepped outside. The wind blew his hair into knots. He was concentrating so hard that his face was twisted into an expression of anxiety. He took hold of Caley's hand and led her behind the walls of the kitchen garden where the fruit had set along the cordons of the espalier trees. Who would jam and bottle them at harvest time, and make the entries in the bound notebooks, nobody knew.

'It isn't easy to say this.' He hurried into a troubled confidentiality. 'But I ought to try and say it before the moment passes. I should have said it at once when I saw you were waiting at the airport, but Neal was there, or I should have said it in your room last night, but I wasn't collected enough. I want to apologise. I was completely wrong and you were right. All the time I was away, when things were going badly, I used to repeat your words like a mantra to myself. *These three are my own people. They're not great, they're certainly not good, but they are mine, and until I feel I can't do any more for them, I stay put.*

'When you said that' – here they turned a corner into a cooler wind that rose up from the burn below, and he put his arm round her shoulder to shelter her from it – 'I didn't pay it enough attention, or I thought the example you were using discounted the theory.

'And, just now, you challenged me again, saying, "Surely something went right in India? Didn't Singh pitch in?" You are predisposed to think positively. Everything's turned to the forward direction with you, the most hopeless situation is redeemable. Onward and upward! That's a power of instinctive optimism I don't have. I can't tell you how, in the silent recesses of despair, I've clung to that outlook and blessed it.'

They stood quietly, leaning into each other while buffeted by the surge of cold outer air. Caley was far from tranquil as she responded to his intensified breathing. What she was doing to this man might be unforgivable. She had her own apology still to make and her private explanation, which she deferred for the same reasons as Thomas. They'd been too little alone for complete honesty, or too much. These moments were very heady, given resonance and dimension by the long time they'd spent apart and the broken memories, sealed together again as they reunited. They had arrived at a sense of dropping time, the infinite moment, the closed eternity. That was the end of dreaming. The actual knowing began.

9

He struts, thought Ruth, watching Neal striding up and down the garden before breakfast, swishing at the long growths with one of the walking sticks he'd taken from the stand.

He's making a list for the estate agent because he doesn't want to be caught out when the man says to him, 'Oh, but, Mr Langholm, she's let the place run down so badly. It's dropped ten thousand in the last two years.' He wants to be upsides with him and smart with his replies. So he struts like a wee colonial. And in a minute he'll come in by the kitchen door and say to me, 'I wonder if I could trouble you, Mrs Palmer . . .' What's the matter with the Ruth that everybody else cries me by? Ruth's the name of friendship but he thinks that'll cost him too dear. He's worried that I'll ask for more than my due when the time comes to leave, and if I'm only Mrs Palmer, at arm's length, it'll be easier for him to say, We couldn't possibly see our way to doing more for you than our legal obligations stipulated.

But he didn't. He went straight into the dining room, whose French doors were ajar in the warmer morning air and where she'd laid out breakfast on the sideboard in covered ashets. He helped himself to a grilled kipper and some scrambled egg and sat down opposite the other two, who fell quiet at his entry.

'I must see about hiring a car this morning. I wonder if Batey still rents out his taxi when he's not got a fare? I'll only need it for the morning while I dot about the town and get through this business.'

'If you want to borrow my car, Neal, just ask me. I'll be pleased to lend it to you and then, when you give me back the keys, you can say, "Thank you", and all's well.'

'Are you staying, then? I hadn't thought to presume.'

'And neither had I. Thomas has asked me to stay on, and so has Ruth Palmer but, most important, Edith did. I know her wishes in a lot of the small things, if you don't mind my carrying them out.'

She might be handy after all. 'What were you thinking of?'

'I'll go to see the minister and the florist, and all the churchy people, the choirmaster, the organist, that end of things. Then put a notice in the paper and send one to the *Scotsman*, though nobody will come all the way down here from Edinburgh, but it should be seen to all the same. Phone calls to the family. Those cousins of yours will want to know first-hand. I'll go through her list of numbers. That's all very dull for you, but I don't mind doing it. I've got to know these people fairly well over the months.'

He didn't disagree with her proposals. 'And, Thomas, what's your brief for today?'

Thomas dragged his eyes back from the garden, where he was lost in reverie. 'I'll stay here and see to this. A day would make it quite presentable again. It's just the edges. The structure's still all right.'

So he would hit the garden. Fair enough. He was the plantsman. As for himself, Neal got out the piece of paper where he'd jotted down his notes during the flight from Hong Kong and, scanning it quickly, thought he'd got it about right. No need to change tack. He ringed the 'Funeral Arrangements' section, pleased he could consign the whole of it to Caley. A figure had formed in his head, however, on the valuation of the property and he added under 'Sale of House' the upset price which he would propose to the local agent. Not quite nine o'clock yet. In a few minutes, he'd go and phone and make his appointments throughout the day with the professionals, designating two hours' maximum discussion time to each.

Thomas watched the rapid eye movements, the flicking, filing mind at work. Practical situations need men like you, I suppose, and I'm glad you're here to see to the details instead of me. His thoughts vaporised gladly into the prospect of the hoe and the shears, clipping and rediscovering the old lines buried by overgrowth.

'Can I give you a lift into the town?' Neal asked Caley considerately.

'That's kind of you, but everything's within walking distance for me. Thank you all the same.'

Thomas smiled. Her politeness could be excruciatingly pointed at times.

They broke up, Neal to make his phone calls, irritated that the solicitor couldn't fit him in until three in the afternoon – and it was probably going to take him all that time to locate the documents in his dusty little back office – Thomas and Caley to the slower pace of what came easily to hand.

Because it was at the forefront of his mind, Neal dealt at the outset with the sale of Carterbrae. The local solicitor had opened up a small sub-office at the northern end of the town, in George Weir's front room, to be exact, with two pinboard panels wheeled into the bay window to make a display of sorts.

There were some very faded photographs of houses on show, Neal thought, while he waited for the estate agent to appear from his bachelor toilette, and that indefinable air of dampness hung in the corners of the parlour which betokened a lack of daily movement. Dank. They shook hands cordially enough, however, Weir remembering that Langholm had a reputation as a sharp man on the business front, so that he must have his wits about him, not to be dunned, Neal hoping that the man had forgotten giving him a clip round the ear one time for thieving the apples from the orchard at the back of his house.

'Trade is slack?'

'Not brisk, I fear.'

'When did you last sell a property?'

George Weir, a dark, disorderly man who'd been every kind of factor you could imagine in and around Langholm for thirty years, thought that this line of questioning was hardly decent on the part of the recently bereaved, and reserved his condolences. 'We had part fee for the sale of the house at Crerar in the spring, with all its policies and furbishments. It was an auction that I personally arranged,' he answered carefully, like a man delivering his credit rating to a would-be lender. 'But these are not handsome times for country properties. You are thinking of asking me to handle the sale of Robert Langholm's house?'

The slip was inadvertent but Neal, casting an eye on him, wondered what sort of time warp the town languished in, to omit twenty-one months so readily from account. 'Quite so.'

'It is a house that has never been sold since the day it was built. Nearly two centuries, father to son. Quite a record, don't you think?'

That rather begged the question but, in deference to a tradition rooted in the good aspects of sentiment, Neal replied, 'I would like to keep it on, of course, but it isn't feasible. It's a chore making this detour when we do come back from the East, and the upkeep would be a self-indulgence if we were to live in it for only a fortnight or so each year. It is a house to be lived in and would soon decay if it was empty for any length of time.'

The man nodded, poor answer though it was. I am talking about his heritage and ours, while he responds with mere convenience. 'What, in detail, did you envisage in your plan of action?'

Neal sat down in the bay window where the bright June light struck his *aide mémoire*. 'House description to be agreed. Price. Viewing arrangements. Secondary advertising,' he read out.

'That seems to cover it,' Weir answered. 'I will go down myself before the weekend, and take the measurement of rooms, and arrange for a photograph in colour.'

'Tomorrow would be better.'

'Tomorrow . . . Oh, I couldn't trespass before the funeral.'

The statement was as oblique as his earlier comment about the first-time sale. Each reminded Neal of some of Caley's stray observations, coming at him at an angle he couldn't grasp and finding their way in under his defences. Why *not* tomorrow? And how did the man know that the funeral was set for the day after tomorrow, Wednesday? He ran into those small-town mysteries and refinements of feeling that were as closed to him as the vernacular. *Why* not? This was business.

'I appreciate your delicacy, Mr Weir, but I am working under time constraints. There is so much to put in hand before I fly back that I am at a loss to know how to accomplish it. If you prefer to work alone, I can ensure the house is empty for the duration of your visit. Or whatever circumstances meet your . . . professional requirements.'

The man complied. 'Nine tomorrow, then.'

'And on price, while we are here. I see that a stone-built house has not shed its premium.' He waved towards the better pictures among the advertisements. 'Two hundred and forty thousand, I would say, is the going rate.'

'Oh, that is rather adventurous, Mr Langholm. It has been allowed to run down a little these past years.'

'Only cosmetic. A little tidying in the garden, my man is seeing to that right now, and a little paint. The structure of the house is still superb. The best plasterwork you'll see this side of Glasgow.'

'And, after all, not everybody's taste runs to a church organ fully installed under the staircase. The surveyor passed that by a hair's breadth. The weight in those pipes, you know. I would err on the side of modest pricing, myself.'

'It only needs one buyer, Mr Weir, and there may be a thwarted organist among prospective viewers who would jump at it. Look on the positive side. But after your inspection we can review the price bracket upwards or downwards, as we see fit. The *Carlisle Courier*, the *Glasgow Herald* and the property pages of the *Scotsman*, as well as the local rag, for what it's worth. You will have a set of keys, and I would ask that you see everybody personally in and out. I will invite Mrs Palmer to stay on for three months, until the end of September. The least that we can do for her. The furniture remains *in situ*, to be reconsidered once she has found another post. You will have three months' exclusive handling, then we must share it round to shift it. Two per cent commission of the full sale price, as normal.'

George Weir nodded, noting these points quickly on his jotter. 'I will put all this in hand.'

'Good to do business with you, Mr Weir, I'm glad we understand each other.'

They rose and shook hands again and the agent showed him to the door, closing it thoughtfully behind him. Hasn't changed a bit, he reflected, still stealing other people's apples, and thinking that they are his own.

At Carterbrae, meanwhile, the gardener, who was a cousin of the estate agent and another Weir, but Albert, called by and fell into a lengthy discourse with Thomas on the best way to treat the ailing laburnum.

'They get sick, Mr Thomas, for no reason that you can suppose. I've nursed that tree the best I can this spring, but it's all up with it.'

'Well, it's a terrible shame, Bert, because it was the finest specimen you could imagine in its heyday and perfectly sited.'

The jobbing man agreed. On a sloping bank outside the French windows, and angled pendulously, its flowering pods had been a magical screen through which to take in the piecemeal view, the soft-shouldered hills, the waters of the Esk, the sombre, solid township. But, turning sick, it had gone brown and scabrous, the leaves limp, the pods dry and not a bonny sight at all. 'They say thirty years is their normal lifespan, so this has performed threefold. Shall I fetch it out? It's an eyesore at it stands.'

'Oh, let me think a while. Let's not be hasty. There's no replanting once it's out. Do you suppose they die of their own poisons?'

Not understanding this exactly, Bert replied, 'I have heard tell that at Bodnant, where they have the great laburnum walk, they cut the seedheads off so bairns and beasts can't eat them. But, surely, the seeds can't harm the tree itself when they fall on to the ground? It's not in nature to poison your own soil.'

'Not a sound evolutionary theory anyway. Do you know, Bert, in India' – here they turned back across the lawn towards the kitchen garden and the old asparagus beds where couch and ground elder had made havoc with Robert's much prized tilth – 'they use no machinery at all to garden with. They use a push-mower, and women weed by hand. So slow, so inefficient. But it keeps everyone in some sort of work. Subsistence levels of employment.'

'They have fine gardens at the end of it?'

'Oh, the finest, but they are dry. Here I am just staggered, besotted, with the colour of the greenery. You have so many greens. I crush a leaf. It oozes sap and I feel profligate doing it. It's so thick, it's like cream. I can't believe the luxury of it. A tree never grows straight up in India. It takes on a rather tortured shape, with the drought and monsoons alternating, until it looks like a corkscrew.' He cast an eye up to a blue sky scudding with clouds. 'I wonder if it's raining there? The rains are due.'

Albert Weir felt it a privilege to be with this man. He had not understood him even as a boy, but one strain of the Langholms ran that way, counter-clockwise; the wheels of their minds moved so fast they seemed to go the other way. In the company of what was larger, or beyond his compass, he observed respectful silence.

It was twelve by the time Neal got in to see the manager of the Clydesdale Bank. This man hailed from the township of Ecclefechan, like the great Thomas Carlyle, and he prided himself on their shared Latin scholarship, gleaned from the same academy. The Clydesdale branch still used systems that might have derived from Rome and the abacus, as far as his client was concerned, or hadn't heard of electronic banking. Neal couldn't take his eyes off the notes, typed on to index cards, which the man shuffled on his desk as a signal of his efficiency.

'As you know, Mr Hammond, I arranged for power of attorney before my grandmother died, although we never had to use it, happily. However, it falls to me to tidy up her affairs. There are three accounts in her name, if I'm not mistaken – current, savings and deposit.'

'Yes, Mrs Langholm derived a good deal of amusement from keeping her current account to within ten pounds of empty. You would have admired the finesse of her book-keeping. She had a sort of trickle system, like the waterwheel at the miller's. If an account accrued any more than her pre-set sum, be that ten pounds or a thousand, she tipped the excess over into the higher-interest-yield account. Then into Savings Bonds. She had great faith in them. I failed to excite her about investing in a wider portfolio. So, although she gained little, she never lost.'

Neal hadn't thought his grandmother was so astute. Her income must have been minuscule, an old-age pension, a little hand-out from the Church of Scotland for Robert's years of service, savings from long ago. He was therefore taken aback when the man swung round the bitty, line-by-line entries towards him for confirmation of their total. The statements were all in order and in credit. Edith had amassed a thousand pounds in her savings account, ten thousand on deposit, and then Mr Hammond found a memo which he'd slipped under the pile. 'We have transferred more than sixty thousand pounds into various issues of government Savings Bonds, accrued over many years.'

'Nearly seventy-five thousand.' Neal whistled mentally. 'How? How is it done?'

Ruth had once told him that in the town Edith was regarded as a woman of some style, although she bought no new clothes ready-made, and had scant regard for personal adornment. He retained an impression of her sitting darning in the evenings, while Robert played at the organ. This she did with as much skill as the invisible mender, patching their tweed jackets with pre-formed leather strips and a square-tipped needle like a dibber, and she would adapt their old garments like a crofter. He used to be irritated by this policy of making over, and often refused to wear the hand-me-downs. Of course, she belonged to the war generation that cut things down of necessity, but she learned to like the process of thrift, so that one of her favourite outfits was made from a pair of Robert's wide-legged serge trousers, refashioned into gores. This was the same as the Brontës turning their worn skirts inside out, sheets sewn side-to-middle, but hardly needful. When she did buy new, he remembered that it was done frugally. From two yards of offcut suiting she had constructed the great Reid and Taylor dress, of plain navy serge, with a set of linen collars and cuffs that she removed for washing, and in the summer months she wore Liberty lawn, one of those inky prints where the flowers were stubby shadows on plain ground. Her hair she washed weekly in Lux pure soapflakes – it was good enough for wool – so that her head was white and downy like a fleece. And that was how the thing was done.

'Thrift, I believe.'

'It's impressive.' It wasn't a fortune, but it was a tidy sum. Neal knew that the life insurance policies paid after his parents' death had been carefully managed to yield their school fees, but by the end of their Edinburgh time that fund had practically run dry. He was truly impressed, not by the quantum but by its strict husbandry. The method was primitive but its proof, as the financier testified, was that she had never lost and never touched her capital.

'You will realise that the power of attorney lapses. The will disables it, and Mr Armstrong can advise you on the various stages of probate and what expenses I am empowered to meet in settlement of the estate's debts, ahead of probate. Not much is pending, I imagine. No bills to meet. She dealt exclusively in cash. No credit cards. No plastic values there. You're seeing Mr Armstrong at three, I understand, so we move fast and all is totally in order. Don't hesitate . . .'

The rest was courtesy but, sitting by himself in the Thistle over a glass of their eighty shilling and one of the locally baked steak pies, Neal felt uneasily that he'd lost the initiative on that one. He was overtaken by surprise, albeit of the agreeable sort, but he resented being given his schedule for the afternoon, as if his progress were common knowledge round the town, and the sense that, within the confines of these hills, his smallest move was watched or known ahead.

At Carterbrae folk dropped in to pay their respects and clapped the young man and young woman to them fondly. Old friends are best. It was the day of the fishmonger's round, while the grocer made an exception to his general rule and made a delivery of a weekly order to the house over the Monday lunch hour when he was quiet, seeing that the ladies had no transport of their own. Rumour travelled in the wake of these initial visits and, with the rising of the warmth in the afternoon, a trail of visitors descended on Carterbrae to take tea, or a glass of something stronger, or a break of half an hour from other rounds of less agreeable duties than to study the view through Thomas's wide-lens binoculars, admire his pretty girlfriend and concede that Ruth Palmer had lost nothing of her lightness in the baking of a scone.

The hills around were scarred a purply blue. There was a light haze which the depth of range in the Zeiss Ikon fieldglasses separated into prismatic light, the blues, greens and yellows, but no reds, for this was the cool climate, and even what was warmer in the stones tended towards brown or grey hues which, as the sun dipped and cooled again, increased their intensity and depth like sombre thoughts after the highlight of emotion.

It was five before Neal drove back up the hill in Caley's Morris Oxford. A long haul of an afternoon it had been with Mr Armstrong. Neal tried to steady himself and hold some firm objective in his sights, that he hadn't actually lost anything, that nobody had taken anything away apart from thwarting . . . his unstated expectations.

The visitors hadn't left by the time he drove up. There was a small throng of people he barely recognised sitting in the lengthening shadows of the garden, as Caley re-created one of her impromptu parties outdoors, pressing into use a tea service that had been long forgotten in one of the kitchen dressers. Out of the Chelsea factory, he recalled, turn-of-the-century. Gold and navy blue. Rather striking. He hoped that nobody would break a cup because the teaset was intact and rather rare.

And then Neal stopped himself. Whatever did it matter to him now?

Caley watched him as he came over the lawn to join them. He was tired. She had seldom seen him physically tired before and was surprised how puffy-eyed it made him, with the heaviness of a child needing to sleep. He stood still in front of her, sturdy in his light woollens, immaculately centred, and held the keys to her car distractedly in his right hand. She held out her hand to receive them while he puzzled at the gesture, forgetting ownership.

'Thank you,' she said eventually by way of prompt.

As he dropped them into her palm, he replied, 'That's quite all right. There's something up with your brakes, by the way.'

'Perhaps it's the way you jump on them. You always were a lousy driver, revving and then braking. They respond to persuasion, you know.'

He took a cup of proffered tea and went to mingle with their neighbours. Now was not the time to rise to Caley's squabbling ways.

* * *

109

'When will dinner be, Mrs Palmer?'

'Seven as usual, if nothing prevents.'

'Seven will do. Would you care to join us?'

'Well,' – she flushed, pleased to be equalised on more than token Sunday suppers – 'that would be most sociable. We have so much to say.'

She thought he looked less tired than baleful as he went upstairs to change out of his outdoor shoes.

As soon as he arrived, Neal saw that nothing had been accomplished in the garden during the course of the day, while he went from one functionary meeting to another making quite stressful decisions. Nothing had been achieved here but chat. He'd had a scratchy and uncomfortable time of it while Thomas sunned himself, more popular, more agreeable, more time-wasting. When was that not the way of it? The seed pods browned and dropped. The edges straggled without discipline. His own schedule was fulfilled, and Thomas's not started. Previously, he'd been irked by this tendency to procrastinate for his brother's sake, thinking it was a waste of immense talents, but now he sensed that Thomas bent towards sociability because he'd actually encouraged him to be slack by being the opposite, that they'd grown away from each other by being too close-planted, in age and circumstance.

'How did things go with the minister?' he asked Caley, shaking out a serviette crisp with starch which cemented its folds into place.

'No problem. We've settled on the hymns. Thomas agrees with the selection, but you should look at them too.'

'You are well able to decide on that.'

'And readings, one from each of you. Not very heavy or very long. We chose them together, the minister and I. I'll look them up tomorrow and give you a chance to practise. King James Bible, of course. Two o'clock. Everyone will come back here afterwards. Mrs Weir, Albert's wife, will stay and mind the house while we are out and help with serving. The flowers are organised. All yellow. Edith loved yellow flowers the best. Nothing too drab.'

He watched her closely as he listened to her outline. She was good at this, the supreme natural organiser. She was reliable and meticulous on detail and possessed what Singh had alerted him to, that instinct for quality. Was never known to choose the second-best. It was a shame she hadn't moved into proper, executive levels of administration. She would have been a good company secretary. The best talents, but the poorest opportunities.

'I think you've had the most successful day of all of us. Mine was – rather chequered.'

He cleared his throat as if he prepared to make a speech, and attentively they turned to hear it, for he was the man in charge.

'I arranged for the sale of the house and then saw the bank manager, who tells me there is some seventy-five thousand pounds in various accounts. By that, I mean solid money. Cash. Not bonds. No fluctuating shares.' Their murmur of amazement, no less than his own had been, interrupted the flow of his exposition for a second. 'And then I saw Armstrong, the solicitor, who's a dry old stick but very proper. It turns out she has been quite dramatic at the end, our grandmother, quite out of character. Or maybe we didn't know her very well. She has left the heritable, that is, the house and all its contents, to Thomas outright, so I was obliged to backtrack to George Weir's office and rescind my earlier instructions, since they have no legal standing. Thomas is the master here. The disposable assets, the money she has divided in accordance with Scots law, which requires that only one third need pass to blood relations. Thomas and I will therefore split one third, twelve and a half thousand each. One third goes to Mrs Palmer in view of her long and devoted friendship. One third to Caley.'

The words were graven out of him as painfully as letters on a granite slab. He rather felt, making his second address to Doddy Weir, that the man had laughed at him behind his back, knowing all along the terms of Edith's will, either because they were broadcast freely in the whirlpools of town gossip or because the solicitor was his business partner and the two colluded beforehand on what property was about to reach the market.

The astonishment round the supper table, soup barely touched, was general. Was it a whim, scrawled in a hasty moment, or was it fair?

'When was the will made?' Caley asked, to throw light on just that point.

'Immediately after Robert died. Nearly two years ago, as soon as we had left.'

So the old lady had made up her mind at once and not changed it again. Good for her. Not a whim, but not fair either. Caley, who'd so often been discriminated against at home in favour of her idle brother, felt the harm of a prejudice in favour of another, of unequal division, whatever the circumstances. Their aspirations had parity, irrespective of their income. 'And are you hurt about it?' she asked Neal quickly.

He rebuffed any displays of concern from her. 'Hurt? What has hurt got to do with it? Those are her wishes. I obey them without comment.'

'You know, she would see it as a measure of your strength, that you are self-sufficient and we are not. It's a compliment to your strength of character.'

'Is it? Did she say to herself, Neal can always manage on nothing, so here is nothing for him to manage on. I am most grateful for that estimation, or do I mean esteem?'

'But, you know, I'm not sure I want it. Do I want this house?' Thomas turned to Caley to clarify the point, as if he'd temporarily lost his bearings and needed someone else to redirect him.

'Don't say anything about it now. You'll only be reacting, not thinking clearly. Take more time. This is too sudden to take in.'

It was his own advice to Albert over the laburnum. He accepted procrastination meekly.

'Now we should eat, not talk or disturb ourselves any more until we've calmed down.' Caley felt that Neal had done again what he did repeatedly to her at Bruntsfield. It was his instinct to spoil a meal or a mood, just as it was with the men in her own family. They came late and pawed at the meal that she'd so carefully prepared. Whatever women made Neal readily destroyed. What need was there for him to divulge his searches at this exact moment and set up a furore? A man she respected would have stayed silent until they all went to see the notary together, or waited until after the funeral. Neal didn't have that clamp on his reactions, however, or was less equable in spirits than she had imagined.

Ruth watched the cold skin forming on her good broth. She could hardly remember the taste of food. 'I am very grateful to Edith, without having to reflect on why. I didn't ask for this. I didn't ask for anything, or expect it. I was paid in my wages and her thanks. And those were earned. In fact, I can almost say I wish . . . Well, there will be those who say I schemed it, and worked on the weakness of an old lady to undermine her family's claim, is that not so?' Her eyes creased at the injustice of the thought. She realised that when Neal invited her to join them for supper, it was in false amity. He wanted her there only to confound her and test her emotions in the open, so that she would feel even more of an impostor in their midst.

'I make no such accusation of you, Mrs Palmer, rest assured.'

'But you may think so privately and imply as much by the least shake of your head. My conscience and my friends know that I did not.'

'I was not here. I cannot conjecture what was said behind my back.'

Caley moved at that. You cynical bastard, she said. Or thought she said. She didn't say it out loud, but the words were so emphatically framed in the shape of her head and the turn of her body that speech was quite superfluous. Ever afterwards, she imagined she had uttered her ultimatum on him and, as he looked round the other faces at his ancestral table, Neal read the same message written in theirs.

'I'm not hungry for this after all,' he said. 'Don't waste more food on me.' He rose and left them with their broken bread.

10

After a tense and silent dinner, Caley went outside and stood by herself in the open porch looking at her car, which was parked where Neal had left it in the afternoon, neatly backed with the bumper flush against a hedge. Every particle of her common sense told her to get into it and drive away. She was generating more trouble for herself in lingering, as well as trouble for them. Ruth had thought she might prevent a breach within the household, but she'd succeeded in widening it to the unbridgeable.

Without turning round, she had the sensation of Thomas walking out of the hall room and coming to stand still behind her, looking over her shoulder at the escarpment. It was nine o'clock, a settling time. They heard the grandfather clock strike in the interior, sonorous and musical, evoking their past connection with this place. It was as if he'd put a magnet at her back and said, Hold on. So many times when he wasn't here, she'd walked out of this house and got into her car to carry on with the schedules of her own life, but now she rocked on the fulcrum of the threshold, adjusting to these unpremeditated facts. Thomas owned Carterbrae outright. That opened up a host of possibilities, the strongest impression being whether Edith's action was just or not. The woman hadn't discussed her reasons, although Caley knew by instinct that it was done to keep the property within the family unit and intact. If it had been given to Neal, or divided between the brothers, the place would have gone on to the market and been lost to Langholm sons in perpetuity. No argument weighed stronger with Edith than consolidation.

The room where Neal had announced the partition of his grandmother's goods was the salon which had struck Caley so impressively on her first visit. The notebooks were still ranged along the radiator shelf, the silver scrolls preserved their parchment, and there were the other odd family heirlooms of no particular value apart from sentiment, and the fact that the people

115

in this household knew who the first Thomas Langholm was, the compiler of the dictionary of Hindi dialect. It was shocking to let that pass into strange hands, an intimate association that was carefully garnered over the centuries thrown to the four winds. She would have done what Edith did, in her position.

And she herself was left with so much money! Caley was still coming to terms with why, wondering if that other windfall, the insurance policy which went astray, going to pay for Oliver's misdeeds, had influenced the old lady's decision. She must have had a strange sort of compensatory mind. Like Ruth, Caley was grateful, wouldn't turn her benefactress's intention aside, although she underwent a similar pang about how the bequest was going to be interpreted at large. Her conscience was clear, but she knew that it looked peculiar, that people would say she'd been an attentive visitor for the sake of her coming reward, and so the endowment, instead of bringing undiluted joy, trailed a wake of doubt and anxiety after it, not least that Edith herself might have felt it was incumbent on her to repay Caley's demonstration of genuine love with money. No, no, the dates ruled out that theory. She was becoming paranoiac, thanks to Neal's wilful misinterpretation of events.

'It makes a difference, doesn't it, to one's outlook? It changes the perspective.' Lit low, the view throbbed.

'Will you stay here now and be a man of property?'

'No idea. I haven't got a single idea in my head. I've just travelled another ten thousand miles around the world today, on top of yesterday's. I'm bursting and aching all over. My brain cells are exploding. I feel I'm being tormented by sleep denial. Can't think any more.'

He came forward, stepping down a level, and put his hands on her shoulders, dropping his chin on to the nape of her neck. Her jersey parted. His beard rubbed against the back of her hairline and the two kinds of hair, head and facial, merged like the bristles of two different grades of brush pushed together, stiff badger against the texture of fine, pliable sable. Sexual idiocy. The trigger mechanism was so quick and immediately responsive between them that it was hard to tell if her shiver was apprehension at his approach, a cool whisper of wind or the upward change of body temperature to passion. She saw herself, in a visual image, dancing with him; he touched her shoulder, propelling them out of a group and, without forewarning, into the rhythm of an astonishing unknown dance, a pattern of steps she followed by instinct without any actual learning. When was that ever a thrill for us? she wondered.

Caley held herself apart from her peers. She wasn't the girl that girls confided in. She didn't encourage anyone to unburden their amours. She was exasperated by the happiness obsession. When her friends asked her, 'Do I or don't I love him?' she was wont to answer, dismissively, 'If you're asking me, then you don't.' For her to find herself emotionally ambivalent like this, or racked with longing, was more uncomfortable than pleasant.

Thomas, too, came unprepared for the impact of their reunion. He'd been emotionally neutered by the demands of his seven-days-a-week work; the daily cycle of moving from laboratory to his Jeep, to the repetitive fieldwork, to supervision of several massive, international water projects, followed by the anticlimax of the elusive and undefined frustration at the end of it – a sense of wasteful seepage – had gradually taken its toll. Sometimes, in India, he'd become feverish with self-neglect, had skimped on his quota of sleep and food and that other restorative, love – be that emotion, the casual fancy for the other sex, or a fascination with his personal identity. He'd lost the creative hold on his own life, which went flat on him, lacking inspiration until it sapped his well-being.

Neither of them was romantically inclined or self-indulgent with their own emotions. Severely practical people, they looked on the partnership between man and woman as a working unit, in much the same way that Caley wiped down the surface that Ruth Palmer had chopped her parsley on. Their sexual life had been practical too, outrageous, funny, satisfying, but physically normal, not transcendental. The last twenty-four hours had supplied that final dimension, however, compounded of relief on his side at her ready acceptance of him and tempered with guilt on hers. He's been faithful all this time, she said to herself, and I have not. I can feel in my bones that, although he's seemed so diffident for months, thoughts of another woman have never crossed his mind. When he kissed her, the memory of herself was on his lips. Shocking, the old new. That Thomas could actually sustain the intimate through their long separation was a chastening proof of the higher nature of the ties on his side. There were no seconds for Thomas, only firsts, to which he returned with a devotion that was unaltered and undiminished. Driven forward by the sensory shock of the reinvented known, Caley was at the same time held back by a strong, despairing insight into her

117

own unworthiness which had the effect of turning him into a moral giant, whose regard she then craved all the more. He was her tempter and redeemer in one.

And so she rocked backwards and forwards on the threshold, feeling him tense along her back as night fell and new experience waited. In his bed, again.

Neal left the house, then hovered on the doorstep for some minutes in a spasm of indecision. He felt completely pent up: he'd no means of transport and thought about borrowing Caley's car again to get him out of the area quickly. He wasn't going back to ask her, but she wouldn't miss it for an hour or two. The keys lay accessible on the table in the hallway, although he checked the impulse in time and forced himself into the pedestrian mode. He went scrambling down the steep path behind the house which led through a shrubbery of woody rhododendrons and silver birch trees to the edge of the water. He looked around him, disorientated for a while, having forgotten the lie of the countryside.

Eventually, he headed downstream towards the point where there was a shingle bank in the middle of the Esk and some flat walking alongside a smooth stretch of current. But he hardly noticed the terrain. It flashed past in the anger that was raging in his head, which possessed and drove him, blind.

The thought that his younger brother had inherited the ancestral home, comprising the ancient, the intellectual and the beautiful, burned a hole inside his head. One impulse said, For Thomas, that's a typical and inevitable development. He always goes back to the same starting point. He's not progressive. For himself, Neal despised the reiterative tendency, in speech or habits, would never allow anyone to tell him the same story twice, and thought that 'never go back' was a fair slogan for love affairs as well as place. Old hat. Why had Thomas rented their old bungalow in Jaipur, down Jai Singh way? Why fallen in again with Caley, unresistingly, bedding her on his first night back? Why been the natural heir for Carterbrae? Because he had no impulse to new beginnings, couldn't launch himself on his own initiative or make a fresh start. Well, he'd tried hard to redirect his brother, but he'd been proved right. Thomas couldn't clear himself of past attachments and was in a cycle of dependency on familiar habits. He wasn't an original thinker after all, and Neal had the satisfaction of having that limitation finally proved. Mentally, he turned round to his grandparents and said, 'Here we have a second rater. He lacks drive.'

But the concept gnawed all the deeper into him, that his brother's ostensible weaknesses should be rewarded in this way. At that juncture in the walk, he came to a more arduous fall away among boulders and rocky pools. He began to slip on the soles of his unsuitable leather brogues and, unused to scrambling, fell over more than once. He was beginning to overheat, as well as being overwrought.

Neal found that he was very hurt indeed. Upset. Distressed. Caley was spot-on there. His hurt would never end. What a rebuff. What a laughing stock he would be in Langholm among their Edinburgh cousins and friends, among mankind at large, who would look on the by-pass of the elder brother in favour of the younger as a colossal and intended slight. Why Edith had done it remained a mystery to him. Impelled by the spirit of the surrounding place, he dipped into his old biblical stock of references for an answer. The meek shall inherit the earth. Was that a workable maxim? He'd never thought much of that particular Beatitude, reflecting that the meek might turn out to be rather incompetent administrators on behalf of posterity. What was so great about the meek, if you please, that they should be promoted above the militant?

To him that hath shall be given and from him that hath not shall be taken away. The parable of the talents was even more obscure in its contrariness, although, when his Religious Knowledge teacher explained at Bible School that the talent was a New Testament coin rather than a skill, he found he could accept the diktat in terms of interest accrued on capital by way of a higher yield. Surely the accurate meaning of the sentence was reversed by Edith's actions: he was the one who had, by right and the title of primogeniture, as well as his proven work record. He should therefore have been left the house, not the weak, lazy and unmotivated second son. Why was the prodigal so highly prized?

Numerate, Neal had always felt that some finesse of language passed him by, occluding sense. Was that it? The words that people stuck together were confusing to him, like unseemly pairs he wanted to prise apart to get at their hidden core. Clichés troubled him, like counterfeit money he had to put through some validation test. Rank injustice. Did that mean bad and evil-smelling, like weeds, or did rank have something to do with status in that context? Both interpretations were apposite here. Edith had saved her assets by the admirable method of thrift but

119

had dispensed those savings by a despicable unfairness. Two meanings in one: oh, the frustrating ambiguity of people!

Had she really hated him so much and loved Thomas more? It transpired that those photocopied sheets which his brother sent back by weekly post were more valued than his own frequent visits – grudgingly short, he did admit, hastily fitted in between the airport and a visit to his Edinburgh broker, but made all the same. Duty done. Or was it something earlier than that, some grudge . . . ? Neal often came back to the letter he had sent his grandmother about Caley and her family misfits in those last weeks at Gillespie Crescent, which might have given offence. Must have done. But to weigh them so unequally in the scales of justice as a result was surely unforgivable.

He came to a halt, exhausted by the heating exercise and his mental turmoil, and sat down on a flattened boulder. He couldn't believe he was this unfit: the man who climbed all the Munro peaks in his teens. He could see his shoes were scratched by sharp rocks, his feet wet through, and he hadn't even noticed himself slopping into the pools in his distracted state. He sensed the waves of rage and dismay and disappointment beat over him uncontrollably like a spring tide.

He couldn't say he was jealous of his brother, because he didn't admire him, although the scene at five o'clock, when he had arrived back in his over-sensitised state, had imprinted itself deeply on his recall. Thomas aseat on a folding wooden chair, surrounded by his admirers spread out over the lawn. His hands hung down or moved into expressive shapes, his accompanying words flew and cast a spell. Why he had this mesmeric effect on other people was a puzzle. Neal thought of his brother as unnaturally sociable or drawn into groups and crowds who exerted this pull over him, as he did them, but it was a slowing pull. Thomas managed to get a ten-minute high out of every person he came into contact with, and then he passed on to the next person for the next buzz. The endless multitudes of India had given him a continuous audience because he was the effortless leader, standing a head taller than most men and with a carrying voice, the minimal assets of authority or what was popularly meant by having charisma. Whatever Thomas's presence was grounded in seemed insubstantial, immaterial, to him, and that was incredibly annoying for his elder brother, to have to measure his own steady attributes of things regularly achieved, and problems solved, against someone who was basically a mass flirt.

And Thomas had worked up such a body of flaky ideas, infused by the school of transcendental meditation, that he was almost unreachable by straightforward reason. He dipped into strange books and was in the habit of discussing the weird ideas they contained, celestial prophecy, astrothought, lines of affinity, ohm: Neal struggled to understand the new world philosophy, but dismissed it all in the end as junk thought. This alternative mode of outlook was increasingly obvious to him during his one respect-paying visit to Jaipur to see Singh and Sonal. It had turned out to be less than a holiday when he picked up a dose of amoebic dysentery from the food served in the best hotel the evening he took all the Nattawats out to dinner. India repaid favours that way, with a punch in the guts.

Maybe that had coloured his judgment. Neal was frankly appalled by the country. It might have a nominal democracy, although the local-government officials were as corrupt as everyone else in the Far East – decisions clogged by bribery, the buckshee mentality – but it didn't have much else in the way of implementary systems. He found the swarms of beggars that settled back like flies, minutes after you'd swatted them away, and the loin-cloth wayside mystics, shrouded in ash, were emblems of a needless suffering that could have been alleviated by some hard work. Indians were fundamentally divisive in their social outlook and would never pull together on a single project. All-India? Impossible. It was politically a loose federation of states linked by a thousand fragmented cults and religions, which had no philosophy in common other than accident.

Thomas had dragged him round so many temples and shrines and monuments, all crumbling into dust. Up a thousand worn marble steps, shoes shuffled off at the entrance, rupees handed over to the doorkeeper, pretty garlands of gold marigold petals and crimson poinsettias, little handfuls of incense to throw on the ever-burning flame. These heathen practices made Neal shrink with revulsion. Thomas, who'd rejected Christianity as a creed, now took up pantheism or worshipped at the shrine of comparative religion. Every morning, during that visit, he'd dragged him at six o'clock round some scene of obeisance to hear indecipherable chanting, to witness mysteries of faith where men worshipped elephants' heads and pursued a medieval path of nirvana, escalating steps of demonstrable present goodness into endless hereafters. A snakes-and-ladders religion. One bad move and you were back down at the bottom again, being an untouchable. It was too much, really, even on the grounds of its meagre interest as sociology. You should always go to the places of worship, said Thomas, because it's there you see the real people doing real things.

And Neal had forgotten how depressing the physical drifting was on the sub-continent. At street corners there were groups of men huddled by the side of braziers for warmth and a bit of company, while they roasted nuts and seeds and paltry gutter pickings of food. At night, they rolled up in strips of sacking on the pavement and slept like dogs. The Chinese didn't sleep outdoors. You hardly ever saw them in rags. The physical dynamism of a crowd in China was different: it had a high specific density. A mass, it moved. It was going somewhere. It had its eye on the future and was arriving fast. The Chinese were smart, in both senses, and Neal admired their corporate impression of push and presence wholeheartedly.

'But,' said Thomas sagaciously, 'they've no compassion. What sort of people destroy their own past in their rush to reach the future? Could the Indians have carried out the Cultural Revolution and desecrated their own heritage, their books and monuments? The oldest civilisation known to mankind, wiped out in five years? I don't think so.'

'So what? The Muslims and the Hindus just desecrate one another's culture instead. Is that any better?'

For his part, Neal despised the way Indians clung to their old myths, unable to throw off the caste system, or move into efficient organisation, because everyone was working under a regime of inherently restrictive practices. There was job demarcation from birth. What hope lay in that? Neal never hired Indians for site work on principle because Parsis wouldn't take orders from Sikhs, Brahmins from Harijans. He disliked those tired temples of theirs. The Chinese, who were an infinitely adaptable people, had modernised their gods into the tangible ones of money and food. If it doesn't move, develop it, and it if does move, eat it. There was nothing wrong with that Beatitude, as far as he could see.

Still punching each other senseless with words, the brothers conceded that the motto wasn't completely fair. The Chinese were actually very good gardeners and good growers. They had the crafting genius – spinning, weaving and embroidery with silk, or printing, their slow, decorous calligraphy of painted shapes, making furniture from hardwood – their hand skills were their best art form. The tone of China was industry, to do what was measurable: the tone of India, spirituality, where continually a man felt himself in the company of a presence, an aesthetic shape that had been built out of a philosophy or an idea, where the spiritual was shaped into the tangible record. Those interlacings.

The brothers knew they were their places. Amen.

Neal got to his feet and, refreshed after his rest, he moved ahead more quickly, remembering that there was a subsidiary path down from the house which came out at a point just around the next shingle bay. He soon found it, although it was overgrown from the days when he and Thomas trampled it flat on the way to fish or swim in the river, but it was still clearly defined, and even hard-packed in the used areas where the overhang of trees had prevented successive rains from softening it.

At length he came off the downslope of the river gulley and found himself close to the frontage of the house, on one arc of the semi-circular drive. The evening was so still he could hear a clock striking the hour indoors. Nine, he counted, as the chimes matched the length of his approaching footsteps.

He came suddenly to a halt. In front of the porch, Caley and Thomas stood in that sort of love-locked trance which made them impervious to others. Two darks overlapped and merged. They hadn't seen him draw near, so he stayed out of sight. Some lights came on in the house behind them, like a radiance. The ambient evening closed round their duo. Upstairs, the woman who had tended the place for so long cared for it still, and lit the lamps indoors, setting evening into the mood of night. The outsider noticed the mature beauty of the house more pervasively than he'd ever done before, and how it was designed so that the linkage of curves broke up its flat-fronted symmetry, with the drive rounded, the single bay window curved, a high circular auriole inset to please and divert the eye from an overall plainness: architecturally, it was perfect. Already Neal missed his mental access to this place with a pang so strong he could have wept at being excluded. They were staking their claim to it before his eyes, man and woman and servant, in a way that was as basic and elemental as an outline or an alphabet – but hued with the sophistication of the actual place which added layer upon layer of enhancing shadows, of which time and belonging were the deepest.

His parents had stood like this, in that shape he'd seen but never known for himself, the shape of love, the double darks he recognised as whole and exclusive of himself, who was its product. He remembered that other moment of loss, while he waited in a subdued house with their ayah, the women servants going back and forth distractedly, with no other purpose than to attend to their family's disaster. The curtain was blowing in from the verandah, where it was shaded and pink, but shadowy at midnight in his perpetual reconstruction of the bungalow. Sonal came in a hearse car, sleekly black, her sari fluttering like the curtain as she broke the news to them. He stood, the older, formally to attention. No emotion broke him. She lifted Thomas on to her lap and cuddled him, pressing her head down on his while she spoke. Her words reverberated through empty, quiet rooms. Something very terrible has happened to your parents. I cannot explain it simply, and the news I have is patchy.

India was death.

Neal stood alone, looking on from the outside to the in. Unoriginal, iterative, slow-thinking and slower-doing, Thomas still had the together quality that bound these diffuse elements into one identity, and to be expelled from that familial, close-knit circle of association irked his brother beyond endurance, although on the downward journey from Edinburgh he had prayed that it might be the last visit to this backwater. That might well turn out to be the case, but the last was often the most unforgettable.

He almost sobbed at the thought of his exclusion, although the sound expressed itself as a choking cough. Instantly, the people at the house moved and split apart, for he had broken their mutual spell.

11

It was well past midnight before Singh arrived back at his own house. He dawdled on the drive from the hunting lodge, partly out of respect for blind bends and the deep water-ditches on either side of the road to Amber, partly in awe at the deep patina of the night. And so dark is that vaulted purple, flowers in the forest rise and toss into blossom 'gainst the phantom stars pale in the midnight skies. He improvised on the lines to make them fit, noticing that it was the Western and outsider's view which expressed the true cast of his mind, not the native one, and that for at least half of the time he thought subconsciously in English.

He parked outside the silently attentive house. He had two servants, a man and wife who'd been engaged by Sonal when he started his practice in Jaipur, and they lived in a small outbuilding that stood a little apart from the main bungalow. In the beginning, Banji would wait up for his master until daybreak, if necessary, simply to light him home, or make an infusion of tea or undress him, or whatever was asked, but Singh impressed on him that this was superfluous, although he felt he wounded the man's self-esteem by being too considerate. Consideration tended to equalise them and was uncalled for.

The house was quiet and unlocked and blissfully uncongested by either real people or their jangling memories. This place had no associations for him except happiness, being entirely of his own making. He didn't entertain his family or friends or colleagues in these rooms. No one knew the layout of his arrangements. He walked quickly through the outer to the inner hall and into the living area which, with some daring, he had instructed the architect to design on two levels to accommodate the slope of the hills. From this room he had a breathtaking view of the valley, surmounted on its northern escarpment by the Palace of Amber, with its jagged gateways and maze of saffron gardens girded round by the natural fortress of hills. Even now,

125

in the black of night, there was a sense of filled space where the Palace was encrusted out of the solid rock, stone on stone, endowing light and shade with a different density.

Quietly she appeared. She stood still, slightly behind his chair, waiting to be noticed. If he didn't notice her, she would go away.

He put his hand up and she held it fast. 'Did I wake you?'

She shook her head. He couldn't see it, but he knew the silent sounds she made.

'Come round to me.'

She obeyed, advancing a yard into view. Her hair was loose and blue-black as jet. She'd put on a silk robe to greet him but its looping didn't disguise the new fullness of her body. Not so round, but round enough for someone to have seen and reported her condition back to Sonal. Who? Not Banji or his wife, not Thomas Langholm, and no one else came here or saw Shalini. Perhaps she'd been indiscreet and gone out to the bazaars herself one evening, taking Banji as her escort while he was working late at the clinic, and been spied out. Ah, well, he wouldn't quiz or condemn her for that. Dwelling on his returns must be tedious, and sometimes women needed to make their own purchases.

She stood on, monolithic, knowing it was known. She waited for the great separation in his attitude, to be banished from his pleasure and driven out into the dark and cruel villages, her clothes thrown after because her wearing had polluted them, and for stones to follow with abuse. She waited for the command to go.

When Thomas Langholm found her and brought her back to Jaipur, she was a child of fifteen and had already survived a week of living in the desert, alone and without food. 'She's the daughter of poor weavers,' said the water-man, 'who married her off when she was eight to a boy of ten, up-country, during Akha Teej. Doesn't he go and die of the cholera epidemic two years ago, before they'd even lived together, and his family don't want her? As far as they're concerned, she's a witch with the evil eye, while her own people can't afford to keep her. She's another mouth to feed, and unmarriageable a second time round. Bad news.'

Singh was bored with the familiar, in the Polo Bar at the Rambagh Palace Hotel. 'And she's a beauty. She's had to fight off her husband's relatives and knows they'd sell her on again if they had half a chance. She's good enough for an old man's wife, or the brothel. The first option's worth fractionally more.'

The doctor was stung, not by the facts of child widowhood,

which were common enough in the illiterate country districts, but by hearing them in Thomas's critical Western inflection. He'd no responsibility to do anything whatsoever about her, but maybe he ought to soften the other's view. 'And she's fifteen?'

'Maybe sixteen now.'

'And she's with you?'

'I've asked Ajit's family to look after her, but that can't go on for ever. She needs work. She needs another start, free of this awful stigma and prejudice. What's she done wrong? Absolutely nothing. She was only born the wrong sex and in the wrong place.'

Singh wondered. Banji's wife was slow around the bungalow and complained about having to do the heavy work on her own, the lifting and carrying of logs and water. The couple were childless. Would they accept a social outcast in their quarters to help the woman with the housework? Or would that make more trouble for them incidentally, people assuming Banji had taken a sub-wife, because his own was too old for service?

'Oh, bring her to the house tomorrow. Maybe if she had some sort of reference from me, she could get work in town.' That was stupid of him. Sonal wouldn't have consented to the irregular arrangement if he'd been wise enough to ask her.

Shalini never left. There was a stray thread of Brahmin in her family, which meant her skin was pale, the all-desirable pale, and she was book-inclined. She was clever and partially educated in letters as well as numbers through one of the missionary schools. He found her turning over his books one day during her nominal dusting, and he let her borrow them, saying strictly she could take only one at a time and it was to be replaced exactly where she found it on the shelf. She must have heeded him, for he hadn't noticed thereafter what it was she borrowed, but sometimes, turning the pages of a beloved author, he would come upon another sense on the pages, a second presence like the ledges of Amber glinting back at him soundlessly at midnight, with a fuller space.

She didn't speak and didn't look at him, but for almost twelve months, grew up in the back quarters of his house, somewhere, down yards and alleys in his absence cared for and respected by his other servants. She bloomed. He wouldn't have called her a beauty when she arrived, chit-child and face all eyes with terror. She filled out, mind and body. She curved out his seeing until Singh realised that he came home early specifically to see her, left orders for certain meals at certain times so that she might serve them, watched her batten up the hillside with a package on her shoulders and listened to the song she intoned, as pure as *raga*. *My lover has gone up into the hills. Shall I follow him?* The moment knotted in constriction while he puzzled how complex ideas and sounds like these had found their way into the pure at heart.

One afternoon he came across her replacing a book of poetry. It was cool, January with wind, and she wore the long Punjabi tunic and loose trousers for warmth. They were made of dark gold cloth and, in the setting of his room, she fitted like a burst of light shedding colours on the carpet, jade and tan, and the ornate carvings of his grandfather's furniture.

'What's that you're reading?' He took the book out of its place again. 'Tagore? Do you like him better than the ancient poets?'

'Perhaps. He's simpler. The legends, the Mahabharata and the Ramayana, are so unkind. But so are the myths of the Greeks and the sagas of the northmen, the men of Iceland.' She touched the places of antiquity, putting her hand on each of these volumes in turn.

He had forgotten the mythologies of Zeus and Thor, ancient and rather crude translations that had come into his possession with a bookcase from another house. Could she really understand such classic prose, or was she confined to looking at the illustrations, which were blood-letting enough in their graphic detail, to be sure? 'Why unkind?' He kept the book away from her, to test.

'Because the gods seem not to love the human race and deal them terrible suffering. Why does the god Shiva suspect his wife of being false and take his own son's life?'

'But he suffered. He paid for it with a life of suffering and atonement.'

'That cannot compensate for one rash deed.'

He went to the window and looked over the layered valley, cooling out of the sun. Strange that she had an instinct for the good, a moral sense as much as for the quality of the text. He had sillier and more sensational books on view, the lurid, gaudy stuff of the pulp press which fed the same appetite as the commercial films, and served to fill a tired hour or two at midnight. But she preferred the epics. Of course, she was a Brahmin, had some genetic strain of learning, even though the dust and grind of village poverty, and her dreadful fate, should by rights have wiped it out.

* * *

Among his friends, only Langholm saw her. Some evenings they came back to the house after work, or a session at the Polo Bar, or a couple of hours' exercise with his thoroughbreds, and he would call for Shalini to join them. She hovered, shadowy, sitting on a very low stool about ten yards from the easy chairs and talked so quietly with her head abased, that they had to strain to hear her. The talk was necessarily simple. She was not ample. Langholm wasn't fluent in Hindi above the level of the practical. Sometimes it was a fractured, three-way dialogue, with English and Rajasthani interrupting the flow of Hindi.

Singh remembered those evenings with a special innocence. He loved to hear them talk together, the shy smile the other man could extract from her, the questions she framed for him. Tell me about your homeland. Is it really always green and always cold in the northern climate? What do your wear to be warm? How can it be monsoon on every day of the year? What do your women wear? What is wool like? What do you eat? This naïve recital was enlivened by her humour, his patience in replies, a sudden joy in the clapping of her hands when her face was temporarily unshielded in its trust of the man who had brought her out of bondage and to whom she owed her life, unashamedly.

She had the devastating simplicity of a child. Her language was recut from his books, without coarseness or blasphemy, or the modern shortcuts which the campus girls in Bombay and Calcutta universities found chic. The manners of Rome and Paris were absurd in Delhi, but still the pace-setters copied them. Shalini had her own textbook of etiquette, thoughtful response, wise silence. Singh watched her more carefully than if he had been alone with her, feeling chaperoned by the other man's presence, but recognised his own direction towards solitude, as did Langholm.

'She must go, Singh. I am warning you. And soon.'

'She will not go. I have offered a dowry on her behalf. She can remarry as Banji's adoptive child and all the past will be wiped out. The girl is a virgin. She is educated. She is a catch for someone.'

Thomas was alerted, listening to the double-edged eulogy. 'You are making a scandal.'

'But who knows she is here?'

'Everybody in Jaipur knows.'

One afternoon in the gentlest season, he took her round the Amber Palace. They walked, leaving the ride on the back of an elephant to the foreign tourists. It was a long, steep climb, he out of puff, she uncomplaining. But at each turn of the access road, the terrain rewarded them with unexpected views, the hills fore-shortened, the empty water-gulleys in the hills as dark as veins against the backdrop of desert scrub and the knots of a parterre garden down below. Seeing round it again after fifteen years, he was struck by its typicality. He'd seen these same outlines across the Middle East as far as Spain, from Kurdish to Moorish palaces, because they were each cut from the pattern of Muslim. The same inner courtyard, the fountains, the stern lack of frescoes and wall paintings which had enriched the European palaces, as well as the stress which that omission laid on the deployment of alternative details, like the wink of inlaid mirrors multiplying the candlelight a millionfold. The severity of motif had stimulated a more exotic invention.

It was the detail of this palace that made it memorable among the forty thousand strongholds ranged from the Alhambra through the Mediterranean to Calcutta and the foothills of the Himalayas, where Buddhism and the dragon shape started to replace Hinduism and the elephant. This style was more restful than either of those, more pure and elemental. And ingenious! In the heat of the year, the walls of the courtyard were shaded by scented curtains of growing jasmine, which servants kept watered from a ring of troughs placed around the edge. The inner walls were set with marble fonts, cooled by the prevailing Jaipur wind and sloped to filter the water that cascaded down them at the optimum rate. The very angle of the ridges maximised this cooling effect. He marvelled at the mathematics of dimension, like the shape of the astrological conceits which Jai Singh II had designed in the centre of the city, at Jantar Mantar two hundred years ago, and which were still accurate at local time to the very second.

Shalini saw this palace, or felt it, differently from Singh. In the maharajah's courtyard there were twelve balconies, one for each of his wives who, on the days when they might receive his company, hung out their banners. Twelve wives, twelve apart-ments, twelve parallel and strictly segregated households living side by side in conditions of appalling jealousy and tension. The multiplicity of sons of these different unions became the army officers in the maharajah's own bodyguard, and maybe Nattawat, in some distant century, taller and cleverer than his peers, had sprung from the deepest loins of the maharajah. But on the death of the potentate, his widow, who was his first wife, ordered the murder of all the other princelings, in case they plotted against her first-born and usurped his throne, as well as the murder of all the other wives. The only woman in the palace to survive the death of the last king was the mother of the next. In these halls of beauty the barbarous was enacted, dark with blood. Yes, the great water spouts for monsoon rain must have run with human sheddings too. The walls of the women's quarters were covered with a plaster so fine it shone, even after five centuries, a plaster mixed with ground-up mother-of-pearl so that, brushing it accidentally in the dark, the complexion of the beloved might not be bruised. At the same time, these unbruising women carried daggers on their persons in case they were assailed by a man from a different retinue in the same maze of labyrinths, touched or insulted. Then she would attack her attacker and, if there was no recourse, she was trained to turn the knife against herself. Death rather than dishonour.

Shalini understood that wholly. She'd drawn the dagger, too, as the men in her husband's village insulted her with words and gestures, the old men sucked their leering gums as if applied to flesh, the boys displayed their immaturity, urinated in front of her, or on her, arching their trajectory in spray, rode as they would ride her endlessly because they were too young to ejaculate but enjoyed playing with her, tease and torment, the way girl children did with their kittens, drowning them in the well when they were bored with their tumbling, or the animals needed too much feeding. The virile men threatened her most, sticking her in the side with suggestive objects and whispering insults which she barely understood. A man took up a round gourd and worked his knife in it until it split in two halves, seeds and water spilling on the ground. Shalini, he laughed, this is Shalini. Submit to that? No, she'd fall on the knife instead. The ditch in the desert had no fears in comparison, clean, safe, solitary after human soil.

At the same time, she half understood their violence. She'd cast the evil eye on her young spouse. In reviling her, the family and the village men confirmed their own manhood and continuity, their superiority over death. Yes, to them she signified the cause of unnatural and premature death, she was the bringer of cholera, the witch, and was to be scourged and driven out, like the disease. But she was terrified that one day they wouldn't stop at metaphor.

Singh watched her face grow dark and bruise. Perhaps he shouldn't have brought her into a setting so resplendent, when it

131

could only serve to remind them both that they were the menials of history, he the bodyguard and she the body.

When had he seduced her, or had she seduced him with her wordless gratitude? Yes. On the surface, he took her like a Mogul, as of right suborning a female dependant in his household. In reality, she was the giver and the greater, ever strong, loving, quiet, quiet like goodness doing silent works.

She undid the sash of her silk robe. Over the months he watched his love grow in her, remorselessly declaring itself. Soon everybody in Jaipur would know. Even Banji looked at him balefully in the mornings as he brought fresh linen, for the tongues tattled in his direction too.

Her belly was round, her breasts heavier with their swelling potential, but she was still the sum of womanhood to him. Her silent, staunch acceptance wasn't simply docile – she was passionate with him now, and reckless, lapping him up – it was a core strength. She was so peaceable after the chattering at Sonal's house, with its arch reaching after effect, the strident and unfinished notes of their harangues, and soothed him after a day when he might have seen a hundred patients through the clinic doors. Balm she was, and rest.

She stood still, while he kissed and caressed the cream skin under her gown, proud that in her fullness he still loved her. But knowing all the same that the room was as crowded as a tail of peacock's eyes watching them and judging. Soon he would send her away to the villages and out of his sight.

He felt the error of his absolute power of decision over her. It would almost have been simpler if she was a concubine, someone he used and threw away. Ten thousand rupees would see such a woman off handsomely. But he had put himself in the sacred role of her male guardian, bound to protect her honour, and that was his major trespass; he was little better than the rapacious relatives of her dead husband whose thing she had refused to be.

She would pass as a caste Brahmin. Why hadn't he informed his family a year ago that he would marry her, not to some moderate gem-grinder in the bazaars but to himself, and heeded Langholm's warning? That was possible before the child. Impossible now. He would be absolutely ostracised by his clan. Or the *raga* evening would be open to him, his mother's son, but never, in any circumstances, to his wife. He frayed at the curbs of his conditioning. In the West, men did as they pleased, and women too, but, like the ancient burial rituals of the Norse and Greek sagas which Shalini often read, marriage to the Hindu was as ineluctable as death. Not to perform the rite was to deny the life of his father, and the peace in life of his mother, on their eternal path to nirvana.

She felt his tension through her abdomen. Very soon, he would say, I have had my last warning and you must leave. She did not resent dismissal, although there was the strange pain of leaving, because from the moment of her arrival she had anticipated it. She would not go back in time. She might have to beg but she carried the knowledge of his love, and the proof of it in his child, to take her shelter in. Beggars had their pride. She would sit on hallowed ground at the temple gates and hold out her hands in beggary there. The poor are free.

He put an ear to the rim of her navel, and then his lips, listening and speaking alternately. My son, he said, my son, help me to decide. He saw this boy, knowing with utter certainty that he would be a thought prince, calm and measured as his mother, quick as himself, priest and soldier classes merged, both spiritual and practical, the mouth of Brama that spoke and the arms that did – the complete and reborn man. Tell me, my son, what I should do so that I can save you.

What Sonal said to him on parting was quite true. He thought of many desperate remedies to resolve their situation. Even mutual suicide but at this the child spoke out and pleaded for his life. Not me, not me. Do not kill me before I have even lived. Must Shiva be condemned to kill his son Ganesh for evermore? Life and death were in his sway. Doctor, father, lover, he could not shed his responsibility and groaned at the enormity of what he had undertaken.

12

When Lionel Cohen was off-duty, between the cases he attended at the law courts in Parliament Square and his regular visits to the police station in the High Street, the Procurator Fiscal liked to go shopping. Or rather he went browsing round the shops. He was proverbially tight-fisted, although his friends put this down to his inadvertence rather than a spiritual meanness. When he was in his fifties, he'd left his wife of twenty-five years' standing and their two sons, who were still being educated out of his purse. But he was also living with a young woman QC only half his age, and it was a guessing game which of the two women was emptying his pockets faster.

So he didn't buy much on these shopping trips. He liked to walk out of the overheated chambers and was often to be seen pounding the streets behind the Royal Mile, up to the Castle to take in a breath of fresh air with the sweeping view, a peek through the Camera Obscura, an admiring stance by the cannon fuselage while it was fired at one o'clock. Or he would go down to Holyrood Palace, or take the other transverse routes that ran towards the Lawnmarket, the Grassmarket and West Crosscauseway, where the ethnic craft and art shops took his fancy. He was a well-known figure on these patrols, buttoned in a clerical-grey topcoat in winter with his head down into the funnelled easterly wind; and in summer, clad in sombre linen, he was still propped forward as if the blast had shaped his inclination.

The streets that ran away from the High Street were medieval, rough, time-slipped, while the wynds which he often sauntered down enclosed an ancient air, blind-ended in big, grey, hewn blocks. There was a low-life toughness about these closes even after they'd been gentrified and given a set of new oak doors, brass bosses, jangling bell pulls, wrought-iron grilles to prove an authentic security system, and generally brought up smart. He could remember when he might have bought a dwelling down one of these closes for the equivalent of six months' salary, if he'd been wise enough to read the trends. This was where the whores and cutthroats hung out, the dark mews, the backstreet dens and gambling houses that ran private syndicates after official hours; he sailed through them in a wrap of impunity – wha daur meddle wi' him? – but it still wouldn't have done for him actually to reside in the sumps of the Old Town. No, he went down the Mound to the New, and took up residence in Saxe-Coburg Place, a sort of second-best Berkeley Square, cruder, colder, with its houses also head bent in the wind.

Nina Brown saw him pass in front of her windows in Bristo Place on this June afternoon. Her heart thumped. A sort of ghost. A sort of omen. She froze, but it was only on the inside that she felt paralysed. Externally, the vision of the lawyer galvanised her into raising a hand to shield her face from his sideways look through the shop front, and she hid even the shy, self-protective meaning of that gesture with a sudden upward pull on a sunblind. Don't see me! But watch me being so busy that I haven't time to notice you.

Why this pounding? She watched herself flicking quickly along some racks of clothes, not seeing what was on the hangers in front of her. Lionel Cohen's face was multiple for her: the man in authority; the sombre critic who'd warned Oliver of the inevitable outcome of his thoughtless way of life, oh, how right he was; the lapsed Jew who extended a ray of hope that she wasn't obliged to join the great local Jewry club, almost a lifeline man whose crags and weathers she admired. Sometimes, when she saw him about the town, she couldn't help projecting, That's the sort of man I should have waited for, and in her mind she matched herself with him.

He saw her gesture out of the corner of his eye and read it correctly. In one action, it both disclaimed and acknowledged him. She was that kind of woman, Nina Brown, completely ambivalent and incapable of being placed.

He knew her very well, by sight and by rumour, although those sessions he spent redirecting young Oliver were their only direct contact. The South Side matriarchs discussed the Brown family doings in scandalised whispers, reverberations that beat against the walls of salons and parlours and lounges and the other institutions of propriety, lending a piquancy to their bland, recipe-enriched encounters. Drifting through his sisters' houses in boredom, he'd often picked up a titbit and filed their hints among the more usable references.

He'd also come across Nina for himself, hanging around the Festival Club unaccompanied at the end of the summer season, and the Overseas Club in Princes Street, and the AA Club, anywhere, in fact, that a woman cruising alone wouldn't be too conspicuous. Was she a barfly? The sort of woman you didn't dare get into dialogue with because she'd soak a passing male for a double brandy and soda, without the promise of any real return? A dead-end woman? No, she was much more subversive than that. She'd opt to pay for her own drink as long as she could have you at the end of her sentence. It was talk she lusted after, the rare interchange of strenuous debate, but talk – as he'd discovered – without the substance of facts or even solid opinions. She was able to proposition a man in half a dozen languages, English, French, Spanish, German, Greek, Russian – and give a good account of herself in Italian out of Latin prose, as well as gutter Scots. It was the languages she excelled in, but she had no import, had many varieties of words and no inner meaning, was that thing known as an empty vessel, the clanging cymbal signifying nothing.

One time, prior to the Oliver episode, he'd run across her publicly before he knew her name. The Procurator Fiscal had been invited to dinner by the Club Secretary at Muirfield, the golf club outside Gullane, which ranked as a private drinking establishment for the Scottish judiciary. A group of them had passed a pleasant evening at Greywalls, with drinks in the book-lined library beside the log fire, followed by dinner overlooking the Gertrude Jekyll gardens and a hint of sea and sand wedge somewhere beyond the Thirties' cultivars, with coffee taken in the lounge afterwards. There sat the Browns with two other couples who were already rather well oiled.

Why had he noticed them? They were half an octave too loud. Their conversation had no nuances. Maurice Brown was entertaining a wholesaler and the Levi rep, with their wives, returning hospitality at an hotel because Nina never cooked at home. He nodded in Maurice's direction on the way in, but Lionel watched the waiter come and go with several glasses of liqueur and brandies in a horrid apprehension. No need to feel so anxious, really. They weren't his clan. Leaving about midnight, the legal party passed in front of the merchantmen. Some affable goodnight words were said. Have you been playing the course today? the Club Secretary inquired civilly. And then Cohen heard Nina Brown say in liquor-thickened tones, No, not today but I'll take you on any time. She shrugged, twisted, went into winking contortions. The comment was so grotesquely louche they could hardly absorb it in transit. A shudder or shiver was emitted, some shedding impulse anyway, and the lawmen moved on, half smiling. But Cohen often recalled that frisson of corporate disdain, which was hardly less than the recoil expressed among her own dinner guests. That moment became the nucleus to which his sisters' stories attached themselves, for he had been the butt of their synagogue criticism no less than she.

There was between Lionel Cohen and Nina Brown a recognition, then, or the potential of a denied attraction which carried its own stimulus.

Caley knew that she'd no status in this fraternity, no passport to social acceptance, no references she could call on, contacts, letters of introduction. She was a white half-caste, wasn't anybody's child, or wasn't anybody's who wanted to own her wholly. Ten years had passed in a twilight childhood, where she spent most of her time either by herself – the solitaire draughts influenced a system of thinking whereby she chose to play the game not the opposition, and had no instinctive sense of beating others, for she only aimed to beat herself – or in the company of adults. She found things out for herself or was shown hastily, in snatches, by passing grown-ups who'd better things planned for the next hour. She didn't share the learning process with other children. In maturity, the idea of share and share alike gained on her, an equalising process that gave her a chance to harmonise talents – which Neal, Ruth and Edith had noticed was her dominant characteristic – and so make a bridge between young and old, clever or canny, drawing people inside an amalgam of acceptance or happiness, which then became the society of her own making, a Caley family.

That notion drove her, underground, but being an outsider to the accepted norms still wounded, however much she turned rejection by the general to her own purpose. She told Thomas when they were crossing the links at Bruntsfield that she felt she was an interloper in her family, a reminder of an error or something that shouldn't have been. Nina and Maurice had unconsciously sanded her down, worn her away to obliterate her and make her small or less conspicuous. When she took Oliver to a Jewish children's party in the Freemasons' Hall, nobody in the club spoke to her. Nobody knew she existed, so how could they speak to her? The gawky thirteen-year-old in a pale-blue dress with a sailor's collar. Who was she? She wasn't one of them. She wasn't in the clique.

Later, when the Brown/Braun invitations arrived for community weddings in the synagogue and barmitzvahs, they were inscribed with three names only, Maurice and Oliver with Nina asked along on sufferance. Caley was a non-person, wasn't on their celebration list, and neither her parent nor her stepparent thought to protect her position. In Jewish orthodoxy, marrying out was bad enough, but marrying a woman who already had a child was a complication which the enclave was strong enough to eliminate by ignoring it. Small, but powerful in the academic and legal circles of the city, as well as the commercial, the community closed its doors against scandal, forgot its wayward sons and snubbed its critics, because it was just large enough to be self-sustaining. It didn't need outsiders. Some women had converted to the faith, a few of them quite notably, and became fully paid-up members of the order of Jewish motherhood, but Nina wasn't one of these. She thought of Jewry as a private, all-male club. Her husband had membership and, although she'd read through his rulebook, which included no voting rights for her, no parity, no benefits for being second-class, she declined to join the gender who sat screened behind the gallery in Salisbury Road. Yashmaks next, she had been heard to say, which didn't endear her to her sisters-in-law one little bit.

Today, Lionel Cohen was heading somewhere. It was four in the afternoon. He'd finished work for the day and took off down the sultry byways in search of something definite. An exhibition of work drew him towards the lanes behind George Square. He was a subscriber to a new arts magazine, liking to keep up with the trends, liking to be known as a connoisseur of the indigenous, and that very morning he'd read an announcement for this show. Six craftsmen were displaying their wares together. Traditional and Scots, it attracted him. He was looking for something unusual to buy for Janey's birthday: he'd give it a go.

Lionel set considerable store by the word-of-mouth process. When somebody said to him 'Have you heard about . . . ?' he followed up the stray suggestion wherever it might take him, to an out-of-the-run arts film, a book by a little-known writer, a new restaurant down the Royal Mile which was still making its reputation, the phenomenal unique. He wasn't swayed by power or position or any system of star rating because, once talent had arrived at the known stage, he thought it was already played out. It was the upward surge in darkness, the creative work accomplished before it was widely recognised, that was the best. Fame stultified creativity as much as power corrupted, and for the same reason, that self-opinion carried too much weight.

Cohen tracked creative people like this almost as an antidote to his prescriptive life. They didn't have to be productive, in the sense of being painters, writers, sculptors, but he looked out for the men and women who were inventive with the raw material of their lives or had collected the interesting paraphernalia of one obsession. Not showy, not verbal or smart, they were the doers, not the talkers about doing.

The magazine article had intrigued him with its account of a local woman who cut up fossils that had been found by Jamie Drew on the beach at Cowdenbeath. What unprepossessing material was this! He was a mite scandalised at the idea, cutting up fossils against the grain to make them into pieces of jewellery, almost macabre, like slicing skeletons to furnish body decoration. It seemed as primitive to Lionel as wearing a bone through your nose. He'd heard of horrible things being made into earrings and pendants, and felt he'd not sanction that brutalism.

But he wasn't disappointed when he put his head inside the hall. The rest of the exhibits and craftsmen were mediocre stuff, pedestrian, uninspiring. Handling the fossil- and stone-mounted pieces, however, he found he was almost moved by the finished objects. The cross-sections were perfectly smooth, cut and gem-polished by a process he didn't wholly understand into satisfying whorls, like enlarged pre-Cambrian fingerprints or the ancient rams' horns of a trilobite, ridged and folliculated round and round. The colours had come up with buffing, each nodule differentiated in brown, cream, grey, black, the glorious plains. Through the process, he was able to look inside these prehistoric, sea-calcified shells and molluscs for the first time, and the effect on him was a powerful sense of tenderness for life. Shell, sinew, the sensate cord of the vertebrae curled embryonically inside each

140

other. These things had lived once and the modeller had managed to make them live again. The phrase which had been quoted in the article – 'I cut the stones to let their beauty out' – had settled on his ear with pompous overtones. But the discs bore out something that wasn't affected, for the painstaking workmanship demonstrated a respect for these long-gone creatures.

The woman had made a setting for each of the transections so that it sat like a coloured miniature inside a frame. He remembered being told that you couldn't heat-solder silver while its inlay was in place, so the setting was formed first, and the fossil set inside and press-moulded round. With a bodkin pin or a loop for hanging, neat fixings at the back, it became a brooch or pendant or an amulet, in which the bright shininess of silver ore set off the handsome darks within. It was a compromise of old and new that pleased his critical eye. The Highland plaid was traditionally fastened with a silver pin, wasn't it?, and the cairngorm which was lifted from the mountainside became its ornament in time. He liked the natural and earth materials, the subdued colourings which sat together in a kind of ingenious simplicity that had no tang of artifice.

One by one, Lionel Cohen laid them aside, like fruit judged to be perfect. Finally, he chose one piece, a single trilobite left grey and dull, and waited while it was gift-wrapped. It was his one impulse buy, a rare event. He felt a little let down that the woman wasn't around in person, and jotted a few words on the back of one of his cards, *Sorry to have missed you. I am full of admiration. I may be able to assist you. Do ring me when you can*, and left it with one of the girls who was manning the stall in Caley Brown's absence.

Being invisible was probably an asset, or maybe Caley had developed another skill, of camouflage. The clever people thought that she was clever, arty ones artistic, managers found she organised well, the dilettante that she idled to perfection. She did feel too anonymous at times, as if she existed only in the perception of other people, an image to which they attached any quality or colouring that they chose.

You network very skilfully, Neal told her once, thinking it was a master compliment. Network? Make contacts, climb on other people's backs, run a mental computer list of names and addresses to draw on when a favour should fall due? Horrors. No.

But maybe she did, in one sense, like all the rest who'd had to make their own as best they could. I inherited a four-hundred-year-old farm on my mother's side: my family are lexicographers: my home is in Sutherland and, before I die, that is where I will go back. These statements disabled Caley with the assurance of a known path to be trodden down the years, because she'd no pre-set course of her own. It was quite hard to say at fifteen years of age, I'm a path finder, a discoverer of the unknown, because she didn't even have those perceptions.

All right, she was dross or a social half-caste, but she wasn't complaining about it, because Maurice's education had given her the words with which to define herself. When they were driving all over Europe, Oliver taking his unlicensed turn at the wheel, Caley was on the back seat observing and taking notes. The Browns went for long motoring tours across the continent of Europe, with no real notion of what it was they were looking for, just being on the road was enough. The there, the back, the never arriving. They were the kind of people who had no mental maps. Caley stood by herself in the middle of the Colosseum and thought about *Androcles and the Lion*, stood on the passes of Roncesvalles in the snow and contemplated Roland and the *Roman de la Rose*. The monologue had already begun, the thoughts that were unshareable, not because they were very special, but because the people nearby were unspecial and wouldn't have understood the words, or listened to them. She knew Europe intimately, through the access of ideas. Europe was her own country. India was too big and foreign, on the scale of the unclaimed.

Seeing that he was so near, Lionel walked on the last few hundred yards to Chapel Street and Lurie the butcher. He still missed the tasty European food his mother used to cook for family meals at home, gherkins, *gefilte* fish, wafer-crisp matzos and dumpling soup, but generally he tried to resist becoming a belly man. On the whole, he wasn't bothered about meat, either kosher or abattoir-slaughtered, but he did harbour a penchant for Lurie's sausages and hamburgers because the savoury additives were well balanced. They didn't taste of meat slurry or preservatives.

He often joined the queue at Kleinberg's, however, and bought up a supply of boulkies, their light, poppy-seed bagels and a sour bread he was partial to, spicy with caraway seeds. Not often.

There were too many sisters, and too many gossips in the queue, so that he had to run a gauntlet of barbed politeness. But Lurie's at the end of the day was safeish. The matriarchs tended to shop first thing, while the little cleaning women buffed the doorstep with tins of Red Cardinal polish.

He was therefore taken aback to find Maurice Brown standing ahead of him at the counter. He felt gripped by a destiny, to run into the three Browns in the course of one afternoon when, year on year, they rarely came his way. His recent encounter with Caley's talent, and the wrapped fossil in his jacket pocket, impelled him to say something outside their normal exchanges of a nod.

'I've just been to your daughter's exhibition. It's very good indeed.'

'You saw Caley?'

'I didn't see her. They told me that she was down in the Borders for a funeral.'

Maurice looked bemused and answered on reflex, 'Nina's daughter.' None of his. He had small winking eyes and ruddy colouring, more like an outdoor worker than a shopkeeper. The Procurator Fiscal noticed some small depredations in the face, the broken veins, a badly healed cut below the eye that ticked. The man was growing old. But then, they'd had their barmitzvah in the same year, so there was no room for complacency.

Maurice didn't know anything about an exhibition, had no idea what Caley was doing with herself these days, nor any interest, although he felt he should when Cohen referred to it. 'Those fancy goods don't sell.'

'Not by the gross, but we aren't talking gross. We're talking about creativity.'

They were served and finished their purchases together. Before he could move off, Maurice made him an offer. 'Can I give you a lift, Lionel? I'm going down to Stockbridge afterwards. I'll drop you off at home.'

'I couldn't trouble you.'

'Not at all. Not at all. It's a pleasure.'

Prompted by the weight of several questions which he could hardly satisfy otherwise about the man's wife, his child and his stepchild, the lawyer accepted. Normally Lionel walked home to Saxe-Coburg Place, or took the corporation bus if fatigued, but on a hot day neither of the alternatives tempted him. It was only when they reached the car that he started to have misgivings. It was a station wagon, packed high with boxes of merchandise, so high that their road visibility was impaired.

'I've just come back from the Glasgow wholesaler's,' Maurice explained. 'I'll be a minute or two dropping these boxes off. I won't keep you a tick.'

Why did he hesitate? Lionel should have excused himself at once. It took twenty minutes to clear the car of the boxes of pillowcases, Cellophane-wrapped, and bales of net curtaining in several designs and widths to suit the sizes of the windows in the tenements round about them. Maurice left shop boys and a torpid manageress in charge of the goods, as some came out on to the pavement to unpack the contents, the crates being relayed hand to hand, while the Procurator Fiscal stood looking up at the decrepit building frontage, feeling foolish. The inside of the car, which was habitually used as a stockroom, was filthy when he did get to sit down in it.

But the last part of the journey was the most bizarre of all. Twice, when he got to the top of a hill, on the Mound and further on down Hanover Street, Maurice switched off the car engine and let the vehicle slow to stasis before he turned the ignition key again and revived the motor.

Lionel sat disbelieving as, in slow motion, the eyes of the bus passengers whom they'd overtaken in the outside lane of traffic a minute or two back caught up with them again. They looked across shifting space at each other in wonderment. Such a practice was dangerous to the point of madness in the rush-hour traffic. To be freewheeling in the middle lane without power? What was the man thinking of? It was illegal. Did it behove him to point that out, or would it sound an officious form of gratitude?

You're *meshugena*.

You're like me, son, you can do no wrong.

What was the point of saying that it didn't even save on petrol, because the carburettor was flooded when he switched on again, cancelling a microscopic gain? Lionel suddenly remembered that when they were very young men, Maurice had been prosecuted for shaking driblets of petrol out of the petrol pumps at a garage down Dalkeith Road. He was an incipient Oliver.

He got out at last, swollen with relief, so that it was only well into the evening that he realised he'd put none of his secondary questions about the remaining Browns, and the mysterious Caley remained a cipher, an econoid, trapped in its extinction.

* * *

Nina, who was marooned on her personal island, watched the drift of currents carrying her children away from her and out of her reach. She saw Oliver sinking, sinking without trace. The payout from Caley's insurance policy was only the first instalment in a system of organised begging. The young man came back time and time again with his hand out, wanting a little more each time for crises of escalating proportions.

A debt of honour, he claimed, that must be met. Which meant the gang of thugs he'd borrowed from would slash his face if he didn't cough up on time. He needed a car of his own when he came of age. There was a girl who needed an abortion, and pretty quick. And then she needed another one. Was he never going to learn the facts of life? He touched the money that Maurice had earned, pound by pound down Causewayside by selling his pillowslips and his yards of curtain netting for pennies profit, sums on which he'd already paid the excise duty and the income tax. Oliver touched it and it vanished, a Midas in reverse. He left an Aquascutum overcoat behind at a party the first time that he wore it, and it was never seen again. Cufflinks unlinked in his shirt sleeves, suits ripped in an affray outside a nightclub. Money spun out of his control without a compensatory whirlpool gathering at a later stage. The money didn't stick anywhere or to anyone they knew. It fell into a void without providing comfort, food or work for anybody whatsoever. It simply went adrift in pointless waste.

As for Caley, she might have no written pedigree, but Nina thought that her daughter was double endowed all the same, and found herself at times piqued with jealousy at the talents that had bypassed a generation in herself: looks and books. Nina yearned for social acceptability. Oh, to be able to tweak those snobbish Jewish matrons who'd cold-shouldered her when she waited outside the high school and made her pallid with their see-through eyes at each of her disasters, well bruited beforehand, she'd no doubt. They fell silent when she approached. They talked in cliquish groups that sidelined her. She ground her teeth in fury at being impotent to hurt them or to amaze them. She wanted something to boast about, but was wise enough not to make it money. The academic life, not trade, that was the capital's impressive currency.

And she still thought she had clout. She'd made the progress none of them was capable of, the biggest house, the most expensive furniture, two children at fee-paying schools. Maurice earned the money, she spent it, but she spent it wisely. Then what did Caley go and do? She squeezed silver into pretty shapes. She threw her assets away on a man who was committed to a moral poverty, to helping the poor, who epitomised the free-thinker, or the new man, that odious individual. Nina was never so relieved in all her life as when his plane took for New Delhi and left Caley alone to begin again with someone else.

On an impulse, Nina went along to the exhibition herself after she'd locked up her premises. She went, not out of interest, but to complain to somebody in front of Caley that she hadn't been sent a formal written invitation, but was foiled by finding that Caley wasn't there at all.

The explanation of attending a funeral didn't mollify her. She'd never understood why Caley spent two Sundays a month trailing down to the Borders to see that old woman, and was peeved at the refusals given on account of it, because it was a fixity of the calendar, although she was most annoyed of all that she was never asked along.

She'd only the vaguest notion of what Caley did with her time nowadays, so the display, which, to anyone with half an eye, was a substantial and professional body of work, took her unawares. It wasn't her sort of thing, and she'd make a point of telling her daughter so when the time came, but it was evidently somebody's thing. The list of sales, inquiries, pre-paid orders, signatures of well-wishers and commendations in a visitors' book were testimony enough. She drew breath, flushed for a moment with a derivative pride. Caley had done this and she could boast about it vicariously.

But when the salesgirl who was holding the fort in Caley's absence handed her Lionel Cohen's personal card, that pride underwent a subtle change into something colder, solidified, as she remembered Cohen's averted face in front of her own shop door. So that was where he was scampering off to. After the younger women again.

'I'll pass this on to her,' she said. 'I'll be seeing Caley this evening, I expect.'

Later, she took the card out several times and read its lauding message. Why was it inscribed to Caley and why not to her? She wasn't jealous, of course not, but resentful that her child had risen without her help beyond her own ability to maximise on chances, and she fretted at that idea of limitation like a tow rope which anchored and restrained her, glimpsing the unknown freedoms out at sea.

13

Where could he get hold of a fax machine? Neal lay awake throughout a second night, feeling disturbed by the pulses from several inner and outer layers of sound, himself and other selves, waves from which he picked up the pattern of his alienation. An echoing space had formed, and that was the shape of his own distancing. The moment he walked away from the supper table the evening before, he felt he'd finished with Carterbrae for good. His family had cheated him and deserted him, whereby his contractual obligation to them was ended.

On to the next item. His mind raced with what was happening back at Kowloon without him. He urgently needed to send a fax and he needed a typewriter, but Langholm was such a hinterland of progress that he couldn't mentally locate the nearest bits of equipment. A mile's radius might not find him the two machines he needed in the same building. Damn, he should have brought his own laptop with him at the very least.

Three a.m. That was ten o'clock in Hong Kong. They'd be at their desks. He got up and, pulling on a heavy cord-edged dressing gown, which was kept historically on a doorpeg, he went downstairs. Outside, it was grey and ghostly. Used to the night-round illumination of the city, he found the tree-shadowed gloom as frightening as if he was a child, and switched on several lamps to dispel it, bringing back the reassuring colours to his eyes. The telephone was in Robert's study, and the mood of childhood stayed with him as he picked up the receiver to dial his office behind Central Square. Phoning across the world was outside the range of feasible activities in this house, barring a real emergency or death, and he felt exhilarated by the prospect of the call, like putting on a space suit and heading for the future. Up and away.

The call itself wasn't quite so exhilarating. He got through at once to his deputy, a Chinese engineer, who hadn't chased up one of their contractors about a late delivery during Monday's

business, it transpired. That was much as Neal had expected, that
Joe slackened off when not directly supervised, but it could
rebound on him in the end for non-performance. What really
annoyed him was how the defensive Eastern platitudes came out,
the whys, the wherefores, the excuses. Joe never apologised. Neal
let him have it at that, not in anger but through a cold, remorseless
system of vilification. He worked his way down a mental checklist
which he'd been formulating for some weeks about incon-
sistencies on Joe Han's part, needing no notes or documentation.
He found it strangely pleasurable to make the man squirm at the
far end of the telephone like this, visualising the wide-aisled office
suite, the resonating surfaces, glass, marble, steel, which picked up
every note of Han's discomfiture and magnified it. Making him
lose face was simpler on both sides when they didn't have to look
each other in the eye. Were disembodied voices, structures of
command, not people.

'See to it, Joe, Things need tightening up. I want these jobs put
right by the time that I get back.'

'On Sunday, Mr Langholm?' He kept a deferential lilt.

'Maybe sooner. I've got through my business faster than I
thought. I may be back ahead of schedule.'

That was an idle threat but, as he replaced the receiver after
forty-eight minutes – it had probably cost the best part of a
hundred pounds to carpet Joe Han and worth every penny of it –
Neal thought seriously about flying back early. Sunday to Sunday
he'd allotted. The remaining business wasn't going to take that
long. He could, in fact, walk out tomorrow and leave Caley and
Thomas to run the funeral without him. He retracted the thought
at once, knowing how bad it would look, although he wondered
why he went on caring about appearances in the town when he'd
been so publicly slighted. His personal dignity was the reason, or
not being willing to offend against it, rather than any implicit
forgiveness of the slight. Besides, he'd carried his barathea suit all
the way here and he was going to wear it into church, come what
may.

But he was itching to be out of the time warp of this place. He
prowled about the downstairs rooms, which was his first
thorough inspection, and found he was ambivalent about what he
saw. Without Edith's enhancing presence, the house looked rather
shabby. Its charm had been an elegant sparseness, like her own,
with nothing allowed to sink below the basic level of
respectability, damage quickly mended, dust settlement removed.

But her crispness had been a thin veneer, like starch on worn-out linen. Without her, Carterbrae sagged back into its old folds, and he noticed, in the glare of an electric light bulb, that the edge of the antique Indian rug was frayed, however scrupulously bound with blanket stitch in a strand of wool that wasn't quite a perfect match, which made it valueless as a piece.

In the morning the four of them split up, tired of being enclosed with each other and the emotional exhaustion of thirty-six unbroken hours together, spent inhaling the stale air of the past. Ruth stayed behind at Carterbrae, to implement the layout of the others' plans, setting the buffet table as slowly and ritually as an altar, arranging the yellow flowers the florist had delivered first thing, making the placement of her neighbours in the eternal funerary scheme of things.

While she was going about her work, Neal stood by himself at the bay window and watched as Albert cut the lawn edges meticulously with a pair of long-handled shears. Clip, clip, and the green clippings fell on to the brown earth verges, making a different kind of mess which would have to be picked up in its turn, to be completely tidy. Didn't the man understand that the most basic principle of efficiency was to have just one all-in process? Why wasn't he using a petrol strimmer which ground up the trimmings so small they'd disappear into nothing? Mechanisation, for heaven's sake! Mentally, Neal fastened a carrying strap on to the man's back and a pair of goggles to shield his eyes. That way, the job would take a few seconds. He fumed on, powerless to impose his will, while Thomas, owner designate, hung about the premises and thwarted him with his purely theoretical alternatives.

Let's have some action round here.

'Abbotsford? Are you sure that's where you want to go?'

'Why not?'

'It's such a gloomy old place to be going inside on a nice, sunny day like this. And it'll be swarming with tourists brushing up on the Romantic Movement.'

'But I've always wanted to go. I don't know how I've missed out on it this long.'

Thomas capitulated, for that was Caley being emphatic to the point of rudeness. He'd suspended his own will power anyway. The day of travel, followed by a day of huge leaps of change and emotional chaos, had sapped him of mental energy. Now they both needed a quiet interval to reappraise events. A slow drift around Scott's baronial halls might be as good a therapy as any.

It turned out, however, that Abbotsford was shut until the afternoon and so they went up on the hills while they waited. It was a heady day, with pools of bright sunshine and almost no wind, the ideal weather for escape, while this was fantastical countryside to run away in, almost too perfect and modelled, story-book tidy, like walking on to a printed page and finding it was real and three-dimensional after all. They took a path up towards Cauldshields Loch, with the distinctive twin peaks of the Eildon Hills acting as an improbable backdrop to the view.

The colours, with the pasture hill grass bright as an alpine meadow, the towers and pinnacles of Abbotsford standing out behind them on a vivid blue sky, were as permeated as hanks of vat-dyed wool. This modular countryside, which could look exotic by night, deep and vast and echoing, became primary-bold by day. It had turned into the elements of a solid, wooden jigsaw puzzle or a tapestry kit. The sheep grazing nearby could have been worked in tufts from a pictorial illustration, the blossom embroidered in knots, the boughs overhead stem-stitched while the ever-present water in the gulley at their side was so clotted and heavy that it fell like padding on the blocked-in stones of the gully. It was a glorious, reconstructed landscape.

They were walking down this unmarked but quite well-trodden path, which led in the end to Rhymer's Gap, when, over the rill, with a noise as steadily controlled as a hive of bees, a large flock of Cheviot sheep came up from their left flank and took over the whole width of the path. A couple of collie dogs kept these ranks tidy, running so quietly that they needed hardly any instructions. The three shepherds walking alongside their beasts were the local bare-headed, dark-faced men, with radial lines around their eyes where they often narrowed them against the strong weather, leaving them sun- and wind-marked. Thomas and Caley fell back to let the mass of bodies through but, as one of the shepherds passed him, he recognised Thomas and called out without stopping, 'Is it yourself?'

'Jock Macinlay?' Thomas remembered his old neighbour from the Langholm settlements. He'd worked as a sheep hand on his farm on and off during the long holidays at school and before he went to Heriot Watt. As the animals slowed down at a narrow filter point, the two men came side by side on the pathway, dumbfounded that this was where they should bump into each other, on the top of an unlikely hill. 'You're a long way from home, Jock. Are you farming here now?'

'No, I'm helping out my cousin for the day. They told me the old lady had died, so I thought I might have sight of you hereabouts. Tomorrow is the day, I think. I will be there. Are you back for good?'

'I'm still in negotiations with my future.'

'It will drive you a hard bargain then. Watch out.'

The flock kept rippling between them. They came to a bridge over the shallow waterbed. As they met an impediment, the animals on the outside edge of the flock tended to break away, until Thomas stood on one side of the causeway, on instinct, to help filter the runaways.

Doing, he came alive. With his long reach, he was able to control three or four of the sheep at a time and he liked the act of herding them this way, pushing, working with one of the dogs on the outer edge, keeping the flock massed and pointing forwards. He laughed at the jumps and antics of the gullible sheep. His hair flew in all directions. He was quick again.

Jock was doing the same on the other bank with the benefit of his crook, grappling and restraining the hurtling beasts to keep the flock in shape. It was hard work, like moving heavy sacks on legs. The sheep could propel themselves, but usually in the wrong direction.

'See, you haven't lost your touch a wheen,' he called across. 'There's always a job at Carter Farm, if you have a mind.'

'As a drover?' Thomas called back. 'Well, it may come to that.'

The sheep had knocked up the dust on the dried-out path. The group of men following the flock were surrounded by a cloud of motes that caught the bright light. It wasn't disagreeable being hemmed in like this, with the newly thickened fleece warm against the legs, and the men calling and whistling softly to the collie dogs, which showed up as black as two jetted rocks through the intermittent white water of rapids.

For a moment, the combination sent up an exquisite vapour, although they were just working men and working beasts, not striving for any effect, and so the hillside meeting made a strong impact on Thomas as a token of the great, plain every-day which India had stopped him from enjoying. The images the sub-continent threw up were too brittle and hard-won, the animals not fat, the men not fed. He was able to relax more, and dropped a little in height as if his bones loosened when he felt the security of the unchanging landscape pass underneath his feet.

All morning, the phone sat tempting Neal to make another call. At noon, he could resist the urge no longer, knowing that Lin would have left her office by that time and taken the long taxi ride back to her own apartment in Shek-O, on the south side of the island and that she would be alone. Or not. Or not?

He rang her just to satisfy himself. There was a long unanswering wait. Where was she? Showering in a tile-sided cubicle to cool off, slowly, letting the chill droplets fall for pleasure? Or sitting out on the terrace with a glass of Green Lizard, which was her favourite cocktail, Chartreuse, grapefruit juice and tonic water filled to the brim with ice? She'd a lot of personal style, and was the sum of the new Eastern woman, clever, quick-witted, a perfectly tailored size eight: and he had found that was quite a subversive mix when the crisp, city-slick outline went with old-fashioned standards of womanhood. She'd introduced him to all sorts of combinations and people in the Territories. But he often had a long wait on the line like this, wondering where it was she'd picked up her recipes.

'Oh, it's you! Are you at the airport? Do you want me to come down to Mid-Levels?'

Such readiness allayed his jealousies. That was all he wanted from her, just one line of reassurance. 'No, no, I'm still in the UK.'

'There's another problem?'

'Sort of, but nothing you can sort out. I just wanted to hear your voice.'

'So now you've heard it. That's easy. What else can I do for you?'

Should he ask her to marry him? It seemed logical just then, as if a magnetic force towards the UK had been cancelled out, leaving him rudderless or looking for a home. Severing his links with Carterbrae affected his decision relative to her. He didn't have to ask anybody's permission any more, or consult Langholm family notions of propriety. Almost certainly, his working life would be in the East from now on, and he reviewed Lin's assets for such a life impartially. She was hard-working, loyal and trilingual, in English and Mandarin Chinese together with French. She'd been convent-educated and came from one of the oldest banking families in the Territories. A good lifestyle was to be had in Singapore if they moved there, with the accoutrements of a chauffeur, a swimming pool, two Filipino maids and a colonial mansion, complete with its row of whitewashed pilasters. Memberships and invitations to a complete social life, tennis, bridge and golf, came pat with ownership of every property above a certain price.

She was silent, waiting for him to ask. It was now or never.

But it was an expensive form of courtship, down the line, and anonymous. The virtue of distance in scolding Joe Han was a contra-indication in the handling of emotion. Or maybe he was skilled at one form of interface and not the other. 'It'll wait. I felt a bit cut off here. I'm looking forward to getting back. To work. To you. So, see you Sunday. If all goes well.'

'And sooner, if it goes better.'

She always capped him like that. Often her elliptical, broken phrases haunted him for days. The future is with women. He turned the sentences this way and that, like a bit of oriental marble inlaid with semi-precious stones which tempted him to dig them out, dense, thick and elusive in the paradox of statement. Her voice had made him hungry for her again, the web of bones he knew as her body, the soft interstices of thought. He sat regretfully for a long time afterwards, wishing that things were easier.

Thomas had been right about the atavistic gloom of Abbotsford, which discouraged any frivolous approaches. It was also crowded with two coach parties of tourists, one French, one German. A couple of guides were competing in different corners of the library for the attention of their distracted group members who would have preferred anyway to poke among the memorabilia of loving cups, inscribed plaques and paintings, and other mementoes from some famous visitors to the house and Scott's international admirers, set in glass cases for all to pore over.

The library was dismal, the study with its recycled notions slightly better, the final exodus through the Great Hall desperate.

'You're being an aesthetic snob,' Caley complained. 'You don't just happen to like his taste in things.'

'That's true enough.' He cast his eye round balefully. 'Suits of armour and halberds and a heavy dose of Gothic pastiche. It's completely phoney. Look at the wood-grained plasterwork on the ceiling. It's been painted on. False panelling on the dado. It's frightful. Depressing. It's about as close to the historical pretence of those dreary books as anything you could imagine. Entombed somehow.'

155

'You don't like Scott?' she asked him, amazed.

'Don't tell me that you do! Does anybody read him nowadays from choice? Even the new edition's ground to a halt from lack of interest. I was force-fed a handful of the Waverley novels for something called the Scott Essay prize at school, but I can't recall a thing about them. A couple of good fight scenes in *Ivanhoe* and that's about it.'

'Well, yes,' she conceded, 'but I did mean the man more than the books. He saved the Middle Ages from extinction, single-handed, or single-penned.'

'Perhaps that's where he ought to have left them. In the dark.'

Caley walked away from such absolute negativism to shield her own view. Why, you are driven by theory, she thought. The light, filtered through grilles and stained glass to stimulate antiquity, fell generously around her on the heavy carvings and the coats of arms. It is here. It is a fact. Respect the historical fact. The reason she admired Scott wasn't for his creative writing, *passé*, clichéd, overtaken by the lighter touch, but for his documentary style. He'd been the man who recorded the local ballads, went about the countryside and listened to the Border shepherds and the ploughmen when they intoned the old songs, and wrote them down by hand. He'd painstakingly edited the different versions before he put them into print. That was what he'd saved from extinction, the last spoken vestige of the Middle Ages. Was that very different from saving an Indian dialect, or only less important to Thomas because it was their personal culture? Had Thomas become a stranger to his home, despising the indigenous because it was to hand?

For a second, she resented that he'd forgotten her own liking for the ballad minstrelsy, or hadn't connected with her particular reason for wanting to come and see the shrine to a great tradition, if not to a great man, although she was able to keep every fact and impulse of Thomas's life in her head for future reference. His value judgments always seemed weightier than hers because they were spoken, and prevailed. So she resented the oversight, although she still said nothing.

'But, you know, this looks quite like another Carterbrae to me. Your house is older and simpler, and all the better for that, but it's the same collection of family archives. And a few national ones. You're not ready to throw the past over the cliff edge into oblivion?'

He said almost apologetically, 'I'm out of touch. It's so dowdy to my eyes now, and pretentious. Like the monument in Princes Street. It was somebody inspired who said that the Scott Monument was an upended pile of bric-à-brac, and Abbotsford's much the same.'

They laughed, but each remembered simultaneously that his reaction to inheriting Carterbrae was a denial. Do I want this house? Do I really want the responsibility for keeping the past alive?

'All right, then,' she challenged him. 'Tell me what you would do differently.'

'Here?'

'At Carterbrae. How are you going to make it yours and not theirs? Bring it up to date.'

'That depends, you know. On what I do next.'

'And?'

They stood outside now in the mid-afternoon heat, beside a swathe of grass with a border of red roses that distracted his eye and lured him towards them in a docile admiration. 'There are a lot of possibilities, aren't there? It needs some thinking through. I don't want to museumise it. Carterbrae must work for its living too. I don't know how.'

At that, Caley wanted to echo Neal's shout. Decide! And do it now or you will lose your chance in life. Perhaps after all, Thomas was a smatterer who dissipated his massive ability in countermanding alternatives, the Hamlet of indecision.

They drove back to Langholm in a heavy, hanging, end-of-day mood, flawed only because it was drawing to a close.

As they walked round to the kitchen door in time for supper, they saw that Neal had taken it upon himself to fell the ailing laburnum tree after all. Albert Weir had amicably refused to carry out the axing himself although, once the lawn edges had been trimmed, the grass mown in stripes and the worst blemishes of the general overgrowth removed, those peri-dead branches had looked more conspicuous than ever to Neal's perfectionist eye.

Eventually, Bert was moved to say in defence of his obstructiveness, 'Mr Thomas and I have already discussed the matter. He thinks the tree may revive and we should leave it alone for now.'

Well, it damn well would not revive. Neal found a handsaw rusting in the toolshed and set to as the gardener looked on askance at such ineptitude. The amateur went and cut it too low to rock the stump free from the soil, but too high to be invisible. Neal also discovered that it was warm work on a baking afternoon, because the sap was green, after all, and the tree had been saveable with some tender pruning and nursing. This did not endear the tree to him. He attacked it with renewed savagery until the weight of the trunk fell away from him with one rending, bark-splitting crash which seemed to echo down the valley to the water in a mocking ricochet. Neal cursed and mopped his sweat in alternation. He was furious that Weir, going ploddingly about his own business, seemed to be laughing at his clumsy approaches with the saw, knowing he was no woodsman.

Felled, the tree grew. It was immense, just as a frail old man could be a dead weight on the floor and spine-rupturing to try to lift. Neal looked at the splayed mess of twisted boughs, which had been quite tidy and acceptable in its upright state, and wondered how he was going to reduce this carnage to a tidy store of sawn logs by tomorrow afternoon. In prime position, the sight was unavoidable to the funeral guests. The whole community would reverberate with the valley's laughter at his expense. And the more he sawed, the bigger the scatter of branches grew, until he turned into the Sorcerer's Apprentice, unable to contain the debris of his interference.

To begin with, he'd only been angry, and pent up because he couldn't drive far away, or wasn't invited to go along in the car for a day's jaunt with Thomas and Caley, or that Weir outfaced him and Ruth ignored: was ever the outsider. He hacked and hacked and sometimes the wood under his axe, as he pinioned it in crevices, took on the feature formation of Thomas's face to be ground down, or Edith's, or even Caley's, the root and matrix of his disappointment, although these incidental likenesses didn't diminish the ferocity of his attack, shoulder to wrist behind the bluntish axe.

In evening light, the countryside around Carterbrae underwent another subtle change, this time turning down several tones until it started to develop the frayed penumbra of a Gobelin tapestry, with cropping deer in the undergrowth and other small woodland animals seen against a carpeting of flowers that were woven in strong antique cords, old and pale and colour-changed. When it was out of the sun, the landscape reverted to the darker references in which it had been recorded by the minstrels.

* * *

O they rade on, and farther on,
And they waded rivers abune the knee,
And they saw neither sun nor moon,
But they heard the roaring of the sea.

It was mirk, mirk night, there was nae starlight,
They waded thro' blude to the knee;
For a' the blude that's shed on the earth
Rins through the springs o' that countrie.

Syne they came to a garden green
And she pu'd an apple frae a tree:
'Take this for thy wages, true Thomas,
'It will give thee that tongue that can never lee.'

The Border ballads, which were partly raw history and partly fantasy, sprang out of this ground like the stones under the ploughshare, and were still there for the lifting. The rough, land-tied characters who could be met on the road round Selkirk every day spoke in the same doggerel as the quatrains, repeating themselves, relying on tedious maxims, burnishing one bright word out of a hundred. But Caley hadn't tired of them. They were describing their own lives like a piece of poker-work or scrimshaw, dark on light, where the power was in rudimentary rather than fine crafting. These people spoke words that sat in the head, sat in the hand, and were portable and practical, in a way that lofty sermons weren't.

'The steed that my true love rides on is fleeter nor the wind; with silver he is shod before, with burning gold behind.' It was poetry even without the indentation.

The streams are silver, said Thomas looking down the landfall of the valley, they really are silver.

Silver and green and gold, horses riding to the country fairs and jingling their bell-heavy manes, the running water under bridges and the far-distant hills that led to Elfinland. She'd never understood how it was that the shepherds, the farmers' wives and cooks, the humble cast list which populated half of the ballad mythologies, had been capable of inventing the other half, who were magical and princely. Who was the real Tam Lin who came out of Carterhaugh? The feel of his personality in that story was as friable as the texture of the earth. He was hereabouts, if she cared to seek him out, the rascal knight, grandson of the Duke of

Roxburgh, seducer champion, ordinary earthperson who was stolen away in mysterious circumstances until he was reclaimed by a human female.

They'd got a limited range, the ballads, just half a dozen elements in the human scenery, man, woman, old, young, good, evil, and the combinations thereof, but it was still a complete vocabulary of word and place and character because, into the routine, the mystical component of silver and gold enchantment did intrude; the close, near view still allowed the wideness of the unlimited and the universal to enter the imagination.

The five notes of *raga*. The infinitely applicable small.

Thomas Langholm was the inherent product of these Border traditions, even if he didn't acknowledge it. From the landowning gentry by birth, he was a landworker by inclination. He was both of those contradictory elements, the humble workman out of grandee. How to reconcile the two, that was his continuing dilemma – the bookish shepherd, the labourer knight? What role in life could possibly yoke the two?

Watching him working outside on the tree stump, Caley recognised that he was seamless in his own terrain. He knew how to fix a hurricane lamp, could keep a fire burning all night in the grate, or in an outdoor camp, with some clever damping down. His hands were quick and knowing as he searched the drawers of the toolshed for the right implement to finish off Neal's botches, and then he used it skilfully once he found it. He had the look of land men and bodyworkers, concentrating on the task in hand. He worked his body without strain, rhythmic and neat. He might well come into his own here at last. Do. Say. Make. Improvise. These were the good life skills. He was a man who could live off the bare land, if all else failed, and prosper.

'You know,' he said, looking round at the dipped hills, worn as boulders rolling towards the water-cut gorge, 'this is the old drovers' country. They fattened up the livestock on these pastures and then took them on the hoof down to the cattle markets in Newcastle and Carlisle. Wasn't that a balanced life? Solid on the land, work with animals, and then a change of scenery when they went down south, a fixed swing like a pendulum. Or roving from a pivot. It's always been lush in the Borders. The cowboy lands, the small prairies, and somehow we've forgotten that fact, except that Scotch beef is good to eat.'

Midsummer rounded the mood: achievement plus the swelling of potential at the halfway point of life's expectancy. It all shifted.

Thomas's hope rose, too, as the future expanded. He had a house and money to go with it. At last he felt he had real freedom of choice. He talked without restraint of the things he might achieve, a teaching post at Edinburgh, or Glasgow, showing others how from the experience of doing it himself in his ideal combination, or some academic writing which would enable him to put right in theory the things he hadn't accomplished in practice, like a second instalment of his life, or turning the negative into the positive. Even medical work attracted him in a lay capacity, even religious, the old mental homes waiting for him to walk in and take possession of them.

He was the fiery idealist again, the thought-achiever, the man who escaped into an illusion that buffered him against harsh failure. Listening, as he sawed Neal's hacked logs into order, Caley was at times inspired by these projections, but more often dismayed that he could talk so wildly, without the correctives of experience, and, above all, that he included her in his forward vistas without consulting her. It was the same process he'd gone through on his journey out to India, assuming that she would come along his route because she'd got nothing marked out of her own. Egotism! And it was harder to resist his driving force the second time around because of the power of his personality to convince others through his proven personal example. She hesitated to decry the prospects he put in front of her, which were a kind of wooing, because she realised this might be the last day alone with him in fugitive time, the last day of innocence before she said, That's enough of theorising, Thomas. I've moved on in the last two years, you know, and so should you.

14

Well, well, thought George Weir, the estates man, as he came through the inner recesses of the house and into the warm and sheltered garden with his tot of whisky, winking rays of colour inside its crystal tumbler, and what kind of a mess is this for guests to walk in on? A pile of newly sawn logs, which no one had had the time or strength to shift, were stacked in several hasty triangles on the gravel pathway, as unceremoniously as grocer's tins. He knew his cousin Albert wasn't capable of such untidy hacking, or Thomas Langholm either, and so the brown twigs and rain of drying leaves on the central patch of the lawn were the older brother's handiwork.

That was interference on his part, the man considered, seeing that Neal had neither sway nor leave at Carterbrae. Of course, he had known the contents of Edith's will all along, not because they were leaked to him in subterfuge or self-interest, but because she asked him openly, when Robert passed away, what was the best way to safeguard the property for future Langholm generations, and they discussed the permutations without reserve. She wasn't firm about Scots law and so he spelled out the various options for her. The distribution of the money did surprise him, none the less, the amount and disposal thereof, when Armstrong briefed him out of the corner of his mouth on their way side by side into the parish kirk. To avoid making any gaffes up at the house, you understand.

The church where they came together to pay their last respects to Edith Langholm was a grand place, and it always made him happy, or at least resolute, to come inside its doors, whatever the occasion, quiet and humble and cool as his mood. It was built on a shelf of land beside the Esk, here broadened out and jutted with boulders, set behind a low retaining wall that was made out of the same water's stones, and it had bright grass verges all round and a pebble drive. Everything was solid, landlocked, made to last. In the lee of the church was the town's memorial to their dead of two world wars and, behind that, the children's playground, the swings hanging quiet today, the roundabout stilled out of respect for the cortège as it passed by. All the old forms were observed, set against the roll of hills and the massive wealth of the foliage into eternity.

Such a combination of land use gratified him, with the youngsters playing in the park, the living church and the well-respected dead laid out harmoniously with each other. The place was a visual interlock, a permanent truth. The town had no special architectural beauties, boasting only one good building or two among many dreich ones, such as the Cottage Hospital that Thomas Hope had made a good job of endowing a hundred years ago, with stone blocks cut into handsome quoins, and the square pleasingly offset, but, out of the ordinariness of his native town, he still esteemed the way the clean streets ran down to the water's edge and gave a view over the sombre church, which was central to every perspective along the riverbank, anchoring it. The town's bridges, which consisted of a two-humpback stone bridge at the northern end, an iron road bridge painted in thick cream gloss and a metal footbridge to the south, were gratuitously unsympathetic to each other, but they worked, didn't they? They got folk there and back across the water without wetting their feet. The place was only so much real estate if you took away the folk who settled here as steadily as rolled stones. Folk were everything.

So in Thomas, son of Langholm, he'd placed a faith he hoped would not be disappointed, for he knew him as a man of scant ambition in the world. In a time of dispersal, when the youngsters left and the work dwindled at mill and farm, sheep not wanted for eating or for wool nowadays, Thomas was a thinker and a man of authority and learning who could bring something back into the locality. A revivalist? Oh, in his way he was. Not churchy, any more than himself – see how his eyes roved up into the rafters now and then, and he mumbled along the hymn lines from rote memory, not bothering with his printed sheet, as if to be here bodily was enough and his mind went free – but a solid citizen all the same. Dressed up for the day, he stood out from their crowded heads because he was a good-looking fellow and his neck didn't bow down readily to God or mammon. A man of character and principle, a leader in the making, they could do with his leadership now.

He couldn't have defined why he wanted Thomas to stay on.

Some unspecified political input. The town was under invisible threat, if only from the pressure of modern systems. There was talk of rerouting waterways and roadways, and George sensed that the precious eco-system of the Borders was under threat after a long period of protection. They needed a spokesman who was informed and passionate, a man used to chairing committees and making written reports that hit the mark, who'd give their local affairs a higher profile in the big world. This was he.

In this way, George Weir trailed him through the afternoon, standing within earshot to gauge Thomas's plans and mood before he made his own approach.

'And will you ride out for us this year at the Common Riding and mark the boundaries yourself?'

'What, George, are you offering me some old carthorse, like last time, that I can disgrace myself on while you all overtake me? I've no stable of my own to call on, remember, or thoroughbreds, like you racing gentlemen.'

Weir smiled. He'd picked up the news right quick. It was true, he did have part ownership of a racehorse that had won several races at Ayr and Lanark earlier in the season, and he was hoping to carry off the better prizes at this year's fair, the Castle Craigs and Eskdale Plate, for, being light-boned, he jockeyed well and would lead out the champion runner himself. 'But you've been riding all this while, and kept your own saddle oiled, or so I've heard.'

His letters home to Edith were broadcast, then, an innocent pastime. But it seemed to Thomas a decade since he'd been out and exercised Singh's racehorses on the polo grounds in Jaipur behind the Rambagh Palace. 'I've had the odd outing.'

'You're looking fit.'

'That's the walking. A lot of footwork I put in. I've covered a lot of miles all these months I've been away, but not on horseback.'

The two men knew that they were parrying with each other. Thomas wasn't going to declare openly what his intentions were for the last Friday in July, five weeks away, in case somebody held him to them, said he'd made a promise and not fulfilled it, while the agent wouldn't stoop to ask him precisely what they were a second time. Ruminating, but guileless in his determination to have an answer, yea or nay, he put the question in a different form. 'It was a good year when you were Cornet. I cannot think of a better.'

Now, this was the supreme compliment in Langholm, to be the

young man chosen to lead the celebrations in July. It was a form of mayoralty. For twelve months, the Cornet was the spokesman and figurehead for the burghers and freemen of the town, and his main function was to lead out the Common Riding, the ceremonial ride which preserved their ancient boundaries against the depredations of the noblemen landowners nearby, and make good any encroachments. It was their tradition, it was a grand series of days out and drinking sessions on the local heavy and eighty-shilling beers and many-prismed tots, with much merriment, symbolising a feeling of solidarity among the townsmen – women had no part in this ancient ritual apart from baking the gaudily iced cakes in celebration. To be chosen as Cornet was an honour. In his year off, Thomas had accepted the title because it sounded fun and a horse didn't often unseat him. It turned out to be a highlight year for him, too, while he was working for Jock Macinlay rounding up his sheep, reading his textbooks, planting the asparagus beds with Robert, improving his grasp of Hindi and of chess – the all-activity twelvemonth.

But to be considered the best Cornet in this man's estimation was an elevation he hadn't looked for, because there was no measure of it. The subjective praise alerted him to Weir's deeper motives in locating a man who would keep such local practices and values alive. Thomas didn't know the estate agent all that well, less well than his cousin Albert, and, apart from being flattered, he felt the unfair pressure of the man's inherent expectations. He wasn't the sworn representative of the town just because he happened accidentally to share its name. He had no mandate and no authority. He was crushed by the weight of too many opinions bearing down on him, Caley unfixed and roving somewhere on his eye's horizon, his personal aspirations in flux, the world turmoiled with his new position in this household like a too sudden change of perspective, from very down to very up. He couldn't support the load of securing the community's future as well as his own.

The approving phrase was doubly illuminating. In its light, Thomas perceived the man's professional influence on Edith's thinking. So I was your nominee, he thought, dismayed at his promotion in the town's esteem. He wasn't seeking hero status from these people, in whose day-to-day lives he thought of himself as transient. Lord, I'm only human. Why did they keep offloading their own spent ambitions on to him, like crosses of guilt he was obliged to carry in their stead?

'Yes,' he answered slowly. 'That was my best year too. I lived in hope. Such years come only once. We should be grateful that they come at all.'

This is the woman who loved me best in all my life: no one will come close. She loved me absolutely, for what I am, without hope of gain. She was capable of that greatness. Let me not forget it. Let me be thankful for what I have received in love and learn from her example, that I may give in turn.

Caley said this, head down in church, as all the prayer she could muster. It had an incantational quality for her, memorised because it was hedged with its own sadness. Partly because mother-love came to her not from its natural source but from an outsider, but also because with more poignancy, it hadn't been wholly reciprocal. She hadn't loved Edith in ratio and, loaded with the ostensible proofs of the woman's devoted loyalty and belief in her, felt guilty that she hadn't been uncritical of Edith as a human being, or even completely grateful for the proofs.

She was washed by feelings of deceit, to Edith, to Thomas, to many people. Now that she knew herself better, Caley could see that her underlying needing to be liked, to avoid a bruising confrontation, frequently led her into cul-de-sacs of dishonesty. Just as Thomas excited an intellectual fervour in others, she struck up an emotional one. They both made other people love and depend on them, and didn't love in return. Was that wicked? The sermon and the hymns prodded her conscience woefully. Possibly it came down to a framing of the word love, for each of them. Love wasn't an exclusive term, with one meaning only. They did arouse a personal devotion but, she reasoned, you couldn't repay that in kind to dozens of people. Such a wealth of feeling they prompted, but they had only one store of energy to satisfy it. All they could give back was a passionate and time-absorbing interest in the human race, which might have to serve as one of the more comprehensive derivatives of philanthropy.

Ian Hammond had a different goal in mind from his fellow professional along the High Street, and left the two brothers well alone. He pursued Caley, as the only one of the beneficiaries who wasn't personally known to him. Naturally, he knew the terms of Edith's testament, for he'd been asked to witness it and, performing what he thought was an incidental duty as her banker, he had tried not precisely to argue her out of her bequests but to ensure that they were staunch and well considered. Money was money, after all, and hard-won.

He had found her unshakeable, and even indignant that he thought to query her wisdom in passing two-thirds of her wealth on to women who were no more than her friends, broadly speaking. Of course, she had every right to dispose of her assets in that manner, but he privately thought it was a matriarchal way of going about things, making favourites and cutting across recognised family claims. It was the first time in their professional dealings that he'd perceived her as unScottish, or disloyal to precepts of fairness and good sense. He would have preferred to see the house protected with a cash lump sum by means of a trust or some well-invested endowment scheme to ensure its upkeep. It was foolish to give the property intact to one grandson and then not bolster it with the means of preservation.

'Ah, yes,' she trounced him, 'and so tie up even more money in fees and commission charges for you professionals to oversee my bequest, year on year. You would say that.'

'That wasn't in my mind at all, and you discredit me to imply it.'

'Well,' she shifted, 'the boys must work at work. A little windfall is nice, but they must put about for the rest. Ruth is not my friend, or wasn't at first. She's given her life's effort in the service of this family and I'm rewarding her work, not out of any sentimental impulse or affections. And Caley is my grandson's fiancée' – she overstated knowingly in saying this – 'but she is a remarkable young woman in her own right. I am supplying her with the means to develop her talents, independently of his. Work. Work. Work. You see, I'm not giving away unearned bonuses. I'm using my savings, my own, my personal savings, to advance the people I admire most with the means of achieving their potential.'

So be it. He argued no more against that fixity of purpose, although several debits collected in a separate column to counteract her arguments. What if Thomas and Caley Brown didn't wed? What if she went off with someone else *pro tem*? What if Thomas didn't want the precious house and sold it on? What if Neal disputed the will and it came to a contest? What if Ruth upped sticks and left for Tain before these terms fell due? Each of Edith's bequests implied a reciprocity of purpose which might well be mistaken and undermine her notions of achievement. A gift should never presume upon its application. Will and testament.

They were two of the most awesome words in the language. They smote and smouldered like swords of justice, pillars of fire, and he – a mere manager in one of the smaller branches of the Clydesdale Bank – cowered from their retributory power.

Caley stopped in answer to her name.

'How do you do? I'm Ian Hammond.'

'Ah, yes. Edith often spoke about you.'

'Did she?' The bank manager was genuinely surprised at being a conversational item between these two women. 'Favourably, I hope.'

'She didn't change banks to get away from you at any rate.'

'And that must serve as my best reference?'

'Permanence is the greatest accolade.'

He was arrested by the sentence, as pithy as a Latin tag, which it took him some seconds to construe. 'Why, then, we all fail in the end.'

'Quite so.'

They were forced to slow down in their walk across the pebble-strewn driveway of the church. Only one official car had been ordered, and it was wedged in the narrow turning street by the press of mourners. Over the low stone wall Caley saw the brothers open the two rear doors of the dark limousine and sit in distant corners, looking out at the crowded congregation on each flank.

'Won't you join them?'

'Hardly,' said Caley. 'That would be inappropriate. Family first.'

Surely it wasn't unseemly if she were indeed Thomas's future wife, although the banker searched in vain for the ring that would denote an engagement. Maybe one of his prophecies had come to pass.

'Isn't Ruth Palmer here today?' He tested a second presumption, that the housekeeper would go north again as soon as she was released from her duties.

'No. She says that where she comes from the women don't go to funerals, and so she's stayed at home with Albert Weir's wife.'

'That's sensible of her. Thieves quite often target empty houses. Lately I heard of a couple who were robbed of all their presents while they were at their own wedding ceremony. I did notice that the Carterbrae address was advertised in the local press with the funeral announcement, so I was apprehensive. You've set my mind at rest.'

These words contained so many affronts to Caley's notions of propriety that she moved off among the throng to lose the man. Worldly and cynical, they carried an implicit blame of anyone who trusted the townspeople with facts which they surely already knew and, as she'd placed the funeral notices herself, the criticism returned specifically on her. Did he know that? Of course not. He was a man who was unexclusively rude. The comments also offended her because they penetrated a mood of concentration which she wouldn't have called spiritual, but was thoughtful, personal, intense and was not to be ruptured casually by his dismal and irreverent talk.

She couldn't shake him off.

'I didn't bring my car round,' he said, 'because I knew it would add to the crush. Could you give me a lift up to the house?'

Caley could hardly refuse this favour, short of outdoing his insensitivity, and so together they followed in a line, some cars behind the official limousine, wending down the back streets of New Langholm, round Reid and Taylor's works, up the road to Eskdalemuir and then across the water to the protected solitude of Carterbrae behind its screen of trees. Caley was tense throughout the drive. There was no reason for her to be wrought, apart from the wary silence that fell between her and the stranger, in an enforced twoness inside the intimate car, together with the burden of sorrow, unlocalised and without specific ground, that someone had passed away, as well as a sense of foreboding which she couldn't clear from her mind, an overall heaviness of mood.

Don't be absurd, she thought, it's only because I'm worried about the arrangements. But she'd organised more complex events than this in her day, so there was no actual cause for anxiety. She'd a nose for quarrels, however, because those years of being caught up in domestic brawling at Buckstone had made her over-sensitive to atmosphere, although no single outburst between the brothers had alerted her to danger. There was a stiffness of manner between them, and the matter of the felled tree, Neal's anger that Thomas had dealt with the débâcle so swiftly, because he knew how to sharpen the saw and the blunted axehead, as well as the fact that Albert stayed on until after nightfall to help the favoured brother tidy up, while he wouldn't lift a hand for the elder in the course of the afternoon. The distance across the back seat of a funeral car measured that alienation precisely, while she herself was resolved to keep well out of it, determined to suffer neither from the rebounds of their anger with each other nor an accusation that she'd accelerated it.

Everything was orderly when she drew up and parked her car alongside twenty others on the semi-circular driveway. She'd been fretting for nothing. Ruth was reliably in charge, and had Albert's wife as back-up, pouring drams into short tumblers, not paltry tea and sandwiches for the folk who'd come a distance and had a drouth, but wholesome meat and drink. They'd baked and cooked all yesterday, and the table in the dining room shone with the egg glaze on raised pies and joints of ham, and the loaves of bread out of Carterbrae's own oven.

It would go well. Everything was fine.

Alec Armstrong, the solicitor, concentrated on having a few words alone with Neal. Since their longish interview on Monday afternoon, he'd had time to assess the situation further. It had one shape abstractly on a piece of paper, but quite another when applied to persons.

For himself, he couldn't fault Neal Langholm. Yes, his brother was a thousand times more personable and charismatic; still in a tropical-weight suit, lacking even that foresight to be dark-clothed, he roved easily among their guests and set off an indefinable movement in their midst, of excitement or buzz. But buzz wasn't everything. Neal, officious in his perfectly finished suit, was also impeccable in manner. Admittedly, it was only the manner of a major-domo, directing and delegating to best effect, but it was the wise and useful habit which, falling into the rhythm of his own metre, the solicitor greatly admired.

They shook hands correctly. 'I am gratified to see you here,' said Neal without a flicker of emotion.

'No more than my dues. Well, Neal, we find ourselves on the verge of change.' A small sound of laughter rippled out from Thomas's corner and the lawyer met it with that concentration of the eyebrows which some might have called a frown. Alec Armstrong hailed from Berwick and the locals thought he was as ambivalent as that non-partisan town, sometimes one man, sometimes another. As an Englishman who'd chosen to qualify in Scots law, he was a hybrid and therefore suspect to the general. 'How will this alter your plans?'

'Not much.' Neal glanced up at a sun-laden wall, as if it were unfamiliar. 'I wouldn't have kept this place on even if she'd left it me outright. I don't want it. So not having to dispose of it is a benefit for me. I may advance my departure and fly out tomorrow if I can book a seat on a Hong Kong flight. I'm very busy. A lot of things are waiting to be finalised.'

The features which the lawyer scanned for their small print were tidy too, or carefully effaced. That quality had stirred him on Monday, as he perceived on the young man a face bared in simple disbelief rather than any of the cruder emotions such as jealousy or anger. Seeing the reins of self-control were well held, he was able to grieve for him, as a man in loneliness. He thought that the family had undervalued his sturdy accomplishments, while he himself had been impressed long ago by seeing Neal's name in a publication about architectural engineers. No, there was no glamour in that profession either, but the quiet structures were a foundation on which society was built; the deeper underground, the more durably they would hold against a strain.

'It is warm, is it not?' the solicitor asked, in sympathy for the heat-retentive capacity of sober suits.

'I'm acclimatised. This is quite moderate by Hong Kong standards. There's no humidity in Scotland. It's the humidity that's intolerable.'

But it was warm all the same. The breeze had dropped. The afternoon fell still and breathless, while the heat, which had poured out of the sun all week, was incubated behind stone retaining walls and a height of overgrown trees. The land shelf throbbed with the contained molecular energy of thermal power. Flies settled irritatingly on sweat. A haze came down and added to the strange standstill of the day, like a slow beat whose repressed pulse gave assurance of resuscitation later on.

The people also dropped pace and came temporarily to rest, heavy with rich feeding and the prisms from several tumblers. There was a pendulum movement across the grounds of Carterbrae, a light note and a dark, like a resonant, waterborne echo, while the woman went between, side to side, from one extreme to another, trying to reconcile the two into a single measure.

But there was bad feeling and she knew it. The two brothers never once stood shoulder to shoulder to present a solid front to their neighbours. Thomas made groupings and Neal broke them up, casting a long dark shadow wherever he stood, a chill which people moved out of into full sunlight. Her nerves began to fray around five o'clock. It was the end of the period for civilities: time to go. Please go now, she began to say in her head to all of the faces she passed. She cleared the plates, picked up empty glasses from the warm stalks of the grass, giving hints on lateness, but everybody ignored her. She went indoors to wash up, just to bury the sight of Neal's visible, tangible outpouring of hatred, but found that Ruth had started on the tea-making, laying on yet another round of victuals with half a dozen Selkirk bannocks ready for slicing and baskets full of assorted teabread. Lord, these mourners were hungry. They must have fasted for a week ahead. On and on the day ground.

Unconsciously, Caley triggered its detonation.

Albert Weir's wife, who'd picked up something of her brother-in-law's intention to root the young couple permanently in their local ground, came round the tea table, which was set out against the back wall of the house in full view of the assembly, and said to the young woman, 'Well, I hope your next visit to our church will be a happier one.'

It was well meant, and spoken privately, but, in that still hush of a dropping afternoon, her voice carried to several ears. Some tutted at her lack of tact. Some smiled. But all of them passionately wanted to know the answer.

Caley hesitated to give it for a fraction too long. A communal doubt formed. She ought to have retorted something bright and meaningless, but the truth had been worming uneasily inside her brain for days and wouldn't declare itself or shape into the escapist lie. Thomas waited too for an affirmative – 'That's right, I'll soon be back in white' – not having wanted anyone else to make a proposal in his stead, but passive about deflecting the moment when it arose spontaneously like this. Now or never.

Neal turned around and answered for her scathingly, 'Is it wedding bells you are anticipating, Mrs Weir? You'll have to have exceptionally good hearing to pick them up all the way from Giffard. Caley's engaged to someone else. A Captain Gordon Strachan. The date is set for – October, isn't it?'

They were static, like jarring figures on a highlit screen.

Thomas took a slow step forward. That fact was immutable once it was stated. And he'd known it all along. It was the unspoken vacuum behind Caley's actions ever since she'd come to meet them at Turnhouse, just the one thing she couldn't say out loud to him. 'There's no need to explain,' he excused her.

Armstrong had admired a certain stoicism in the older brother, but his version constituted a denial of his emotions. The younger was crestfallen, racked, desperately hurt by the private revelation which was made in this public arena, but he didn't disguise the rawness of his feelings. He revealed and rose about his torments, thinking primarily about the woman. The simple words as he said them carried an explicit forgiveness, but they also confirmed a widespread astonishment that he was ignorant of the facts and as fooled as they had all been in the character of this woman, who'd come among them for many months under a false assumption. She was a hussy after all. Caley turned aside, knowing no explanation would make her seem less despicable at this moment in their eyes.

In that second, she missed a key connective movement. Thomas's slow step forward had been in Neal's direction, as he stood isolated beside the tea table. The older read it as a threatening gesture, not conciliatory, for he imbued his brother with his own antipathy and, on an instinct, his hand went towards the knife that lay on the table top, ready to cut the bannock for the feast. This was no ordinary knife, but a dirk, sharp and pointed. Ruth had made a picture feast with the fruited bread laid on the wooden board and set on top of a pewter platter, with the skean-dhu bared beside them in still life.

Thomas saw the knife go up. His out-turned hands came back in, just a simple reflex of self-protection and inquiry, patently amazed that in the space of one minute his lover appeared to have deserted him and his brother was making hostile moves to attack his person. He couldn't analyse such swift turns of attitude, only react to them in the heat of the moment.

There was a general movement round about them, shrinking in horror at the sight of raw malevolence between kindred or a hurrying to intervene by some of the braver souls in the group, before this moment passed into their communal history with bloodletting. But Thomas got to his brother first. He put his right hand around Neal's wrist to try to disengage the weapon, but Neal was stocky and very strong-shouldered, game-fit rather than walking-fit, and could out-muscle his brother at close quarters. The two men, coming together awkwardly, knocked each other off balance and they fell in an ungainly sprawl against the edge of Ruth's careful set piece, pulling at the cloth until half a dozen items from the navy-and-gold Chelsea teaset spilled on to the stones of the terrace with a crash as the knife was knocked away under the table and out of their reach.

The guests who hadn't noticed anything awry heard now. The two brothers grappling with each other: what could have caused such an ugliness to erupt? The base instinct to crowd around a dog-fight was irresistible. The latecomers into the circle were just in time to see a sudden end.

Their blood was up. Thomas and Neal were both afraid by that time of what the other might inflict, blindly self-protective, and they wrestled with each other in a tussle that was mental as much as physical. Threshing wildly, Neal's suit became dirty with the twigs and withered leaves of the felled laburnum, while Thomas's flimsy jacket was torn around the armhole and hung loose on his shoulder like a dislocated joint. The two came to a full stop against the untidy pile of logs. Thomas slipped a fraction and, in that second's grace, his brother lunged at him, pinning him firmly to the ground. Thomas scrabbled away from a series of well-landed blows, hands scraping on the ground. Unconsciously, they'd trapped some shards of Chelsea porcelain under their bodies, and Thomas's palms went down on these, embedding half a dozen long splinters in his hand. One sliver found a deep vein near his wrist. The pain was effortless. Thomas looked across the span of his own body to see his left hand gushing blood, pumping as rhythmically as a well-head. It was as if the axe had fallen again, only this time Neal did it in reality, the wounding and the savage cleaving on flesh. Hate flew out and made the indelible stain with an element that would never rot down in time in the soil of Carterbrae, shed blood, the deeper for being shared.

George Weir came over and removed the pieces of china from the surface of Thomas's blooded hand, for he was good with beasts as well as buildings.

'Flex your fingers,' he ordered, and watched attentively as the five digits clenched into the palm, if rather feebly. 'There's nothing severed. You'll live. Now get up and let us find you a human doctor. You've got long splinters that will need surgical removal.' He put out his hand to help the young man to his feet.

Neal was as bemused as anyone in the crowd. He didn't know that he felt this degree of animosity.

'You have disgraced us all by this,' Weir judged him in passing. 'We will be the speak of the Borders. A man comes to a family funeral and is wounded in a fight with his own brother. What a tale that will make on many tongues.' It was the dark and feuding ballad, ripe for incremental repetition.

He took Thomas in his car to the Hope Cottage Hospital. The crowd departed slowly. Caley packed up her portmanteau with what little she had brought, ready to leave at once. Neal made a hurried phone call and found that he could travel out from

Heathrow on an early-morning flight. Charitably, Caley offered to drive him up to Edinburgh for his connection, while Ruth stayed behind to clear up the debris of the day in a trance, knowing that the harmonising spirit laboured in vain.

15

When he woke, Singh looked out each morning at the Jaipur sky with the intensity of a professional augurer, seeking signs. The water shortage was becoming more acute day by day. Every twenty-four-hour delay in the onset of the monsoon rains was critical, with wells drying out to their muddy residue, the countryside parching until even his own eyes, as they searched the horizon hills for rain clouds, were blistered, white, hot, his lids closed over the swollen veins which felt as hard as grit or as if the desert sand had blown into them. But every day, the sky was the same unblinking blue, hard and hammered out, promising ferocious heat even at six o'clock in the morning. There was a massive atmospheric tussle going on between the earth's drag and the sky denying water. At the hospital, the blinds would not be raised or the fan arms switched off all day, while he clung to shadows round the clinic.

One more day's reprieve. Another day before he had to deliver his decision to Sonal. What shrivelled the surrounding hills into walnut-hard cracks gave him a chink of hope that something would happen to deliver him, over which he had no control.

Shalini waited for the temperature to fall before she ventured out. The curve of these hot, cloistered days was doubly intolerable to her, like being bound on a wheel of fire, never cool, sometimes roasted. She went downstairs to the dark underground store-rooms that were cut into the rocks, to read or sew, but there was no air in them and no natural light. At midday she ate and showered again and lay down to rest, but got no rest from the intolerable wrangling heat. Time had become as meaningless for her as for Singh, measured only in discomfort or his return to Amber. She lived when she was with him in the late evening and at night as she lay in his arms, but died during the day or was empty of consequential thoughts.

At five o'clock, when the sun dropped from its zenith, she escaped with Banji into town. They hired a motor rickshaw for speed and drove with the canopy down, enjoying the rush of air through their flapping clothes and hair.

The streets were dusty, pink with a gentle haze where pedestrians had grouped at corners and beaten the ground into a loose powder. She hid a little in her thin veils, drawing the end of the sari carefully over head to be anonymous to the crowd. Banji walked beside her; he handled the money and the bartering and carried her purchases, as well as his own, in a canvas shoulder sack.

They spent a long time at the spice merchant, buying fresh supplies of turmeric and coriander and chili. Banji was exacting about the source of each of these powders, pinched and sniffed and haggled endlessly while she was bored, sitting on the rug-cushion seat to one side of the stall. She waited through twenty different orders, twenty different paper spills rolled into a cone and folded tight, before the spice merchant wrote out the label to seal it with, apothecary serious over his prescription.

Her eyes wandered up and down the lanes, wishing she had a friend to visit, or accompany her on these shopping trips, wishing she could call in at the clinic or see the water-man, wanted him to come that evening to the house and make her laugh again. She was hungry for talk and occasionally imagined, with a sense of daring, how she would be able to talk freely to her son and read to him when she spelled out the pictures in the legend books, passing secret words between them. She held that steadfastly in view.

Banji finished at last with his condiments, and the two of them proceeded into narrower lanes, catching a welcome breeze of night, where the wind was filtered over awnings and cooled by their slight movement.

'Perhaps tomorrow it will rain,' he hoped. 'Lay this dust at last.'

She held up her hand to test. 'There is wind, isn't there? The wind will come first before the rains.'

They passed one of the jewellers of the city. Shalini knew that Singh put his money into diamonds because he was afraid of hoarding rupees. She did not exactly follow why, but thought the diamonds were more beautiful than coins or paper money when he showed them off to her, and therefore more worth saving. They were uncut rocks he invested in, some quite large, bigger than her thumb nail, and he explained what was the special quality in each.

This one was absolutely clear, a true brilliant. This one was very valuable because it had a pink tinge. This had no flaw and, once it was cut and set, would sparkle with a wonderful light.

Rolled round in her palm, she couldn't imagine that provisionary sparkle but held them up to the light to seek it. Lozenges of red and blue and green shot out at her. Was this what men prized, and women? Fought, stole, killed for the artificial lights in gemstones? Why, the dazzles in the air and in the water were brighter than these. So she said, but he laughed at her, holding the pink diamond to her throat and picturing it set in a collar necklace.

On the pavement in front of the jeweller's shop, a man sat crouching, with his legs folded away under him. He was quite an old man and not the best diamond-cutter in that business, although he had been excellent in his day, but they kept him on for his eye rather than his touch, as a prop for passing tourists, the moving model at the doorway. He worked on a rudimentary grindstone with a pedal mechanism, shaping the diamond facets against the wheel by hand.

Shalini stopped and watched, mesmerised while Banji explained the process. He often accompanied the doctor on his gem-hunting and had picked up the basic science of the diamond-cutter's art. It was better to have two men in the dark lanes. Two men bartered more successfully in unison against the dealers and their cartels, keeping up their own dismissive dialogue to bring the prices down.

'He can feel the shape of the facet with his fingertips. In Europe, they have to do this with a special cutting machine. There, the operators have to wear glasses to shield their eyes and they are made to sit in locked rooms so they can't steal tiny diamond chippings. And all their clothes are changed, in and out, every day.' Banji was amused. 'In India, we have the best craftsmen. This man can see with his fingers better than foreigners see with their eyes.'

Shalini bent down until she could hear the whirr of the grindstone against the hardened carbon of the diamond face. The stone rubbed against the cutter's fingertips. Every day, the whetstone wore away his skin until the flesh bled raw. At night, he applied betel leaves so that the tissue would paper over by the morning, when the whole process would begin again. She felt for his silent suffering, flayed by poverty in this way.

* * *

To be considered for fitting with a Jaipur foot, most patients had to be young, certainly under forty, and capable of work. The artificial foot was not inexpensive, so had to be cost-effective, while incidental surgery was more traumatic for the aged and, in a world of strict resourcing, Dr Nattawat and his colleagues made what they thought was a fair system of priority.

But some complex cases came his way. One day, the last time he spent the evening at the Rambagh Palace with the water engineer, he'd seen a man about sixty years of age. This man professed to be older, or not to know his precise date of birth, because he was one of the city's best-known astrologers. Soothsayers, Langholm called them in disdain. The man made himself timeless deliberately, because proclaiming his ancient reputation enhanced the present one. He'd had an accidental tangle with a rickshaw and damaged his tendons, upon which rheumatism had set in, deforming the foot into a difficult club shape, which was painful to walk on and to keep shod. Singh didn't think this patient was a candidate for full-scale amputation, but that a simpler straightening of the tendons would be beneficial. He X-rayed the foot and told the man to come back in a week's time.

Strangely, the man spoke English to him spontaneously, as if to prove that he too was an educated man, scientifically trained, not just some booth palmist who worked at fairs and festivals, telling women what they wanted to hear about strong-armed lovers and impending fertility. Perhaps conceding this, Singh thought he would seek his professional advice. He passed him a piece of paper. 'This is my birth date. And the one below is the date of my intended. What day should we settle on for our marriage?'

'I need to know the time of day,' the astrologer objected. 'And I have no charts with me. I must take time to consult my charts at home.'

'I was born at four twenty in the morning, my intended at noon. When you return next week, it will be soon enough to tell me. I will have your answer about the operation, and you can give me mine.'

Today was that day. The consultation went well. The tendons could very easily be severed and the toes made to lie flat again. The ball of the foot would then rest on the ground, all being well. They made a tentative estimate about how long the old man would have to wait for the operation to be performed and how long recovery would take.

'Now, you promised me a good date in return. Have you forgotten?'

'No. I did not forget.' The man pulled a slip of paper from the waist fold of his dhoti and handed it back.

Singh saw the dates of birth exactly as he had written them. 'And what is the most favourable conjunction?'

'There are some things,' said the astrologer, 'that we may not foretell.'

Singh's face was thunderous. The man was blackmailing him, wanted to be paid for his forecast like a street fortune-teller after all. He put his hand towards his jacket pocket to find some coins.

But the patient held up his hand defensively. 'No. I cannot predict what it is you ask of me. Excuse me. That is all.' He salaamed with exquisite grace and politeness, before retiring through the open door of the consulting room.

Singh sat on, dumbfounded for some moments, black with the worst omens of foreboding. The old man wasn't prescient at all, hadn't consulted his charts at home but some gossips down Jai Singh way, who'd passed on the situation regarding his intended. His scepticism at human nature was stronger than his faith in augury, and he was furious with himself for falling into the ploys of superstition, while Thomas Langholm sat above his shoulder, spirit in air, and laughed and laughed to see his sour expression.

Shalini wandered down the bazaars, enjoying the populous.

More walkers came out, breathing the scents of evening. The rickshaws thickened on the road, coming and going, a large matron with a basket of live chickens, beaks poking through wicker, who exhorted her driver to go faster to speed their imminent beheading, a solemn man with a briefcase who sat bolt upright staring into space, reviewing the case he had just represented to the circuit judge. Business was at its most brisk in the two hours before nightfall. Shalini picked up white kid shoes stitched with spangles and touched the tempting bales of cloth, not meaning to buy anything, but because it was a pastime.

She turned a corner and ran across the path of Singh's mother, walking five feet away. Banji had stopped and spoken to Sonal on a previous occasion, so she recognised the woman at once, and would have done so anyway because mother and son were distinctive in the crowds. The height of the forehead, the shape of nose and chin were not Rajasthani features. Shalini sped on, putting her head down to avoid catching the woman's eye but remembered that if she went too fast, she would lose Banji somewhere behind her in the crowd. She stopped to look round for him and, in doing that, observed that Sonal had halted, too, and gazed back in her direction.

She knew that she was known.

No point in hiding, then. Sonal Nattawat's face was uncovered. Why not hers? Deliberately, Shalini took the end of her sari where it fell behind her left shoulder and unwound it from her head, letting the material fall like a long, loose scarf in front of her. I will not hide, she thought. No more hiding or running away for me. Desert or city, I am free.

Sonal swayed in indecision. She was struck by the young woman's dignity, her absolutely correct demeanour as she turned slowly on her heel and walked up the wider boulevard. There was plenty of space to follow and watch her without being conspicuous, so she did follow and kept her in her sights under the shade of the banyan trees. In doing so, the older woman recognised that she was in the grip of a large presence which was not exclusively the girl's, but was her enigmatic son's, to which Shalini might provide the clue. What did Singh like? His mother did not know what Singh liked, so every detail of the girl's costume intrigued her as something newly apprised. She wore a silk sari in a shade few Indian women could carry off, terracotta, almost bronze, the deep-city colour, red of reds, which showed up glowingly against a skin so fair it was next to cream. Well, she might have guessed at that taste after all, invaded by a rush of understanding, which was strength, and with it weakness to fight his choice of woman to the last.

The girl wore no jewels and no make-up. These were the prerogative of consort or of concubine, and to see her bare of decoration moved Sonal, and warned her of the unusual. Why so quiet, lacking in ostentation? For a second, she found herself thinking that her son had not treated this young woman properly, as she deserved, and was in turn confounded by her foolishness.

Other men eyed her. Bold without her head covering, blindingly fair, she was a magnet. She had powerful outlines, the body of a worker, strong, round, shapely, but the delicate head of a thinker which vendors and purchasers caught out of the corner of their eye, squat on stools, and followed like the tail end of a comet, flashing gold at the hem. Until Sonal felt she was practically her chaperone, felt in herself an urge to dart forward if anyone had been so impertinent as to make the slightest approach or pass a rude, suggestive comment.

But the girl had an imperial carriage and learned something, living in the shadow of the palace at Amber. Commoners did not approach but rather separated in her path. Sonal was consumed with a new longing, to come close enough to hear her voice. At moments, she watched herself watching, overcome with shame at the gross unsuitability of her behaviour. Following a woman of no principles down the bazaars, she whose father had been a minister to Nehru, whose brother had held ambassadorial rank. She imagined her own mother doing such callow snooping. Impossible!

In this case, instinct was stronger than example, although she trembled at her own audacity. Surely Shalini must notice any moment, or already knew she was being trailed, and would report it back to Singh. Any day now he would drive out to the lodge to deliver his final decision, and she argued lamely to herself that observing the girl from afar had some material relevance, since it would help the assembled family unit to dispose of her more tactfully.

But the child she carried was not to be disposed of. Sonal tracked her with a sense of heartbreak about the first of her second generation, thinking inexorably to herself, My child's child is twice my child. Neither Shalini nor Singh had any hold over her imagination compared with this unknown unborn whom she began to shape precisely in her mind, down to his name.

They came together. For a second, a long moment, they hesitated beside a stall that sold trinkets and ivories. Shalini slipped on a solid bracelet, Sonal admired a small fillet of pierced lattice-work that could make a cover for a favourite reliquary book, standing four feet from each other and wholly uninterested in their respective purchases. Speak, thought the older woman to the vendor, just make her say something in reply.

'How much is this bracelet?'

'One hundred twenty rupees.'

'Ah,' said the girl, sighing, 'too much.'

Sonal listened to the quiet sigh of wind over traceries and was satisfied. A strict choice she had made, and a strict rejection. The stallholder pitched his price far too high, and there was a minute pleasure in that, because he had assumed by accent and deportment that Shalini was well-to-do and pushed up his opening bid to match. When the girl walked on, Sonal took up the self-same bracelet and, checking its absolute smoothness, its matching cream, managed to haggle him down to fifty.

Banji, meanwhile, was in a swelter, padding up the lanes with his load of purchases in the suffused heat. He thought of dinner waiting for the turmeric, wanting to go home before it was dark or the demand for rickshaws too heavy. He was puzzled, seeing the old mistress follow the young mistress, as if their positions were reversed. With the wide gap between himself and Shalini, she might not realise he was following at a distance, be actively looking for her own shadow round and round the acres of bazaars but, with Sonal in between them, he feared to overtake and catch her up. They could go on like this for hours.

And deeper thoughts troubled his immediate, practical one. Why was Sonal behaving in this furtive way? It was so odd, to tag her son's servant, that it was sinister. And whatever else he felt personally, it was his primary duty to protect Shalini from threat, even of verbal abuse. If the two women talked, if they argued publicly, it might fall to him to intervene. Heavens! The shame of it. The difficulty of appeasement. Even if all passed off agreeably, was he in any way obliged to report the evening's strange coincidence to the doctor? He did not think he should mention it without provocation, for it smacked of tittle-tattle, which he abhorred, but Shalini might complain behind his back that he had neglected her and it would all come out. What to do?

So he went round and round distractedly. It was an incalculable relief when he saw the two women come together at the trinket stall, stop and part again. He darted into a side lane and soon caught Shalini up.

'Where have you been?' she asked with fake irritation.

'And where have you? We have walked halfway to Amber and back this evening.'

16

'How did you know about Gordon?' Caley asked Neal once they were clear of Selkirk, and her rage and shame at the post-funeral events at Carterbrae had subsided into base curiosity.

'I met him a couple of years ago. I'm surprised you've forgotten about the evening. You were there.'

She took her eyes off the road to scan the profile that was only two feet away from her in space, a mile in outlook. Even the recall of memory was competitively ranked with Neal: I can remember things better than you do. What was the absolute test of such a boast? Should she retort, Well, you've forgotten that I ever sat beside you in First Ordinary Geology? Hardly. She wasn't the type for cheap one-upmanship, but something still asserted itself.

'No, I haven't forgotten that evening. Thomas was there, and Singh. I've always thought it was ironical that it was Singh who introduced all of us to Gordon, just as he brought me to Gillespie Crescent in the first place. It was at the Hawes Inn at Queensferry and we were celebrating the end of year. You'd booked your flights. When we got back to Bruntsfield, there was a telegram waiting to say that Singh's father had died. I can go on, if you like, and tell you what we ate and what I was wearing. I haven't forgotten it at all. I asked you how you knew *about* Gordon, not how you knew him in the first place.'

He wasn't in the least chastened. She'd only proved that he was right on these details too. 'He works for Smythe and Carruthers in St Andrew Square. They're my stockbrokers. One of the partners told me when I was back last month.'

'Well, he told you wrong. I'm not engaged. Not to Gordon. Not to anyone.' She held up her ringless left hand as proof. 'And I haven't set a date to ring the bells in Giffard, or Fairmilehead for that matter.'

'But you will.'

Caley had a very long fuse. Not only was she bad at being

angry, but, logically, she felt it achieved nothing as a means of persuasion. She tended to trust her grandfather's maxim that whoever lost his temper lost control of the situation as well. Capable of absorbing all of her own tension and most of other people's, she was determined not to let Neal rile her, but somehow he managed it. He made her blood boil, just because he stayed so cool, critical, always in command of his own range – or limited to it.

'Who knows what I will decide?'

'Not Thomas obviously.'

'I've never lied about it. Never promised. Never cheated.'

'Only lied by omission.'

'You're right. I've not been completely frank. These last few days have been too heated for clear thinking. But we've both hurt him needlessly, and I much more than you.' The picture of Thomas hurt, being hurt, palpably wounded, swam up in front of her eyes. How could she have run away and left him to the care of strangers? His hand bleeding, his feelings racked. She witnessed again his gentle form of pain, without recourse to screams or smashing, the indrawn converse of the norm she was familiar with in the tempestuous tantrums of the Brown household. Breaking strain. Thomas would be wondering where she was and looking out for her. He'd be looking round the house, searching in her room, wondering why she'd absconded without explaining herself. The moment that the balance of her emotions reasserted itself, she wanted to turn round and go back to Carterbrae and make it up with him. But how could she? Now she was committed to getting Neal to the airport and away from the argument. 'Why do we treat him so badly? Why can't we behave better to him?' She shrank in her own misery and felt small.

Neal shrugged. 'He's one of life's victims.'

Yes, the phrase said everything about the cast of his own mind, dismissive and self-exempting. 'Then that makes us into victimisers, which is rather worse.'

'I've no particular scruples about what I did. I only defended myself from his attack. Don't you do that? Turn away from the attacker?'

'Rarely.'

'Then you are a fool.'

'Most probably I am.'

She understood how frustrated Neal must feel with her: she'd rehearsed all these arguments with Gordon himself for the last few months, about plain speaking and clearing the air. Anxious to have a straight answer for his own sake, he thought the first step was for her to reach a personal decision on where she stood with Thomas. But Caley couldn't bring herself to write the letter of dismissal, as cold as an employer setting out the end of a contract, and had let it drag on until they met again, at which point she discovered she couldn't say it any more easily than she could write it, and so she went on compounding the situation until its hidden tension was released with that audible bang of calamity an hour ago when fist met flesh. Fool, yes, she was that.

But had she been so very wicked? Most of those girls who'd floated through their Bruntsfield years had more colourful records than her own. For some reason, however, Caley's doings excited active comment. For other people, a remote past lover and a nearer replacement was so normal that it would have passed for dull. She seemed to be some kind of standard bearer, or others heaped her with their own vicarious expectations, much as they did Thomas. Still, neither of them liked to disappoint those aims and were also culpable in that they went on being loyal to quite unworkable ideals. Mythic figures, they found it hard to be heroic round the clock.

'Have you seen Gordon again since that first meeting? Do you do business with him?'

'No. Never.'

'So it was mentioned at Smythe and Carruthers quite by chance. How you must have gloated, and sat mulling over it all these weeks. How to detonate it to best effect, like laying a mine?'

'That's to overstate. I'd no notion of how the land lay between you and Thomas. I didn't ask. Didn't greatly care. So I was staggered to see you sitting waiting for us at Turnhouse and then to find you so cosily ensconced at Carterbrae, rather acting the young chatelaine.'

'At least this gives the lie to your suspicion that I'd ingratiated myself with Edith.'

'It gives the lie to nothing. I said no such thing.'

'You didn't need to. You breathe what you think. You can imply it by the least shrug of your shoulders. The woman got that right.'

Further debate was pointless and Neal, whatever Caley thought, disliked the vapid dispute, if not the actual process of arguing, which he invariably considered he had won. He'd no wish to trade slanders with her and so, partly to distract her attention and partly to relieve his own incumbent boredom, he changed the topic. 'Do you keep in touch with Singh?'

'The occasional letter. I haven't heard from him much recently. A short note about a month ago. Why?'

'I wonder what's happening out in Jaipur, and how he's extricating himself. Not easily, at any rate. What has Thomas told you about his situation? Or are you mum on that imbroglio as well?'

She turned to pay close attention, alerted by the different timbre of this impersonal malice.

After the splinters of china were removed, the doctor in duty at the Hope Cottage Hospital ordered an X-ray of the punctured hand, but said the plate wouldn't be processed until the morning. He didn't think Thomas was an at-risk patient needing to be kept in overnight, so the hand was merely bandaged. He ordered rest as well as a sedative to make him sleep, which Thomas disregarded, although he did promise the doctor and George Weir, who kept up his solicitous guardianship of him, that he would go back for the diagnosis first thing on Thursday morning.

This was delayed. The morning wore on in lengthening queues while an emergency road accident was attended to. At last, he was pronounced semi-fit, warned that he ought to protect the hand from knocks and continue the course of anti-tetanus injections once he flew back to India. Thomas took note of all this. On no account was he to drive, ride a horse or flex the hand unnecessarily before the wound healed over.

He didn't go back to Carterbrae after his appointment. He walked up the High Street to Jim Batey's house to ask if he could hire the car, unless Jim was already booked for a taxi fare.

'How long do you want it for?' asked Jim.

'A day. Maybe a day and a half.'

'And you'll bring the car back? You'll not dump it at Turnhouse and have me hoick all the way up to Edinburgh to get it home again? Folk have done that on me before now. And I've had to pay the airport parking charge.'

'I promise,' said Thomas. 'I'll be back tomorrow night, Friday at the latest.'

Driving back north again to Edinburgh, however, Thomas had his misgivings. His hand hurt as he manoeuvred the gear stick, a sensation which he could readily discount. Exercise had got to be good for the muscles and, if it wasn't, the stab of pain was therapeutic in itself, in minimising recall.

It was obvious to him that, within twelve hours of the funeral, he and Neal and Caley were indeed the speak of Langholm and its outer boundaries. There was a current of watchfulness along the hospital corridors in his proximity as his neighbours made their own assessment of his state. Jim Batey and the consultant had asked for no explanations because rumour had supplied them ahead. He looked back on the fight as an outrageous accident which didn't wound him in a personal sense, except that it made public those feelings which were grotesque even in private. He didn't exonerate himself in the settlement of scores. If Neal felt such antipathy, then he must have encouraged it because those passions needed a rich soil to grow in. He ran his mind back over the last few days, the last few years, looking for retrospective clues as to why animus had got the better of them both and supplanted the more natural bonds of brotherhood. They hadn't always been at odds like this. Their holidays together were agreeable, the recent exchange of visits went off passably well, the old Munro expeditions had been good-humoured and team-supportive as trips on the exposed, capricious mountains had to be. Differences there had been, of approach and timing, but no open arguments.

His disquisitions came back to one sticking point, which coincided with Caley's arrival on the scene at Bruntsfield. Was Neal sidelined by the pairing, which was undesirable in his own judgment in spite of its finding favour with Edith? Was he smitten by her himself, not so much by her attractions as a woman, as by her disdain of exercising them on him? Pique only? Surely his brother's grounds for entering into local mythology were stronger than a lasting huff?

After all, those two people weren't irreconcilable, Neal and Caley. It wasn't lost on Thomas that they'd driven away, and voluntarily, in each other's company. He itched to know what had been said along the way, about him or not about him.

Could it really be true that Caley was engaged to someone else? It was almost immaterial compared with the problem of what she must have been thinking about all the time that he was in Jaipur. Getting on for two years. Surely not that long! It was an unconscionable time to keep a girl waiting, but there had been talk of meetings between the two of them, travel arrangements made and then broken, a crisis here, there an unexpected development which sidetracked him, whereby in his own mind there had been no real or irreversible falling off – just a preoccupation with the current train of events.

She'd found another man. Well, why not another man? He hadn't offered Caley much in the way of emotional security. He'd been a lazy and inconsiderate lover, driven by his own career needs and the excision of the demon duty from his roster. Captain Gordon Strachan from Giffard. He remembered him distinctly: he was the type of man known as well set up, ex-Army, ex-Northern Ireland, DSO for some piece of mindless heroism like going across a bomb site to rescue a wounded civilian. It was good for PR, he could recall the officer saying about the citation in the course of that evening when they were introduced at the Hawes Inn. I wouldn't have got it for attending to another soldier. That's only the line of duty. Doesn't earn headlines or points. Even saving a life is political. He was wry, then, as well as having a cool head under fire. He had money, looks, position: the amalgam of success as defined by an address in the chic satellite village outside Edinburgh. Thomas could almost hear Caley saying that with that ironic twist in her voice, I'd like to see the man my parents chose for me: and this is him.

He drew gradually north of Galashiels and felt the countryside change by imperceptible degrees, implying the largeness of a city on which roads now focused in a radial concentration, conduits to a flow. There was less luxuriant wandering in the terrain: stranded in a field blindfold, Thomas would have been able to pick up the direction of magnetic north by the current of purpose towards a more dense molecular structure, like a vibration over the horizon, pulsing them towards it.

When he crested the final hill above Dalkeith and saw that bizarre, unique mass of geology known as Edinburgh, as familiar and idiosyncratic as his own bones erupting from the loose linkage of flesh and memory, he wasn't moved so much as dismayed. Trying to locate Caley in the immense carcinomatous eruption was as hard as pinning her down emotionally. Elusive and enigmatic, the power of both city and woman was notional rather than actual, something resting in his imagination. He wasn't sure he had the will-power to search and dominate. Where to begin? In setting out, he'd only thought about the end, not the means, having no starting point but her family address in Fairmilehead where the warmth of his reception was in doubt. Nina Brown might well be uncooperative or obstructive on Caley's whereabouts, and then what would he do? He had no lead. He knew nothing whatever about her personal life.

The city, as he drew finally inside its range, sat as grey and inscrutable as the riddling Sphinx over his destiny. What questions should he ask it, and how should he interpret the replies? He'd spent the longest period of his life here, so that it felt his personal, emotive home rather than Carterbrae or the township of Langholm, which denoted his ancestral and native community, his inherited ties, the thing he couldn't alter in his make-up. Genetics. Genealogy. The third location, Jaipur, arguably exercised the strongest pull of all on him, because he'd chosen that of his own free will, and his feelings about the place were ratified by duty, charity and the powerful word ethic, which implied morality and ethos in one. He could ignore a super-imposition, or reject it, but not an open choice. He was committed to such in perpetuity. These three places also happened to line up with the three dominant people in his life, Caley, Neal and Singh. That shape had a monolithic simplicity about it – simple except that it was split tripartite. He recognised that having a duty-encumbered home and personal inclination and work, the triangular pattern of a life, wasn't as splintered as this for other people. For the lucky, all three angles or options occurred in one locality, which struck him as an enviable neatness.

But that was the nature of Scots in general: to cross the globe, to emigrate, to bide from home. As the world went on contracting, merging the customs of East and West indiscriminately, with each half trying to use the other for a trade-off between technological expertise on the one hand and the resources of raw materials and low-cost manpower on the other – computer chips versus cheap textiles – more and more technocrats lived this kind of wandering, dislocated life. Singh was another man like himself, cut in two. The status that his people attached to a Westernised university degree in medicine had probably unhinged the remainder of his life because he couldn't reconcile the two philosophies, or resolve the conundrums which were implied by the rational palmist or the scientific layer-on of hands. Singh's standards were so schismatic, part blind faith, part logic, that he could never perform to his own expectations.

Neal likewise. Who was Neal's perfectly harmonious partner? Someone who was a compromise of Eastern mores and Western education, or a rare mix, the hybrid, half-caste, nomad or misfit which they were individually consigned to pursue in order to match the mismatch in themselves. Hopefully not that awful, self-

191

seeking Lin he had in tow, the chirpy one. Her small-boned slightness, her irritating Chinese voice like wind in reeds, always humming, sounding low in the background like the noise pollution from a motorway. Surely he wasn't planning on a future with her? Neal wasn't her meal-ticket so much as her guarantee of a British passport and an exit visa before the handover. That wasn't cynical of him. Hong Kong was full of a new breed of superior Chinese girls urgently on the make, mopping up the spare Europeans who were out on short-term work contracts. Their finishing schools included a course on how to hook susceptible fools. How to make the most of their sexual assets or of what Western girls didn't know about the well-managed orgasm. How to close the deal.

Of course, Neal might well be wedded to his work and need no one at all. Soberly, Thomas acknowledged that his brother had the makings of greatness, in the mould of the giant Scottish engineers, Watt, Telford, Stevenson and McAdam. They were the road and steam and transport men of an era, the globe-shrinkers. Why not a Langholm immortalised alongside them in the history books? There was a great project waiting for Neal somewhere, if time and opportunity served him well. When he went out to visit him in Hong Kong, Thomas had been impressed by the vast earthworks he was taken round on tour, equivalent to the Pyramids, the Aswan Dam and the Suez Canal all in one. The spars had already been sunk which would support the wide approach road to Chek Lap Kok, while a man-made island was being dredged up from the China Seas to carry the runways of the new airport, and the harbour was in process of enlargement to absorb the new business that the airport would generate. He thought land reclamation was the most formidable act of global restructuring, in polder drainage or the raising of sea dykes, which was wholesale genetic engineering of the face of the earth. But was it for the long-term good any more than the human variant? Well, that was a matter of principle on which he had suspended judgment.

Neal, incidentally, had the survival hardiness of great men, to be able to live by himself, away from home and the known comfort states. There was something succinct in him, nett. All right, he was blinkered in his outlook, but that could be the price you had to pay for achievement at the highest levels. The most able people of all, in terms of raw ability, had too much peripheral vision and were easily distracted, like himself. In comparison with Neal's accomplished bridges, harbours, airports, the concrete structures lifted high into the witnessing air, what was digging a few bore holes to keep village drought at bay until the next monsoon? Not a lot. It was merely practical, however humane, and lacked dynamics or vision.

Thomas acknowledged, as he made the final tangled approach inside the city limits, that he'd mixed ethics too far into his own idea of employment. That was the missionary strain coming out in him, the doer of good works, goddam him. But, different as they were, he and Neal were still the new breed of colonials, the engineers, the technocrats, the oilmen and riggers, experts in satellite telecommunications, who went out to conquer new worlds and markets, and put them under the dominion of the English language, even if that was a form of jargon computer-speak, and the Western philosophy of progress. They were the consultants who kept the developing world up to scratch, according to a code of practice which they neither observed or personally admired.

'Caley isn't here,' said Nina. 'She hasn't lived here for almost two years. I'd have thought you'd know that.'

The words, baldly said, were quite dismissive. Time to turn round and go. But two things detained Thomas. Nina had ushered him inside the house quite welcomingly and, when she delivered this astonishing information, he was already seated in the Chinese-yellow drawing room. Therefore she wasn't actually showing him the door. And a subtler change was manifest, in her and in the room which was the projection of her identity. Both sagged, looked tired, lacked the refreshment of recent input, a new coat of paint about the skirting board and the eyelids. He occasionally lighted on a stain on the sleeve of her sweater, then on a wrinkled chair cover, which at one time she'd have dispatched quickly.

She hesitated to tell him any more and he to ask for it, inviting a refusal.

'No, I didn't know. She never told me she'd moved on. I sent all my letters here.' He suddenly misgave. Maybe Caley hadn't received his letters at all because her mother had intercepted them. Immediately he cancelled the twitch. Caley had replied to them, hadn't she? That presupposed receipt.

'Yes, I forwarded them.'

'Unopened?'

She didn't reply to a question that formerly would have

provoked a tirade, and he knew without telling that all his missives had been censored by this woman before they reached Caley. Steamed open at the kettle spout, read, carefully resealed. But was that any worse than Edith broadcasting his private news to each one of her weekly visitors in turn? He let it pass, having surfeited on the judgmental.

Nina waited for the reproof and eyed him differently when it didn't come. Yes, she'd read those photostatted letters that came weekly out of India, looking for something to scoff at. She encountered tales of hardship, tales of frustration mixed with his quick thumb-nail sketches, word and drawing, of Muslim buildings and villagers' faces in the corner, and was won over by his narrative power in spite of herself.

She looked at him anew, as either the traveller returned or the man of property but, at any rate, not a man her daughter was associated with, and that improved him out of reckoning. She saw Thomas Langholm for the first time as a man in his own right and not as a suitor. Oddly, she found he'd picked up a sexual aura abroad, an attraction that wasn't in her line of liking but was undeniable all the same. He looked – distinguished. The word surprised her. Burned and bearded, he had a glamorous air and, however disregarding of his merit at one time, she was impressed by the improvement on the surface.

Thomas noticed her sense of wonderment as she reappraised him. He'd only met her a handful of times in passing while he picked Caley up for the theatre, or at lunch once in a wine bar in Rose Street when she ran across him and asked him over to join her table, although she'd made her disdain obvious in front of her business colleague by cutting across his conversation, cutting him out of her line of vision. A total nobody. Now he perceived the absolute opposite in her regard. She was waiting for his lead, was quiet and attentive even to his pauses for breath. He'd never underestimated this woman's capacity, although it was for something that had always stayed qualitatively undefined: hard work or indolence, insight or insensitivity, sheer fickleness was what Caley's mother was best at.

He saw himself, in her readjusted focus, as an oddball but a man who'd at least stepped out of the constraints of normality and done the unusual thing. Boredom was Nina's worst enemy. She was deeply bored by most of Edinburgh's antics because its wealth was too unshowy for her to compete, and its culture too limited or derived. It demanded the intangible ticket of recommendation before she could enter the cliques of power. She didn't have a coterie mind, being incapable of manoeuvring with allies, so she stayed permanently excluded from the society she craved, as Neal had predicted. And yet she could have graced its inner sanctum by her sheer eccentricity, a polygonal quality that stored oddness, the serape thrown, the Evil Godmother blackness of her habits. Maybe they should have spoken in another tongue to generate excitement. In French or Latin the two of them might have struck a bond.

While she still waited for entry to the inner circle, other aberrants from the social scheme of things had been a painful reminder of how she personally was debarred by those on the inside: but, now that she'd abandoned all hope of entry, because of the scandals that piled up on her family's record sheet, the rejects were a form of solace. She actively sought the company of peculiar individuals. Thomas's strange clothes were old fashioned and well worn; not the sort of man she wanted to be seen dead with, in terms of a blood link, but as the scarecrow outline of a passionate individualist, then she liked and admired him, and even coveted his friendship. Thomas Langholm was a one-off and they were the rarest breed of all, because they despised club-manship and never joined.

To his surprise, she didn't ask the intrusive questions people had been putting to him ever since that arousing phone call on Sunday morning in Jaipur. When are you going back? What are your long-term plans? Are you here for good? The fact that he had choices, was multiple in outlook, was a source of such intrigue to Nina that she didn't want to curtail its scope by the delineation of a single answer. All questions were interesting, but all answers dull, because they narrowed choice and carried the deathly obligation about enactment. Thomas read her obliquity, well versed in it, for the woman was half way to Caley.

'It's quiet here,' he noticed. The city traffic bypassed this street, but there was also a lull of oblivion about the rooms he hadn't perceived on his earlier visits. 'As if you've got somebody sick in bed upstairs. There's nothing wrong is there? Where's Oliver? What's he doing with himself these days?'

She was breathless at the rush of his deductions. Yes, the rooms were as enclosed as an invalid's house. The windows she kept shut against the heat of midsummer, her unkindest season. 'He's travelling,' she said brightly. 'Taking a year off. He's in Israel.'

'Ah, the homeland. Is he working on a kibbutz?'

'Something like that.'

Thomas had an image of the recalcitrant youth doing the tedious jobs he'd been allocated when he himself had a spell at Yakum, south of Tel Aviv, during one university vacation. Oliver would be asked to mould plastic bottles, repetitively by hot pressing, for filling with the farm's export quota of Jaffa orange juice, or to clean the oil in the tractor engine which only the expert, resident Israeli kibbutzim were allowed to drive, or to tend the huge greenhouses for the tomato and salad crops that furnished the communal meals in the refectory. Would the fastidious, plate-pushing youth consent to eat that wholesome, raw or water-boiled food, as plain as prison fare? Not on your life. He'd starve, or steal, instead.

'I must go,' he said, and got up. It was almost six o'clock. Some end-of-day urgency impelled him into town as his body clock turned towards evening and more urgent thoughts arose about where he was going to spend the night. The basic instinct. A dozen friends would put him up, pay for his Indian tales with a supper at the Ship on the Shore, a round of drinks, a bed in some back room.

'Yes, you go and see Caley. You may catch her. I know she's got a big party on this evening.'

He wasn't going to ask for her address because it might well turn out to be embarrassing, a Giffard-shared retreat.

But Nina Brown took pity on him in her way, for she had an awkward sense of fairness. Lionel Cohen's card prompted a small burst of penitence. She'd appropriated its well-wishing message in every sense, rationalising that he'd only written it because of the Brown family connection, because he'd glimpsed her in Bristo Place on the way to the exhibition, felt guilty at not popping in the door to speak to her – in other words, she had effectively convinced herself that the man wrote it for her, Nina, and that Caley was merely a pretext, a catalyst to a larger event. She'd kept it in her bag and pored over it at hourly intervals as thoughtfully as a love letter.

'Caley took on the lease of your old flat in Gillespie Crescent when you all went off to the Far East. I suppose she thought she was keeping it warm for you, although it hasn't turned out that way, has it? You'll none of you ever come back.'

Who would have thought it? he reflected, turning Jim Batey's car into the main thoroughfare, so well known that it seemed like an axis of his own mind, from Morningside to Churchhill, a right bend at Bruntsfield, swelling and amplifying and then turning off irresolutely like the camber of a good idea, rich with incidental detail. Caley had turned out to be a returner like himself, and maybe a sentimentalist.

17

After she'd dropped Neal off at Turnhouse, Caley drove back to town and parked in a line of cars opposite the flat, a little above the showrooms of the Blind Asylum, but didn't go indoors at once. Night had settled imperceptibly down the city walls, a thin darkness punctuated by the warm street lamps that curved along Gillespie Crescent. In June, it was still balmy between the enclosed stone buildings, and she sat on in the car for a few minutes, reluctant to activate the next sequence of events by going inside, switching on the internal lights in the hallway of the flat, picking up the mail that would be lying waiting for attention on the doormat and the resulting, routine business of her own life, suspended for three days at Carterbrae.

It was almost midnight. The pubs had closed. The last revellers had staggered out of the Golf Tavern and dispersed home over the Links. The streets became her own private grounds again, silent, resonant and personal to herself. She locked up the car, hoisting the tote bag over her shoulder, and hesitated for a second before taking the few steps towards the junction with the main road. On her right was the hill at Bruntsfield, culminating in the open green space at the top of her sightline, and reached by a curve of specialist shops where she often went in to buy last-minute supplies of food to serve the people who dropped in at the flat. On the opposite side of the main road there was a small, off-street petrol station, several restaurants and bars, the Kings Theatre looking dark and emptied after the evening's performance, with the metal grilles locked back in place. Below that and the Cameo cinema, the road bent round on the convex route towards the central clock at the Tollcross intersection, stranded pale and high on its traffic island. The hands beat up towards twelve, closing time together.

That was her entire span, from the clock up to the Links. It was a complete world, offering her a domicile, food, entertainment, transport, an eco-system, complete with long-term memory and association, in half a mile of cityscape. I am so small, she thought, as if the word implied inadequate. Something ached over the horizon towards her which she felt little able to encompass. Singh! Man Singh Nattawat was in such dire trouble. The enormity of his situation swelled into its unknown circumstances and defeated her ability to understand it because the predicament was off her personal map.

Seven, eight years Singh had spent measuring the span of this one arc of central Edinburgh, looping up as far as the Royal Infirmary and the medical schools behind the Meadows, which made a strong, shared space between them. She'd been able to re-create the man very intensively while Neal went on spelling out the wicked lack of choice for any high-caste Indian who failed to conform. Almost sensually, she could feel him walking beside her again along these streets, teasing public opinion about their possible coupling. Of course they'd flirted magnetically, probing and feeling the internal shape of each other's mind with words. Half a dozen kisses they'd shared, she and Singh, not simply curious, but full and knowing and satisfied that there was enough to sustain them if they went further into passion. That he drew back from a casual, sexually diverting affair with her convinced Caley that the impious drive towards this outcast servant was the one involvement he couldn't resist. She felt dismally sorry for him, as well as jealous about the complexion of the woman who daily grew heavier with his child. She put her hand on to her own womb, realising its emptiness.

Something familiar wafted to her off the empty streets and filled them with Singh's actual presence. She was longing to see him and touch him, put her hand on the impeccably tailored sleeve and feel empowered by his personal polish, the absolute finish of him. Hear, feel, absorb the complex being of the man. It was a form of lust for his immediacy. She was shocked not so much by this hunger as by the depth of his bodily imprint on her, which combined the smell of sandalwood, the ironic contrast of white surround and dark iris in his eyes and the fluted inflection of his English. Arches and lines into infinity.

Ever practical, her first thought was to interpose herself and solve the problem by doing something for them first-hand. She could phone, she could write, she could even go in person . . . although that came out in words as a fatuous idea. Hadn't she enough dilemmas here at home without dashing off on a hurried interventionist spree? It would be just like her to turn down the travel option for her own well-being, the eternal stay-at-home, and then fly out to Jaipur on a whim for the sake of someone else. Be sensible, she enjoined herself, and take stock.

The light glared across a square, dadoed entrance hall that had defied any softening efforts at curvature. There were at least two dozen envelopes waiting for her on the floor, which she shuffled mentally into the routine and the interesting as she went to boil a welcome kettle. There were a lot of greetings cards among them. A lot of congratulations on her displays of jewellery, following on less from the fact than from the article promoting them in the arts magazine at the weekend. Acknowledgment at last. Some of the signatures she knew, but some were those of strangers to whose courtesy she nodded in passing.

The water came to the boil. She poured it on to leaves of herbal tea and sipped the brew, while she went on sifting papers into the discard pile. One of the last confused her. It was a formally typed business letter. She was tired by now, had hardly slept since the weekend, and was bemused by the look of the strange letterhead and a name – Alastair Renton – which she didn't latch on to at once. The letter ran:

Dear Caley Brown,

I must confess that I was profoundly daunted by the arrival of the manuscript you sent me at the end of May. Normally, I would not look at a handwritten collection of papers but your introductory letter explaining their source and the motive for publishing them, as well as prior knowledge of the great Langholm lexicographer, drove me on. They were, in any case, remarkably lucid to read in style and presentation – no worse than many an italic typewriter. There's an attractive, story-telling quality I took to at once that reminded me of Stevenson, not the *Kidnapped* and *Treasure Island* novelist but the observer we come across in *Travels with a Donkey* and his American journals. A clear eye, a clearer style.

I am beguiled by the idea that Edith Langholm considered these extracts – terminology is one of my problems with this mass of documentation: diaries, letters, clippings, whatever – should be printed as a family keepsake. The cost of typesetting would have been prohibitive. But you are right, they are worth a wider circulation than a family archive, although they are hard to categorise in book form.

Are they publishable in any commercial sense? They ought to be, heaven knows. Quality, variety, scope, it's all here. But we learn never to make promises in this trade, in case they turn out to be misleading. We hardly dare to praise. But there's something very remarkable here, though I'd be hard put to tell you what it is. My opinions are completely subjective, and are further constrained by the small resources of this publishing house. It may need to go to a larger concern. Today, the book industry is in a notoriously fickle state. The strangest books succeed – I mean, certain quality books sell for no good reason I can define or reduce to a formula. Somebody ought to take this on as a grand project, once it's edited down. It's far too unwieldy as it is. But the fact is, however good in theory, nobody may take the risk on it because you cannot classify such a text.

My last query: does the author know you've sent me his writings? Would he approve and cooperate in their publication? Questions of copyright arise and would need to be cleared before we type/edit/circulate. I will mull on this and talk the script up to some influential people to create a climate of acceptance.

By now Caley was wide awake with excitement. Edith had been talking about carrying out this exercise for a long time, for months if not years, but only at Easter had started to press her urgently to take the thing in hand. Reluctantly, she did it and was as daunted as Renton at the mass of verbiage Edith presented her with.

She'd chosen to approach this man because he came from a long line of Scottish publishers. His great-grandfather had helped to found Chambers' educational imprint, while his grandfather worked at the Aberdeen University Press, and his father published for Thomas Nelson before they closed down the splendid Parkside printing works. Alastair Renton was the last of the clan, and was trying to revive one of the small houses by building up a distinctive, Scottish list, although he acted as scout for one of the London conglomerate publishers as well. Caley had taken opinions and heard he was a sound man. The instinct to publish was in the blood, although instinct might not be enough to make a rational decision on this amorphous bundle.

There were maybe a thousand items altogether, the

photocopied transcripts of Thomas's diaries, interleaved with letters to and from his family and friends. Caley hadn't counted them. If it hadn't been for the open, black-edged clarity of the handwriting, she'd have abandoned the attempt sooner than Renton. They weren't enumerated like a normal script either, but were meticulously dated, and Edith had put them into careful chronological order. There were some items written a quarter of a century ago in a boyish hand, his letters home from India, not just duty missives to his grandparents but witty, accurate observations. Even as a child, this person was endowed with the gift of knowing and writing the truth. While they amplified her own store of letters, Caley had no idea how to place the work, travelogue or philosophy or daily chit-chat, often quite humble stuff except that it was about a monumental change. Thomas Langholm had caught the curve of something, the meteoric sweep of his personal development, and of the epoch. Grounded in the past, he brought to the twentieth century a historical imagination matured in the nineteenth. There was a fibre of excitement in his writing, while he achieved a thing rare among Scots, who tended to be parochial in outlook however widely they roamed; he evoked a sense of the larger, universal scheme of things, a continental drift on which she had cast herself as reader, unresisting.

Reflective. Impassioned. Diffuse. Disorganised, which was a mental richness. On the page, Thomas had made a new impression on her, or she got to know him better than ever before. His development was laid before her undissimulated, eager for experience and vulnerable to it at the same time. Occasionally she caught her breath while she was reading, fearing for him as he described wild forays into the desert where nomadic tribesmen with broken teeth pressed against an unguarded stranger with too much inquiry, or when he fell into impotent despair about the systematic water abuse of villagers. His obsessions entered her own psyche, and he won her over by his word power as much as if he were a Cyrano or another Othello.

> My story being done,
> She gave me for my pains a world of kisses . . .
> She wished she had not heard it, yet she wished
> That heaven had made her such a man.

For two weeks of reading and assimilation, the sheets had

dominated her life. Night and day she'd read them, hardly slept and hardly ate, turning each page with ponderous gravitas. Before I die, I will boast of having seen these pages in this room. When she needed a break from their sapping intensity, she went out and walked round the Links, blowing out her congested thoughts, but even then her mind was preoccupied with tangents radiating from the central theme. What was an apt title? *The Last Missionary* was too fanciful and arch. *Port Out* or even *Starboard Home* too intractable. She was still searching for the all-encapsulating phrase and had spent spare moments in thumbing through her old school poetry books looking for the title. Emily Dickinson might serve, something of the dense elasticity of her style – doom's electric moccasin – or even Milton. Caley was struck by the unlikelihood of such a pairing until she located a connective similarity in their emphatic, Protestant fervour, even if they were centuries and worlds apart.

The project crystallised into hard covers, and would be better for being illustrated. Delacroix's North African journals came to mind, where the text was intercut with the artist's own line drawings, making a balance on the page because the eye was right. How was she going to sell it, not to this man Renton who was already geared to support it, but to Thomas himself? Thomas didn't see himself as a writer, or only indirectly. He was interested in the content, an Orwell who wrote to proselytise, to sow his ideas in prose, and was a man of fairly similar outlook, for whom writing about what he hadn't personally experienced was immoral or unproven, mere guesswork. Thomas would think of a career in publishing as effete and self-indulgent. He had to work, produce the tangible. There would be no more casual words.

She blazed with these thoughts, a follow-on from the letters themselves. In a sense, reading them had primed her for Thomas's reappearance. When he stepped off the plane, she was half way to falling in love with him all over again, mentally attuned, saturated with his thoughts, so that it took only the winning appeals of his behaviour to make her accept him in the attic room at Carterbrae.

The night wore on round about her. Nothing moved. Caley felt embalmed in a suspense of waiting for the morning to arrive and activate tomorrow's schedule, after which she would have to try to contact Thomas again to put these new developments to him.

What would he say to her? Was he going to berate her for a lack of faith? Would these efforts on his behalf act as any form of palliative?

Thursday's schedule included a party, she remembered, and it fell to her to organise it. Almost by way of therapy, to ease the build-up of her congested, unproductive thoughts, Caley set to at one o'clock in the morning, to make a mental clearance before she went to bed. She pushed the furniture around, a table back against a wall, a sofa wide of the fireplace to increase the circulation space. The other exhibitors were coming in the evening, all eight of them, plus several of their friends who'd helped to set up the displays, with their partners and a few family members . . . probably thirty to forty in all.

While she rearranged the living room, adapting it to well-established routines in this accommodating flat where corridors were rooms and the internal stairs were only a feature that afforded extra seating, her mind went on beyond the enclosing boundaries.

Why was she doing this? Why was it always her? Was it only because her flat was at the crossroads and she made herself into a too willing workhorse? At a certain point, she began to feel put upon, as if the people she coordinated into a party mood had started to take her input for granted, assuming that she'd the natural force of energy to be a perpetual catalyst. For once she was resentful that nobody else had appeared on the scene to take a turn in fairness.

At intervals between heaping strategic piles of plates, wrapping sets of cutlery in napkins, polishing the box of glasses she'd picked up from the wine merchant with her order, sale or return, in a frenzy of over-preparedness, she would suddenly weary and sit down on the chair arm, lapsing into a five-minute coma of reflection.

She would catch sight of herself in a mirror and think, God, you're looking awful. She stopped to rake her hand through her hair, made her sweater symmetrical or re-centred the heavy necklace impatiently. She'd let the overall shape get out of balance. She'd been so distracted between attending to Edith, the script, the craft show, that she'd hardly had any time to give to herself for months. When had she last had a day of self-indulgent spoiling, a visit to the hairdresser, a long soak in a bath or a spending spree down at one of her favourite woollen mills? The fun of making fifty pounds stretch to do the work of two hundred with the access of ingenuity! But she'd lost her grip on fun of late and sat on rather morosely, depressed from some elusive cause.

Family, partner, friends. She traced the dipping mood back to its source in that phrase and understood that the reason that she felt unloved, albeit temporarily, was that she felt personally unsupported. Yet again, she was doing her thing single-handed and in a climate of complete indifference. Which of this troupe of people had stood by her, or reciprocated her efforts on their behalf? She passed into a crisis moment when she realised there was no one she could turn to at this point. Ring, write, go. There was nobody who'd turn out to help her. But, very quickly, an answer came back, Oh, yes, there is. There's myself. I have the capacity to be my own resource.

Fortified by her staunchness, she recognised that it left her lonelier still. She'd ended up as partnerless or, having split her affections, was between men. Thomas didn't know anything about her craft fair or this party afterwards, but that didn't prevent Caley, in the irrational insomniac hours, from blaming him for *not* knowing. Gordon was on a week-long business trip for Carruthers and Smythe, but where were the proxy bouquets and the cards? Her mailbag was void of his congratulations. Should she have invited the Brown family up to swell the throng? Hardly. Nobody knew about the inside of her own life, and nobody damn well cared.

When she was sixteen, she'd won a prize at school. What was it for? General excellence, which probably implied an incompetence in the specifics, that she was merely an expert swot. The prize-giving was held in the Usher Hall and Nina promised to come along. After the ceremony, while the amphitheatre emptied of the admiring and proud parents, the siblings who'd been roped in to show solidarity, all the family clans, Caley waited on the pavement outside to meet up with her mother and go home together, sharing a rare moment of success. And she waited. Her friends came by in a loose gang, on their way down to one of the cafés in Princes Street for an end-of-year celebration. Are you coming too? No, she said, I'll wait and find my mother. But Nina never came, had never set foot inside the Usher Hall, and Caley travelled home to Fairmilehead on the bus alone, looking down at the covers of her pile of prize books, tied up in pink cotton string. Where had the woman been? She didn't divulge that but said airily by way of excuse when she did come back later that evening, I thought you'd have another ploy on. The word ploy ground itself into Caley's soul as one that was ever afterwards unusable.

She'd put the books down coldly in her room, and hadn't enjoyed reading them after they were tainted. There they were on the bookshelf, almost in mint condition. At least she'd tried to be loyal to the woman who was her mother by the accident of birth: tried too hard, according to both the Langholm brothers. She should have given up on it long ago. The gravamen of that truth was almost bitter. To have no illusions left at sixteen was sad, and she wondered at what point the tear ducts had dried up in her. No child and no tears: did that mean she was dysfunctional as a woman? That was almost the first thing Singh had said to her: Why are your eyes so sad? She'd put the phrase down to his clever flirtatiousness at the time, a skill in finding the remark that haunted with the aura of his intense interest and insight. It was a compliment a thousand times more subtle and pervasive than the banal 'What beautiful eyes you've got', which didn't haunt at all.

Already, her mind had escaped from the ennui of self-analysis to the pleasure of doing something tangible. She was compiling one of her interminable mental lists . . . bread, butter, chicken, flowers . . . and then, when the list grew too long to carry in her head, she found a slip of paper and jotted the items down.

Written, the word flowers brought back their heady perfume on the day she'd filled the flat with the reject blooms from an exhibition at the Waverley Market, and Neal had quizzed her on the cost. Sumptuous banks of white blossoms she'd arranged, some glorious droop-headed stephanotis and jasmine, hot-house-forced to come into flower out of season. Wonderful, spacious things. But he'd spoiled even that free showing with his grudging parsimony.

The room was pale with reflected light as she re-created the luxuriant scene. It took her a while to realise that the windows were actually brightening with the increase in daylight. Dawn was imminent and she'd worked herself right through the night.

Going to bed at last to snatch a couple of hours' rest, but in a mood largely unrelieved of tension, Caley traced its source further back than the paltry instance of having no one turn up to her prize-giving, and came ultimately to Neal. It was he who'd made her feel stranded this last long evening, or inadequate, or even more profoundly wrong-thinking. He who would not have given a moment of his unpaid time to a communal cause, would have criticised her for doing so. He would have pointed out that the sense of being put upon was entirely her own fault, because she was unable to distinguish between what was owed to others and what was owed to self. She was profligate, uncontrolled, excessive, self-deceiving on the goals of charity – often and often she had flailed herself with the truth behind his taunts.

She hated him with a passion, for hatred was the most knowing of the emotional states, had writhed and contorted herself with the tensions he set up in her, as much as if the searing, self-review were carried out in love. It wasn't lost on Caley that she didn't find Neal's bullish, square-set physique repulsive, any more than he was blind to her attractiveness, but that they stayed mentally distant from each other by enforcing an old incest taboo. He was perfectly manly, utterly solid and unshakeable in outlook, and only a fraction away from being what she might otherwise have admired.

The fact was that the three men whose flat she had taken over, whose lives in it she'd re-created from afar, were in the perfect balance of symbiosis. Any one of them could have been her chosen man, and she came at last to a comprehension of another one of Singh's studied, oblique aphorisms, so cryptic it might take years to unravel: that she was the mistress of them all, all three. She hadn't managed to free herself of their corporate identity, any more than they had shaken off hers.

18

The valley went on shrinking down to its original shape. The hills closed in at evening. Ruth worked on alone, pushing back against the sense of pressure exerted on her thoughts by the cooling, creaking walls of Carterbrae.

After the last four hectic days, her life resumed its old self-contained proportions. She listened out for footsteps on the quarry tiles and hoped that somebody was following her across the kitchen floor with a question or a kettle to fill, something pending; but when she turned round, she saw the space was empty and the cast of shadow was her own.

She was suddenly desperately lonely and more isolated than at any time in her life, much more than when Lachlan Palmer died and left her homeless. Then, a buoyant thirty, she was only impoverished, but had plenty of reserves of mental stamina to work for her living and make a new start somewhere else. She told nobody about the humiliating debts her man had left her with that, in honour, she'd paid off before she set out for Carterbrae. To immerse herself in a new household, a new burgh, was cleansing, baptismal. She'd subsumed herself in Langholm gratefully.

Seven o'clock was a lonely hour. The work of the day was done. Companionship beckoned, a relaxant as compulsive as the early glass of sherry from the decanter. Still Ruth kept at it in the kitchen by herself, going from scullery to pantry in obedience to the greater disciplines of order. She'd cleaned the house from top to bottom during the day, stripping off the beds with violent, sweeping gestures, and washed the bedlinen in batches. In and out to the drying green all morning she'd gone, and bashed the creased corners of the sheets into place with the pressurising steam from her iron, angry, puzzled and frustrated that she was left to cope with the clearing up single-handed.

But the sun went down and, with it, her anger cooled to sadness. She missed Edith, who might have been housebound latterly but wasn't otherwise diminished because she was a strong and calling voice in the corner, regulating the day-round hours with her determined point of view. Her mere presence had set off other sub-currents, the morning post, the daily callers, which were the small hum of an interminable activity. But that had stopped, like a pendulum come to rest, and Ruth paused every so often to check her own heartbeat as if to confirm she was more than Edith's defunct shadow, for, after all, they'd been yoked together for a quarter of a century. I'm all right, she thought. I'm still going strong.

In the kitchen, there was a lot of food left over from the funeral buffet. Ruth rationalised it methodically. There was still to be no waste, even if the only eye scanning her housekeeping budget was her own. Some of it she froze, some she refrigerated, some she made into the amalgam of soup. Preoccupied by labelling and liquidising, however, she was haunted by the sound of that external presence, the missing sound of others.

Neal. Thomas. Caley. They'd been so very real for the past three days, filling up the beds and rooms, the spaces in her head, that their sudden leaving was a pain as sharp as vertigo. Sometimes she fell over with the imbalance of it. So much longing. So much anxiety about their welfare. It was worse than having children of her own because they owed her no actual allegiance and had walked out of this house, one, two, three, without offering an explanation to Ruth Palmer, who was only its keeper. Where they were in the world she didn't know.

She'd made breadcrumbs in the grinder from the stale loaves and spilled some accidentally on to the quarry tiles. She went to the broom cupboard and put her hand on the dustpan and brush to sweep them up. But someone had been there before her. The pan, when she lifted it, revealed the broken fragments of the Chelsea teaset, bounced off the paving stones. Ruth recoiled from the fracture but also from a lazy-mindedness that hadn't finished off the job properly. Briskly, she found some sheets of newspaper and emptied the shards on to them, four cups, two saucers and a jug whose cheeky fatness had always pleased her. They'd made their last appearance for Edith's and Robert's golden-wedding party and before that, she recalled, the graduation celebrations for one of the boys. The navy-and-gold flowers had seemed imperishable then. She pushed two of the pieces together to see if they would glue, but there was no mending them now. She pursed her lips in total disapproval of the breakages but, as she held the expression fixedly, she felt the muscles start to tremble at the corners of her mouth. Oh, not tears, please, no crying! She'd done too much lonely weeping in her life already. Quickly, she folded the layers of newsprint into a firm packet and sealed it with some brown parcel tape before she put it in the bin outdoors and out of her sight.

It was at that point that George Weir came round the corner of the house and almost collided with her.

'You've left it very late,' she accused him.

'I've been at work all day. I came straight on.'

'Of course.' Ruth softened the edge of her hostile-seeming surprise. 'I meant I'd been about to lock up for the evening and wouldn't have answered the door to you in another half an hour. You should have phoned me first to tell me you were on your way.'

George cast his eye backwards across the hinter valley. The sun was still bright. The light would last another two or three hours in these northern bands, but the shadows in Langfault Woods were impenetrably deep. It wasn't a place to linger after dusk. He followed her gratefully through the glazed door to the warm and busy kitchen.

'I came to see how Thomas was with himself.'

'Thomas? Well, he's not here. He went off to Edinburgh after they discharged him from the hospital at lunchtime.'

'By train?' George was daunted by the logistics of such a journey alone.

'No. He went and borrowed Batey's car. He won't be back tonight.'

'But he shouldn't be driving with that hand of his! They told him so expressly in Casualty. Why did you let him go?'

'Let? I haven't the power to keep him. He doesn't heed me – or anyone, for that matter.'

The man took an impatient turn about the room to exorcise his annoyance that he hadn't foreseen this flight. 'I'd have driven him up to town myself if I had known. What harm he does himself.'

'I don't think you'd have been welcome on this journey.'

'So. He's gone chasing after Caley. That's the greatest harm of all. What a whimsy miss she's turned out to be.'

Ruth's heart pounded in making the defence she'd realised would have to come some time, as much as if it were her own wrongdoings she explained. 'You judge only by the appearance of it.'

'Then you must know more about the insides of the business than I do. You and Neal and she disguising the truth of things together for so long. You should have intervened somehow to stop this foolishness coming to a head, and served our interests better.'

Ruth thought it rather harsh to be blamed twice over in this way: for letting Thomas go back to the city, and for not averting the expression of their characters in the first place, towards a final falling out. George was a man who had mastered the fabric of a building but knew nothing of its inhabitants, the way they moved, sighed, fell apart. 'And how was I to do that, pray? By betraying their confidences? I did what I could to warn and smooth things over, but where there's such bad feeling between brothers, common sense is powerless. They would have quarrelled about something, those two, in the end.'

'And Edith was equally in the dark about this other man? This fiancé?'

'I told no tales. What she knew, or guessed, I cannot speak for.' All the same Ruth was suffering from a growing sense of perfidy, enlarged by the dowry gifts. To cheat a man was one thing, and allowable in some straits. To cheat on him was another. That modern syllepsis unsettled Ruth's position, so that she recognised she was sure of her monetary soundness, but not of her sexual one. What many people wanted from Caley was affection – herself included – and maybe she'd been less than direct in her criticism of the young woman in order to safeguard her continuing visits to Carterbrae, which would have been a bleak place without her.

An even greater guilt hedged her truthfulness. At the back end of the year, she'd left Edith to the care of Bert Weir's wife and gone on the Monday morning with Caley into Edinburgh. Some serious shopping fell due: a nephew's birthday, a wedding present for the children of some friends. Ruth met the call of the second generation.

To her surprise, Caley didn't drop her off in Princes Street and run. She came with her, gave discreet advice she heeded, carried her parcels. Thus unencumbered, the chores were quickly done. What to do with the rest of the day? Come and have lunch with me. I'm meeting an old friend and then you can come on to the studio and see what it is that I get up to that I call my living. That'll be fun.'

The stern city was benign that day, its autumn foliage as soft as froth against perpetual masonry, sun-washed, rain-blurred.

Perhaps her attitude was only a matter of mood and heady escape. When Caley introduced her to the old friend in a wine bar off St Andrew Square, she was as ready to be charmed by him as any other woman might, or had suspended criticism for the sake of a good day out.

And he was effortless on charm, this Captain Gordon Strachan. He was a different man from Thomas, or any of the Langholms. She'd no doubt about the lie of things between them, but couldn't find it in herself to condemn a man who found the common element this readily. He knew Sutherland well, it turned out, had organised a military exercise on the Army shooting range near Tain, played golf at Dornoch, Nairn and Lossie many times, and she was carried along unresisting by his manliness and worldly ease. He revived the map of her past and made it real again for her. Although self-mocking, he wasn't self-questioning. Strong, square, objective, he was a man on the rise.

How did she know that they were lovers? They didn't kiss, or not lingeringly, there was no snuggling up or even an eye caress, but they had the air of realistic settlement between then. Had Caley married him already in her mind?

The thought pumped its own adrenaline through Ruth. During the long coach journey home, however, she had plenty of time to castigate herself as much as Caley for fickleness. Yes, she was shocked, afraid and at times sneakingly jealous that Caley moved from man to man without a hitch. But she didn't judge and said nothing to Edith apart from opening up her packages by the fire, opening up her thoughts about Caley's workshop on a South Side mews: the silver smelter with its temperature controlled by electricity, the making of the individual moulds, how the fixings were attached, what silversmithing marks were stamped on every piece, the signatory initials, ₢, like a four-leaved clover with its last good-luck petal missing.

It was a clever industry and it came as a surprise to her. Caley had made so little fuss about her own talent because she expected fuss from no one else. The two women talked about why this was, and promised they would foster her talent between them. Edith often discussed her own ideas about fostering, a word that translated imperfectly into French as adopt, favour, stimulate, encourage – but no amalgam of the total English looseness, the embrace, of it. It was hard to get that cuddling right.

On Gordon, however, silence. Ruth permutated her own initial prophecy: there will be no other woman for our Thomas. He is a once only man. But that doesn't mean to say they will end up together. She shouldn't have said that out loud, for fear it carried on the air to other ears and delivered its own enactment.

This evening, however, faced with an inquisitive critic, Ruth was uneasy about the way she'd suspended her own judgments. Of course she'd sided with Caley, women against men, but that had turned into a futile bravado at the funeral when the sombre, duty-laden men were in the preponderance. There wasn't a man present who wouldn't have smiled waggishly at the temptation of another love affair, but condemned the girl for succumbing to it. A grim spirit of mafioso retribution hung on in these hills.

What they were condemning was a female frailty. Each of the men present yesterday, even Jock Macinlay, would take it for granted that Thomas had had a woman out in India, as a normal, healthy sexual outlet and a man's right, while Caley was, by a sense of honour either Calvinistic or chivalrous, doomed to an interim chastity pending his return. Lang, lang, may the ladies weep wi' their gold combs in their hair. That the reverse situation might be true shocked even her, and she was restive inside her own duality. Why shouldn't a woman have two lovers? She couldn't uncloud her mind of her own confusion.

So Ruth, too, shifted with the weight of the majority and asked: What if? What if the three inheritors left for good? What if Neal went back to Hong Kong, Caley wed her captain, Thomas vacillated in his disinterested state, so that not one of them set foot inside Carterbrae again, leaving her to interpret their third-hand directives by letter, cablegram and phone, a proximator still? Had Edith, foreseeing that outcome, bought her loyalty to the place when she could buy no one else's?

'I came by this evening to talk to you about the arrangements for the Common Riding. Maybe you're in no mood for celebrations. Our sadness draws us down.'

The echo was that of a human person, the shadow someone else's after all.

'Now's as good a time as any.' Ruth drew off her tied apron and washed her hands again before she sat down at the deal table, in one of the drawers of which she kept her notebook. Year on year, she was responsible for the making of the traditional barley bannock. Carried aloft at the head of the procession, it was decorated with emblems rendered in dough, fat salt herring, a spade, thistle and crown. The festivities went on all day, with the hotels and bars in town supplying most of the provender for the events, and separate committees organising the closing ceremonies and the final dance. It fell to Ruth to supervise these women's groups discreetly. George had come to rely on her steadiness on that front, glad there was no dissent or abuses of precedence, the ladies being touchy on who was allocated what tasks. The male hierarchy went more smoothly, left-hand man, right-hand man, Cornet, but, lacking system, the womenfolk were known to jostle for places undefined.

Ruth turned to a fresh page in her notebook, headed it with the year, dated the entry in the margin, while he admired her good order. Partly native to herself, her system had benefited from the annotating skill of Edith and the scriptory household at Carterbrae. He took the jotter from her with a quickened interest, flicking back over the archival last quarter of a century. How fascinating it all was to him! The colours that were selected for the annual horse ribands and rosettes, and those gaudily iced cakes that went on sale in the town bakeries, unlikely and unappetising greens and blues, were the same ones that were sported by the Derby winner of each succeeding year. Ruth had chosen to decorate the pages of her notebook in these simple hues, which achieved a garish charm. The programme for the ceremonial was on sale at the local newsagent's, but she'd added to each year's list of races the name of its winner, highlighted in the racing colours. His own name, as gainer of the Blue Riband for several years, was picked out in green, yellow, rose, purple and red, as was appropriate.

'You've made a proper document of our proceedings. I like your touch. You make your record with some style.'

Ruth retrieved her notebook, eschewing praise, and waited for his further deliberation. It wasn't monumental stuff, detailing only the small passages of their ritual, but for her it was the enlarging dimension and an escape. Her hand flew along the lines in response to the numbers he anticipated on the day or the small adjustments from last year recommended by the main committee. She filtered suggestions through her own experience of the procession: no, that would create a bottleneck but if they got Jock Smail's agreement to use the short cut over his allotment, it would save a long corner for the party following on foot . . .

Out in the hallway, the clock chimed eight. George looked up, alert. Several doors stood open in a long run of rooms, like thoughts and sequences logically following each other towards a conclusion and the outer porch. He knew the interiors of the house space by space, but was glad he wasn't called on to measure it with his tape, for the moment.

'When is Thomas coming back?'

'Tomorrow.' She put her pen down wearily, for, however much they filled the hour with the details of the Common Riding, they both knew the day was incomplete without the missing man. 'But you do realise he has a return fare to India? He hasn't severed himself from his United Nations work and it's all up in the air until he does. Like it or not, we wait for him to decide before we can move on.'

'What about yourself? What will you do?'

'I would like to have a grand scheme ready worked out, but I don't and what I thought I wanted half my life ago, I don't want now. I've waited on other people all this time. I ran my father's manse from the day I left school. I was his housekeeper and did the needful, for my mother was an invalid. And then I married Lachlan Palmer and turned into the unhappiest woman that ever lived. But he grew sick from the cancer, and I nursed him to the end. The dirt of him. I hated him and what he spent his life on, that I was yoked to a coarse man. To come here was sweetness after sour. I like not to be noticed, just relied on for the things that I can do. So I am only a functionary, although that's better than nothing.

'What I am seeing for the first time is that for forty years I've been a minder, as you might say, a steward for other people's gifts. Each time I took one of these posts, I thought I was a stop-gap, that I was keeping a household or a person together for a while and, however unpalatable it was for me, I could meet it by thinking, This is only for now. But now went on a long time and became for ever. At each change, I was a substitute for someone else, first a stand-in for my mother, then for a nurse, lastly for a missing set of parents. But who was I? Who noticed Ruth Palmer as she let herself be moulded into this space or that?

'Maybe I never was anyone in the first place. Or maybe I've become institutionalised into other people's expectations of me, biddable, not troublesome, easy to squeeze. That's why I concern myself so much with Caley Brown because I see the same agreeing tendency in her. Why should the women be left in limbo while masters opt for other priorities? A bit of me rejoices that she doesn't hang about waiting for one man's return. So don't call her a whimsy miss to me, for, given her place, I would have wanted the courage to do what she has done.'

This long harangue astonished her companion, as an answer which ill fitted his question.

She spoke it slowly and thoughtfully, pausing between sentences, looking around her to draw resource from the familiar objects of the kitchen, the things that strengthened as well as detained her. Why should cups matter? Why should she feel it necessary to take down the cahiers and add in her own hand the exact weight of strawberries she'd picked that morning and turned into freezer jam? *Fraises, groseilles, mirabelles* were written up in the notebook, the farmhouse quantity recipes from the Auvergne, hints on how to crystallise fruits in season, how to sun-dry pears, all copied out in an elegant foreign copperplate. Another hand for Ruth to forge as best she could.

George Weir, however, noticed only the copying neatness of her, on the page and in her well-starched blouse. He admired it because this was a facet of himself. While she spoke, in her second-hand passions, he found he was repeating every word, for it was his life too, in brief, derivative and often dull in its respectability. The lilt of her Highland voice gave it a new appeal, however, like the crayon colours she added to the programme of events.

The light was still clear. From where he sat, he had a view through the glazed porch to the town and the settlements. He picked out his own chimney in the distance, a speck but distinct because he had the eye of a cartographer. He saw his house was dusty and untidy, the photographs of unsold property faded and fly-blown on the screen, but instantly, as if superimposed on it, Ruth's hand shifted and organised and replaced the scene with something fresh.

His mind raced at an unexpected proposition. How much had he and Neal settled on as the upset price for Carterbrae? Two hundred and forty thousand. Of course, the outlandish place would never reach such a premium. Say £200,000 for the sake of argument. His own domicile would fetch about half of that, free and clear, and – though few knew it – he owned a brace of cottages at Selkirk that were rented out. The sum total, together with Ruth Palmer's windfall, would meet the outlay without recourse to mortgaging. Himself and Ruth. The idea clicked in place with the neatness of a certainty.

He remeasured Carterbrae as theirs. What could it be? The place must be productive. A school, a nursing home, a small-holding. It must have a yield of sorts, and he sat in a dwam for some minutes putting up different pictures on to his eye screen to see which one he liked the best.

'It's getting late,' he said. 'I've an early start in the morning. I'm auctioneer at the Polworth estate.'

'It's a shame to see all that go under the hammer.'

'The curator of the Museum of Antiquities came down and took the best of it, only two pieces for the nation. The rest must drift about like flotsam, landing where it will.'

'Ring tomorrow,' she said without rising, as if he were an intimate seeing himself out. 'About eight or earlier, and I will ask Thomas to reassure you if he's here, or let you have an update if he's not.'

'Well and good.'

When he went outside, the valley had cooled appreciably but was all the fresher for that. His head seemed to clear and he was much occupied with the notion of the development, and angled to himself on the way home how he could make the expedient thought into an attractive proposition.

19

In the small hours Singh woke, disturbed by a sense of vivid colour rather than the actual bang and crash of an electric storm. He got up and pulled the wooden shutters back. The valley of Amber was floodlit by the cataracts of lightning, which forked like brilliant rivers into the blackened, drought-stricken sky. The wind was high. The scene outside moved and became animate before his eyes, swaying under the power of the blast, while loose objects were picked up and thrown across the window pane, a branch in flower, disjointed from its tree, a boll of bindweed clinging to itself that careered madly over the road and into nowhere.

'It's come,' he said, torn between relief that at last there would be water in the city, dams filled, crops harvested, a plenty that stretched into next year, and a halt to the epidemic sickness – the reprieve from widespread disasters – as against the tumults of his personal sorrow that today he must fulfil his undertaking and go out to deliver his answer to Sonal. 'Will you sleep again?' he asked Shalini.

'No, I don't think so. It's nearly dawn.'

She slept under a sheet on these restless nights, a meagre covering that showed up the outline of her limbs and her ripe body. Her fertility was magnificent, its swelling almost spiritual like the great temple statues of the Jain followers, which were a celebration of life with their splendid torsos and bosoming. Not erotic, certainly not pornographic, but subliminal to those who were capable of reading their message with enlightenment. It was the beautiful degree of finish on Shalini's form that moved him, the subtle endings of her body, as she stirred to meet him, half awake. His desire for her was unassuageable, was heightened by the love he felt for his impending child or because he couldn't understand the lust he felt for what he owned, for what had no power of refusal, in any sense. I want you, was a declaration he reaffirmed in wider terms, as he reached down towards the fruit of her loins, caressing them with his words and with his being. He wanted to see this child, and to love this child, with a hunger and an impatience that was sometimes painful. The moment of fusion, lit by the engorgement of the window light, re-created all the other intensities of a passion which he, supposedly in control of, was ruled by.

'What will you do today?'

'Read. Sew. It will be cooler indoors if it rains.'

'I will be late back this evening. I promised to go out to the lake. Not very late. Maybe ten.'

'I will be waiting.'

After a single drenching, the countryside had revived. The terrain he drove through had been arid only a week past, seeming dead or no better than dormant. The refreshing showers that had come and gone kindly all afternoon, leaving pauses for the doctors and patients to scuttle between the buildings of the clinic without a soaking, or to readjust their protective canopies in liquid sunshine, had changed the landscape. Already specks of green were appearing on the panorama of the desert, like a nondescript sheet of marble that someone had diligently inlaid with flower motifs in the semi-precious stones, garnet and carnelian and lapis lazuli and malachite. These colours were subdued, tints only inches deep in the soil but had a sombre, thought-provoking glow, less lustrous than against the milk-white tones of the Taj Mahal. The bougainvillaea provided a stitch of colour against the drab of India, threading its way through gardens and parks down to the roadside.

The double doors of the hunting lodge were open and Ajit's father was nowhere in sight. Each of the succeeding doors along the corridor stood ajar, so that Singh was free to walk without impediment down the length of halls to the inner hall of pleasure. The house waited as tentatively as he did, catching at stray winds to cool its airless passages.

The rooms were unnervingly silent this evening as he passed, giving rise to the joyous notion that Sonal wasn't at home, had forgotten or misunderstood their appointment, extending him another day's grace, or another week's. But as he rounded the last corner, traversed the last portal, he saw that his mother was indeed in residence while, opposite her, legs crossed on the carved, high back chair and reading a newspaper, sat his uncle V.J., placed like a patriarch or judge.

Singh was livid that his mother was resorting to such strong-arm tactics on him after all or, trusting him to keep his word and come, had not trusted further than the shallowest observance of his undertaking. V.J. was the guarantor of his good behaviour, as he embodied the memory of their elder brother who was the ambassador, not to be dishonoured. What would they threaten him with if he didn't comply with the family diktats? Were they really going to ostracise him? In admitting that she lacked the moral authority to enforce such a banishment alone, Sonal had reduced her status in his eyes. He was ready to heed her pleas but could ignore her strictures. But when he looked at her more closely, he saw that her face was drawn with the strain of waiting, too, and he pitied her in a moment, realising how intimidating she found him. He felt older than his mother, with the gravitas of alternatives that had not beset her, in her day.

Well, there was no avoiding the unpleasantness as V.J. rustled his paper into an alien set of folds, and took off his half-moon reading glasses to concentrate on what his nephew had to say.

'Have you eaten?' asked Sonal, having some sympathy for the interviewee.

'Enough, thank you.' He sat by the window, closing the triangle.

'I sent the servants out. They have their own ground to till and make the most of this downpour to catch what water they can. It may not last, of course. But there is cold food if you would like.'

He waved his hand impatiently. Let me have my say without so many interruptions. 'I told you I would give you my decision today and am glad you are both present to hear it. At the beginning of the week, I spoke to Lata, in this room. She confirmed her cousin is coming for a visit very shortly. Perhaps the matter of approach and conditions would be aired more conveniently with the girl directly.'

Ah, he wanted a modern arrangement, one to one, minimising family involvement. Nothing so crude as bride viewing or a Nattawat mass inspection of the intended. 'Through you personally? You want to speak to her alone?'

'No, no. Through the proper channels. My grandmother, if she will consent to undertake the office, as my speaker.'

Sonal's relief was unbounded. What joy! Lata's cousin! She remembered that the two had met very briefly at a polo match the previous year. University educated, well bred and well-to-do, already vetted and approved in that the families had existing contact; she could not imagine a more suitable match. The rain cooled their faces after all but would not wash away their soil.

'I wish you every happiness on the favourable acceptance of your choice,' said V.J. and was done. His part in the business had ended.

Oh, heavens, save me from the obsequies. Even the soothsayer will not predict the harbingers of my future. No wonder he wanted the woman who spoke to him without veils, took his body without pretence or even politeness.

'And Shalini?' asked Sonal, unable to ignore the real undertow of the unspoken in their dialogue.

Singh looked straight ahead down the length of corridor in delivering his condition. 'When I marry, I will need several more servants. There are plenty of rooms in the back quarters at Amber. Banji's wife is not as agile as she used to be. We will retain her services.'

Reasoned, plausible, the clause defeated her. She couldn't stop her eyes from catching her brother's in an appeal for help, as she accommodated her son's real intention. That Shalini would stay on as his paramour was elided. This was a preposterous answer. How could Sonal Nattawat advance the idea to her mother in those terms, and ask her to negotiate the disgraceful? The existing family link through Lata would ensure that some pointed questions would be asked about the other woman's status, and rightly so. It wasn't fair to ask this of an intending bride.

V.J. said nothing. He was in the role of nominal paternalist, the oldest extant male and Sonal's closest relative. He was there to remind of the demands of duty, if Singh turned recalcitrant; he had been asked along to provide an emotional buffer between two people who were afraid of being alone together. But his nephew had made the proper moves, come down on the side of right in spite of his wanderings, and he, family spokesman, had already given his blessing, the most that he could be expected to do. All this marriage brokerage was women's business, anyway. He couldn't care less how the young man conducted himself in private, as long as it didn't end in scandal, so he resumed his glasses ready for the next page of newsprint.

Sonal, finding no response in him, came back to her son. She could read in his face the depth of his affection for this woman whom she had only glimpsed between stalls in the early evening. She read the pain and, behind that, the pride she must not wound. He had striven to compromise, an effort from which she balanced her range of choices. She could refuse outright, and lose him altogether, or she could follow his suggestion and see how it was received by the girl's family, stage by stage, over the next few months. He had done as she'd asked in maintaining the façade of ritual observance and, like V.J., she thought the rest, the qualitative core of the proposed alliance, was not her problem. Over to Lata's cousin.

'Yes,' she said. 'We must have some tea to quench us.'

While she was gone, V.J. took up his paper and Singh got to his feet and looked out of the small-pane windows which gave on to the inner courtyard. Rain had started to fall again, in huge white slashes that streaked the view of the disused fountains and left deep puddles on the paving stones. In minutes, the rain water would be absorbed into the ground, filtering through wide cracks that had appeared in the water-lily beds. The whole garden ought to be lifted and relaid to correct the settlement of a century. Would he do it when he inherited the lodge? His friends used these fringe palaces for their parties and family shoots, restocking their lakes with duck and game, or for debauches, whatever sport their taste ran to, but at this moment he was so disappointed and disgusted with himself that he couldn't fill the house mentally. He had killed his own best happiness. These rooms wouldn't resound again to singing and laughter in his time.

Even now, fearing his mother's final opposition to his plan, he could back out. The attraction of iconoclasm was strong. Other men did it, not as public or as well connected as he, but in Delhi and Calcutta and Bombay more progressive lifestyles were prevalent. Should he strike a blow for freedom of choice in the provincial town? His family wouldn't shun him for long. Just a few years. He groaned unconsciously, thinking he might have borrowed a share of courage from Thomas Langholm and his New World ways, but sensed he was eternally alone in this torment because even Langholm didn't know what it meant to be a lapsed Hindu.

He remembered a story by the English writer Somerset Maugham about a rubber planter in Malaysia who contracted for a bride to come out to the East by ship, sight unseen. In good faith, the young woman made the long journey by sea from England only to find – and this was written in a tact so hushed it only accentuated the shock of her discovery – that the planter already had a native woman installed in the quarters behind his

223

bungalow, a native woman and their mutual child. The Englishwoman left at once, not willing to be woman number two behind the swarthy. That was the only way to tell his story outside the sub-continent, where the ramifications of caste were incomprehensible. He was the same as a white man who had gone native, as if it were the next worst thing to bestiality, or a king who imagined that his favour would by itself elevate the commoner to royal privilege.

The rain switched off again. In the space of watching, the sky cleared and turned a blue almost as violent and colour-struck as the midnight one in storm. The country staggered from one extreme to the other, drought deluge, peace riot, eternity and damnation bonded like the self-destructive components of an atom into one single, vastly reproductive cell.

The paving stones dried even as he watched. They were ancestral stones. Nehru had walked here, on a visit between New Delhi and Bombay. In fifteen years, they would substitute Gandhi himself, to make a better legend, and nobody would know the truth of it. Maybe he should re-lay the flagstones when the time came. It struck him, as he heard Sonal's footsteps grow closer down the long length of passageway from her kitchens, that this was a fine position for a woman's house, secluded, unpressurised for a woman living alone with a few faithful servants. Maybe Shalini would like this place and it could be her private abode.

Sonal poured and Singh passed a tea glass in courtesy to his uncle.

'Now we have had a rest and time to consider,' she spoke frankly, 'let us shed our inhibitions and call things by their proper name. We are a family. We are one. We have no secrets and nothing that passes between us will be conveyed elsewhere, outside these walls.'

'I am not even listening,' said V.J, holding up a prohibitive palm.

'I am delighted to ask my mother to make the first approach on your behalf. I recognise your delicacy of feeling, and think it would be very wise for the two of you to meet, as often as you wish, until you are both certain. But it is out of the question for Shalini to continue at Amber. It will make talk. It will make trouble. If all goes well, and the match is arranged, it is unfair to expect Lata's cousin to accept such a condition, and for you too. You must give yourself a reasonable start. What I suggest is that Shalini comes into my household for a time. She will be comfortable and well cared for. She won't work. She won't be a servant by any means. She will be – my companion.'

She had found the secret resource to meet her crisis, and her son was humbled by the scope of her magnanimity. They both bowed down before her greater spirit. But she couldn't keep the heartbreak out of her voice, knowing better than he did how, shouldering the scandal, she would be held to blame for it, that for every friend who said, brave and wise woman, there was another who said, unprincipled.

She was encouraged by two prospects. In separating man and woman belatedly, she might loosen the bond between them and regularise it. With a contrary passion, she foresaw the little boy, the brown-eyed, brown-haired child, Singh himself reincarnate, reborn in this lodge, her double child running through the chain of corridors with both of his mothers in pursuit, and watched as her own life began again, like flowers colouring the desert sands. She knew she would not be able to let go, but anticipated, with an equanimity born of acceptance, how she would be locked into her fate.

For his part, Singh was overwhelmed by the neatness of her proposal, which prepared the way for his own vision of how the future would evolve. These halls would sing and dance again before the year was out. He cheered up visibly as his mother came halfway to treaty and lifted his eyes to meet his ancestors along the walls.

When the two men left, Sonal walked to the outer door to see them off, and bolted it after them, shutting up each subsequent door as she retreated into her inner sanctum. She faced a night alone without her servants, perhaps the last night of her life alone.

She didn't know if the impulsive offer of a home was premeditated, in the moments when she trailed Shalini through the lanes, mesmerised by the elegance and charm of her physique. Remembering her purchase on that day, she found the drawer where she had placed it and drew out the bracelet Shalini had admired. Wore it too, clasped it round her wrist for a few seconds. When she arrived, she would make her a gift of this in welcome, acknowledging that she must have intended something by way of reconciliation in the act of buying it.

But fingering the smooth and polished surface of the ivory, like perfect skin, she felt it in herself to feel sorry for Lata's cousin, knowing or unknowing, who was destined to marry a man with such a charge upon his soul. He had not uttered a word of enthusiasm at the prospect, or even her name.

20

Neal caught the last shuttle from Turnhouse to Heathrow and the last Tube on the Piccadilly Line into the heart of London. He put up at Brown's Hotel and woke up on Thursday about six o'clock, paralysed by the diversity of choice.

Sunday to Sunday, he'd said. One week to do the business. That meant that he still had three days in hand. He didn't need to be back in the Hong Kong office until Monday morning, and hadn't even lost part of his holiday allocation, a week being the standard company leave for attending a UK funeral for the next of kin. He looked out on the pre-rush-hour London pavements, sluggishly unpeopled compared with the East, although it was already broad daylight, and thought through the alternative allures of the capital: there was an interesting exhibition at the Royal Academy, Simpson's sale where he could browse for a tropical-weight suit, he could drop in at the Overseas Club, drift into Hatchards to see the new bestsellers, or he could enjoy the small shops around Mason's Yard, admiring the sealed jars of pomade, silver-backed bristle brushes and ebony accoutrements of a gentleman's estate. It was his own village in London.

Today, none of it fascinated him. Pleasure always seemed non-productive to Neal. He couldn't imagine anything duller than three days of sybaritic spending. He dialled through the hotel exchange to British Airways and established that there were several flights during the course of the day, at ten, four and eight p.m. The last plane would get him into Hong Kong early on Friday evening, local time. That would leave him a whole day in London, followed by a long night's paperwork in-flight, and he'd still be in time to spend Saturday morning at the office, seeing the inscrutable smile of hatred written on Joe Han's face, writhing from his ticking-off. He'd settle for that unique combination of pleasures.

* * *

He squeezed in all his shopping before noon. Simpson's resident tailor managed to alter the length on some lightweight wool-and-linen-blend trousers, a good cut, rather raffish, while he went down to the ladies' department and found a pretty, sleeveless dress for Lin, a straight shift he knew she'd suit, then went for lunch across the road in the Royal Academy. He called in at the company's London offices about three and made himself useful there, or made his presence felt.

A valuable Singapore contract had materialised while he'd been on leave. He'd been chasing this deal for months and smiled to see it yield at last. Would he have time to check it out? Certainly. He made a few brisk and bristling phone calls from the managing director's desk, peeling back some ambiguities of phrase. Meanwhile the office girls noticed the labels on his holdall and his designer parcels, and he laughed too. He liked to laugh with the people he wasn't working alongside. He didn't feel he lost anything by it.

When he did eventually get back to his own desk in Hong Kong, he was pleased to find that Joe had exerted himself to good effect since Tuesday. A rollocking always paid off. The contractors had been chased up, and the revised delivery dates were confirmed. Not one minute of their four days' advance on deadline was allowed to slip into the backwards abyss of time penalties. In his own department, at any rate, they were up to scratch.

He rang Lin, surprised at his own nervousness, and arranged to go out and join her for lunch in Shek-O. She was going over to Chessie's for a barbecue. He'd be welcome to join in. The more the merrier was the Hong Kong calling card. Before he caught his taxi out to the south side of the island, however, Neal made a small detour inside the Hong Kong and Shanghai building. He took the escalator to the viewing platform on the thirty-seventh floor. It was halfway up the skyscraper, and quiet on Saturday at twelve.

Stimulated by buildings, Neal still found this one the most exciting place he hadn't had a hand in constructing himself. The viewing room was a grey glass cube, with three or four severe, black leather settees against the walls as loungers, the stereotype modernist, minimalist structure, all angles and monochrome and boastful of its sky-defying linearity. Hubris, the Greeks would have called it, to reach so far into the privileged territory of the gods.

But the view was divine. Ahead of him, the straits lay choppy and blue in that bold, primary light of the East, with rays that hit the air at a slant different from that of other latitudes, bounding and bright. He never tired of watching the shipping ply the waters of the archipelago in their strange, oil-like limpidity, island to island, with a marine fleet so diverse it wasn't likely to be found anywhere else in the world, the canopy-fringed ferries that bussed the traffic lanes, the grey warships sliding eerily by under flags of convenience, the cargo vessels piled high with stencil-highlighted containers, the asymmetrical junks sailing against logic, a flat hydrofoil shooting off to Macau, pleasure yachts off drowsing bays, cracking little smacks with outboard motors: the whole of the world's waterborne traffic was filtered through these channels. To be encapsulated in the temperature and atmospherically controlled building of the Hong Kong and Shanghai Bank, looking out at the hum and throb of the South China Seas, well, it beat St Andrew Square as well as Piccadilly Circus, and it sure as hell beat Carterbrae!

Behind and slightly to his left lay the Governor's Residence, as artificial as a wedding cake. Double-tiered, white-pillared, protected by a greensward garden lawn which had been savagely reduced in size since its colonial heyday, it looked exactly the anachronism it was, dwarfed by the skyscrapers that crowded round it. They blocked off the view to the sea which he was able to enjoy from the lofty heights of the thirty-seventh floor. Britain in parentheses. He burst out laughing at its ostensible shrinkage, power along with lost dimension, and 'Serves you right' were the words that came inexplicably into his mind. He thought this with glee, in spite of being proud of the invitation to the next Governor's garden party in the Residence grounds, which was lying on the coffee table at Mid-Levels. At the takeover, the Chinese would probably raze the phoney palace to the ground and build half a dozen skyscrapers on the site, increasing its usefulness ratio a hundredfold as they went.

He loved the city, whether that was because of the liveliness or the missing harmonies of it, the wing-tip clearance of life on the edge of the known, safe world when he touched down on the old Kai Tak runway, so fractionally close to death that he could actually see people cleaning their teeth in the crowded apartment blocks alongside the airport. He even loved the smell of the East which had started to haunt him, living inside his head as well as his nostrils. His clothes reeked of it until, occasionally, he'd fancied it was his own pervasive body odour he was picking up.

Thomas had noticed it, too, and said it was one of the by-products of pollution, created by a massive concentration of chemicals and effluents from the world's biggest factory complex, slip, dyes, oozing chicken giblets, the soupy brew of civilisation which added to the slow burl of the water in the straits and made that limpidity oil-like. Neal dropped his nose to the back of his right hand and sniffed. It came up sweetish, acrid, but not unpleasant. He could live with his own stench.

The taxi dropped him off in the centre of Shek-O village. It was only a muddy square with road cones syphoning off a few undistinguished areas for development, but Lin had chosen to live here because the rents were cheaper than in Hong Kong, the properties larger, often with private gardens or a roof garden, and it was popular with the Europeans who were her friends. Pink, green, lilac-washed, the village had a Spanish air when the geraniums were in bloom, and he glimpsed the snaking causeway out to the headland down a maze of food-strewn alleyways.

Neal headed on foot towards the sea, noticing in passing that the Thai restaurant was packed out today, at the start of the weekend, and had attracted a patient queue of customers who were willing to stand without cover in the insufferable heat, drinking from long bottles of Chinese lager beer to cool themselves. The cooks served up the specialised glutens of oriental food, that gooey, gunky mix of sugar, vinegar and monosodium glutamate which wasn't entirely to his taste. Perhaps that was the smell which had entered his own body stream, not pollution so much as the recipe of ersatz and synthetics, or the concomitants of modern.

He walked on past some shanty cafés which, in France, would have been chic with shady umbrellas and wicker or wrought-iron chairs. But in Hong Kong there was no pavement and no pavement-café society.

After a couple of hundred yards, he came to the patch of allotments which had been scraped off the beach into cultivation. God knows what the Chinese put on the sand to stabilise it and make it bear these intensive crops – untreated sewage, Thomas had told him, but he didn't wholly believe that, or want to. They were beautifully maintained, at any rate, and produced admirably variegated, bursting mangoes, verdant spinach leaves, a glorious, frothy-headed crop of carrots. Then on past more tumbledown sheds and shacks where the allotments owners lived, only

230

marginally more tidy than the cafés in the square, until eventually, along a ditch-sided earthen pathway, he came to a single brick arch. Its solid, embossed wooden gate demarcated a semi-formal garden along European lines reclaimed from the wilderness outside. This was Chessie's place.

As he walked into the inner compound to meet the hubbub of voices, Neal found that his heart was racing with apprehension. He felt changed, or charged, as if he'd been bombarded with cathode rays and was radioactive, a dangerous catalyst for the other people who stood near him, a carrier of death. But that was absurd, he reasoned. As you were. He'd only been away on the same business trip he went on every six weeks, eight times a year. Without the crepe and armbands, nobody would know the difference.

It was a large lunch party. A lot of familiar faces, a few newcomers. They were barbecuing chicken in the shady portion of the garden, beside a long, patterned, tiled table which had a grilling trough built in at one end. He felt a touch of welcome as Lin detached herself from the throng. She stretched up and kissed him. Her lips were very warm from standing near the coals, but she stayed cool herself. She was looking marvellous, in a slub-linen dress that didn't seem to crease on her slender shape. Its pale-lemon colour was striking against her straight fall of iridescent hair and the permanent bronzing of her skin. The local experts in ethnology told him that she wasn't straight Chinese, but what the rest of her was she didn't proffer. He was fascinated by the precision-tooling of her flesh, how she touched him on the shoulders in her balletic way, making a ritual of her smallest gesture, *à point*, the index finger and thumb arched minutely as a Balinese temple dancer's. She looked very brown and must have been sunbathing on her balcony again, although he'd warned her not to do that for too long. But she had a foolhardy disregard for her own perfection and thought she was immune from harm.

'A day ahead?' she asked him quizzically.

'Oh, I wrapped it up early.'

'No surprises? No sly clauses in the will?'

'Plenty of those. Later.'

It still felt hot under the skin and, sensing the prickliness in him, she found him a shaded lounger on the verandah and brought him out a glass of iced tea as well as several different people to speak to, in case he grew bored with his own company. She managed to serve him without being servile.

He found this house rather lovely and relaxing, apricot walls, a steeply pitched roof with steel cross-beams, and it was furnished indoors and out in the informal, beach-house style. Throws, hangings, a daybed covered with kelims, the multi-ethnic aggregate favoured by the world hippie. The cane seats happened to be sodden and rain-split, the hammock was looped lazily between trees, terracotta pots sported palms and fronds which wilted in the heat. Nobody expended much care on it. It was an illegal structure (buildings with walls being permitted on this site, although no roofing was allowed) and Chessie herself was an illegal tenant, being a sub-tenant and, while he was away, she'd taken in a sub-sub-tenant, namely Marian Kirkwood. She was small, dark, intense, the lonely newcomer.

Lin brought her over, innocuously enough, because she was a fellow Scot and, worldwide, your birthplace was as good an introduction as any. But a couple of sentences into the conversation, Neal discovered that, incredibly, she'd given up on a messy marriage and a first-rate career in Edinburgh only the month before, and knew one of his architect cousins quite well professionally.

'Aren't there easier places in the world for you to run away to?' he asked her.

'Where else do you suggest? It's been good enough for you to run to.'

He panicked unreasonably. What was the matter with him that he kept having these palpitations? It was the cousin connection. Douglas Langholm had been advised of the funeral arrangements as one of the names on Caley's list, but had sent his apologies. Neal knew he was over-reacting, imagining that some hint of the fracas at Carterbrae had leaked out this far to sea, like a wave-assisted oil slick, and sat convinced that this woman knew something and would broadcast it, to his disadvantage.

In the meantime, he managed to laugh it down. 'Escapism? Yes, it often feels that way in the New Territories.'

'But I'm not running away at all,' she enunciated over-precisely while Neal knew that, however long she spent on the island as Chessie's paying house guest, he'd try to avoid her socially another time. These wound-up women were no good in the south. Women needed an equipoise in their make-up to survive the rigours of indifference: men, climate, the sexist culture, they were all punishing on a nervous temperament. 'I went to school here,' she corrected him. 'I was at school with Chessie. My father was stationed at Stanley with the Royal Fusiliers for seven years. Hong Kong's my home. You see, I'm running back, not away.'

A woman called Eva came out on the verandah and joined them, lightening their fractious mood. She was tall and blonde and Swedish, very beautiful. She was in love with an Englishman, Mike, whose two dogs, an idiot pair of mutts, roamed round the garden, rooting at the base of the fragile bark. They'd been out hang-gliding that morning, launching themselves into the basking thermals off The Peak.

'Brilliant today,' she said. 'Perfect conditions. I got all the way down to the beach and I've never managed that before.' She confided so much in strangers. Last time they were here, Eva had told him how she'd been propositioned by one of the Thai ayahs in the ladies' room of the Marriott Hotel. Imagine that, she said out loud, do I look like a lesbian? He'd never have made that sort of declaration, knowing how, in the incestuous social climate of Hong Kong, a denial turned overnight into undisputed fact.

It was that sort of community, quickfire friendships, association by accidental pairing, a kind of human snap. People talked about their travelling as the most important experience they had in common, being permanently on the move. They all admired his London-tailored clothes, which were still held in higher esteem than the Chinese copies. Marian found her rhythm at last and told them some tales from Scottish folklore. So it went. It had its hypnotism, the drifting continent, the mythologies of flux and impermanence so that Neal could see why Europeans had been drawn for five hundred years to the outdoor, free and easy culture of the East. It was the society without rules. This was where lovers met on the periphery of the Western world in Somerset Maugham, or where a heavy-limbed, somnolent beauty was captured by Gauguin.

Neal relocated the words hippie and traveller in the context of the day. Maybe this city was a microcosm of the New Age world of drop-outs. Your pedigree was what you could do. History was now. The future was next month's trading figures and success was money, not spending it with style, not inheriting it from your family estates, but making it gross.

He came to about three a.m. covered in sweat. It was a remorselessly humid night, and Lin's air-conditioning must have fouled up again, leaving him drenched. Then Neal remembered in visual replay how, seconds before, he'd been rolling down a flight of whitewashed steps on to the impeccable lawns of the Residence, locked in a fierce and fighting embrace with the Governor himself, who was decked out in his Prince of Wales plumes, his colonial pith helmet, a white tropical mess dress, the lot. Behind them, down the cascading ripple of the stairway, was a trail of blood, magnified into a river by the pristine setting. The garden party guests screamed and parted in an image so pure and diagrammatical, it was like a bit of classic cinema footage he knew by heart, arranged but real.

He sat up in bed and instantly Lin was awake too, responsive to his slightest movement. She got up and found the light switch and a cotton wrap. In seconds, she'd made some jasmine tea.

'What happened?'

'Only a dream.' He took the glass and sipped at it while she balanced neatly on a folding chair. All her furniture seemed removable.

'What happened in the UK?'

'Not a great deal. I lost my past.'

'That hardly qualifies as a surprise. You're getting careless with your past. You've lost it twice before. So it doesn't matter. It's not like losing your passport.'

This was eloquence from Lin. She didn't go in for discussion. She only stated a point of view or gave him the resumé, the bottom line, of her reflections. This brittle, trading-floor approach to sentiment was sobering. His fever cooled under its stern draught. Don't ever indulge your emotions with me, she implied. Find the nobility in suffering. She had rather haughty looks, arched eyebrows, noble nose, and got away with this much arrogance. More profoundly, she seemed to speak with the voice of the cheated, harassed but indomitable Han nation, so that her lightest words came to him burdened with the weight of broken dynasties and kingdoms drowned in gore.

And how well she knew him under her elisions! She meant that his family past went a long time ago down a Nepalese ravine when a gang of hill brigands murdered John and Mary Langholm for the sake of a leather pouch full of rupees and an inscribed gold watch. Never found, these personal belongings confirmed the violent act in Neal's own mind. But his own personal, associative life he'd walked away from consciously when he left to take up work outside Britain. He'd survived that compound loss. He'd survive anything which the past could dredge.

As for his passport, well, that was his own statement of identity and purpose. They could steal it, or impound it in some immigration wrangle at a Third World airport, forge it, fail to acknowledge it – but they could never actually destroy his own licence to manoeuvre. It was his personal sovereignty and, as such, was inalienable.

Half of Lin's implication was philosophical, half practical, as she signalled her continuing interest in a man who was going somewhere, globally, in real space and time and advancement, and whose key to the future was the mere fact of his nationality which afforded him these travel options. It was the Eastern translation of his potential.

'You're right. I was only interpreting my dream.'

'Leave that to the old women, to live in dreams. You can afford to live first-hand.' She got up from her chair, clapped it shut as easily as folding an umbrella and placed it against the wall, out of her busy way. She lifted his empty glass meticulously from the bedside cabinet and went to look out of the long window that opened on to her balcony, examining the density of the air outside. 'Today will be insufferable. We must have a swim. Who'll be having a pool party?' As if to implement the thought, she threw off her wrap and stood, an unembarrassed nude, beside the open window.

Her words reflected her body. There was no archaic voluptuary in her. He admired the lean carcase, the fleshless structure of her shape. Ribcage, navel, a bone-tight knee. Nothing excess or ponderous. She was the streamlined new.

Lin was thinking about a friend of Mike's who had a good swimming pool. They'd get in there somehow. Who could she ring? She noticed incidentally that the houseboy had been skimping on the watering and her containers were looking flaccid. Only when she'd filed these simple thoughts for action did she turn to the complex issue: this man.

She liked him. She went on liking him. He was straight. Unlike a lot of whites who came out to the East for cheap kicks, he didn't graze down the boulevards off Causeway Bay looking for clean prostitutes, or take the street boys into bed when she wasn't looking. Compared with most of the expat, ex-colonial, exile Brits, he wasn't a bad bloke. And he was good to her. She liked the dress he'd bought her in London and, on instinct, she put her hand up to caress it where it rested on the back of her wardrobe door on its padded coat hanger. The Simpson's bag was still conspicuously in place, looped by its handles over the back of the hanger like an enhancing frame. These small impulses didn't weaken her general aim, to organise their future in parallel.

'It's time to move on,' she said decisively, and he recognised that he would move at her bidding, wherever. 'You'll have been here two years at the end of next month. Quite a lot's happened while you've been away this week.' She leaned forward without actual propulsion and opened a small drawer. She pulled out a sheaf of papers which were strewn with her personal emblem, an outbreak of little yellow sticker notes. Universal, she made these seem unique because she outlined the notelets in felt-tip pen as if they were a printed card or an invitation, something more important than the mere addenda of her comments.

'A brilliant job's come up in Singapore. You ought to go for it.'

He read the outline of the advertisement with a growing sense of confirmation of his own trends. It was exactly what he would have wanted for himself. Lin watched and gauged his interest in the job spec, almost glad of the final breakaway from Britain which he had implied. Now that the venerable grandmother was dead, he wouldn't need to go back to Scotland so often – or, indeed, ever again.

The pool was bright and blue, a sweeping kidney shape with a dazzling whitewashed surround and lawns luxuriantly green and broad by Hong Kong standards.

Lin had wangled them an invitation to Mike's friend's pool party in record time. How did she wield so much influence for somebody with no money and less power? Lin handled some of the big accounts as one of the credit controllers at the Hong Kong and Shanghai Bank, and she gave the impression of being in the know, of holding privileged information which she traded against her social entry to the grand occasions. The fact that she divulged nothing whatsoever in return, was as impenetrable as a numbered safety box in some bank vault in Switzerland, wasn't held against her, or nobody complained because market confidentiality was as tightly guarded as the membership roll of a Masonic lodge. Her friends hoped she would crack, and were continually disappointed by her hold on secrecy, or encouraged by it.

Eva plunged and surfaced in the sparkling, chlorinated water as smoothly as a mermaid, although, in a grey gingham bikini, she was more like the young Bardot, the only woman in the world who looked superb with wet hair. Mike's two dogs gambolled on the lawns, panting and untidily long-eared in the heat, ran through the oscillating spray, then flopped their wet coats down on to his tolerant feet.

Lin was wearing a one-piece costume and a matching overblouse, this season's outfit, and was as smart as anyone could be in a state of undress.

But it was the rather peppery woman dressed in an unbecoming black who took hold of Neal's attention on the lounger where he lay dozing. She was a powerful swimmer and covered the fatuously shaped pool fifty times with long graceful strokes before she hauled herself out on the rim below him, frowning hideously as she claimed the sunbed next to his.

'I remember you now, or I remember meeting you once. I came to a party in your flat somewhere near Tollcross.'

He turned and looked at Marian Kirkwood with all the welcome of a bad omen. Her racing costume, inscribed with the crude lettering of Warrender Baths, her deeply creased face, pasty and out of place against their communally toned suntans, gave him a shiver of apprehension.

'I'm sorry I don't remember that. We held a lot of parties there over the years.'

'Caley Brown asked me along. She was going out with your brother at the time. It was stupid of me not to think of it at once. How are they getting on?'

How was he going to shake himself free of her gratuitous attachment to him? What memories and relationships was she going to dredge up to embarrass him in a setting where he was the coming man, his own man, independent of his dreary heritage? 'She's engaged to someone else,' he lied. 'Or so I heard. I don't keep in touch.'

'Not with your brother?' she inquired a second too sharply, and he had an uncanny sense that her information was more recent than his own, that she had made a call to the UK during the weekend to check her facts. She was just that sort of tiresome, knot-tying woman who loved to trip you up.

'Not with Caley.' His brevity in reply was laconic, his smile dismissive. Time to leave. Her, the party, the colony, the past. This evening, he would sit and make out his application for a transfer to Singapore, and as Neal went to collect Lin on the way out, he thought that he would take her to dinner in their favourite restaurant at The Peak, which was the most romantic, dew-settled location he could think of to ask if she would seriously consider going to Singapore with him. Ahead, he tasted her surprise.

21

Someone else inside the flat opened the door to Thomas.

He couldn't see Caley anywhere in the downstairs rooms that were crowded with partygoers, and so he browsed round his old habitat for a while, wondering if it really was his own place. The same address. Probably the same landlord. Once he'd recovered from the surprise that Caley had taken over his lease at Gillespie Crescent in the first place, Thomas started to recognise the odd bit of confirming furniture, the noble junk that went through auction rooms because it was too big for modern houses.

She'd shifted things around imaginatively: a beaten-up desk was moved behind a settee, transforming them both into something handsome. There were better light fittings, or they were more sympathetically angled into an interesting chiaroscuro, as well as some new pictures and well-hung curtains which gave the rooms a sense of style they'd not quite achieved during the Langholms' tenure. He'd never seen a place of Caley's own making, and found himself taken by the strong plains she imported, dark walls, square cushions, the geometric layout of her possessions which gave a surface depth as marked in high relief as if it were a texture of antithesis. Completely modern: utterly traditional. Fresh paint. Throughout there was a touch of lightness with a pulse of warmth behind it, like the smell of cut freesias on spring days, something cool but living too, with the natural ozone pungency she habitually carried indoors.

The overlay of styles was disturbing because it was the superimposition of her own character on top of his, her small improvements to him personally, like her reinterpretation of his domestic lair with what was known as the woman's touch, or the tantalising outline of what might have been. The sense of déjà vu became rather poignant. A frisson of sensuality, of liking what he saw, only added to his dislocation. He'd set out for Edinburgh at lunchtime with one specific objective, to find Caley and make it up with her, or make sense of the confused situation, although he wasn't sure if his mood was angry or apologetic to start with. This changed subtly when he talked to Nina. The straight line to Caley became a circuit. Why had she moved to Gillespie Crescent? And why was she holding this party? Was it her birthday? He realised with a pang that he couldn't remember the actual date of that, and felt bad about turning up empty-handed if it were indeed some sort of festivity. That would look like an unforgivable omission, and he would lose the advantage of being badly treated by her, having deserved it.

It had called for a certain courage on his part to climb the familiar spiral of stairs and press the bell. After all, walking into an engagement party wasn't improbable, so that he was relieved it wasn't Gordon Strachan who opened the front door to him, although unconsciously Thomas trailed the other man through a suite of rooms as much as he trailed Caley. Was he heading towards another argument, another vulgar brawl?

The guests who hung about the rooms were as familiar as the furniture. A number of them were old acquaintances of his and Neal's and Singh's – the people who'd been dropping in for years and who just kept on coming. There was a different host, a different layout to the rooms, but the flat was still a good central location near the crossroads, an open hostelry. They'd changed their allegiance while he was away, the engineers, and doctors and geology men. Now they were Caley's friends. They hailed him distantly, trying to remember how long he'd been away. How are you doing? Good to see you back. Are you home for good? He was waylaid for quite a while by giving out more stalling explanations. For the first time in his life, Thomas faltered socially. His charisma failed him; he wasn't confident enough to project a compelling image of himself, composed of the work, the remote place, the non-European time zone he carried in his head, and the wide sweep of internal countryside in which he dwelt.

He read the withdrawn puzzlement in each pair of eyes, as if they were signalling that he'd become a supernumerary in this town and in Caley's circle, the outsider because she'd stayed inside it, giving it a new pivot or a new dynamism. They were looking at him warily, shiftily, and this made him apprehensive because he still hadn't located the two main protagonists in his focus, and he began to feel increasingly an interloper in a setting where he'd turned into a stranger, uninvited, unwelcome, even ignorant of the basic reason for the celebration, and so a killjoy.

Between the doorways of here and there, he underwent a mind change, a spasm of alternative identification, and knew for a second what it felt like to be Neal: this is my natural environment, but not quite. To be the one who was ousted, the de-privileged, the second favourite – it was a disagreeable state of affairs to be an also ran in your own household. Caley had upstaged him in the present.

A younger man than the rest was standing by himself smoking, managing to give the impression that smoking a cigarette was a complete and sociable activity which absorbed the whole of him. He looked down at the ash almost attentively, as if it was speaking to him in reply. Admittedly, they were very expensive cigarettes, Sobranie Black, smoked for effect rather than quick nicotine inhalation, and they perfumed the eco-system of the interior air which Caley had balanced to perfection with an alien substance, the narcosis of the young man's personal selfishness.

'Oliver,' he said, approaching him.

The other looked up, although his face didn't change at all in recognising Thomas Langholm, not interested, not pleased, or even marginally taken aback. 'What are you doing here? I thought you were in India.' Said without pleasantness, the words sounded abrasive, almost hostile.

'Was. Will be. My grandmother died. I flew back for that.'

'Oh. Sorry.'

Thomas hesitated for a second, reappraising the young man, asking himself if it was worth exploring their instinctive distrust of each other for long enough to turn it into dislike. Probably, in this instance. 'I thought you were abroad too. Working on a kibbutz. I was speaking to Nina only this afternoon about you. That was the impression she gave me.'

That drew blood all right, and was worth the effort. Oliver's smoke screen thinned as he forgot to puff his fag, so letting the long grey ash from the Sobranie fall unnoticed on to the carpet. 'I gave the kibbutz up as a bad job. Literally. It was only filling in.'

'You didn't enjoy it?

'Slave labour, isn't it? And it's not my cause.'

'Judaism?'

'Work.' Oliver laughed lightly and, for a second, he reverted to being young. He was better-looking when he laughed, looser and more carefree. He just had handsome muscles, but Thomas picked up a new, underlying nervousness in him and saw that the fingers were brown-stained. A chain-smoker at twenty. 'I got back this morning. I'll be casting around. There are lots of openings.'

What a talent for evasion Caley's brother had! He slid through facts and money and the precise statement of things with an assurance that was almost convincing. He had all the sterling qualities, strong looks, the rudiments of an education, a personable demeanour made up of a shrewdness that was more diplomatic than his blunt mother's and more diverse than his single-minded father's: he could have been the great all-rounder but he had missed, ending up a con man, too hesitant to press on into achievement because of the double-track mentality of the cheat who habitually kept something back for himself. He'd never declare the whole of it.

It dawned on Thomas that Nina hadn't known the young man was due back in the city. The sense of someone sick in a spare room upstairs at Buckstone was the vacuity of her hold on her son, a space she kept waiting and ready for him, bed made up, towels folded, just in case. But he didn't go home: Caley's was his safe house, where he hid from his parents as much as he hid from the Procurator Fiscal. The thought was complex and occupied a good deal of Thomas's reckoning. Perhaps its deviousness explained why Caley didn't tell him she'd taken on this flat, why she left her letters to be forwarded, possibly why she hadn't come with him to Jaipur in the first place, that there was a larger imperative in her scale of priorities, and this was it. She was providing a safe hiding place for her brother. What a strange girl! She went out of her way to protect a young man who had done her no good, and never would stand by her to any reciprocal degree. At the first sign of trouble, he would ditch her, walk by on the other side, wouldn't call her name across a line of traffic if it deviated one yard from his own chosen direction or his gain. Do her down, do her a disservice. And she must already know that in the bone. A sentence of Neal's came back to him, that some day Caley would have to choose between seeing these people alone and not seeing them at all.

The two of them were standing in a corner of the downstairs living room. People were eating and Thomas, suddenly ravenous, remembered that he hadn't had a morsel of food since Ruth Palmer's Selkirk bannock the previous afternoon. In front of him, a plate of untouched supper lay rejected, shoved on to a deep shelf of the bookcase. These were Oliver's discards. A chicken leg barely tasted, some carefully shredded coleslaw, a fresh baguette thickly buttered and then left with the teeth marks showing up as clearly as in a dentist's pink amalgam. Yes, it was Oliver's way to pick and choose, turning up his nose at the meals Caley had wrought, spurning what she did for him. The young man followed Thomas's famished eye and commented, 'That stuff's a bit fatty for me now. I've got used to lighter meals. I don't know why I'm filling up my system with all this cholesterol.'

What would you like for dinner? Caley asked him once in Thomas's hearing at Fairmilehead.

Lobster Thermidor.

I was thinking more along the lines of mince.

The words surfaced again: Oliver had started to cultivate the preferences he couldn't afford; he took away the taste of plain-fare normality with the whiff of something exotic that had blunted his palate.

'What's this party for? I wasn't strictly invited, just happened to be back and came along.'

Again, Oliver sent the stranger a look of baleful surprise. 'It's for her exhibition, of course.'

'Which exhibition? I've been a way a long time. Don't forget, I'm a bit out of touch.'

'It's a craft fair. She's been putting her silver jewellery on display. Sold everything. Wiped clean. She's the talk of the town, small talk though it is. Small town.'

'When was that on? The exhibition?'

'This week. It's on all this week. She's got a TV interview booked for Monday. Not any old Scottish TV programme. The BBC. The works.'

Thomas measured the Brown terms of approbation and success. Critical as he was over their overtness – high sales and good publicity, with no reference to the objects themselves, the workmanship, the inspiration, the research that had gone into the basic finding of her raw materials, or what she'd really achieved by way of synthesis: the sum total of originality – he acknowledged that at least her brother had an inkling of what was going on in Caley's life, whereas he was gloriously ignorant. 'Have you been in to see it?'

'Yes. I popped in this afternoon. Stuff's a bit ethnic for me, but someone likes it, obviously. You've still got time to catch it before it closes. She's kept the display going and only sold from stock. There's still plenty to see.'

Thomas nodded. His time left in Scotland shortened while the list of his commitments lengthened. He hurtled towards the minuted deadlines, a ticket out on Sunday at the latest, but came no nearer to an actual decision. He hadn't even set eyes on Caley yet. There was a strange pulse through the room, created by his unbearable anxiety, the tension surrounding her actual appearance downstairs, whenever it might eventually happen. The implicit intimacy of shared space was a powerful drag on him. Next to this room, on the other side of the wall, was the same bed waiting and Thomas still couldn't absorb the fact that for the last two years she'd been sleeping in it, waking up in the same window-shuttered room, but without him or with someone else.

'Tell me, is Gordon here this evening?' He put it out as casually as he could.

'Gordon? No, he's away all this week in The Hague.'

'Holland?'

'Yes.'

'On business?'

'He handles all the finance for one of the company accounts in the arms trade. Delicate negotiations. The international venue. Hard to detect. They like dealing with a military man for the hardware. Questions of national security. Stumm.'

Vague, unquotable, carrying a spurious glamour, the words conveyed the essential of Oliver's character. But they were also effective. Thomas was practically crawling on his hands and knees to ask for more details, why the retired captain chose to go on negotiating deals in the arms trade when he'd left the Army behind, how much of his workload it comprised, how often he went abroad. The bait had been dangled in front of him tauntingly, but he let it hang, realising these overheard snippets were all that the young man knew. If he did press on, he'd get another vapid dissertation culled from third-hand sources, as on the building of the Faskally Dam, and a fistful of unconvincing theories.

'If stumm applies, it may be safer not to refer to the fact at all. The wartime adage is still useful. You never know who's listening.'

But Oliver couldn't be shamed into a discreet silence. He only pulled the corners of his mouth down into a grimace, which was one of Maurice's facial gestures, both men intolerant of the least correction. 'This is peacetime, isn't it? Doesn't really matter. The relationship's a bit iffy anyway.' He wobbled his free hand, to imply the shakiness.

Of course this was music to his ears but, again, Thomas knew the young man said it only to provoke, or inflate his own importance, airing a smattering of superior knowledge. Any stable state was as flat to him as it was to Nina, and so he'd happily imply the love affair was in peril, true or not. As he walked away, Thomas thought it still seemed inconsiderate of Gordon to be absent during this crucial week for Caley, so maybe there was some solid foundation to the rumour. He was able to smile at himself, clutching at straws, as if the other man's temporary absence excused his own larger indifference.

Caley had remembered her neglected guests below and came downstairs at that point from the more popular sitting room above. She was looking tired, maybe strained. Carterbrae had taken up three days of her time and energy. She'd called in at Alastair Renton's office and talked to him until midday, then shopped and cooked for the party in the evening, which had been arranged long ago and so was unavoidable, although she wasn't in the right frame of mind for jollity or the streamers of self-congratulation. She'd sunk to the bottom of her own priorities again, and her own self-esteem.

She was still managing to smile, although Thomas recognised that smile of old, the controlled corners of it, not relaxed, as if it was a convenient mask for the busy, organising mind. He watched her for a long time, hidden behind the shade of a standard lamp and her habitual kitchen bowls and impromptu jugs filled with branches of decorative foliage, thinking, She must have watched me like this the first evening when Singh brought her along. Same room. Same people. But a turnaround in their positions.

Compulsively sociable, Caley was demonstrating her skill in ways he was better placed to judge at this remove. He knew the sifting and blending attributes, the hostessing technique of finding the connective theme or a common topic which would serve as an introduction, her long, quiet, assessing wait while the rest of the group was talking before she picked up a new strand, chosen from the threads and stray opinions idly thrown away by others which she'd collected for a useful future. Memories, the ambitions of long ago, shared holidays, old love affairs: she stored them all. She was better at total recall and social grafting than he was. He dazzled, but she burned slow and steady. He promoted himself, she promoted others. Altruism had a more enduring thrust to it than egotism. Because it encompassed other people it had a larger scope, and lasted well, sparking off new contacts. Even if he'd stayed in Edinburgh, Thomas suspected he wouldn't have kept this group of friends together. He'd have grown bored with them, as a simple, reflective surface of himself, and let it show before too long. He had to keep moving to be interested in his own development, and that precluded being interested in other people's.

Was it important in the first place, promoting this feel-good factor? Maybe. Harmony was the invisible component of the cooperation he respected and relied on in the workplace, which got the well bore sunk, the water drawn, the social fabric repaired day after day. It wasn't a major greatness, but the strongest of the minor ones.

He admired Caley's calm, and the complete lack of hysteria in her mental outfit. Still not thirty, she had the aura of a *grande dame*. The phrase came to him ready-made but it also jolted him. Of course, he recognised her intimately, made up from one chromosome of himself. She was Edith reincarnate, the harmoniser, the arbiter, the stayer at home, the stickler for standards of decency and personal behaviour – traduced time and again by Neal's and Oliver's, but still she went forwards with her methods and equilibrium intact. Any tangible reward was immaterial to the woman's longer-sighted purpose, which was the common good.

She moved closer into his own orbit of shared eye space. The light fell directly on to her dress. She was wearing pink, which looked startlingly fluorescent on somebody who almost never wore bright colours. It was very fetching, but she didn't look herself in it because Thomas knew it was a garment chosen for her by another man, and therefore he disliked it. An unprecedented jealousy fired him. He was ripped in two by anger at her near inaccessibility. He wanted to take the dress off and see her breasts for himself, wanted to lose his hand between her legs again, because he was powerless to be completely rational in her presence and anyway his main hold over her might be simple and unthinking chemistry. Nudity made her his.

She saw him. She came towards him eagerly, although her eyes were lit by an emotion more complicated than happiness because she dropped the semblance of her fixed social smile and looked serious, if not actually alarmed, at the sight of him.

'How did you get here? How did you know? Well, you're all right.' She glanced down quickly at the bandaged hand. 'Will you stay on? Stay over. I'm on my own. Wait until all these people go, then we can talk. Are you hungry? There's still some supper left upstairs in the kitchen. You look – rabid. But I'm so glad to see you. I wanted you to be here but was afraid to ask you. I'd have come back down tomorrow to Carterbrae and sorted things out. I panicked. I shouldn't have left you in the lurch, I know.'

She passed on. Someone else made a claim on her attention, and she gave it without stint.

There was a square bay window in this front room, where Caley had arranged a desk of sorts. She'd put it together herself from two glass-fronted cabinets, stacks of shallow drawers, and then she'd fitted a piece of chamfered mahogany across the top of them to act as a bridging work surface. That was her idea of a piece of furniture, a happy find plus a bit of make do. He wondered why there were glass fronts to the drawers instead of wooden ones. Thomas pulled the top one open and realised they were a pair of old shop fittings, throw-outs from a refurbishment of Maurice's drapery, probably Edwardian, certainly pre-war, but nicely jointed pieces where the drawer front was hinged in brass, and dropped down on a ratchet for each access to the folded shirts and stud collars and ties, while the glass insert let you see at a glance what was stored inside. A very sensible design.

Inside, she kept gems and samples, and any fossil finds that weren't suitable for redeployment as ornaments but had taken Caley's eye in a mineralogist's shop or on a rocky shore in Fife. Some of them were as smooth as commercial paperweights, looking like a skein of bubbles trapped in an outward glaucous substance, while others had strange crystalline extrusions, and there were things like pillars of salt but in very odd colourways, a pale luminous mauve, phosphorescent yellow, amber resins, underwater blues and greens; it was altogether a strange, encoded, inverted world which she could interpret better than he. Thomas stood and stared into them, but read only the surface. She knew the meaning.

He didn't touch them, afraid of leaving follicles of skin behind to dull the gleaming surfaces, but he pulled out drawer after drawer of sample trays, rapt with enthusiasm for fresh evidence about the way she thought, while the rest of the room seethed round about him in the unproductive chat and posturing of parties. It was a real insight, and the collection baffled him as much as Neal's revelation about the army captain and Oliver's about her exhibition of work. All news to him. So many lives she led, so many talents for people and for doing. He wasn't envious, only admiring of the variety of skills.

He replayed an image from the one time they went together to Jamie Drew's cavern in Cowdenbeath, which turned out to be a dusty outhouse in his garden, full of heaps of old, unlabelled rocks stored in shoe boxes. The three of them went down to the beach together afterwards, and the man showed them where he'd been lucky in searching for graptolites and starfish echinoids and sea-urchins in his private, hidden seams. They watched him pick up normal-looking rocks along the shoreline and handle them, examining them for evidence of a fossilised life within. If he came across one he liked the look of, he wedged it on top of a boulder with his foot. Using his chisel and a neat geologist's hammer, he hit one side of the unprepossessing rock with an expertly positioned blow: it sheered in half as neatly as the shell of a drained coconut, and yielded up a perfect ammonite, as pale as sandstone and curled tight around its central, spinal cord. They were silent, he and Caley, stunned and moved by what the man had brought to the surface out of an impenetrable stone.

How do you learn to do that? he asked.

You can't learn it. You either know the lie of it at once, or you stay in the dark.

Thomas came upon a lot of good, useful words along the way, glacial till and gault and polymath, which Drew used when he talked about the first amateurs of this science, who were often clergymen, often women, the Renaissance hunters after knowledge. He pocketed the words quietly to look at later. For a while, he'd been obsessed with Caley's collection of geological maps, which described the heave and tilt of landmass in the making. It was a slanted way to look at things, like a contour map of familiar territory, or marine charts for offshore banks and reefs: not the whole truth, but the key to a complete understanding.

He was smitten all over again by Caley's plural occupations: she was both private and peopled, focused and diverse. There was an all-encompassing ability here, a range he hadn't properly grasped or credited before. He projected her future development, in terms of the manifest raw talent, and found he couldn't follow the arc of it into infinity. There was no knowing what she might achieve. She had the capacity to change and modify every decade or so, whereas he might do no better than re-create his own past, or his family's past. He was only eccentric: she was original. She'd been described as a sensible child, and then a capable girl, but was on the threshold of being recognised in her larger milieu as an accomplished woman. That was an impressive escalation, and unstoppable.

He pushed the revealing trays back into place and waited for herself.

22

They came to the best part of an evening, when all the dinner or party guests had gone home and the dishes were piled high, ready for treatment in the morning. The two of them could sit back and relax, drain the half-empty wine bottles, forget whether it was night or daytime outside because there was something lit inside their heads. It turned into their own place again. They were together and alone. That was intimate enough. Caley kicked off her shoes. Thomas took off his pocket-drooping jacket. Late last night, Ruth had hurriedly stitched the shoulder seam back into the armhole to make it serviceable again. Underneath, he was wearing black denim on top of a T-shirt.

'You don't wear black as a rule.' Caley watched him closely. He still rated as the most interesting man she'd ever come across. The cheek bones, the haggard, intensive look, a hint of impending eye strain in somebody who'd read and concentrated for too long. Here, two years ago, he'd been irresistible to her, but since then he'd turned into the apotheosis of himself, more haggard and driven than ever. Black deepened his unconscious effect. The sharp lines it threw into his face and the overall darkening were like the sepia tint on a photograph she'd been carrying around for years in an inside pocket. It had turned engraved without being looked at or brought into the light of day. Time alone aged.

'Yes, I started wearing a lot of black in India. It cut down on the dhobi man's bills. That and indigo blue. They're meant to have alluring connotations, by the way. Be attractive. They're the colours of sexuality.'

She laughed, folding her bare legs underneath her on a peeling leather chair that had had a few turns around the salerooms before it landed here. 'So that's the mega-selling power behind the success of blue jeans! You're kidding me.'

'No. I really mean it. Black and blue are supposed to be erotically charged. Indians are keen on depicting the god Vishnu with a blue face. One of his most common incarnations is as the Water Purifier. He's painted standing balanced on one leg, with a fountain spouting out of the top of his head and he's got a bright blue face. Which, I admit, looks a bit ridiculous. Hinduism is a hard-to-take sort of religion, isn't it?'

'Why the fountain?'

'Oh, that's meant to be the purity of the Ganges as he perennially filters the meltwaters. He must have a great plant installation up in the Himalayas. The rest of us would like to know about it.'

She pulled an incredulous face. 'The purity of the Ganges? I thought Mark Twain said the Ganges was the river so polluted that even the microbes couldn't survive.'

It was his turn to burst out laughing. 'I haven't heard that one before, but it's spot-on. Anyway, Singh calls me the water purifier when I get above myself and too deistic, or even idealistic. That's almost as objectionable to him.'

Reminded about the absent doctor, Caley put her glass down among the growing line of empties on the coffee table. 'You know, you didn't tell me about Singh and Shalini, and you should have done. He didn't tell me anything himself, although I had a letter from him only a few weeks ago. Is it so bad that neither of you can talk about it?'

'So Neal has said something to you.' That salacious bit of gossip would fill the road nicely all the way to Edinburgh. 'I suppose with a fairly negative inflection. Singh should have known better than to get himself boxed in. Yes, it's that bad, or it's insoluble, which is roughly the same thing. I've been distracted all this week, wondering how he's getting on in Jaipur. He's got to decide soon what he's going to do.'

'And why isn't this girl acceptable to his family?'

Thomas looked down the enormity of explanation. 'You'd need to know India to know that. The wrong caste. The wrong set of circumstances.'

'And that makes marriage between them impossible? There's no compromise?'

'Pretty well. For high-caste Hindus like Singh, marrying is more of a social mechanism than it is for us, or a religious one. Personal choice has got nothing to do with it. It's like Antigone burying her brother so that his soul can finally be laid to rest. It's not a rational exercise. More of a compulsion. You life isn't your own. You're in a family chain, and a cyclical one in relation to your

karma. For those of us who don't share it, it's one of the most
bizarre aspects of the faith. Weirder than blue.'

Caley turned sombre hearing this. Everything Neal had said to
her in the car, before she offloaded him at the airport, reinforced a
first impression: that she was a hair's breadth from being a
Shalini. Illegitimate, she'd be roughly the same caste-slave as a
child widow on the sub-continent, one of the social untouchables,
the woman who had the misfortune to have no man's signature
at the bottom of her pedigree to verify it. What saved her
personally from the same outcast status was her higher education.
That was her own freedom, her passport, her ticket out of
oblivion, the thing she travelled on. Caley Brown was able to
stand up independently of men because she had the vital scroll
after her name, which served her better than a father's or a
husband's testimony.

'So, they're very unhappy?'

'Yes, and they'll be unhappier in the months to come, whatever
he decides.'

'What's your best guess?'

'That he sees sense and picks some sloe-eyed beauty from
another town, who doesn't know the score, and pensions off
Shalini at least for the time being. That's as the Nattawats would
have it. They're the old school, very correct. For him, Shalini's not
so expendable even short-term.'

'You mean he is completely devoted to her?'

'I suppose that's true.'

They were both silent, Caley remembering the detached flirt
that Singh used to be, dodging the serious as well as the improper
relationship, steering a middle course as an accomplished escort,
the man with a pretty woman permanently on his arm for show –
while Thomas reflected on how far the example bore on his own.
Single-minded devotion was an uncomfortable state. It threw out
the self-corrective balance.

'And what's the worst?'

'Limbo. That they go on as they are. Once she gives birth to
their child, he's a social outcast too, or he's permanently
damaged. Already, they're marginalising him in Rajasthan. First
of all his family life will suffer, then his professional. The clinic
rooms will start to empty down his side of the verandah.
Nothing's secret there. Remember Proust's Swann. The Paris
coteries have got nothing on Jaipur's. He'll be hounded to
extinction.'

This pained her excruciatingly to hear, unfair and wasteful of his precious skills. 'Why doesn't he come back to the UK and put it all behind him? He can start again. His job prospects must be international. He could practise as an orthopaedic surgeon anywhere. The States. What does the New World care about these prohibitions?'

Thomas grimaced too at the theoretical escapes that he and Singh had exhausted months ago. 'For a start, his surgical techniques are pretty specialised. The nearest thing might be working on limb casualties from abandoned minefields, say in Iran or Cambodia, but he's not going to opt for all that upheaval unless he has to. And anyway he's got a commitment to his city. That's another thing I can't put easily into words. They're citizens as well as being members of a caste and their own established family group. That's the sum total of their notions of belonging. It's very hard for an Indian to be really independent unless he sheds all his worldly goods and becomes a holy man, a *saddhu*, wandering and begging and suffering. But even then he suffers for himself, on his personal pilgrimage, and not on behalf of mankind. Others purge themselves by giving alms to the beggar. It's so unChristian, it's quite an alien concept to us. Singh is consigned to a term of loneliness whatever he does from now on. He can't just cut himself off.'

Thomas was suddenly tired. It had been a long and tortuous day since he went into the cottage hospital for his appointment. Talking in turn to Batey, Ruth, Nina, Oliver and a roomful of his lapsed friends – that was a huge expenditure of effort. 'I shouldn't be drinking all this wine, you know. I'm on anti-something or other.'

'Does it hurt?' She lifted the damaged hand that was hanging limp in the chair next to hers.

'Not as much as it did. Let's have a look at it, shall we?'

The hospital bandage was only a light, protective covering of gauze and lint. Caley peeled it back quickly when there was no plaster to rip the skin. The wound from the piercing splinter of china was neat, inflamed but not infected. He'd had a lucky escape. A centimetre on either side would have slit one of the tendons and only a small proportion of the splinter had pierced his skin. 'It's lucky it's your left hand. You can still write.'

'That's a priority, is it?' At two a.m., penmanship seemed a long way off.

'It could be.' She drew a deep breath, anticipating more of his displeasure, maybe more of pain. 'I went to see a man this morning called Alastair Renton. Have you heard of him? He's a book man. Edith asked me to see to this a couple of months ago. She wanted me to arrange to have your letters published, your diary extracts. I think she had a mind to pay for them to be printed herself, just as a family curiosity, a sort of Langholm scrapbook, but I wasn't so sure. I thought they might be commercially viable.'

'Yes, I know who you mean now. Renton's a cagey type. Canny. The family have been publishers since the back of beyond. His father took something ecclesiastical of Robert's.'

'That's right. Nelson's Parkside works. Well, he liked your extracts. He's asked me to talk to you about what he ought to do next. The copyright's not completely yours. I don't know whose it is now, but the initiative is yours. Your final say.'

'But what was it I wrote? I can't even remember. A few letters. Drivel, and such personal stuff. Who I met and what I ate. It's surely not book material?'

'He thinks it is. I can tell he's quite fired up about it, although he tries to stay low-key, and I assume he's been through the stages of a manuscript often enough to be mercenary about the process. No, not quite, not mercenary, more objective than we are. More commercial.'

What a confounding proposition! Thomas got up from the cosy chair, fired himself, although it wasn't by enthusiasm, more by a transcript of dismay. This wasn't his personal goal in any sense, and so his first reaction was to feel imprisoned by another second-hand set of expectations, Edith's and Caley's and Renton's, each of them working on his behalf, admittedly, but not towards his perceived ends. He thought of those pages as layers of old skin he'd shed a long time ago or last year's growth of hair. It might have some anthropological significance in years to come, but to collect the debris was positively unnatural and maybe unhealthy. He took a turn about the living room, lifting a book, dimming a light distractedly. 'Today you saw him?'

'This morning. There was a letter waiting for me when I got back yesterday and I rang and got in to see him at once. I was with him for a long time, or it felt like a long time.'

'I'm overwhelmed. Let me get used to the idea.'

She obliged. As if she were breaking the line of her concentration on him, which was draining the expression on his face into blankness, she got up too and, with a nighttime shiver, put on his discarded linen jacket over the bright pink dress.

She looked better that way to his eye, was more subtle, double-layered.

He asked himself, What was he complaining about? This was exactly what he'd imagined as a perfect futurescape just a couple of days ago at Abbotsford: a modern application of the ideal monastic composites, eight hours' body work, eight hours' mind work, eight hours' rest. What he'd envisaged then was academic writing on a research topic, however, not his scrappy letters home. Warily, he approached such a collection as a statement of himself as an individual and nothing more instructive, a typecasting that he might not be able to shake free of in the years ahead. He had aspired to being much more than himself. Never write your autobiography, cautioned Auden, because you're using up your capital. This felt too soon, and too presumptuous an expenditure. While Edith backed it, he knew that his sterner grandparent would have utterly condemned the project as wanton and self-proclaiming. He wouldn't have wanted to read it, and why should anybody else?

Caley watched him while these scruples played out over his features. Gaunt, riven, haunted by illusions of a greater being. What a state of affairs! Most men of Thomas's age and disposition fancied themselves as writers, had toyed for years with the idea of a script and their persona as the author-hero of it, the great unpublished me, without having a shred of the necessary graft to put ambition into deed, word on to page: and here he was, handed the effortless opportunity to be – nothing more than he had already given proof of, and he spurned it as an idle vanity, not his proper medium. What was she going to do with him? He knew himself so little.

'I'm honestly grateful for your concern, and for the time you've put into it already,' he said, 'but I don't like manufactured books. They cheat. This would have no theme, no drive. It would be immoral. I don't know that I could subscribe to that.'

Over to Renton, she thought. He'd have to work hard himself to convince a reluctant author that it was worth the candle.

'I'm tired now,' he said. 'I just want to lie down.'

Thomas lay back on the familiar and accommodating bed, with his hands folded behind his head. It was so late that the street lamps had switched off but, in a Scottish midsummer, the low natural light was enough to see by: the gloaming. Inside its penumbra, his mind moved along the silent street prehensively, revisiting its attic garrets and stout main doors, the angled bays and reticent, respectable architecture. Boring, it was safe, and after hazard he was more able to appreciate its unchanging face.

Caley came back into the room behind him. He turned his head a fraction and there she was, easy, smiling and accessible. Marriage must be like this: an excited predictability. She sat down on a side chair and shrugged off his loose jacket like a shell. The pink dress looked better in diffused light, only warm or rosy, a reflection of mood more than a forcible, statement garment.

'Gordon bought you that?'

'Yes. Not altogether my style.'

He smiled as she unzipped the long back of the shift and let it drop on to the ground. 'Why do you wear it then?'

'It's a cheerful colour. I wear it when I'm feeling down or stressed. It's a good form of camouflage. Rose-coloured, you know. It sheds a glow.'

She came and stood by the bedside. She was unabashed in her body, like a boarding-school girl who was used to public showers and changing rooms and altogether plunges. Her underwear tended to be decorative. It was almost the only thing she cared about in clothes or took real trouble over. The pieces matched and were the same colour as her outerwear, navy, black, or broderie anglaise white for summer. Now it was peach and lace-edged, as if she were a Puritan who concealed a cavalier frivolousness underneath.

She took his hand, stroking the fingers separately. He shook his head a couple of times against the pillow, implying a negative response to the gesture, he wouldn't play, but also the futility of trying to deny himself the magnetic nearness and the sheer pleasure of her touches. It was his left hand she held. She placed it on the middle of her ventral plane, so that the wound coincided with her navel. And strangely enough, the hand seemed to hurt less for her ministration. He lay still.

She sat down on the edge of the divan and looked at the shadowy face. 'Where do you rewind to, when you go back over things?'

'You mean at what point did we start to go wrong? Oh, round about the beginning.'

'You're that cynical?'

'That inevitable.'

'I won't settle for such a downbeat version of things. You can be more interventionist in the way events turn out. Attack without aggression.' She swung round and leaned on the headboard beside him, from right angle to parallel.

'That's your new motto?'

'I'm growing into it. I'm not so easily put upon now.'

He remembered her layabout brother, accepted back without question and given generous house room. She'd hidden, fed and protected the unrewarding youth more than once. 'Are you sure about that? Haven't you just expanded your capacity for tolerance?'

She smiled back at him without a trace of enmity and proved his point. 'OK. Attack without visible aggression.'

He'd no resilience against her nature, which was predominantly sweet and indiscriminate and rather winning. She was that rare person, a natural lady. The result of such a widespread, harbouring quality – that she cared about everybody in equal measure – he tried to overlook because it was as immaterial as their disjunct past. He probably ought to be working himself up into a tirade of wounded masculine pride, be petulant and stomp about the room, but the late hour and too many drained glasses on top of his tetanus injections sapped his energy for anger. He couldn't grasp the edge of hatred in Caley's company. In a sense, she was inevitably right: by looking for the better motive in others, she found it. Behaving badly in her presence offended against the most basic decency, self respect. She was conscience.

She lay down beside him as companionably as a dog on a hillside, and pulled the coverlet up over their shoulders. It was so quiet round about them, they felt alone in the world. Resist this impulse, he said, but he couldn't obey his own commands. He lay frowning with dismay in the dark while she smoothed the frown as gently as she'd healed his hand. He watched himself slipping under the influence of her power as their kisses changed momentum from casual to intended, general to local. Was he going to make love to her after all? Probably. Fidelity took some peculiar forms. He could argue that her loyalty to Edith in her lonely widowed years, and to his own talents in his absence, was worth more than conventional sexual morality. Caley needed to serve other people directly when they presented her with an urgent crisis, a now, more than any remote ideals. She still puzzled him with her oblique priorities, and she tested him to the limit of his forgiveness, which might be his own definition of love.

They were quiet and calm, in a harmonious mood. He took off

his black and underneath was pale-strong. She caressed him, the pliable surfaces, the bones, the ridged vertebrae. There was no point in resisting her moulding powers after all. He was her thing and she shaped him.

They closed round. Thomas thought that sexual intercourse for Caley might be the ultimate acknowledgment of someone else's need, a sort of charitable giving. This didn't gratify his vanity one bit, that she was a contemporary Manon Lescaut and he was only the preferred among several lovers in the past. It was rather humiliating to think that she'd chosen serially from among men, not finally, so that all the time he was engaged in what ought to have been a mindless passion, one cold brain cell recast himself as Gordon in her arms, or as the men who, for all he knew, had chanced along in between the two of them, or as the men she'd loved before she knew him. She was already experienced by the time he met her, so his chastened, once-and-for-all restraint hadn't counted for much. In fact, his naïvety had made him more susceptible to a woman who reviewed men coolly, and meant he was less able to judge her with dispassion. Their chief attraction might be raw sexual energy, or the relationship was distinguished for its quality of physical rapport, a total accident. But why should he start to argue with that?

The light began to come up behind the shutters. It was already dawn.

'Where is it that you rewind to, then, if not the beginning?' he asked in turn.

'Oh, I don't go in for post-dated analysis. I prefer to fast-forward.'

'So what's next on the tape?'

She rolled away from him and over on her side. 'You want me to tell you what I'm going to do. I've no idea, any more than you have. I'm a day-at-a-time person. Or maybe you want me to tell you something about Gordon, what he means, what I mean, but I'm just as vague on all that eternity stuff as I ever was.'

'Will you stay with him? I would like a hint.'

She touched the jetted face sadly. Someone had described the Cairngorms to her recently as granite cathedrals and Thomas had the same quarried isolation in his features. 'You're asking if I like him more than you. Or which of the angles of tension will take the greater strain. I'm not sure. When you're here I prefer you and when you're not, I forget what I think. Because you feel so powerfully about uniqueness, that there should just be one and that the best, you imagine that I feel the same, but you're wrong. I can't make comparisons between people. I don't like comparisons. All I know is that I can simulate a sort of happiness with anyone, and your happiness is more important to me than my own, while it lasts, or while I'm with you. I'm not an idealist.'

'You'll have to be a bit more clear-cut than that, Caley. I'm leaning on something that keeps giving way under me, and that's not fair.'

'I know. I'm still being too objective about men instead of properly sentimental. You'd need to give me another yardstick apart from what I want, or what you want.'

Was she very strong or very hard? 'You're dodging the issues. There's an ultimate preference. A qualitative difference you can't brush aside. Or am I wrong? Maybe you don't feel anything at all.'

She sighed. The more he pressed, the more she fragmented in her response. 'Sometimes I would like to know what it feels like to be cherished. I haven't had much cherishing in my life.'

This wasn't said at all tearfully, but was self-pitying enough in tone, unlike her normal self, to startle him. He picked up the desperate disappointment of the undervalued. She's a woman who will always be badly treated, said Neal, because that's what she expects.

'Does Gordon manage to cherish you?'

'No, he never does that, but he's quite a clever man-manager. He makes me think. He stops me from postponing indefinitely.'

'It's a shame your own father didn't stick around to give you some moral support. That might have made a difference.'

The phrase struck her with some force because it was unexpected. 'My father? And who the hell was he?' she asked dismissively.

On impulse, she leaned over sideways to the bedside cupboard and brought out a shapshot to show him. It was a badly taken photograph of a tall man in the distance. His features were blurred to the point of being anonymous. 'Do you know him? Recognise him? He's the tall, gaunt one, with the bony shoulders and the traveller's kitbag slung over his back heading for the far horizon. Kiss goodbye and leave. Well, I've kept choosing the same man ever since, the walk-away type, like father, like lover. It's my known male pattern, to choose the one who'll abandon me, pick up and then let down.'

He studied the perfectly identifiable outline of himself and didn't disagree. She'd not shown him this before, or even alluded to the missing man. It was the last of her surprises. But, seen, the image took on life. In what country was this picture taken, what continent and when? Was this man still alive, the indifferent passer through, and did he visit her here as casually as her stepbrother did, making a complete latch-key family? There was no point in asking her these questions because she wouldn't tell him, or not in a knowable way. He might have to wait a long time to come to the palpable in her.

It was already six in the morning and they hadn't slept a wink. The street was starting to move. The milk float made its slow, whirring progress along the crescent. The birds chorused in the quiet of a full and sunny morning. The equinox had passed into another quarter phase. It struck him as entirely possible that they were two people so perfectly attuned that they simply cancelled each other out; their mutual indecisions reduced their lives to stasis. They needed to put behind them the urgent wanting to be liked, even by each other, and go on to accomplish the unpopular thing.

'What is it you want me to do?'

'I think you ought to go back to India at the time you said you would. Meet your schedules, and then you've nothing to reproach yourself with afterwards. Singh's going to need some looking after. Don't run out on it. Tidy it up. Serve out your three months' notice or whatever it takes, and then see what presents itself. Good lord, you've got choices. Feel sorry for the people who haven't.' She looked out at the sky, wondering only how to dress to meet the weather, whether it was warm or hot. 'As for today, come back and see Alastair Renton with me. Why not? There's nothing to lose. If you're a celebrity to one man, why not bask in it for an hour? I'll give him a call. You don't need to decide. You can still say no after you've met him.'

At the ebb of his own will-power, he submitted to hers.

23

Singh took the longer route to Amber, looping south of Jaipur to cut back across the sleeping city. It was a retrospective. He stopped the car periodically, feeling the wafts of solitude as sombrely as his mother did, enclosed within the tiers of her lake house, locked down many layers. He didn't get out of the car to walk the familiar routes, but he visited several places and buildings with a long, backward look of association and nostalgia.

All round him, the streets and the bazaars were empty. A few people were asleep outdoors on the pavements, rolled in their bedding like winding sheets, a bundle of dusty rags, while others congregated at this late hour over brazier fires, alight on the street corners. These filled the air with a pungent, acrid woodsmoke, less noticeable than it was in winter, when the dense fumes turned sulphurous and whitened the surrounding roads with specks of ash. The street-dwellers didn't seek the comfort of the open fire for the sake of its heat but for its implied companionship. They stood and roasted a few nuts or seeds in the bottom of a tin, pierced to form a canister, and told stories or jokes to make the night pass more quickly. He hoped it wouldn't rain too heavily on the street-dwellers tonight or douse their charcoal fire.

Everything was quiet in the compound round the clinic as he drove past. The caretaker nodded off on duty. The lights burned in the laboratory. Ajit would be working until midnight, hoping to ingratiate himself with Langholm when he returned or with Langholm's successor if one was appointed. And if no one came, the laboratory would be embalmed in the unchanging until the posters were fly-blown and the pile of English magazines turned yellow and the water samples, carefully stoppered, evaporated down to the dry spores of their particular algae none the less.

The lights were still playing at the Rambagh Palace Hotel, laughter and the tinkling of glasses reaching him across the grey and ragged lawns. The doctor was invaded by the great loss of change. Such diversions were a thing of the past, and he underwent a spurt of irritation that the water engineer had, with his sudden removal, accelerated their demise. We're letting too much time pass in the enchanted city, he used to say inside these halls. The enchantment lay in not counting up the months, in not being responsible for the sum total, a euphoria that had vanished overnight with such a violent act of maturity that the merriment and flow indoors seemed not only out of place but obscene in his present sullen mood. Death for Thomas: birth for him. Who joked now?

The wild, roaming street monkeys slept, the monuments were still, the vendors had left the alleyways. He passed, the solitary moving atom, across the compass of his universe, feeling the burden of a solitude so great that it made his heart malfunction by racing, slowing down, hurting with needle-like pains deep in his chest.

He watched himself delay the moment of telling Shalini about his decision as long as he could, meandering aimlessly across the city which, in its dormant state, reinforced his role as an outlaw, offering no door for him to knock upon except his own. Which cousins, which friends would hear him out? The love affair had made the normal inaccessible, too dull for him to find resource in.

He rehearsed his speech and his decision to Shalini a dozen times, finding new entries and approaches, none of which softened the delivery of Sonal's stern ultimatum – she must go. Only as far as the lake to his mother's care, to an alternative condition of loving kindness, but still she must go from the centre and creation of his existence. He couldn't imagine the rooms at Amber without the flute of Shalini's presence, the dark gold, the colours of danger she carried, the leather-bound books she readdressed him to. His sadness at the summary end of postponement and of his youthful years drained him. Even as the wells filled all over the city and men gave thanks, his own ran dry.

V.J. reached home by an opposite route. His private house was more sumptuous than Sonal's, and more ancient, with remarkable carved wooden shutters and balconies like dark lace against pink stucco, and a series of splendid marble floors, now lifting at mistaken angles after two centuries of rising damp and an accumulation of neglect and cheap repairs. Sonal was lucky to have been connected to the family members of Nattawat, who served the maharajah: his kingly generosity had been carefully managed to lose nothing in the passage of time, apart from some slight seepage of water through the paving cracks. Her three children were handsomely provided for, while the doctor was said to be a very wealthy man in his own right through his astute purchase of diamonds on the open market.

On the other hand, V.J. and his ambassadorial older brother, among whose more illustrious postings had been numbered Cairo and Paris as well as London, served the more distant kingdom in Delhi and had found themselves reviled locally for every mistake and change of policy during the semi-dynastic rule of Nehru and his daughter and her son. Now, with their pensions frozen, their lands confiscated, they made up a new class of poor, the people who lacked the assets to maintain their personal holdings, the more decayed by being more obviously so. When his son married Lata, V.J. was relieved that he was able to share the burden of upkeep by giving the young couple the ground floor of his house. As he walked past the open doors to rooms where servants slouched and furniture was ranged untidily, heard the fitful crying of small children, in escaping upstairs to his own apartments he had misgivings that all this dismal sharing was no good.

Not so fast. Lata waylaid him. Had she been sitting under the staircase all evening, waiting for his return? He drew his jacket collar tighter in indignation.

'You didn't get wet, did you?' she asked pleasantly. 'You managed to dodge the showers?'

'Only just. A torrential downpour is beginning. I am merely damp, spirits as well as body.' This was the politest imprecation for her to leave him alone, but she held him by the direction of her gaze which strayed upward towards their mutual concern, the state of the roof over the great flanks of the double-sided marble staircase.

Sure enough, a drip started, while they watched the length of its fall on to the irregular tiles. 'We can't delay this any longer,' she complained.

'No, indeed. We will have the builder see to it in the morning.'

Lata knew that this answer procrastinated indefinitely, rambling around the hypothesis of which builder and which morning, but did not feel the moment was right for precision. Another answer prevailed. What had been decided between Singh and his mother? The import of V.J.'s mission that evening was known through the chatter of women in the household, her mother-in-law to her sister-in-law to her own gossiping cook, as powerful a downward filtration as the drip, although she was too much in awe of this man to broach him directly. But, after all, her cousin's name had been mentioned and her own family's dignity was involved. She thought she had a right to know.

V.J. thought differently. The scene at the lake was disagreeable enough without reliving it under a shower of raindrops. Whatever he thought personally of his nephew, rather spoiled by too much endowment, looks, wealth, cleverness, as well as a Western education which made him arrogant towards discipline, always his own master, he did admire his skill and his dedication. He actually found himself envying his surgical work at the clinic and his ability to mix in the world of men and of public affairs. The old man found retirement and women's doings did not suit him. The confrontation with his son's wife at the bottom of the stairs was typical of the modern lapse in standards and of his own diminishing authority.

'So, if you will excuse me . . .'

But still they held each other in the trance of inactivity. They were saved from absolute rudeness on either side by a violent gust of wind that torn open one of the verandah doors and crashed it against the inner wall. As she turned to fasten it up, he moved away.

Though Lata shut the banging door, the house reverberated with disquiet. They hadn't eaten yet downstairs. Pans clattered. His unmarried daughter, who took the upper floor for her own use, played music loudly. It was like living in one of the squalid blocks of flats in New Delhi with neither privacy nor peace.

Wistfully, V.J. recalled the undemocratic days of elegance. He missed having access to his own grounds, missed having a team of gardeners with whom he consulted daily, had loved the carpet neatness of their flower-beds planted out in spring, and walking on to his own verandah in the early morning to view the night's refreshment over the dewy lawns. He was wishful about the times of greatness, when Rambagh was still a princely palace and he went there as an invited guest to the wedding of the last maharajah. Then, there had been street festivities at which the whole population of the city was fed, a munificence that lasted for a week. There were firecrackers by night and feats of horsemanship at the polo ground by day, men astride who were so nimble in their turns, they moved like centaurs, man-mind, horse-body as one. They held jousts and tourneys in the streets and squares for all the people to see. Floats of flowers, banners waving, teams of men running in the streets, colours high and strong, yes, he had seen the last of chivalry in his time. All this dismal sharing was no good.

The sad involvement of his nephew was a case in point. In the past, men did as they chose and no one asked why. The maharajah himself had been married three times simultaneously, all his wives bore his children, no stigma to any. But men of their standing should not engage their heart with the low-born. There was a discernment to be upheld in the quality of choice, especially in the choice of women, and democratisation was not possible in all things, or desirable. In marriage, men should rule.

But then he paused, adjusting his own bony discomfort in a hard and narrow chair, and recognised that he might really mean the opposite of what he was thinking. He was envious of Singh's passion because that colour was of old. The hour of magnificence had gone; now they were required to lead careful, pennied lives without extravagance. This girl he had rescued from death in the desert was an emblem of the passing day and, for a while, the two of them had resurrected the displays of greatness.

The same downpour drove Singh home to Amber. It wiped out the scenery as he nosed, blind, along the northern highway, between weather-made ruts and ditches, relieved that no other maniac was likely to be travelling tonight under such pelts of rain. He parked the car under the protective roof slant of the house and dashed round to the door, but even that twenty-yard sprint left him soaked to the skin, through his jacket and shirt. He took them off and rubbed himself roughly dry, putting on a robe for comfort.

As he moved into the darkened living room, he saw that Shalini had fallen asleep while she was reading. Several of her favourite books were left open, scattered round her position on the carpet. She had fallen asleep on her left arm, which was bent underneath her head like a pillow. She'd have cramp when she woke up. He was surprised at the evidence of her carelessness. Normally, she was tidy and particular about returning his books to the shelf, according to his first instructions, and had promised to be waiting for him when he got back from his mother's house. He thought that meant awake, alert, receptive. But carrying the child must tire her out. He left the lights off to let her slumber on, and sat at the picture window some feet away from her in the dark, watching the rainstorm flicker white and black across the valley floor, as he waited for her to wake up and open her eyes, open her arms to greet him.

He waited for a long time, might even have dozed off himself or became entranced with the monotonous, time-reductive drumming of the rain. When he came to, nothing had changed in the room. Shalini was still asleep in the same position.

But her body didn't move in conjunction with her breathing and she was silent. Even in sleep a body moved. He got up and went over to her, suddenly anxious. As he touched her arm, he felt it stone-cold in reply to his warmth. His trained instinct took over. He put out a doctor's hand to feel her pulse, but, as he moved her a fraction, her body fell back from the sleeping position and allowed him to see that she had taken her own life by rolling on to the point of her dagger, the same dagger which she'd kept for her protection in the villages and in the desert. She'd placed it knowingly under her heart. He knew that she had it whetted to a razor fineness and it must have gone in deep when her weight went down on the blade. Her death would have been instantaneous and mercifully short of pain. A mercy killing.

He put his ear down to her abdomen, the way he'd done half a dozen nights before, to hear his son speak, but his son was stilled into silence. Nothing. He said nothing. The child had also died and had no answers to give back about how or why. Singh was overwhelmed immediately that his base thoughts of suicide had been fulfilled like this, as if he'd communicated a feeling that he'd wanted the two of them gone, to rid himself of trouble, while his eyes poured helpless tears. Only this morning . . . Why hadn't she waited for him? She must have been dead only two hours or so. If he hadn't driven the long route round the town, if he hadn't spent that time taking tea with Sonal and his tedious uncle, he'd have been back here to prevent it. If only, on and on.

Surely it was an accident. She must have fallen asleep with the dagger hidden underneath her for her own protection, still cautious for her personal safety, and had rolled on to it accidentally. No other explanation was possible. But common sense ruled out that expedient answer. The knife had been placed with surgical accuracy. Her death was deliberate.

He began to realise, crouching beside Shalini's curled form, that he'd explained nothing at all to her about what was in his mind. That while he loved her to the ends of his being, he hadn't told her so. Their child was a separate source of joy to each of them, not a shared one, or not discussed openly. Maybe that was how he'd failed her. It wasn't enough to love. You had to convince the other person of the love's existence.

He took her hand, still gracious in its pose, and felt the hugeness of what he hadn't been able to convey. Not knowing what else to do just then, he spoke to her about the future as he had planned it to himself, describing Sonal's attitude and her spontaneous suggestion and the lake which he was sure she would enjoy, cooler than Amber, how the lilies when they flowered were pink not white, as he started on the endless monologue of regret. But he saw how each of the pictures he projected of their necessary division had been tolerable, even to himself, as long as she was at the end of every mental day. Without her surety, the compromise which he and Sonal arrived at had no value. Without a fixed point, the doors flew open and let the weather in.

Why did she do it? The tumult and confusion of blood dinning in his head meant he couldn't clear himself of the essential questions. It would have been better if she'd died in the village by stoning than by her own hand in his house. He was sure she hadn't meant to die, or hadn't planned it – and yet she kept her dagger and waited until he was away for the whole day. Maybe she really did know in her intuitive way what Sonal intended and how he must comply, was able to read his unconscious flesh, and had taken her life thinkingly because that way she was the least impediment to his ambition. She'd served him to the end, to make his way easy, so that the family didn't ostracise him or the patients desert his clinic-surgery.

He sat alone for a long time, one set of tears drying on his face and neck before another followed. What a small world he'd confined her to! The space of these rooms, one foreign friend, two servants and himself. The area described by her sari was all there was of her. And the enlarging books. He picked them up one at a time, preciously, and looked down the page at what she had been reading two hours before. Was there any clue in these? She was obsessed with the over-coloured legends, which were her fairy tales, her nursery rhymes, so well known they turned incremental with retelling, the ten incarnations of Vishnu, his consort Lakshmi, the forbidding spirit of the female Kali brooding over all of them. She didn't tire of the limitations and their childish crudities.

He put them face down as she had left them. But under the last he was surprised to find an envelope. It was addressed to Shalini herself and held only one sheet of very simple, blocked writing. It was from Thomas and must have arrived that morning after he had left. Was this the trigger to her unhappiness? He read it quickly, discovering no more depth than in the legends, its only interest for him incidental, for it confirmed that Langholm had arrived safely and made family arrangements that no one would quarrel with.

He returned it, unavailing, to its envelope. Inside Thomas had tucked a photograph which, at first glance, shocked him because he couldn't remember when it was taken. But there they were, all three of them, he and Thomas and Shalini, on the terrace after one of their laughter-invaded English lessons. Banji had been called up to take the snapshot, protesting he knew nothing about cameras. So it transpired. It was overexposed and badly centred. Still, it caught the mood, and Thomas had written across the back of it 'In memory of all our happy times'. He realised it was the only photograph or memento of her that he owned. He hadn't thought about recording it while it was happening, or her while she was alive.

He read the letter again, putting his grief to one side, and saw how it flowed on a natural wave of concern and kindliness. The man was kind and he had been thoughtless, letting him depart without due ceremony. Perhaps there was something latent in the message from abroad, carrying the waft of gentler climes and of friendship, from which Shalini knew herself to be excluded for ever.

Futile conjecture. But he would cremate the letter and the beloved books with her body, and keep the photograph. Reality pressed. He must make funeral arrangements of his own, as he had done for his father's last rites. Thousands had come to that to pay their respects, not to the man but to the servant of the state, the last counsellor of the last maharajah, obsequious to passing godheads. He would be the only mourner at Shalini's funeral and carry out the rites alone, casting petals and lone words in the wind. No tears must be salted on the face. No undignified weeping, which was self-indulgent and would trouble the spirit of the departed in their passage to the next life.

It was morning, somehow. He had sat alone throughout the night, flayed and desperate and unforgiving of himself. At six o'clock, Banji crossed the courtyard to wake his master up and inaugurate a normal day. When he came into the living room and saw the static scene, the blood-dark sari, red of reds, he fell down on the ground and abased himself, forehead and knee.

'There is nothing to be done, Banji. I found her yesterday when I came home. Will you call the women who dress the body? I've a long day ahead of me. Several operations and a clinic. And I will have to go out to the lake first thing to see my mother and tell her what has befallen.'

He showered and shaved and dressed in white, noticing the discarded shirt of yesterday as it lay stained with rain and sweat and unawareness. Only yesterday. Only yesterday morning he had held her. He started to catalogue infinity when, in the courtyard, the wailing of the women reached him. He didn't know his own eyes in the mirror as he wondered how he was going to share the disappointment with his mother who stood even at this moment at the gates, full of false hope, while she waited for him to arrive with Shalini and the future on his arm.

24

By midday, the suite of offices was overheated. The publishing man threw open the window after his clients had gone, and then remembered, when the wall of sound from the traffic at the foot of the Royal Mile hit him, why he'd shut it in the first place. Thomas Langholm and Caley Brown had come to see him together. That promised something.

The apparent synthesis had enough cracks in it to worry him all the same. Thomas first. Subdued and rather diffident, he admitted he'd come along reluctantly, and his attitude during the morning's discussion was almost non-partisan. Not used to having to activate enthusiasm in a writer, or pulses of egotism, Renton had felt himself floundering and stuck to the practical problems.

'The text would benefit from editing down.'

'And you still think a chronological order is the best?'

'On the whole. If you section a manuscript like this into topics, you fragment it, stop the narrative flow. And then there will be items that don't belong under any of the headings and end up under miscellaneous. A patchy book.'

Thomas was more interested in the long room at the bottom of the High Street, split by a set of connecting doors with a screen of books and the view from either side, and paced restlessly about the office. 'All that preparatory work. What if it doesn't take?'

'Let me face that risk. I appreciate your point about manufactured books, and I agree with you. This doesn't read that way. It feels like what we look for in the trade for years without finding it, a real book, a book about reality. Whether it succeeds or not, it's a chance we ought to take. It's the good good book.'

This was overly biblical for the layman. Thomas came to a halt, considering the last of his quibbles. 'I can't commit any more time to it personally. You might want me to edit and publicise the thing, and I've no relish for that sort of task. You'll have to excuse me from any further involvement.'

More eager than he would admit for the end product, Renton was ready to accept a package of unconditional means. 'We'll leave that open-ended. Whatever you have time for will suffice.'

He compared this genuine disinterest with the majority of first-timers he met on the publishing circuit who said to him unabashed, What is it that I have to do? To be rich and famous was implied more than what do I have to do to produce a very good book? He ought to have been less unnerved by the personal strangeness of a man who wrote strange words. His eye took in the bandaged hand, the hastily resewn seam, the dust of mental travel on him and wondered how much self-neglect a body could withstand.

He compared him with the man he'd watched arrive at Turnhouse last Sunday evening, and wondered what had happened in the interim to the trio made up of two men, one tall, one stocky, and one girl. It was quite a shock when the dark-clothed girl whose table he'd hovered next to, pretending to read his Sunday paper, had walked into the office on Thursday morning. Of course, of course, it fitted. He already knew about the Langholm brothers from the close-knit Edinburgh nexus, but hadn't known their faces. Now they slotted into place with the impact of the unavoidable. It wasn't luck to have run across them at the airport while he was still in the process of reading the manuscript. In a city of half a million souls, not to have met someone from the same social register was the larger coincidence.

After they left, Renton went out over the lunch hour and walked in to Holyrood Park. Walking was his only form of exercise. He kept his car garaged and normally clocked up under five thousand miles a year. His normal means of transport was by plane or foot.

This fact, as he threaded his way along the tourist-crowded pavements outside Holyrood Palace, recommended Thomas to him all the more because he felt, in the reference frame of Turnhouse to Munro peak, that those were his parameters as well. He liked the two rhythms of this man's character, the very wide given variety by the very small, like a camera lens that changed from the panoramic to the zoom in seconds. Near and far. The writing often had that pulse as well. He lived in Thomas a little, filling out the man he'd glimpsed in a transit lounge as unusual, off the beaten track. To someone who'd lived safely, that was an enormously attractive option and if, at the point of middle age and accomplished in his own, routine sphere, he could have poured himself into another mould, it might have been the erratic figure of the traveller. He didn't think that Langholm's was a freakish talent. That sort of maturity came late, like second thoughts.

He went on adjusting his perspective. At the first meeting, Caley had picked up his reference to Stevenson in passing, and she didn't disagree with his point about the clear-seeing eye and the classic style. R.L.S. was a fine analyst of men and places, when he stopped turning a pretty phrase and left it plain. Ultimately, the second name she mentioned was more telling. They both considered Thomas Langholm was inherently Orwellian in his approach to the written word, biting and bitter, the social commentator who was politically committed. In retrospect, it struck him as uncanny that both of these men were tubercular, although Stevenson, wealthy from the immediate success of his books, was able to protect his failing health in the softer climate of Samoa, while Orwell battered out the last of his lung power on another island, Jura off the west coast, a stern place and inhospitable to talent.

Had Caley noticed the inbred potential in this man of hers for being very ill because he was very driven? She was certainly more nervous in his company than the day before, no doubt because she was anxious and felt responsible for subjecting him to ordeal by publication. She looked calm enough, but it was the mock serenity of someone who was supremely self-controlled.

Renton found he envied the traveller, for his talent and his woman, neither of them in his view esteemed at their true worth. Young men, what did they know? They'd no sense of hold or what was remarkable in women. She'd forced a turnaround in his own attitude to the prospective book. Originally, he'd meant to press for its publication by one of the larger houses who could afford to take a risk: now he wanted it for himself. Make or break. Caley had provided the fulcrum, the essential additive. If she would edit the manuscript in Thomas's stead, or illustrate it, or simply talk it through with him, he was willing to take the chance and prolong his own professional contact with her along the way.

In the few hours in his office rooms, Renton felt he'd got to know Caley Brown thoroughly, the mental variance, the grasp of things, a strong sense of compassion without sentiment. He wasn't disappointed in his own judgment of the quiet, centred woman at the next table whose looks had knocked him off his feet.

He'd spent four days in a pointless infatuation with a woman who was already spoken for, just a hundred hours of idolatry. He looked down at himself more critically as a result thinking, The cut of this jacket is all wrong. Tomorrow I'll wear a quieter tie. Vicariously, he had absorbed her standards and her influence.

Using his own key, Oliver opened the door to Caley's flat about two in the afternoon. He rang the bell and waited for a decent, nominal interval to give his sister time to answer it, but he was quite relieved that the place was empty. Caley had a way of hovering nearby, nagging at him with her eyes.

He made himself at home, raided the fridge for some cheese left over from the party and found a couple of bottles of Alsace beer to wash it down with, surprised in passing to see how neat and tidy the kitchen was, with piles of clean dishes stacked up on the table. He only took this in as an irregular state of affairs because he was used to tackling mounds of greasy washing-up on the kibbutz. He conceded she must have been up early to see to all of that.

He pulled one curtain across against the glare before he switched on the TV set in the downstairs room and watched half an hour of an American soap opera while he was eating his late lunch. The cheese was good but crumbly. Messy stuff, cheese. He looked round for a handy plate but there wasn't one, so he swept the fragments off his clothes on to the pale carpet. The crumbs didn't show that way. He flicked round the channels for a while, but it was all housewives and shift-workers, vox pop stuff, ugly people airing their dreary and ill-formed views, about as mesmerising as a slow drip. He landed on a programme with girls surfing, and stuck with that, but soon grew bored with the feeble plot and low-grade dialogue.

His eyes grazed round the room, looking for something to distract him. He'd been for an interview that morning and it was a pretty edgy experience. They wanted his dates of employment end to end, and a job description for each of his previous periods of full-time work. It was all so serious! Had he any criminal convictions, apart from driving offences? That startled him. He'd made a few things up, exaggerated a couple of the details, nothing too colourful. All the same, he had an uneasy sense of things catching up with him, empty spaces on his CV that were already sending off a strange pulse, like sonar detection waves under water, searching for the hidden facts. How to fill the empty space differently? How to invent a truth?

He felt frayed and pent up. He wished he hadn't sold his car before he went away at Christmas, but it had made a handy sum of money to go travelling on. Now he had no wheels. He was on his uppers and he was alarmed at the prospect of being incarcerated for any length of time inside Caley's four walls up a communal staircase, with its rotten outlook. Out of the window some park railings confronted him and a scrap of greenery. High roofs hemmed him in.

He was desperate for the break. Just one good break and he'd be all right. He knew he could work hard. All those boring months on the kibbutz proved that, but he'd got real initiative to do something of his own, something big, if he was just given the right chance.

A stray impulse about Nina swept over him and he felt his own facial muscles contract in response. Was it a smile or a grimace? He had the impression of the long, lie-in mornings at Buckstone when they'd both gone off to the shops, Nina and Maurice, with the sun coming gradually round the two right-angled windows of his bedroom, a skin-warming layer of inertia in which his thoughts basked too, about what to do with the remainder of the day. He really needed that quiet time to himself every morning, to sort things out.

Sitting where he was now, in a sunny window, was nearly as good. His thoughts percolated slowly. The process of thinking was fascinating, like shuffling cards, rhythmic and rather soothing, almost an end in itself. But after half an hour he started to feel uncomfortable, as if he had cramp in his hands. His mind was going through the motions, but nothing happened as a result. No action was taken. He felt bad somehow, stiff, and the badness went very deep, immobilising him for even longer, like a net he'd put his foot on which tangled him up the more he tried to shake himself free of it.

Then he bestirred himself. Of course, he was only cold because the sun had moved round the angle of the bay, leaving him in shadow. He just needed to get his circulation going again. The trouble was, he was missing the warmth of the Med: the swimming, the easy life. He hankered suddenly after what he'd had and not appreciated at the time.

Got to get going. He patted his pockets abstractedly and heard the empty sound. What he needed more than anything else was a cash flow. He'd been quite surprised when he came away from the interview to pass a gemmologist's shop, and he had stopped for ten minutes or more looking at the samples in the window. So that was what they fetched! Real money. Not meaning any harm, he leaned forward to Caley's double stack of drawers and pulled the top one open. A large mauve crystalline piece, built up like a skyscraper, took his eye and he fingered it analytically, remembering how Thomas had studied them too the evening before. Had he been thinking the same thing, that they must be worth a bomb? Oliver put the mauve one back as too conspicuous to remove, and found a slatey fossil that he liked the look of. Small, he was able to slip it effortlessly into his empty waiting pocket. Plenty more where that came from. She'd never miss it and meanwhile it might make all the difference in the world to him. Hurriedly, he picked up another couple of items, so quickly that he hardly noticed the sleight himself, and pushed the remaining pieces on the tray around until they filled the vacant spaces proportionately.

He went out at once, noticing that the sun was warm outdoors, which encouraged him to slow his pace and soak it up. Stop that tan fading.

In the late afternoon, Ruth left George Weir's house, heading back to Carterbrae. She'd worked hard in his offices and got the place redd out, shifted the dust and felt she couldn't make a better job of it in the time. He himself was away at a land auction in Ayr. She preferred to work unhindered and was quite touched that he left her the run of his house and private papers.

She didn't peek or pry at them. There was nothing she couldn't ask outright. Even the surface arrangement of things told her George was a man who had no system and, on the way home, she seriously examined herself about whether she wanted to supply it. It was easier to separate the two ideas when Weir was out of the place: the system she could mend easily enough, the man maybe. He had no side to him, no guile. Like a lot of the local farmers and landmen, he was almost innocent, a straight man, so she felt his dusty corners were the worst of him, with no behind-hand dirt. They might battle over detail but not over principle.

This thought occupied her all the way down the High Street, through the square, where she stopped for some fresh meat and an evening paper, before heading for the bridge. As she crossed it, however, she drew in sight of Jim Batey's house and saw that his taxicab had been returned home safely, and stood tidily parked on the verge. So Thomas had come back after all. Her heart leaped up for joy in spite of herself, a feeling of fullness that arose within her body's frame like a stronger pulse rate, just at the moment when, on her right, the waters of the Esk and Ewes met and merged, with the noise of two tributaries becoming a whole river.

The car and the swollen spate changed the direction of her own thinking. She would always give way to Thomas's claim on things, her personal time included, and went with a quickened step up the steep brae, throbbing with the heat of her own energy and concern. The wayside stones were bright, the dykes as marked as known signposts counted out along her way. She crossed the last causeway to the escarpment of Carterbrae, and was astonished not at what she saw – which was the same half-moon drive, the same backdrop greenery, the stern fascia of the stone-built house – but at what she could hear.

It was heart-stopping because someone was playing Robert's music at the organ, and for half a second she imagined it was himself. The porch door was left ajar to cool the house, and from the open hallway the sound of the organ fell like the torrent from a second waterfall about her ears, the notes cascading past her down the hillside. She recognised the piece. It was the sixth of the Brandenburg Concertos. She'd long admired the perfect harmony of the grave background chords and the motif that went on surfacing among them like an elusive ray of happiness and sunshine. Allegro. The happy man. Often, when Robert played it, she'd chased that motif down a maze of barriers, always trying to reach it, glad of its re-emergence like a known face, elusive in a crowd of strangers.

There it came again. Five notes made to yield infinity. She smiled in spite of herself as she recognised his theme.

Thomas played the organ less well than his grandfather, who was his impatient tutor at the instrument, but he'd the same instinctive handling of a phrase. There was more trial and error in his playing. First a fast-flowing sequence, and then a passage so broken and hesitant it almost improvised on the score as it was written, but that had its own charm too, as if he was feeling the music too deeply to play it straight off. They were arpeggios slowed by the limitations of his hand. She waited at the front door, nodding in encouragement, albeit reluctant to interrupt his flow.

By what surge of inspiration had he picked up the same sheet that Robert had been practising from when he died? She remembered the old man's frustration with the difficult, interlocked notes and his own feel for them, made harder by his stiffening fingers. In the morning, he cracked them free of their overnight arthritis. Why, Thomas's own hand had gone intuitively to the very place where the other had left off, and he began again.

She took in that Caley was standing beside him, turning the score. One of her hands rested on his shoulder. They looked very young to Ruth all of a sudden, but that was because they'd both missed a connective generation and came straight from their ancestors without the gradual middle ground that led up to maturity. Or they were very old with their responsibility. Caley's other hand turned the sheet music but, because she couldn't sight-read the music perfectly, Thomas had to nod at the bottom of the right-hand page to signal that she ought to turn.

They noticed Ruth and stopped, while Thomas swivelled round on the stool.

'I didn't see your car,' said the woman.

'No, I drove Batey's taxi down here. Thomas doesn't do his hand any good at all by changing gears.'

'And how will you get back?'

'We'll worry about that later. I bought some fresh trout at the fishmonger's seeing that we'd given you no warning about supper. I hope it doesn't upset your plans.'

'I had no plans.'

The three of them moved together into the flagged kitchen, which was also cool from the open door, although the sun beat up to it. On the worktop was a baking dish with three fresh fish laid out, neatly filleted and stuffed with lemon wedges, as pretty a sight as the salt-herring emblem cooked in dough or painted on a flag to carry at the Common Riding. The baked potatoes were scrubbed and scored ready for the oven. The parsley butter was mixed in a sauce boat.

Thomas had been investigating the kitchen garden in the afternoon and found some leeks that had bolted but would do to grace the stockpot. 'I think it's a waste of time trying to clean out those asparagus beds,' he judged. 'We'll put in some early-crop potatoes to clear the ground. What would you like to grow instead, Ruth?'

'I've a taste for those purple onions,' she said, 'and my own broccoli.'

Caley had been under the strawberry beds and located a skimpy handful of fruit. The warm weather had brought them on fast, but she eked them out with the early raspberries and made a compôte with some spoonfuls of cassis. Quite a royal feast.